OLD PYBUS

OLD PYBUS

WARWICK DEEPING

CASSELL · LONDON

CASSELL & COMPANY LTD
35 Red Lion Square, London WC1
Melbourne, Sydney, Toronto
Johannesburg, Cape Town, Auckland

First published 1928
This edition published 1965

Sole distributors of this edition

G. BLUNT & SONS Limited
North Acton Road, London

Printed in Great Britain by
Lowe & Brydone (Printers) Ltd, London

402583-0

TO

THE MARY

IN MY WIFE

I

MR. CONRAD PYBUS collected pictures, and being the possessor of two "Constables," and three "Cotmans," he had some right to stretch out a large hand and to indicate the picture that was hung against the blue horizon.

"That's Castle Craven—over there. Rather like a thing by Constable. What?"

In spite of the largeness of his hand and the largeness of the car in which he sat, he spoke with an assurance which failed of its effect. He was shy of the woman beside him. She was leaning forward in the coupé, her dark thinness and her pallor joining to disconcert Mr. Conrad Pybus's vague yet ample correctness. She was smiling, and when she smiled the angles of her long and expressive mouth curved deep into either cheek. It was a curious smile, showing a gleam of teeth, but not as the conventional beauty displays them, all to the front as though advertising a musical comedy or a dentifrice. As a small nephew put it: "Aunt Ursy laughs in her cheeks." She did, with a kind of slanting upward, ironic swiftness, as though the two corners of her mouth were retracted by a couple of hooks.

Mr. Pybus's hand, sheathed in wash-leather, seemed to fascinate her. Extended, palm turned towards the landscape, it suggested the hand of a policeman on point duty, pontifically presenting a whole street to some hesitating motorist. But with the gloved hand the illusion ended. The blue-and-white-striped shirt-cuff, nicely protruding from the blue sleeve, marked the particular Pybus. No man could have been better tailored. His hats came from Pont's in St. James's Street.

She examined him with one swift and inclusive stare while he remained for a moment in that attitude of civic dignity, presenting her to Castle Craven, that hill town, grey under a kind of blue murk, the lapis of a horizon that was tumbled with clouds. She saw the red gold gleam of a wheat field, ripe on a green hillside. The world seemed a welter of hill-tops, green and grey and silver, or bewigged with smooth beech woods. The distances appeared immense.

But beside her and very much in the foreground was Con-rad Pybus, solid and obvious, all black and white, a heavy man who could not sit comfortably in her presence. He had been trying so hard to impress her. He wanted her to marry him. And she, with the merciless eyes of a woman who had no illusions, saw him as a glorified and rather flashy stockbroker's clerk, a morning-paper man, worth perhaps fifteen thousand pounds a year. He had a place—Chlois Court—in Berkshire.

She allowed herself to agree with him.

"All those clouds massed up there. Rather fine. How much have we done?"

"Oh—about seventy. You wouldn't know it in this 'bus, would you? An hour and a half. No so bad."

His large, white face, with its unblinking blue eyes and a very black moustache, reminded her somehow of the face of a chef. But why a chef? How oddly one associated things! Only—that particular sort of face seemed to call for a chef's white cap. She smiled.

"You are going to give me lunch there!"

His right hand reached for the gear lever.

"Of course. Saracen's Head. I wired them before we started."

The car went softly down into the valley where the Brent ran under the grey span of an old bridge between the steep greenness of overhanging trees. "Aunt Ursy" was peering into a little mirror. She had one of those ivory skins that are proof against sunburn or worry, and neither her skin nor her hair needed attention. Conrad Pybus was showing her how he could handle a car on the narrow steeps of the ascent into Castle Craven. He was very conscious of her sitting there, squinting at her sleek face in that provoking little mirror. Yes, she was "it," as much "it" as the car he was driving, but she would take more handling, oh—yes—much more handling. He might be a new man, but Chlois Court had a ripe and proper atmosphere.

While she, consummate wordling, but coolly honest, as many worldings are, watched a high stone garden-wall glide by, its greyness tufted with golden St. John's wort and draped with Campanula. Colour! Of course! The man had no colour. Moreover, he possessed one of those heavy white skins which resemble greasy vellum. Hence the "chef complex." Yes—that settled it; for, whatever she might be, she was like most women, richly fastidious, a saint in her æsthetics, if something of a vagrant in her morals.

Meanwhile Conrad Pybus's blue car, with its black coupé and silver snout, climbed the steep and tortuous Bridge Street into Castle Craven. He drove with a confident care. He was doing the thing well, and it was no use doing things badly in the presence of Ursula Calmady.

"Might be the Brooklands test-hill. Oh—you idiot!"

Baulked by a Ford van that pulled out in front of him without a by-your-leave or a signal, he had to hold the car on the steep hill. The lady glanced at his face. He had the air of saying to himself things that in her presence could not be said.

She smiled to herself.

"No—my dear, no. You are not a bad sort, but in six months you would be saying those things aloud."

The car moved on, and she allowed herself to feel self-revealed in the dignity of Castle Craven. Its very steepness was dramatic and Shakespearean. Between little grey crowded houses, the cobbled streets swept up and through the black throat of an old gate. There was a sudden enlargement of the sky. The tall houses drew back under the smiling white clouds. A church tower with six pinnacles, each topped by a gilded vane, made a glittering against the blueness. In the centre of the great space a market cross rallied the town. There were houses of stone and houses of Georgian brick, and a row of pollarded limes shading the fronts of a line of shops. On the left a golden head swinging on an iron bracket overhung the broad pavement. A little farther on the White

Hart Inn wore upon the top of its white-pillared portico a turban of flowers. Two red 'buses, and half a dozen cars were drawn up by the Cross.

The obvious Pybus drew in towards the Saracen's Head.

"Well, here we are."

He was made to measure.

2

Double glass doors opened from the vestibule into the hall of the Saracen's Head. Directly opposite to you as you entered was the office, with the registration book open upon the counter, and the fluffy fair head of Miss Vallence—the book-keeper and reception clerk—visible between a green-baize letter-board and a time-table of the local bus service. A strip of faded red carpet stretched from the glass doors to the office. Four cane chairs and two smokers' tables were arranged symmetrically, one either side of this red strip of carpet.

On the right and the left, passages led to the lounge and the coffee-room. A flight of stairs, covered with the same red carpet, disappeared between two green china pedestals support-ing aspidistras in cherry-coloured pots. Between one of these pedestals and the office window, with a big brass gong hanging behind him like a halo, a little man in a black alpaca coat stood for some eight hours each day.

He was the hotel "boots," but his activities were various. He was a sort of watch-dog and cicerone. Whenever a car drew up he would go out to meet it. He carried up luggage, and carried it down again. He sold odd stamps, and provided luggage labels, and distributed the morning papers, and was sent upon errands. The Saracen's Head knew him as John. His rather big and well-polished black boots had—in that par-ticular place between the china pedestal and the office window —impressed a blurred, worn mark upon the carpet. His digressions were frequent and various, but returning from them he would resume his place by the brass gong like a spider re-turning to the centre of his web.

His appearance was not a little remarkable. Imagine the head of a Roman emperor upon the body of a boy of fourteen. He was old, how old nobody knew. His brilliantly white hair fitted his big head like a legal wig. He had very blue eyes, and a grey, inscrutable, resolute face.

"John——!"

"Yes, miss,"—or, "Yes, sir."

He had manners and dignity in an age which is peculiarly lacking in both of them. Understanding people put him down as having been a servant in some house of quality, a footman, or perhaps a groom. There was something about him that suggested horses. Moreover, he could stand quite still under the eyes of the hotel's loungers, and such stillness is rare. He might appear a funny little old fellow in his black alpaca coat and grey trousers, and very clean as to the collar, but not so funny as many a young fellow-my-lad might think. You took him courteously or you did not take him at all. Those blue eyes of his could be as disconcerting as the eyes of Marius were to the slave.

3

It happened that this old Roman was standing in his usual place in front of the brass gong when Mr. Conrad Pybus's car pulled up at the kerb. The blue bonnet was the colour of a French soldier's tunic. Every sort of car pulled up at the Saracen's Head, and their cargoes were as various as the cars. But this was a car of quality, and old John walked along the strip of carpet, and out down the two well-whitened steps. He did not hurry. He was both brisk and deliberate.

"Allow me, madam."

The lady was in the act of opening the door of the coupé Old John saw her and not the man, for—in the act of leaning forward she obscured the figure of Mr. Conrad Pybus. She was a gentlewoman—as well as a lady. She exhaled an indefinable perfume, and was smart with an exquisite and simple rightness. Her dark and jocund eyes smiled at old John from under the brim of a black hat. She was wearing a simple tweed suit in which purples and browns were blended.

John held the door open for her.

"Any luggage, madam?"

There was something roguish in her glance.

"No; no luggage, thank you."

"Very good, madam. The lounge is on the left. I will show the gentleman the garage."

She crossed the pavement and went up the two white steps, and old John stood holding the handle of the coupé door. He was looking at Mr. Conrad Pybus. His blue eyes seemed to grow very large with a staring, challenging intensity. Mr. Pybus stared back, but his eyes were the eyes of a man profoundly astonished and nonplussed. Also—he was profoundly disturbed. His big white face seemed to hang there in the interior of the coupé like a bladder of lard. A gloved hand rested tentatively on the knob of the gear lever.

There was an extraordinary stillness. It may have lasted for ten seconds. Then the interlocked glances of the two men seemed to fall apart, or rather—the younger man's eyes flinched from the older one's. Old John was closing the door when a voice intervened.

"Oh, I have left my bag."

She had come back for her vanity bag, and old John recovered it from the seat, and closed the door of the coupé with a gesture of crisp fierceness.

"The garage is on the left, sir, through the arch."

Mr. Pybus, staring straight ahead through the wind-screen, pulled the gear lever over.

"Are you taking lunch, sir?"

"I am."

"You'll find a side door in the yard, sir. Gentlemen's lavatory just inside, first on the right."

Old John, turning with deliberation, walked back into the hotel, and his white head regained its yellow halo as he resumed his place in front of the brass gong.

4

That he as a man should sit calmly down to lunch after cutting his own father was beyond Mr. Conrad Pybus's capacity. Obviously he was not himself, or rather—he was too much himself. He had reverted—and without realizing his reversion—to the little barbarisms of the struggling 'thirties, when he had scuffled with life in his shirt-sleeves.

Moreover, he was so very conscious of Lady Ursula, sitting opposite him at the little table in a recess by the window. A card with "Reserved" printed upon it remained propped against a vase full of purple and white asters. Yes; she too was so confoundedly reserved, such a woman of elevation and of quality, poised like Diana before his moon-faced homage. For the last three months he had been trying so hard to place himself on some sort of feeling of equality with her, to impress her, to realize himself as Conrad Pybus, Esq., of Chlois Court.

Then—consider the immoderate obstinacy of that absurd old man! How could a fellow have foreseen such a damnable coincidence? To hear yourself saying: "Hallo—Dad," to a little old fellow who cleaned the boots, and saying it in the presence of that most elusive and ironic goddess. Besides—it wasn't as though he and Probyn had not attempted to do something for the old curmudgeon.

The head-waiter was standing at Mr. Conrad's elbow.

"Lunch, sir?"

"Take that card away."

"Certainly, sir."

"I ordered lunch by wire—a special lunch."

"Yes, sir. I know all about it, sir. The wine is on ice."

George, of the Saracen's Head, had a soothing voice, and a sleepy and humorous eye. He knew his world. Obviously the gentleman was in a fractious mood, being the kind of new gentleman who raised his voice and made a fuss when things were not going well. George's sleepy eye observed the lady. She was putting one of the asters in place with an air of doing what came natural to her. Her face had the glimmer of an inward smile.

"Soup or hors d'œuvres, sir?"

Mr. Pybus was posed. He bungled his French, and realized that he had bungled it when his lady made her choice. And he was most absurdly annoyed. First—a wild oddity of a father bobbing up like the ghost of his own past, and then a fool of a waiter tricking him into speaking of hors doovres! He became throaty and self-conscious.

"I must apologize for this—place. Had it recommended to me by Pelham. Doesn't do to take an *ipse dixit*."

She looked him straight in the face.

"Don't you like it?"

"Flyblown—like most of these country pubs."

That something had upset him was as obvious as was the heavy white solidity of his countenance. She wondered what it was. Not that it mattered. The loutishness in certain sorts of men is easily rediscovered. He glared; he examined the table silver; almost she expected to see him take up a spoon and polish it with a corner of the tablecloth. And she was amused. Always she had loved mischief, but mischief without malice, and it seemed to her that she was watching a materialization of the real Conrad Pybus, of the man who sat in his office chair in his shirt-sleeves and smoked rank cigars, and bullied people. His voice appeared to slip back into his throat and to become thick and aggressive. She was vividly aware of his crudities, of the inherent vulgarities of the man, and suddenly she wondered how she had been persuaded to spend the day in his car. She hadn't been persuaded. She had been provoked by an impulse, an ironical curiosity. And here she was sitting opposite to him, and feeling the hot waves of his extreme discomfort pouring over her. Moreover, what was the use of ordering wine to be iced if you had not been schooled to suppress the common heats of the body?

She glanced over her shoulder at the window.

"Don't you find it very hot in here?"

He did. He was perspiring. He expended a further portion of his heat upon the waiter.

"Open that window, will you?"

"Certainly, sir."

The window was opened, but he continued to give her the impression of a man lunching in a London grill-room on a hot August day. She surmised that the salad would be flat, and it was. And again he expanded more heat upon the waiter, quite unnecessary heat. She was feeling the freshness of the hill-town air whispering round her shoulders, and she had all the essential and clear coolness of her breed, but she began to be infected by his flushes and his discomforts. It was like travelling in a stuffy and crowded railway carriage next to some stout person who mopped and panted.

"Beastly lunch—I'm afraid—I'm sorry."

She assured him that the lunch was excellent. But what had upset him? Not that she asked the question. She had ceased from wishing to ask Mr. Conrad Pybus any questions. She had become too conscious of his incongruities. He continued to remain in a heat of frettings and apologetics, and while applying the coolness of her easy voice to the fevered forehead of conversation, she considered Mr. Conrad Pybus as a social specimen. He reminded her of some common child who had been carefully drilled and prompted for some social occasion, and whose niceness crumbled and fell to pieces under the stress of sudden publicity. She saw him as a moist, awkward figure, eating with uneasy ferocity, using its table napkin too frequently on that very black moustache, pulling bread to pieces with its bolster fingers. She was reminded of the simile of a man sitting upon a hot plate. He fizzled.

"Hang it—this meat's a bit off."

"Is it? Really—I think you must be just a little unfortunate."

Her incorrigible self was conscious of inward whisperings. A bit off! Oh, delicious and splurging Pybus! Almost she feared for his aspirates. And with the cool air on her neck and shoulders she thought of Chlois Court, and his pictures, and his library with its multitudinous classics all bound in red leather. Culture—culture spelt with a very big K, Teutonic, a little pathetic. And yet, in spite of his carefulness and his contrivings, the trotter protruded in proximity to the trough.

But she began to wish for the end of the meal. She decided that the day's adventure had reached its climax, and that he needed cooling under the trees of Chlois Court.

"Really—it has been a delightful drive."

He asked her if she would care to wander round Castle Craven. There was the castle, and the Master Mostyn museum—"Prehistoric stuff, you know." Smiling her own smile she assured him that she had to be back for tea. Could he manage it? Of course he could manage it. He showed a sudden restiveness. He brought out a black leather wallet and put it back again. He asked her if she would like a liqueur with her coffee.

"A Kümmel, please."

He called the waiter.

"Two Kümmels and two coffees."

"In the lounge, sir?"

"No—here."

His restiveness seemed to increase. Frowning over his Stilton he actually missed a remark of hers.

"Wonder if you'd excuse me a moment. I'm a bit doubtful about the petrol."

"Of course."

"My chap's a careless idiot. There's a petrol pump in the yard. I'll get the fellow in charge to fill me up."

"Please do."

He placed an open cigarette-case in front of her, but forgot the matches.

"Won't be a minute."

She smiled at his departing back.

5

Mr. Conrad Pybus appeared in the hall of the Saracen's Head rather with the air of a man who had pocketed some of the table silver and was determined that no one should know it. He strolled. He lit a cigar. He had come out in search of the little old man with the big white head and the black alpaca jacket, but the father of Probyn and Conrad Pybus had gone to his dinner.

The son strolled to the street door, stood on the white steps for a minute, and listened to Castle Craven's old heart beating to the new rhythm. A dirty young man in a blue French cap and a soiled brown mackintosh passed by with his modern music and his odours; the detonations of his machine seemed to strike against the faces of the old houses and to reverberate from one side of the square to the other.

"Filthy things," thought the man on the doorstep.

Certainly. Filthy, yet useful. But where was that incorrigible old man, that Diogenes out of his tub, that John Pybus of the invincible blue eyes? Was it possible that he was still a little afraid of his father? He—Conrad Pybus, Esq., of Chlois Court, afraid of an hotel "boots!" But was it not the unexpected and the incalculable that one feared? Yet, he wanted to explain. It was necessary that he should explain Ula Calmady, and the awkwardness of the contretemps, and the need for shutting one eye. His father had always been such an uncompromising old devil. He had always insisted upon keeping both those very blue eyes wide open.

Mr. Conrad strolled back up the strip of red carpet. He was for tempting a second encounter. He spoke to Miss Vallence in the office.

"Excuse me—porter anywhere about?"

"Gone to his dinner, sir. I'll ring."

"Oh—don't bother. It was about some petrol. I can manage."

He took the passage leading to the old coaching yard, where the blue car stood in the shade of a high wall, and as he emerged into the yard he saw a little figure crossing it. The son removed the cigar from between his thickish lips.

"Here—I say—one moment——"

John Pybus paused, turned, and looked at his son.

"Did you call, sir?"

Mr. Conrad strolled heavily across the cobbles. He was

very conscious of that grey, resolute face with its incorruptible blue eyes. As a man of the world and a man of business—big business—he would have chosen to wink at his father—but then—you might just as well have winked at Jehovah.

"I say—just a moment——"

His voice insinuated. It suggested a smooth yet stealthy gesture. The yard appeared deserted.

"Just a moment——"

Old Pybus seemed to stand very square on his heels.

"I don't know you, sir."

And he went on and by his son, looking up slantwise into his face like a veteran marching past some very young general who had seen no red blood spilt.

CHAPTER II

I

OLD John Pybus's father—Peter Paul Pybus—whom someone had nicknamed the "Cato of Booksellers' Row"—had—as a counterblast against his own parents' partiality for apostolic names—christened his own son John Julian Apostasius. For Peter Paul had gone beyond mere noncomformity. He had been a Bradlaugh man in the days when such hardihood might seriously damage a man's pocket, and in associating his son with the Emperor Julian—called the Apostate—he had defied both his wife and society. Peter Paul had relented so far as to allow the "John," for as Mrs. Mary had asserted—"How could a boy go to a Christian school labelled Julian—Apostasius!" Peter Paul had agreed that it would not be fair to the child, and that a good, stout simple name should be added as a sort of handle.

In those days, before the coming of Kingsway, and the "Waldorf," and Bush House, Peter Paul Pybus had had a shop in Booksellers' Row. Boys from the city schools had come to Mr. Pybus for secondhand copies of Ovid and Thucydides, but they had been obliged to go elsewhere for their cribs, for Mr. Pybus had held strong views upon education and had refused to pander to the lazy. A little, brown, snuffy shop in the very narrow part of the street, it had had a certain reputation with collectors of first editions. The reputation of the shop had been the reputation of Peter Paul Pybus. Packed full of literary gossip, obtained from heaven knows where, he had taken an interest in all the literary scandals and sensations of two generations. He could have told you just how and why Buchanan attacked Rossetti, and how Tennyson liked to administer rhythmical smacks to a pretty and feminine shoulder when declaiming his own verse. Mr. Peter Paul would never allow Tennyson his poetry. "Suburban stuff, sir. Give me Browning."

One of John Julian's early recollections was of a certain shop that was opened in the Row directly opposite the bookshop of Peter Paul. John was fifteen at the time, and the shop had puzzled him. It offered you French novels of a sort, and queer little boxes of artificial sweets. It was a surreptitious shop, and people peered into it surreptitiously. It a*tracted the schoolboys who came to buy school-books. John Julian would sometimes catch two or three of them sniggering outside it, and waiting for some other boy who had sneaked in to buy photographs.

John remembered asking his father about that shop, and his father's frozen face, and the rasp of his voice.

"There isn't any such shop, sir——"

"But—there is. Haven't you been across——?"

Peter Paul had gripped his son by both shoulders.

"Dog's vomit—my lad. Step over it. I say there is no such shop."

And for Mr. Peter Paul Pybus there was not. He had a habit of mind that was Cromwellian, and he passed on a part of it to his son.

The elder Pybus and his wife died somewhere in the 'eighties, and John Julian inherited the business, and took to himself a wife. And he, too, was something of an oddity. He stood five feet three, and he married a woman of five feet eleven. It was said in jest by their intimates that John Pybus had to fetch the step-ladder out of the shop when he wanted to kiss his wife. But her height was her only distinction, and it is more than probable that John Julian was disappointed in his marriage. Poor Edith Pybus was both weak and argumentative, and she argued at the wrong moments. She set out to spoil the two boys whom John Julian had given her, and over the upbringing of these two boys there were many clashings. Not for nothing had John the head of a Roman emperor. And he was a Victorian. He had a sort of moral earnestness, an extraordinary sense of honour and of public duty, and like his father he was absolutely fearless. The mother, sentimental and flabby, had set herself with the boys against the father. She gave them sweets after their canings. She tried to smuggle their offences out of sight.

"Boys will be boys, John."

Whereas John Julian believed that most boys—his own included—were little savages and howling egoists, and that no man is made without good and appropriate lickings. Nor should this be set down to hardness of heart. He tried to be more wisely kind to his two boys than was their foolish, conspiring, jealous mother.

He sent the two youngsters to a goodish school, but he was never on such terms with them as he had been with his own father. They were big youths; they appeared to take after their mother; at the ages of sixteen and fourteen they were able to look down upon their little Roman-headed father. During those earlier years, when he had felt more the mate of his wife, John Julian had allowed her to choose the babies' names. Hence Probyn and Conrad.

John Pybus had trouble with them from the time of their going to school, and as they grew taller and more full of the arrogance of the awkward age, the trouble increased. They had inherited the concentrated, lower middle-class snobbery of their mother; they had a loudness; they quarrelled; they purloined each other's ties and collars. Conrad was a bully. Both of them were perfectly familiar with the secrets of the shop across the way. In fact, at the age of seventeen, Probyn was the possessor of a collection of indecent photographs which had to be hidden away under a loose board in his bedroom.

So that when the wife died, and the two young bounders were put out into the world—Probyn with a wholesale woollen firm, Conrad as a clerk in a shipping office—John Julian felt a little weary of them, and of the narrowness of the Row. In fact, it is probable that it was the pulling down of the Row that sent him into the country. He sold the London business, and took over a shop in the Dorsetshire town of Winterbourne. For many years he sold books to the Dorset folks; but the market was limited, and if he managed to keep himself and his housekeeper, he did little more. He wrote regularly to his sons, and saw them occasionally. More than once they borrowed money from him—or rather—he gave it, and would not hear of its return. Probyn married the daughter of a speculative builder who was scattering villas about the Surrey suburbs. They had one son, Lancelot, prophetically shortened by his mother to "Lance." Conrad was unmarried. He liked his adventures, but he liked them cheap. A fellow could be a very devil among the shop-girls on Yarmouth beach, and if you were careful— Conrad was careful.

2

But of John Pybus's ultimate and final quarrel with his sons no one knew and no one cared.

Why should they care? John Pybus had never asked for pity. As a gladiator he had gone down fighting, and fate had dragged him out by the heels, and finding him still alive had decreed that he should live as one of the arena slaves and scatter sand over pools of blood.

On that August day he had met one of his own sons in the arena, and the man of the 'forties had fled from the man of the 'seventies. Old Pybus had watched Mr. Conrad get with some hurriedness into his car and bundle out into the market square. Mr. John resumed his halo. He was on duty by the brass gong when Conrad, having recovered the lady, shepherded her with heavy impressiveness out of the Saracen's Head. They passed Mr. John Pybus standing by the gong. They went together down the strip of red carpet. Mr. Conrad was still apologizing.

"Beastly place!"

His father was wondering whether a woman with that dainty and whimsical face could bring herself to bargain across the counter with a shopman. He felt a liking for the gentlewoman. She had smiled and looked at him and spoken. He was an old man. His impulse was to accost her and to say: "That fellow's a rotter. Turn him adrift." But, then Conrad Pybus was not exactly a rotter, but a person of property, and it was probable that a woman who could wear her clothes as the lady wore them had her own philosophy.

George, the waiter, coming out for a few words with old John, who was treated rather as a sage and a great man by those who worked with him, spread a palm in which lay a shilling.

"Gave me that—he did, for a special lunch, and the wine iced, and him with a lady."

Yes, Conrad had always been careful, and old Pybus's thoughts went back to the occasion when he had quarrelled finally, and like a Cromwell, with the carefulness of Conrad and the punctiliousness of Probyn. It had happened during those Winterbourne days, in the second year of the war. Mr. Pybus had been in difficulties at the time, for his selling of books—never very brisk—had languished with the war. But the quarrel between John Pybus and his sons had had nothing to do with business, though business had been at the back of it.

For John Pybus was old English. When there was war there was war, and if his country was involved in it, then it was his—John Pybus's war, and his sons' war. He was an old-fashioned patriot. Also—he was—or had been a bit of a Puritan. Also—he was blue-eyed and resolute against the bully, were he emperor or Bolshevist. So Mr. Pybus had been able to speak of the war as Armageddon without cribbing an obvious bleat from the popular Press. St. George for England!

Absurd, great little old man, facing bankruptcy, yet able to lose himself in the great tragedy, and to get up at recruiting meetings and speak to the young men. "I am a man of peace—but I charge you—take up the sword." For a year he was a kind of fiery cross at Winterbourne, and so successfully fiery that he was sought for to set alight other and damper districts.

Meanwhile his own sons procrastinated. Probyn could not be spared, but he was doing his best to be spared, though he was thirty-seven and a married man. Conrad spoke of joining the Royal Naval Reserve. The letters that old Pybus wrote to them were not models of tact. Your Cromwellian soul does not trouble about the squeak of a boot. He could not understand at first why sons of his had not been among the first hundred thousand, but when he did understand it, he took up the scourge. He bought a third-class return ticket to London, but he had to follow Probyn to Yorkshire, in order to have it out with the elder son. Probyn, a little sheepish and sententious, had very good excuses. It appeared that he had become indispensable; his father-in-law had put up some money, and Probyn had interests. Wool was a necessity—you know, and so was a man who could give the army what it wanted. Conrad, unearthed somewhere near Fenchurch Street, was less explanatory than his brother. He was busy, arrogantly and perspiringly busy. Ships—you old fool—ships and more ships! He did not call this meddling old fire-eater a fool, but he implied it. Besides, he was a careful fellow; he was out to make money.

John Pybus returned to Winterbourne with a very fierce blue eye. He had said things to his sons, things which would not be forgotten. He had called them shirkers, gun-shies, opportunists. Such burs stick even to sleek jackets.

And then—when speaking at an open-air meeting in a certain rather backward town, old Pybus met the New English. He was heckled. A young man with a little ginger moustache and prominent teeth, who was something in a Somersetshire coal mine, reared a head and asked questions.

"I'd like to ask the speaker—whether he has any sons."

"Two," said old Pybus promptly, like an old Roman confronting the Gauls.

"And are they in the army.?"

"No—they're not. And be damned to them."

3

Early in 1917 John Pybus sold himself up, lock, stock and barrel, and after paying all his creditors, disappeared from Winterbourne with some twenty-five pounds in his pocket. He disappeared, too, out of the lives of his sons. He had cursed them and, without wishing that the old fellow's curses would come home to roost, they found it convenient to remain estranged. Not that they made no effort to find the old man, or failed to make a magnanimous gesture. Probyn, softer-fibred than his brother, happening to be in the south-west on business, broke a journey at Winterbourne on one reeking December day, and found the little book-shop in other hands. Squeezed in between two bigger buildings rather like a child in a crowded railway carriage, it reproached Probyn. It looked cold and grey. His father's name had disappeared. The paint was cracked and peeling, and Probyn was wearing a fur-lined coat.

He had made inquiries. His father's putting-up of the shutters had signalized a voluntary bankruptcy. John Pybus had departed with honour, but no one knew what had become of him. It took Probyn three months to discover that his father was earning a living as a tram-conductor in a midland town. Probyn held out a filial and magnanimous hand.

It was repulsed. John Pybus was not to be pitied. He was quite capable of working. He had no intention of accepting three pounds a week and obscurity in a south-coast watering-place or a London suburb. He said in effect: "You can keep your money; the money that ought to have gone to the men out there in the trenches."

Obstinate old man. After that there was silence, and the silence lasted for ten years. The two Pybus sons had made use of their opportunities. Probyn had bought and sold mills; he had a place at Windover in Bucks.; in 1920 he was knighted; Dolly Pybus became Lady Pybus; Lancelot was at Eton. Conrad, still a bachelor, and in the cream and the plumpness of the forties, had translated sundry shipping deals into a country estate and culture, and some two hundred thousand pounds safely stowed away. So did some of our great men arrive during those extraordinary years, while old Pybus drifted about England, an obscure and resolute philosopher. He came to rest at last at Castle Craven. He liked the large sky and the rolling country, and the cheerful human bustle of the inn, and the little stone cottage he was allowed to occupy between the garden of the Saracen's Head and the Castle Field. He had a niche. He was both a nobody and a somebody. He had books, and one or two intimates. He had a patron and protector—though he did not need one—Mr. Backhouse, miller, seed and cake merchant, and man of property, who owned the Saracen's Head, and kept Pounds, the cockily-servile young manager, very much at heel.

To some of the irreverent know-alls Conrad and Sir Probyn Pybus were referred to as "Shipping and Shoddy." But no one knew that they had a little old curmudgeon of a father who was "boots" at a country hotel. The paternal Pybus was supposed to be dead. He had become a mythical figure. Lady Pybus allowed it to be known that her father-in-law had been something of a literary man, a connoisseur, and a merchant who had traded in rare books. Oh, no, there had been no soiling of the Pybus fingers. The Heralds' College had traced the Pybus family into Lincolnshire, good old stock with a somewhat Dutch flavour. Lancelot was to go to Cambridge—Trinity, of course. He was a dear boy, and so clever. Lady Pybus's father had built himself a mansion on a Surrey hill. All was well with the Pybus world.

4

After his tea each evening, John Pybus fed the pigeons. White fantails, blue rocks and half-breeds, they came to him from the red roofs of the inn's stables and outhouses, and from the ruins of the castle. They swarmed and fluttered about the old man, alighting upon his shoulders and his hands, and often his white head would be crested with one of the birds. He fed them with bread-crumbs and odd handfuls of corn. With his short pipe stuck in his mouth he would stand in the midst of these wheeling, fluttering, strutting birds, and so thick were they at times that he appeared as in a cloud of living snowflakes.

Any time of the day he had only to take his stand in the stone-paved yard or broad passage between his cottage and the inn garden, and whistle his pigeon call, and half a dozen birds

would come to him. There were some of them ready to
follow him into the cottage, but since the fantails shed white
feathers and John Pybus had a passion for tidiness, he allowed
them as far as his doorstep, but no further.

The cottage was half stone, half red brick, with a pantiled
roof. The kitchen faced the inn. The window of the living-
room looked out over John Pybus's patch of garden, and
beyond it to the green slopes of the castle field and to the castle
itself, with its walls tufted with wallflower and snapdragon.
Some very old ash trees grew among the ruins. The Hart
Royal tower still showed its crenellations black against the
sunset. Beyond it the ground fell steeply to the river, the
banks deep with the shade of beeches, and always there was a
murmuring of water and the play of the wind in the trees.

Mr. John Backhouse had put Mr. John Pybus into the
cottage. In the old days the head ostler had occupied it, but
since hardly a horse came into the inn yard, and the garage
attendant had seven children and lived out in Bridge Street,
the cottage was at Mr. Pybus's service.

Mr. Backhouse had—with characteristic abruptness and a
twitching of his grey eyebrows—announced the fact to Mr.
Pounds.

"I'm putting Pybus into Castle Cottage."

That was in the days when Charlie Pounds had believed
that, as manager of the Saracen's Head, he had a right to argue
with Mr. Backhouse.

"I thought of sleeping the girls in it. There are three rooms,
counting the sitting-room——"

Mr. Backhouse did not argue. He was laconic, and wasted
no breath. If a person disagreed with a statement of his he
just repeated the statement.

He said: "I'm putting Pybus into Castle Cottage."

Pounds, who had a face rather like a cake of Castile soap,
with two sultanas for eyes, had begged to object.

"It's waste of good room, sir."

Mr. Backhouse had twitched his long eyebrows, and had
asked Mr. Pounds if he happened to be deaf.

"Did you hear what I said?"

"I did, sir."

"Well, don't waste my time."

John Pybus made his own bed. It was a very simple affair: a camp-bed of green canvas, with one army blanket below and one above and a pair of cotton sheets between them. His furniture, too, was of the simplest; a couple of Windsor chairs, an oak table very worm-eaten, a five-tier deal book-case full of books, a basket-chair with a red cushion, a square of green cord carpet to cover the floor. His bedroom floor had no carpet. On the living-room mantelpiece in front of a little gilt framed mirror he kept a calendar, his pipes, a tobacco tin, and three photographs, the photos of his wife and his two sons. It was an ironic, yet human touch.

He fetched in his own water and swept his own floors, though help was available. The women liked John Pybus. He was a clean and handsome old man. They spoke of him always as Mr. Pybus, and in an irreverent age that was no light tribute. One of the chambermaids—Sally Summerscales, a sturdy little dark-eyed thing, insisted on occasional tidyings up, more for the love of the thing than because the cottage needed it. But she darned John Pybus's socks, and patched his shirts, and fussed over him as some women fuss over a man for the sake of human self-expression. She was a mixture of shrewdness and of unsophisticated curiosity. Mr. Pybus was an oddity, but to Sally he was an interesting and picturesque oddity. She chattered to him and told him about her love affairs, and asked his advice about them, and never took it when it was given.

From the first she had been interested in the photographs on Mr. Pybus's mantelpiece. She had asked about them.

"My wife—Sally."

"She's dead, is she?"

"Thirty years or more."

"And who are the gentlemen?"

"My two sons. They were killed in the war."

"Poor fellows," said Sally, going closer to look at Conrad and Probyn, and stroking her square chin with a crooked first finger. "They are not a bit like you, Mr. Pybus."

"They took after their mother."

"So you're all alone?"

"Yes, quite alone, Sally."

"It does seem hard."

"No company is better than poor company."

Sally supposed that it was. And Mr. Pybus was not quite like ordinary men. She had discovered the gentleness in him, but it was the gentleness of some stout old tree sunning itself in the light of a tranquil evening. He had his thoughts and his books and the belief that nothing could matter to him very seriously any more. He put on spectacles to read with.

He read a great deal by the light of a paraffin lamp with a green shade, sitting in the basket-chair with the red cushion, and wearing horn-rimmed spectacles. He read poetry and philosophy. He was a great admirer of Blake. He was both classical and modern. He subscribed to one of the London libraries, and each month he had a box of books sent down. He was amazingly up to date in his knowledge of social tendencies and of scientific thought. His interest in life as life was deep and unabated.

CHAPTER III

I

M R. CONRAD drove over to Windover.
Mr. John Pybus's presence at Castle Craven within a morning's drive of both Windover Hall and Chlois Court was a family complication, and Conrad was a cautious fellow.

Turning in at the lodge gates, between two stone pillars capped with griffins, he saw before him, the famous avenue of beeches arched like a great green tunnel. Always there was a soft, cool movement of air under the spreading boughs of the old trees. The grey trunks were spaced like the pillars of a temple, and the cool drift of the air between them made young Lance Pybus imagine that he was feeling the breath of the divine afflatus.

He was an imaginative lad; he had a temperament.

Mr. Conrad Pybus, proof against all such fancies, saw the redness of the Queen Anne house glowing at the end of the avenue. The old brick-work had the sun upon it, and the sashes of its windows were very white. Chlois Court was bastard Gothic, conceived by some early Victorian; and though Conrad's house had a more dramatic exterior than his brother's, Conrad was a little envious of that old red brick-work. It was so mellow. It suggested that Probyn himself had mellowed more gracefully than had his younger brother. Yes, there was something Georgian about Probyn. He had developed a country manner, or what he conceived to be a country manner.

Conrad stopped his car on the gravel, to the east of the yew hedge and the terrace. Through the square openings in the yew hedge he had glimpses of Probyn's lawns, and the flower borders, and the pleached limes of the Dutch garden. It was all very still, and slightly autumnal, with the dew yet upon it, and some of the old trees showing here and there a tinge of yellow. Conrad's broad nostrils seemed to narrow. Always it appeared to him that Probyn's head gardener got better results than his man did at Chlois Court. Damn the fellow! Still, his dahlias were always better than Probyn's. Jealousy can include the most trivial of details.

You might be jealous of your brother, but you entered his house informally, and Conrad walked towards the terrace; but in the angle that the yew hedge made with the south-east corner of the house young Lance was reading Noel Coward's plays. He had tucked a deck-chair into this sheltered corner. His flannel trousers were well up to his knees; his dark blue socks were the socks of a rowing man. He wore a white, blue-edged Trinity blazer.

"Hallo, Conrad."

"Hallo, my lad."

There was a sulkiness in these salutations, for Probyn's son had the knack of making his uncle feel aggressive and uncomfortable. Eton and Trinity! This second edition of the Pybus text-book had received the author's corrections. It was a more complete and polished product. It could lounge in a chair, and glancing up casually address its uncle as "Hallo, Conrad." Young prig!

"Father in?"

"Try the library."

Lance Pybus resumed his reading, and his uncle walked on towards the french window of the library. He disliked his nephew, because Lance—even as a child—had been a creature of queer aloofness, the kind of boy who watched you and listened to you with a mysteriously grave face, and remained insultingly silent. At least Conrad had felt his nephew's silence to be an offence. It had given him the feeling of being spied upon, criticized, ridiculed. The boy had never been anything else but a reticent, conceited, embarrassing young brute, and the young man looked like being worse than the boy. Probyn and Dot had spoilt him. Obviously. But Lance's very looks were very disturbing to his uncle. There was something challenging in the eager, upward lift of the head. His dark hair gave the impression of being blown back. It was like the head of youth running swiftly against the wind.

His broad face, with its large and sensitive mouth and short nose, had a young matureness, a reticent but sparkling obstinacy. And there were those very blue eyes, either very bright and near or very distant. They were the eyes of that incorruptible old man—his grandfather.

Meanwhile, Lance turned his head to watch his Uncle Conrad's progress along the terrace. Conrad turned his toes out; he had the walk of a man who would be very fat at five and fifty; his neck was too short; he had a greasiness.

Yes—that was it, a suggestion of greasiness, for if Lance was an offence to his uncle, Conrad was far more subtly unpleasing to his brother's son. It was a question of temperament, of fibre, of vibrations. Lance might baffle the older man, but Conrad Pybus was no mystery to the nephew. It was as though those very blue eyes looked right through Mr. Conrad's thick and soapy skin, and saw—— Yes, what exactly did he see? Perhaps it was more feeling than seeing, a shrinking, a scorn, an indignation, a revulsion from a nature that was essentially garish and vulgar. For as a boy Lance had been absurdly fastidious; he would shrink away from the touch of certain people; he had loathed fat meat, or the smell of vinegar. Conrad had been one of the persons who had nauseated him.

Beneath a lounging exterior there was swiftness and fire. He had a dignity of his own, a very definite attitude towards life. It included a mental bearing upon his father's business, the "Jason Wools," and the "Sign of the Golden Fleece." He disliked the Pybus advertisements in the daily papers. They were not redeemed even by their publication in the advertising pages of *Punch*. Why tamper with an old Greek legend? Why throw Medea overboard, and stamp a golden fleece in red upon your packing-cases? Why commercialize Jason? No doubt Jason had been nothing but a fighting merchant adventurer. But these modern Jasons with their custard powders and their pills, and their blatant shoutings, and their quite foolish, cheap exaggerations! What a modest age! Language was ceasing to be able to express the stupendous virtues of soaps and motor-cars and bottled beer and shoddy.

Lance might have a temperament, but he was a fighter.

There were certain people and properties that he could not abide, cheap people, louts and their loutish English voices, all raw and crude creatures, the sploshed faces one sees in a city, faces that Nature did not think it worth her while to finish. In fact, he hated ugliness. He had been known to fly into sudden passionate rages. It was known among his intimates at Eton that, mocked at by three louts who had come in a chara-banc to see the house the King lived in, he had fought the three of them in a side street. And though the three of them had set upon him in chorus, having the peculiar sense of honour of their class, he had come away prettily battered, but with his young male pride in the ascendant. He had seen the three flinch from him and from his berserker scorn of them.

Nearly ten years ago he had seen *Cyrano* played in London. Cyrano was one of his great men.

Meanwhile it occurred to him to wonder what Uncle Conrad wanted with his father at ten o'clock on a September morning. Mr. Conrad must have left Chlois Court directly after breakfast, and he was a late riser. He was one of those fellows who got out of bed like a wallowing beast emerging from a mudhole.

Lance frowned. There are occasions when a young man has qualms, and an unpleasant realization of what those qualms imply.

2

Sir Probyn Pybus was writing a letter when he became aware of his brother standing at the open window.

"Hallo, Conrad."

Probyn was red where his brother was sallow. Tall and ruddy and rather spare, he had a smooth geniality and very fine manners which, though put on like the shop-walker's frock coat, fitted him with some naturalness. His right eye had a slight cast in it. His eyes were of that colour which is neither blue nor green nor grey, but a blending of all three. He smiled a great deal. He had what Ula Calmady called "the civic manner"; you might count upon seeing him in

mayoral robes, and upon his having his portrait painted in
those robes. As a matter of fact, his portrait had been painted
by Wycherly, and had been hung in the Academy.

"Come in, my dear fellow."

He had become a euphuist. He had got into the way of
speaking as though he was receiving endless deputations, or
presenting prizes. When he shook hands he did it with a kind
of genial éclat, bending slightly at the hips, but keeping the
upper part of himself rigid.

"You are early."

He smiled at his brother. His strabismic eye, and his
grizzled, clipped moustache, and his ruddiness, and his general
air of condescending prosperity were very familiar to Conrad.
He had been called "Collars and Cuffs Pybus" at school. But
now he was very much the merchant prince and country
gentleman, wearing his Harris tweeds and floppy hats, and
boots with thick soles to them, and decorative waistcoats. On
the estate he carried either a gun or a thick ash stick. He
bred cattle and took prizes at agricultural shows. Every morning at eleven, accompanied by his agent, he went over the farm
and the gardens. Yorkshire saw him less and less these days,
for he had been lucky in his subordinates, and he liked to think
of himself as the great man in the background.

Conrad looked out of temper. He threw his hat into a
chair, and chose a cigarette from the silver box on his brother's
writing-desk. Probyn's library was not so full of books as
was the library at Chlois Court. Its atmosphere was different;
it suggested, rather, the country gentleman, the squire, farmer,
fisherman, sportsman, knight. It had a mellowness, the
vague and genial shrewdness of its owner's swivel-eye.

"You do a devil of a lot of writing, Probyn."

"Necessity, my dear chap. Responsibilities——"

Conrad sat down in a leather chair. When Probyn talked
of his responsibilities—the younger brother was moved to
exclaim "Bosh!" He was inclined to be abrupt with Probyn,
perhaps because his brother's civic manner irritated him.
There was too much clanking of gold chains.

"I've seen the old man."

Probyn put down his pen.

"Our father?"

"Our reverend parent—if you like. He cut me dead."

Probyn looked shocked.

"You don't say so. But where——?"

"Castle Craven. He's 'boots' at a local pub. I'd turned in there for lunch with Ula Calmady. Beastly awkward."

Probyn got out of his chair and went and stood with his back to the window. He had a liking for being on his feet when any alarm was sounded.

"By Jove!" he said. "By Jove. What a predicament! And he cut you?"

"Dead. That's to say——"

"You spoke?"

"I wanted a word or two. He spat in my face like an old tom-cat."

Probyn made a smooth, deprecating gesture with one hand. Conrad still retained so many of his crudities. He was apt to go off the deep end. He had not cultivated a nice, gentlemanly restraint.

"My dear fellow! Awkward—of course. But then—mark you, he is—our father."

His brother's eyes gave him a transient, scornful glance.

"Obviously. I thought you ought to know. I thought you might like go to over——"

"It's conceivable——"

"You'd look a fool——"

"My dear fellow—that point is debatable."

In moments of stress John Pybus's two sons differed in their attitudes and gestures. Conrad sat heavily and aggressively in the club-chair, his big hands spread upon the padded arms like two bunches of bananas. Probyn, looking down and to one side, stroked with his fingers the left lapel of his brown tweed coat as though smoothing the fine nap of the cloth. He was for conciliation, smoothness. Conrad was both cautious and truculent.

"It made me look a fool—caught with a woman like Ula Calmady."

Probyn raised his eyebrows.

"But—you didn't——?"

"Is it likely? But how the devil——? Well, you see—when I drove up—the old chap came out and opened the car door. We just glared——"

"Very awkward. But—my dear fellow, it makes me feel conscious of a kind of humiliation. 'Boots.' He's an old man."

"He's still a damned tough one."

"My dear fellow, I think we ought to remember——"

Conrad gave his brother a stare, and became explanatory and aggrieved. Yes, it was a fact that he and Lady Ursula Calmady had been seeing a good deal of each other. He had been minded to bring the affair to a climax on that particular day, and the last thing that he had expected was an anti-climax such as the resurrection of old John! Because you couldn't do anything with old John. He had no instinct for life's business subtleties. You might have tipped another sort of man the wink, a man who was capable of seeing the humour of the thing. "Say, dad, I want to hook this fish. Mum's the word. You take me?" Conrad did not put it quite so baldly, but he made Probyn look a little uncomfortable. After all, who was Ursula Calmady? A woman of good family and of the world. Might it not have been better if Conrad had been bold and frank? Taken the situation by the collar.

Conrad looked contemptuous.

"Well, would you have done it?"

He had Probyn straddling a fence.

"Very awkward. You remember, when I attempted a *rapprochement?* I sometimes think that he was a little bit touched in the head."

Conrad threw the end of his cigarette into the grate, and reached for another.

"He began it. After all, a fellow needn't lie down under his father's curses. Besides—the whole business was absurd. But there it is. Of course, he thought me a beastly snob. But why should I pick the old beggar off the pavement at such a damnable awkward moment—? 'Say, Lady Ula, this is my old man. He's a bit of an oddity, of course.' No, damn it, let's be honest. The old chap cut us adrift. Ridiculous rot, too. I believe he was a bit jealous of us. He was always a rotten bad business man. But the question is——"

"Exactly," said Probyn, as though meeting a deputation. "The situation must be considered."

3

Lance had left Noel Coward's book of plays lying face downwards in the deck-chair.

He happened to be wearing tennis shoes, and in strolling along the terrace towards the Dutch garden he came within the range of those two voices. He was thinking of other things. Had he been asked the question he would have replied that there was but little likelihood of his being interested in anything that Uncle Conrad might have to say to his father. At that critical moment, when he was about to pass in front of the library window, he had paused to watch the sunlight making a chequer on the grass under one of the cedars. He observed such things. It seemed to him that life might be spent observing birds, and the effects of sunlight, and the changing colours of the year.

Somewhere, at the back of his consciousness he heard Conrad's thick voice saying:

"It made me look like a fool, caught with a woman like Ula Calmady."

Lance came back to his realities. He had no intention of listening to his uncle's confidences. The very suggestion that there should be any relationship whatsoever between Conrad and a woman could be nothing but an offence to a young man who had gone three times as a boy to hear Gwen Ffrangcon Davies sing in *The Immortal Hour*. Ula Calmady? The name had the flavour of a night-club, and Lance could associate his uncle with night-clubs. Well, it might be humorous. That fat bounder! And Lance was about to pass on when he

heard something more singular. He could not help hearing
it. With one of those flashes of intuition he realized that he
had a right to hear it.

They were speaking of his grandfather.

But his grandfather was supposed to be dead.

Lance did not remember old John Pybus. As a very young
child he had seen him but twice, and the memories had faded.
There was no portrait of the old man in the house.

4

Beyond the old bowling-green that was now a tennis-
court, and the brick and stone Georgian shadow-house with
its lead cupola, someone with French feeling had long ago
planned a "Bosquet." Planted with old yews, box and holly,
it held at the end of its little secret path a dim and windless
space paved with worn flag-stones. The white figure of a
marble nymph poised upon a pedestal, and half lost in the
dark foliage, seemed both to advance and to retreat. A moss-
stained stone seat stood in a square recess.

Lance stared at the figure of the marble girl, but at the
moment it was no more to him than a white blur contrasting
with the dark foliage. His face was very grave. The Bosquet was a favourite retreat of his, with its shadows and silence
and its moist green gloom. It smelt of box. It seemed to
symbolize the change that had come over him during the last
year; he had been conscious of a withdrawing, of a significant
aloofness. He had retreated so much more into himself, a
new and rather mysterious self. There were times when in
one of his fanciful moods he could see himself as a young faun
lurking in these thickets and peering out at those other human
figures moving in the unmysterious sunlight. He had had
qualms, doubts, discomforts. He had a new pair of eyes
and a reinformed consciousness. He had been seeing his
mother and father as strangers. He seemed to have been
making rather shocking and disturbing discoveries. These
people of his! How was it? And how beastly of him! To

be suddenly ashamed of your father and mother, to be able to see all their weak points, to be vividly and hotly conscious of certain defects! Was he an infernal prig? He had not wanted to see that which a something in himself was compelling him to see. He could not help it. And at times he would feel a sudden rush of tenderness and compassion, impulses of affection that alternated with moods of silent hostility.

Ten minutes ago he had been standing outside the library window listening to the self-revealments of his father and his uncle. His grandfather was alive. That unknown and rather mysterious old man whom he had been brought up to think of as an eccentric bibliophile continued to exist as "boots" at a country inn. An anomalous figure, a figure which appeared peculiarly disconcerting to those two other men! But how, and why? What were the motives that could persuade a man to cut his own father?

And what of his own father? It would appear that Sir Probyn regarded the situation as one that required tactful handling. They ought to do something for the old man. Certainly. But what?

"Well—if you think you can resurrect him after all these years! Have him to live with you, what? Besides, he'd turn you down."

This had come from Uncle Conrad.

"Most disconcerting, my dear fellow."

"Call it—an infernal complication. I'd put down three hundred a year to pension the old boy—but I'm damned if I want him living within a morning's drive of me—as 'boots' at a pub. No, it's not our fault——"

Sir Probyn had allowed that such proximity could not be permitted. Something would have to be done. Should the situation become known it would create a false impression, an unpleasant atmosphere. The world could not be expected to understand old John Pybus's eccentric stubbornness. The world would think——

"It likes to think its bloodiest," said Conrad; "especially about successful men like us."

5

Lance sat down on the moss-stained stone seat. He still seemed to hear his father's voice suavely conspiratorial and bland. Sir Probyn had said that he would drive over to Castle Craven—by himself, of course—and visit the Saracen's Head. He had suggested the making of certain proposals to John Pybus, proposals that included independence, a settled income of—say—£500 a year, and a little house on the south coast or in the suburbs. Conrad had agreed to the proposals, but had shown a scepticism. You might take this old horse to the water, but you could not make him drink.

And to Lance Pybus hidden in the Bosquet came the consciousness of shame. His father and his uncle were ashamed of their father—while he——! But was his the same kind of shame? Was he not ashamed of their shame? Yet, what did he know of old John Pybus, this grandfather of his who was "boots" at a country inn? Might not the old boy be a shabby reprobate, an impossible old man, a very solid skeleton hanging in the family cupboard?

A fellow had to be fair. And in fairness to those others he had to remember those qualms of his own, those very personal memories of the stuffy, stuccoed, semi-detached house at Putney which had been followed by a very new and raw red villa-mansion on the outskirts of an industrial town. Eton and Trinity and Windover Hall, and these beech woods, and the pleasant spaciousness and beauty, and the intimate aloofness of this very Bosquet had come to him as the result of his father's climbings. Material success. His father had always been generous.

What right had he to criticize his father? He could remember the double and secret shame of the last May Week when Sir Probyn and Lady Pybus had put up at the "University Arms," and his people had met the people of his friends, and he had been conscious of torturing differences. His mother talked too much and too loudly. His father——! What a beastly sensitiveness was his! Surely you ought to be able to respect your father, and especially the human foibles of your father? Wasn't it a question of affection? Why these hypersensitive qualms, this feeling of vague antagonism?

Which was the more vulgar, a pretentious shame, or snobbish mortification in the presence of that shame?

For Lance was in the first flush of his season of ideals. He meant to take life with immense seriousness. He was serious. There were the realities, or what seemed to him to be the realities, love, beauty, endeavour, the following of your inspiration, accomplishment. He had a young dignity. Youth can have a stateliness of its own, inward pageantry, a graciousness of movement. It is the age of protest, of a passionate questioning, of eyes that look up and out. Its very defects are active, not passive.

"A man ought to know. I—myself—ought to know. Let's be honest."

He was a far more subtle creature than his parents, and perhaps he knew it. Their reactions were so obvious. And a part of his trouble was that while he saw—or thought he saw—these two people as two rather mechanical figures moved by the most simple of impulses—they understood him not at all. Their visualizing of him was arbitrary and conventional. He was the son, the heir, the gilded youth, success in the flesh, Eton and Trinity, the future dictator, the wearer of the Golden Fleece. They had no knowledge of the bird in him, of the musician, the saint, the child of original sin, the scribbler, the dreamer, the rebel. They wanted him to be the conventional son, the "Lance, old lad"—the nicely polished product of their material union. And he wasn't.

Well—what of it? He got up off that Roman seat, and walking like a young prophet full of inward stirrings out into the sunlight, turned instinctively towards the Dutch garden and the splash of its little fountain.

6

His mother was there.

She, too, liked glitter, and was pleased as a child is pleased by it. Lance could remember her in a purple dress all covered with silver sequins, but now her stoutness had to be more decorously draped. But at night—on state occasions—she had taken to wearing a tiara. It seemed that any bright thing or any gaily-coloured object had an irresistible lure. Had she had her way she would have covered herself with pieces of lace, and ribbons and scarfs, and brooches and bangles, but the sophisticated simplicity of the day and her modiste had compelled her to refrain.

The french, panelled drawing-room of Windover had not satisfied Lady Pybus. She had filled it with lacquered furniture, and brilliant cushions and tuffets, and painted shades with gold fringes, and orange and blue rugs upon a black and polished floor. Her exuberant taste had invaded the Dutch garden. Liking comfort and shelter and the splash of water she had had erected upon one of the little panels of grass at the end of the water cistern an orange and black striped hammock bed. She was in the act of settling herself under the awning when her son came to one of the openings in the pleached lime hedge.

Lady Dot was very plump. She wore very short skirts. Her bobbed head of very fair hair stood out like a nimbus. She was one of those women with a high colour and a beaked nose, and eyes of hard, bright blue. Her voice was rather high pitched, decisive, and a little brusque, never changing its tone or its timbre and, like her voice, she was without modulations. She was a woman who always set out to manage people or a situation with the same assurance with which—had she been a cottage woman—she would have washed her children and put them to bed. She was utterly without shadow effects. She said at once and with confidence exactly what came into her head.

And her son, standing there at one of the green windows, saw a very stout pair of legs in flesh-coloured stockings, and that atrocity of a hammock bed, an orange blot in the centre of the sunk garden. It was an atrocity, insulting all those old tired, gentle colours, the grey of the stone, the soft rust red of the old bricks, the lily leaves; the grass, the dark clipped yews, the lavender, the water.

He had dared to call the thing an atrocity.

"My dear, you're too squeamish. Besides—if I want to be comfy——"

She might have had it put anywhere but in that perfect little garden made for the gentlewoman of another day, and for brocades of old rose and grey and lavender, the subtle shades of twilight moods. His mother was all full noon. Had he tried to tell her some of the intimate truths that a young man never tells to a mother, she would have exclaimed, "How —absurd! Really—my dear—you ought to see a doctor." Having no reticence, and being a woman who was quite ready to discuss her husband with other women, she did not understand the reticences of her son. In fact she was not aware of his reserve. Lance had silent moods, and silence to Lady Dot was merely the absence of anything that needed saying.

Her son watched the swaying of the hammock bed, the subsidence of the cushions, and his mother's very large and flesh-coloured legs arranging themselves. He thought "She shouldn't wear those stockings," and while he was thinking of it she looked up and discovered him. She was able at all times to find an immediate use for anybody.

"Lance, old lad, I've forgotten the oil of lavender. Get it— will you?"

"Yes, mater."

"And you might see if Mills has put a man to mend the holes in the stop-netting. The Ashleys are coming in this afternoon."

He was half-way to the house when he heard her calling:

"Lan-cie—Lan-cie."

He hated being called Lancie.

"Hallo."

"If Conrad's still there—tell him I have a bone to pick with him. Send him down here."

CHAPTER IV

I

JOHN PYBUS had gone to the bank.

At half-past eleven every Saturday morning he would appear at the doorway of the Saracen's Head wearing a hard felt hat and a black coat, for this was both an official and a personal occasion. He would cross the cobbles of the market square and, passing between two of the pollarded lime trees, enter the Castle Craven branch of Barclays Bank. John Pybus had a banking account. He received a pound a week, his cottage, and his food; and his tips amounted to quite a comfortable little sum. His needs were few; tobacco and his books his only luxuries, though to John Pybus they were necessities.

The sallow young cashier treated him with respect.

"Good morning, Mr. Pybus."

"Good morning to you."

John Pybus would bring out of his pocket a canvas bag which, when emptied upon the counter, would produce a pound note or two, some silver, and a few coppers. He carried the paying-in-slip separately, all the details neatly filled in, and the cashier knew that there was no need to check Mr. Pybus's figures. The old man had a cheque-book, and it is possible that he wrote three cheques a year. He had never been known to draw a cheque to self. The money remained on the right side of the counter.

"Very muggy to-day, Mr. Pybus."

Mr. Pybus would reply with a "Very" or an "I agree with you," and after giving the cashier a nod and a glance from his blue eyes, would walk out of the bank and back to the inn, and hang up his felt hat, and change from the cloth coat to the alpaca. He would be away for ten minutes, never more. He was not interfered with. Mr. Pounds, the manager, had realized that interference was neither necessary nor advisable.

John Pybus was hanging up his felt hat when Miss Vallence hailed him from the office.

"John——"

"Yes, miss."

"A gentleman's called to see you. He's in the lounge."

Mr. Pybus gave her a stare.

"What name?"

"He didn't give any name. He said you'd know him."

That she was curious about his visitor John Pybus was well aware, for Miss Vallence was curious about everybody. It was part of her business to be curious about people, especially when you never knew whether a lady and gentleman were man and wife. "It's always the man that looks sheepish. The women are as bold as brass. Besides—a case is such a noosance. It isn't nice." Miss Vallence made John Pybus think of a very yellow canary shut up in a cage, ever ready to pipe "Sweet-sweet," but keeping a black eye brightly upon the realities.

John Pybus changed into his alpaca coat and walked towards the lounge. He had his suspicions. A gentleman who gave no name when inquiring for the hotel "boots" would probably be a Pybus. And after all—a name was superfluous; but when John Pybus saw Probyn sitting alone in the lounge, with that swivel-eye of his pointed like a gun over the top of the daily paper, John Pybus was not surprised.

He said, "Good morning, sir. Anything I can do for you?"

Probyn rose rather hurriedly, leaving the paper on the round table. It is probable that he saw his opportunity in the emptiness of the lounge. He held out a hand.

"After all these years—surely? I heard from Conrad. I was—distressed."

John Pybus made no attempt to take his son's hand, and Probyn, with an expostulating and embarrassed smile, withdrew it.

"Well, as you please. I wished to make the first move. Are we unreconcilable? It seems a pity."

Old Pybus watched his son's face.

"Lunching here?"

"No, at the White Hart. I left my car there."

"You'd get a better lunch here."

"You think so?"

"But you wouldn't enjoy it. Conrad didn't. I'm just going to have my dinner."

Probyn had the air of a man being heckled at a political meeting. He continued to smile; he looked hot; he stood, bending slightly, with his hands on his hips.

"Do you know how many years——?"

"About ten," said old Pybus promptly; "my memory and my digestion are as good as ever. As I was saying—I was just going to have my dinner."

Probyn made some sort of polite noise...

"Usually—I have it with the rest of the staff; but if you have anything to say——"

"Believe me—I have."

"Very well. I'll take my dinner to the cottage. You can come and see me eat it."

2

So, Sir Probyn, looking rather like a man who had lost his chauffeur, had to stand in the coaching-yard while his father was collecting his dinner in the kitchen. Old John came out of a side door into the yard, with a plate of roast beef, greens and potatoes in one hand, and a slice of bread with a piece of Cheshire cheese on it in the other. He jerked his white head at Probyn.

"This way, sir."

Incorrigible old derider of the higher conventions! The plate was very full of gravy, and old Pybus walked with great deliberation, assuming that his son was treading on hot pebbles.

"Musn't spill the gravy—you know—sir."

Probyn cleared his throat.

"You always loved irony."

"Not a bit of it. Gravy's gravy. Like to soak my bread in it at times. So they made you a knight."

"They did."

"Saw it in a paper. What did they do it for?"

"As a recognition—I gather——"

"Public services, patriotism, self-sacrifice. Didn't buy it, did you, Probyn?"

"The gibe is unworthy——"

"Ooops—mind the gravy! Boiled potatoes to-day—you see. Personally, I prefer them mashed—with butter. Plenty of butter."

And Probyn, following in step behind him, was thinking— "You old devil! Just the same as ever. What am I doing here? Wasting my time—of course. But I'll do the generous thing. I can always remind myself that I did make an effort. Why on earth can't the old fellow be—respectable. No tact, no consideration. Never had."

Over the grey cobbles between the ancient red brick walls Probyn followed his father, who persisted in going at a snail's pace, talking the while as though wielding a playful scourge.

"Democratic age, sir. But a handle is as much a handle as ever. Your dustman has to be Mr. This, and your brick-layer's labourer Mr. That, when they are mentioned by the local Press for getting run over when drunk, or for growing a prize pumpkin. And the scullery-maid is Miss-So-and-So. Bosh, isn't it? Better a plain Bill Sikes and a Nancy Lee. Mr. John Pybus! What use—what bloody use—as the vulgar would put it—is the Mr. to me? But then—of course—a knighthood——"

They had reached the green door of Castle Cottage, and old Pybus turned and looked wickedly at his son, though there was no wickedness in him.

"This gravy. Both hands full. Mind opening the door, sir?"

Probyn opened it. He saw the red-tiled floor, and the Windsor chairs, and the dahlias in the little garden on the southern side glowing like velvet and cloth of gold beyond the lattice windows. He was thinking at the moment of that saying of Conrad's that old John was jealous of his sons, and had always been jealous of them. Big fellows looking down at him. Yes, little men were often touchy and self-centred and arrogant.

"Take a chair, sir. You'll excuse me going on with my dinner. Have to be back on duty at a quarter to one."

Probyn let his father pass, and then closed the door, but he did not sit down. He was looking at the two photos on the mantelpiece. John Pybus saw the look.

"My two sons, sir; killed in the Great War—both of them."

Probyn made a movement as of pulling down his waistcoat and settling his collar.

"You won't accept sentiment. Can't we delete the irony and come to realities? I'm a business man."

"Exactly," said his father; and sat down to his dinner. "And what's the business to-day? I think I know, my lad. Much better leave me alone. I shan't interfere with you."

His son, standing by the window, and looking out at his father's little garden, felt the muteness of a discredited motive. As a boy Probyn had been a plausible youngster, full of florid yet ingenious excuses, but always his father had poked a finger at the fabrications, and the thing had burst like a bladder. Besides, few motives are single and direct, and Probyn's motives were mixed. He had good nature. He liked to feel well with himself, and he was wishing to feel well with himself in his attitude towards his father. He would rather do the generous thing. Moreover, there was Lance to be considered, and Lance's mother, who had said with abruptness that she would never have the old man in her house.

Meanwhile, John Pybus was contentedly eating his dinner, and Probyn knew that something had to be said. He turned and sat down in one of the Windsor chairs.

"May I put it to you, father, that I should like to make things easier."

"Easier?"

Old Pybus paused with a piece of potato on his fork.

"Easier! I'm not complaining. I've got all I want. How could you make it easier?"

"There is no need for you to remain——"

The blue eyes fixed him.

"Pension me off. Put me comfortably on the shelf some-where? I'm quite contented here. You need not worry my lad. I am not going to complicate the new coat of arms."

Probyn winced. For with unerring aim his father had thrown a stick and knocked down and marked out the prin-cipal motive.

"You're not fair to me. If you remember—on a previous occasion—I attempted——"

John Pybus gazed at him fixedly for a moment, and then went on with his dinner. He had every appearance of en-joying it.

And then, while Probyn was trying to sort out his motives and to make a respectable pattern out of them, his father asked him a question.

"How's your boy?"

"Lance. He's up at Cambridge."

"Putting him in the business?"

"It's there for him. You won't be offended if I say that it is a very fine business."

Old Pybus broke bread.

"Hope he'll like it. Though making money's not living, Probyn. I suppose—he is all—that you want him to be?"

"I have no fault to find."

"Splendid. The perfect little gentleman, God bless him! Got his own car—I suppose?"

"He has. It's justified. Lance isn't——"

The blue eyes observed him.

"I wish you luck with him, Probyn. There is no bitter-ness between me and your boy. Don't spoil him."

Probyn's colour seemed to come quickly.

"Really—father! You did not spoil us, did you?"

"But your mother did. There—there—let us leave it at that. I suppose when a boy is up at Cambridge—he wouldn't be pleased to have it known that his grandfather—— Quite natural. I'm not quarrelling with the prejudice. What do you make the time?"

Probyn pulled out a gold watch.

"Five and twenty minutes to one."

"Thanks. I must eat my cheese. You need not worry about me, Probyn. Never was better in my life. I shan't intrude. No wish to. Besides—no one here need be told—that because my name's Pybus—you take me? No obligation anywhere."

His big white head caught the sunlight. He smiled.

"My good wishes to your boy—anyway. He's·young. A fresh start. New blood. Hope he'll miss our mistakes. Good luck to him!"

3

Lance had been writing.

This room on the third floor was very much his own, impulsively untidy; the room of a young man who, with a freedom of gesture, distributed his belongings where and how he would. Furnished much like a college keeping-room, it had an additional door which communicated with his bedroom, and a south and an east window, each filled with that green English landscape. For writing he used a deal table covered with a powder-blue cloth, which he could move from window to window as his mood shifted. The east window gave him more open country, the south the beech avenue, the park and the distant woods. The general colour of the room was a soft and indefinite rose. An oak bureau, in which Lance kept his private papers, stood between the passage door and the south window.

"My son writes—you know."

Lady Pybus allowed the information to be broadcast. It was an interesting and refined fact, or a kind of gentlemanly trick which was allowable, provided it was not taken too seriously. Lady Pybus was a little proud of it. Lance helped to edit one of the Cambridge magazines. He spoke at the "Union," gravely and a little fiercely on subjects that were in the empyrean so far as his mother was concerned. She had never read any of his work. He never showed it to her. He was funny and secretive about his scribbling.

That morning he had written at the top of a page—

"Who will hold up the sky for me when I go for the Apples of the Hesperides?"

What a question to ask! And for a Pybus! His mother would have looked brightly blank over it. If the apples were golden apples, and there was any difficulty about them, Lance had better ask his father to write a cheque.

But Lance himself had got no further with it that morning. He was standing at the east window looking down at a car that was standing on the gravel. So his father was taking the Buick. There were three cars in the Windover garage, the Daimler, the Buick, and Lance's little Talbot. His father was going alone. Lance saw Wyman the chauffeur standing aside, and his father at the steering-wheel pulling on a pair of wash-leather gloves. It was unusual for his father to drive a car, especially so without Wyman beside him. Sir Probyn drove rather badly, and was helpless when trouble occurred.

To Lance the suggestion was irresistible. His father was driving over alone to Castle Craven to seek out old John Pybus and to persuade him to be respectably buried in some suburban villa. Youth confronted one of its problems. What manner of man was this John Julian Apostasius Pybus? The name had the flavour of old vellum. For to Lance the fiercedly sensitive, with his almost uncanny insight into the workings of his father's mind, the discovery of his grandfather had quickened certain curiosities.

He watched the blue Buick slide into the black slot of the beech avenue. He was conscious of a restlessness. Standing idly beside the table and tapping it with his fingers, he looked at what he had written, and at the white space below it.

"Just what I am," he thought, "a question and a blank sheet. What does one write on the page of one's self? What can one write without knowing."

He turned the page. He was in no mood to sit in a chair and scribble. Going down and calling one of the dogs, he made for the open country.

4

Sir Probyn was back at Windover by four o'clock. He looked tired. He glanced at a picture paper while he drank his tea; and Lance was as silent as his father. Lady Pybus, who treated her menfolk like children, was yet full of rare refrainings. She read the daily paper, yet she could never refrain from reading portions of it aloud, and from making comments upon the tendencies of the day.

"Really! I call it absolutely scandalous! They ought to do something," the "They" being the Government, or Scotland Yard, or Public Opinion, or the Press. Lady Pybus reposed upon public opinion as upon a pillow.

Lance escaped. He strolled round to the garage where the Buick, covered with dust, was standing under the glass shelter for Wyman to wash her down. Lance happened to know the Buick's mileage, for he had driven her the previous day. The speedometer recorded the fact that his father had driven 113·6 miles. A map and route-book spread upon the tail of the twoseater gave the distance to Castle Craven as 66 miles.

The coincidence appeared conclusive.

· Windover dined at 7.30. Lance, on his way downstairs after dressing, heard his mother's door open. His father came out, but, turning back with his hand on the handle, answered some question of his wife's.

"What? No other alternative. Well, one could not have done more. He always was a little eccentric."

Lance heard his own name uttered by his mother's voice. His father's back was turned, and Lance continued a swift and soft descent.

"Quite so. Much better that he shouldn't."

So they were not going to tell him. He was to be given no key to the family cupboard and, somehow—he resented this exclusion. What did they mistrust? His common sense or his curiosity or his youthfulness? Or was it parental consideration? He had no wish to be considered in that sort of way. But parental prejudices are regular and universal, a part of the social scheme. Fashions change, but the passion to possess and to cover up is always in the picture.   His mother danced and wore short skirts.   That was about the only difference between her and his maternal grandmother.

After dinner, Lance went up to his room and shut the door, but he did not switch on the light.   He carried a chair to the open south window and, straddling the chair, looked at a sky that grew brilliant with stars.

"I want to see for myself," he thought.

Yes, that was life, seeing things for yourself.

CHAPTER V

I

LANCE drove fast. He had youth's swiftness and its love of swiftness without youth's recklessness. He had too much imagination to be reckless, for the reckless are those who cannot see round life's corners. With the chalk hills and high beech woods behind him he crossed Oxfordshire, going west. He had no great love for flat country, with its root crops and its stubbles and its endless cattle in endless fields. He was out upon adventures; he pushed the little Talbot hard; his hair, blown back from his bare head, made the swiftness of the adventure visible.

Then, with the hill country rising to him once more, he came to Castle Craven. Capturing its steepness, and captured by its soaring austerity, he pulled up in its market square. He sat there a moment, conscious of the grey town's atmosphere, as of something splendid and spacious, yet intimate. Those six soaring pinnacles, each with its gold wind-vane, the blue spaces of the sky, the white clouds sailing, a wind ruffling his hair. The town made him think of a ship at sea, sailing that rolling landscape, with the wind alive in her rigging.

Over on his left the portico of the White Hart wore its turban of flowers. The Saracen's Head was a little lower down. Lance parked his car by the Cross, and walked across to the White Hart. He was drawing a bow at a venture.

In the office of the White Hart a girl, looking up from a ledger, saw this young man with the wind still in his blue eyes and his hair.

"Can you tell me whether you have anyone named Pybus here?"

The girl came to the office window. She had a rather sullen face.

"Staying here?"

"No, on your staff."

He smiled, and she felt compelled to smile back at him.

"Oh—you must mean the Saracen's Head?"

"Do I? Thanks so much."

"Old John—the 'boots.' Everyone calls him Mr. Pybus."

"Out of respect—I suppose?"

"Well—I suppose so. I've heard——"

But her sullenness hid a sensitive self-consciousness, and overwhelming her suddenly, it sent her back to her ledger.

"The Saracen's Head's a few yards down."

"Thanks so much."

She watched him walk towards the hotel door, and she allowed herself to wonder who he was, and what he wanted with old Pybus. Such a good-looking lad and not in the ordinary way. Interesting. He had a mouth that was irresistible to some women; they thought of him as lying with his head in their arms. Moreover, he had the "County" look, that indefinable air. It was probable that he belonged to some family which had employed old Pybus, and had remained interested in him. Not like this beastly ledger! She scratched in a "bath" and a "breakfast," and wished that she had kept Lance there a little longer. He had one of those faces which seem to light up from within. Most of the faces that the girl of the ledger saw were so dead.

Lance went back to the Talbot, and drove it into the "Saracen's" yard. This time he varied his approach shot. He returned to the squre, and entering by the front door, saw John Pybus in his usual place with the brass gong like a halo behind his big head.

Lance said:

"Can I get tea here?"

He had a pleasant, quick courtesy, because he felt a natural respect for people, especially for old people.

"Certainly, sir. Would you like it in the lounge?"

"I should—please."

"For one, sir?"

"Yes, for one."

Old Pybus looked hard at him, but knew him not from Adam.

"I'll tell the waiter, sir."

"Thanks.   Are you the manager?"

"No, the 'boots,' sir."

"I have left my car in the yard.   If it's in the way——"

"I'll see the garage man, sir.   Plenty of room to-day.   Not staying?"

"Not—not staying."

Lance walked into the lounge thinking "So—that's my grandfather!" But what an unexpected figure! And so unexpected did Lance find it that he sat down in one of the lounge chairs with his blue eyes staring. He was conscious of a curious excitement. He had come over to Castle Craven, with a self-created image of an old man in his mind, and when he tried to recover that image he found that it had vanished. All that he could remember about it was that it had been large and murky and just a little sinister, and that it had included some of the features of his uncle and his father. It had been a composite image. And instantly the reality had effaced it— that vivid little, upright figure, so clean and alert, with its striking head and fearless eyes.

He was both astonished and excited. There were other people in the lounge, touring motorists full of chatter; but Lance was conscious of a stillness, a kind of inward silence. It seemed to him that something incalculable and significant had occurred. He was still on the threshold of the adventure when the waiter came and stood by him.

"Tea, sir?"

Lance came out of his stare.

"Yes, please."

The waiter was turning away when Lance detained him.

"I say, I have left my car in the yard.   There's a map in it. Would you mind asking the porter."

"Gone to his tea—I think, sir."

"I mean—the little old man with the big head."

"Yes, sir—old Mr. Pybus; gone to his tea, sir."

"Never mind, I'll get it myself."

He went for the map, but saw no sign of his grandfather's big white head. He was a little disappointed. It was possible that this was going to be a rather baffling business. How did one get to know an old man who was "boots" at a country hotel? How did you approach him? For to Lance the inspiration of the adventure lay in the temporary hiding of his own identity; he wanted to approach his grandfather as a stranger, to look at him with clear, impartial, yet eager eyes. For the situation was unique. Here was the original and almost mythical Pybus, a rather mysterious old fellow, waiting to be discovered and explored by his own grandson who had appeared as a casual young man in a car.

Lance's excitement had its tinge of emotion. Also, it was sublimated curiosity suffused with a sense of the picturesque and the singular. He had the qualities of an artist, a quick eye for the dignity and the spacing of a situation. He sat down to his tea. He reviewed his first impression of the old man, and it was that of a white head seen against a background of gold. A venerable head with a halo. Yes, that was the inspired word—Venerable. From that moment he christened his grandfather—"The Venerable."

2

When, after hurrying through his tea, Lance went out into the hall, his grandfather was absent. He strolled to the door, filled and lit a pipe, and considered the situation. Too direct an approach would appear clumsy. If he waited it was probable that his grandfather would return to his place by the brass gong, but how public would be the opportunity! How could you ever begin to talk intimately to an hotel "boots" in such a place?

Well, why not explore? He might happen upon his grandfather in one of the passages, or in the coaching yard; he could get into conversation with him, ask him about the castle. The way to the castle ruins lay through the Saracen yard. Lance followed the inspiration, but it failed at first to show him that little old figure in the alpaca coat. He strolled to the end of the yard, past a group of loitering chauffeurs who were chaffing one of the Saracen maids. He both saw and heard a fluttering of wings, and rounding the red angle of an old brick coach-house, came suddenly upon his grandfather, the centre of a cloud of birds. Old Pybus was feeding his pigeons.

Lance's head went up. He had a way of throwing it back when anything arrestive—a face, a landscape, or a picture—caught his attention. His eyes lit up, and in the smile of them there was a sudden quality of tenderness. Father Time and the pigeons! He saw one bird perched like a living crest on the old man's white head. The birds were on his hands and shoulders and round his feet, and old Pybus's face wore an absorbed and meditative smile.

Lance had paused, and when he walked slowly on, it was with a feeling of exultation. Here was his chance, and what a chance! It seemed to him that he was going to speak to someone who straightway would be a friend, an old man whose hands were stretched out to these fluttering birds. How unexpected and how suggestive! But would the birds be shy of a stranger?

Again he paused, standing a little way off.

"Shall I frighten them?"

Old Pybus looked up and round.

"You sir? No. They are only shy of children."

"The catapult boy. Little beasts."

"I was one, sir. It's natural—at that age. What's natural—has to be thought of."

Lance drew nearer.

"Wonder if they'll come to me?"

"Hold out your hands, sir."

"But there's nothing in them. Wouldn't that be swindling?"

Old Pybus gave him a quick, attentive look.

"There's a piece of bread in my coat pocket. Right-hand side. You can have it."

"That's very good of you," said Lance with eyes that saw John Pybus as his sons had never seen him.

He felt for the bread in his grandfather's pocket, and standing beside him and crumbling it became a part of the cloud of

birds. His impressions were quick and vivid. The birds had
no fear of him; they settled upon his wrists and shoulders even
as they settled on his grandfather's, and it seemed to Lance
that he and his grandfather were sharing some beautiful
rite.

"You have made them very trusting."

"I have fed them like this for seven years."

"Every day?"

"Winter and summer—but in winter I feed them before
dinner."

"Where do they come from?"

"Our pigeon lofts and the castle. The castle's full of the
blue birds."

"I was going to look at the castle. Can I get to it down this
yard?"

"Yes, sir, past my cottage and over the field."

Lance wanted to say to him, "Don't call me 'sir.' It is I
who ought to call you 'sir.'"

"Is that your cottage?"

"Yes, sir."

"Looks out on the castle."

"It does. The barbican used to be there in the old days.
They have filled up the ditch."

"Very peaceful. A place to read or write in."

"That's so," said his grandfather; "I read a lot. Books
stay with you."

Lance, with a smiling softness of the eyes, looked down at
his grandfather. But inwardly he was looking up to him.
What a man of surprises! With that venerable head and
thoughtful face of his, full of the humility of service, yet
resolute in his pride, with birds and books for his friends, and
that ruin close to his windows.

"What books do you read, sir?"

"The "sir" slipped out, and old Pybus's blue eyes gave a
curious flicker. This young man was unusual, very unusual.
There was something about him . . .

"Solid books—most of them. I read a lot of poetry, Blake
and Whitman."

"Blake's great. And novels?"

"A few. Conrad. There aren't any more Conrads left for me to read. And he's dead."

"I know that feeling. And Hewlett's dead. What a book—'The Forest Lovers'!"

"'Rest Harrow' was bigger."

"Different. And what a figure—with his flowers and his shepherds and his Wiltshire downs!"

"Talking of figures—Hudson—now."

"Ah, Hudson," said Lance, with a little thrill in his voice.

And—then—suddenly—they looked at each other, and in that look there was a kindling of the emotions, a question, a wonder. Each had a feeling of subtle infection, of a drawing together, of some mysterious spiritual relationship. To Lance the thing was becoming exquisitely real. For the old man the feeling had a disturbing, puzzling strangeness.

"Care to see my books?"

"I'd love to."

"I'm free from four till six. They treat me very well here. A lad comes in to help."

"I'm glad of that," said Lance.

His grandfather's blue eyes seemed to grow big and strange. Why did he say he was glad? And he was glad. You caught the vibrations of it—in his voice.

3

John Pybus had five shelves of books, but the first things that Lance happened to notice in that austere little room were the photos of his father and his uncle on the mantelpiece. They had been taken many years ago, but even from the doorway Lance had recognized the flabby pallor of Conrad's full-moon face, and his father's oblique glances. But he paid no heed to them. He was all for continuing to be the unknown young man until he and his grandfather should have come closer to each other. Meanwhile, he crossed towards John Pybus's bookshelves, but paused by the window, one of those broad, low windows that one finds in old cottages. It gave to Lance the sheaved splendour of dahlias and tall asters, with the grey walls of the castle and the gracious curves of the ash trees rising to a blue and white sky. The outlook from his grandfather's window had beauty and tranquillity. It offered you glimpses of distant hills, and of the Castle Field, with its banks and hollows very green in the sheeted sunlight. It had the spaciousness and the dignity of a fine picture.

"That's a good thing to live with, sir."

"Yes, you go out to it," said old Pybus, "and it comes in to you. The older you grow—the more beauty gets you."

"Always?"

"Depends on your eyesight, doesn't it?"

"Insight, sir?"

"That's what I mean."

They smiled at each other, and Lance went on to look at his grandfather's books. He felt that he would be knowing his grandfather in reading the titles of his books. They were of all ages and of all kinds, many of them books that Lance had never heard of, queer old volumes in leather coats, histories, herbals, gazetteers. There were the old and the new, Chaucer and Swinburne, and one or two little volumes of war poetry. Lance glanced at the modern, Shaw and Oliver Lodge, and Masefield, and Joseph Conrad, and a few of the younger school. The Venerable's taste was both catholic and varied. Imagine an hotel "boots" reading D. H. Lawrence! Moreover, in a place by themselves, Lance saw books on contemporary science, sociology, psychology. The Venerable read Freud and MacDougal.

Lance picked out Hardy's "Tess."

"Ah, I remember that being published," said his grandfather, "and the fuss over poor 'Jude.' I saw Thomas Hardy once."

"Did you?"

"I used to sell books. Yes, and I had quite a lot of first editions. Got some of them still. Up—there. Stevenson's 'Treasure Island,' and Conrad's 'Nigger of the Narcissus'."

"I say—have you! May I look?"

"Certainly."

"Have you ever written a book?"

"I—sir?"

"Yes."

"No. Had a try once. Who hasn't?"

"I scribble rather seriously."

"You do. Published anything?"

"No, not yet."

"Tried to?"

"No. I'm not satisfied—yet."

"What's the matter with the work?"

"It doesn't strike me as real. I just seem to miss things—at present."

"Plenty of time yet," said the Venerable with a smile. "Generally, youth is in such a devil of a hurry."

For twenty minutes they discussed books, and handled them, and confessed to their intimate, individual passions and prejudices. The Venerable could not, and would not, read Meredith. The man was too clever, boringly clever. An artificial person. They argued about Butler's "The Way of All Flesh," and went on to discuss Aldous Huxley. Lance was a romanticist. No, not of the Monsieur Beaucaire school. But wasn't the life of the day full of pungent romance if you had the eyes to see it?

"Yes, things happen," said his grandfather. "You can express them in black and white—or in colour."

Lance was for colour. But looking out of his grandfather's window he saw beyond the reds and golds and purples of the Venerable's garden the shadows of the castle and the ash trees stretching far across the green of the castle field. It was half past five, and he had sixty miles to cover, and a secret to keep both at Windover and Castle Craven.

"I shall have to be going. I've enjoyed this immensely."

"Far to go?"

"It won't take me long. I say, sir, if I happen to be this way again—may I come in and talk?"

Old Pybus looked at him queerly.

"Any time you like."

"Thanks—ever so much."

The Venerable walked up the yard with him and watched Lance drive off.

"See you again, sir."

He waved a hand, and old Pybus stood looking towards the arch of the gateway. He had a strange feeling of kinship with the lad. It was as though something that he had always known, something that was his, had dropped down out of the sky.

4

Lance drove home with the sun behind him.

In leaving Castle Craven he seemed to be coming down from a height, and was reminded of Italy and one of those Tuscan towns with a shrine or a campanile soaring against the sunset. His pilgrimage had been to the feet of the unexpected. He had discovered a sage.

His own grandfather! A little old man with the head of a Roman emperor, an imperial philosopher, a kind of little Marcus Aurelius, with his flowers and his books and his pigeons. The Venerable! The polisher of boots and the bearer of burdens! For in Lance was that rare virtue, a passion to reverence men and things. He carried a flame. At that time he had the audacity and the élan of the idealist. Also, he had the essential cleanness of a flame. To the sex-obsessed and the unpleasantly clever he might appear something of a fool, lyrical and tiresome, a fellow who never looked higher than a garter.

He was back at Windover by a quarter past seven. He rushed up to his room to change. It was a warm, still, September evening, and in leaning out of his window to look at the world, he observed his father sitting in a deck-chair on the terrace. His father was reading a paper, the *Financial Times*.

Lance drew back. He had felt himself above his father and able to look down at him with sudden impartiality.

"Poor old pater!"

Yet he was conscious of antagonism, contempt, compassion.

At dinner they asked him where he had been, and accepted his vague answer—"Oh, just knocking around, seeing things." Neither Sir Probyn nor his wife had sufficient imagination to penetrate beyond their son's silence. Besides—it was usual. He would disappear for the whole day and have nothing to tell them when he returned.

The poetic age! Sir Probyn's swivel-eye gazed rather dubiously at the versifier. Poetry, useless stuff. The pursuit of it was quite gentlemanly, but not very productive. Sir Probyn supposed that it came of Eton and Trinity, though you did expect a young man of this tennis-playing, sports-model, slack-trousered generation to be a little more practical. Still, Lance was a good oar. He might be a scribbler, but he rowed in the Third Trinity May boat and at Henley. That was a solid performance. You had to allow a lad his head of steam.

But it never occurred to Probyn and his wife that their son had discovered his grandfather, or that in discovering him Lance might wish to keep the Venerable in a niche apart from the lares and penates of his parents.

CHAPTER VI

I

SEPTEMBER mist.

Lance, standing at his bedroom window and brushing vigorously at his insurgent hair, saw the beeches draped in vapour, and the grass grey with dew. Also, he saw the Daimler below on the gravel, with Wyman standing beside it smoking an early and surreptitious cigarette. Sir Probyn was driving up to town to attend a board meeting.

Lance and his father had had a passage of arms over this very board meeting on the previous evening. Sir Probyn, pouring out a second glass of port, had called his son back from the half-opened door. Something had occurred to remind the elder Pybus that Lance would be in his last year at Cambridge, and that the serious business of life was approaching. Probyn was an opportunist. It may be that right eye of his had persuaded him to approach life obliquely. Also, he was just a little afraid of his son.

"Lance!"

"Yes, pater."

"Just shut the door a moment, will you?"

Lance had closed the door. He had come and stood by the table with that air of alert gravity which was so disturbing to his father. The lad was so full of silences. Sir Probyn, very conscious of his son's eyes and of the fact that Lance was being detained there like a dog called back when it is bent upon some adventure of its own, had smiled and tried to make an easy movement in his chair.

"I have a board meeting to-morrow. Care to drive me up?"

"The Buick?"

"No—the Daimler. Good opportunity. I'd like you to come with me and get an idea."

Lance had waited in silence.

C

"See how these things are done. Can't begin too early. You'll be in your last year."

Sir Probyn had glanced at his son, and then had removed the band from his cigar. After all, to an intelligent lad like Lance a hint should be sufficient. Probyn was very fond of his son, though with a rather puzzled and slightly diffident fondness. He had given the lad plenty of rope; he had not interfered with his scribbling. Sir Probyn always thought of it as scribbling. But he had plans for his son, quite gentlemanly plans. The young Jason should travel; he should be a man of languages, he should carry the Fleece into foreign lands. Experts! A young merchant prince and director! But first a year in the mills, and another year in the sales-manager's office.

Lance had stood looking down at his father. Only of late had he begun to visualize himself as a business man; life had been so easy. Moreover, there had been a vagueness about the future. Probyn had not been very definite in his suggestions; again, he had preferred the oblique method.

"I don't think I should be any good in business, pater."

His father had said, "Oh——! What do you know about it?" and had looked at his son, not directly, but as though his glances diverged and met again behind his son's back. He had been surprised—as parents always appear to be surprised—by Lance's abruptness, an abruptness that had sounded aggressive.

"Don't know much about it, do you, Lance?"

"Not a great deal."

"Thought that you understood, my dear boy. It has always been in my mind——"

Lance had pulled some grapes from a dish, and had begun eating them. He supposed that he had understood in a way that his father had intended him to go into the business—but never had he given an inward consent to anything. He had been too young to consent to anything. He did not know. He had urges, prejudices, predilections. He had been full of his rowing, and his inspirations, and his explorations into the adventure of life. He had taken things rather as he had picked up those grapes.

"You see, pater, it's not easy."

He had frowned, while eating skin and pips, and thinking of that other Pybus. No, it was not easy, especially for a lad whose man's cry was to be, "Give me something difficult. Not the easy thing. The easy thing's so fatal."

"I have been thinking a good deal lately."

His father had raised bland eyebrows. Surely it was not necessary for Lance to think! The proof of the pudding was in the eating, and if Lance's eyes were not open to the advantages of business—well—he had only to look about him.

"Your mother and I have taken it for granted——"

He had been caught by a sudden swift glance. Such a strange look.

"I don't think you ought to, pater."

"My dear boy! Don't you appreciate the fact that your mother and I——"

"You have been very generous."

His father had smiled over the apparent concession.

"Of course—naturally. We wanted you to have every advantage. It's our wish——"

Again he had been the target of that steady, searching stare.

"Do you want me to do—what you want me to do, or what I——?"

"We want—what's best, Lance."

"Yes, that's just it, pater. What's best! But isn't that just about the hardest——"

"Well, use common sense. I'm not going to say—that I'm a good deal older——"

And there Probyn Pybus had left it. He had never been a man to push an issue to immediate extremes. His nature was bland and circuitous. Conciliation. Allow a few suggestive persuasions to soak in. Besides, he supposed that most young men began life with bees in their bonnets; and if you were a shrewd person you allowed the bees to buzz themselves out. He had said, "All right, I'll take Wyman to-morrow," and felt that he had been tactful and kind and rather subtle.

So Lance stood brushing his hair. His father had ordered

the car for nine, and Lance was late for breakfast, and the Daimler—standing on the gravel—suggested that it could carry a compromise. Sir Probyn, with the morning paper propped against the coffee-pot, was wondering whether his son would come downstairs and say "Morning, pater, I'd like to drive you up to town." While upstairs Lance was passing through one of those experiences that may appear trivial at the moment. Being sensitive, he found the doing of certain things difficult; but also he had youth's ruthlessness and its scorn of compromise. He had changed very much in a year. He had become more acutely self-conscious, and also more aware of people and their proclivities. He had seen people through the eyes of other young men, and he had begun to see his own people with a very disturbing clearness. His father was a far more vivd and comprehensible figure to Lance than Lance was to his father. Youth sees things freshly, with a cruel impartiality, wide awake to all the tricks of soul and body; and by his son Probyn was seen as a caricature of himself. Lance had not asked to see him like that. It happened so. It was one of those inevitable discriminations which make life both humorous and tragic.

"I can't go."

He went downstairs in flannels, and met his father's oblique eyes looking up at him over the top of the paper. He helped himself to porridge while his father finished his second cup of coffee. They had wished each other good morning.

Probyn Pybus got up as his son sat down. He gulped his coffee. He folded up the paper with a crumpling testiness.

"Lot of mist this morning. Meet my board at eleven."

Lance, with a spoon in the sugar-bowl, supposed that the mist would lift very quickly. The day promised to be hot.

Sir Probyn—with a chracteristic swerve of the right eye allowed it to be seen that he was nettled.

"You'll spend the morning scribbling—what?"

Lance looked out of the window.

"Very likely."

His father went out of the room saying something about

life being a serious business, and that every man—however young—should learn to face responsibilities, the kind of thing that thousands of fathers have said to thousands of sons.

2

Lady Pybus was a late riser. When the maid carried in the breakfast tray she would find that large, fair, overflowing creature yawning under her lace cap.

"Sir Probyn left for town, Wills?"

"Yes, my lady."

"Where's Mr. Lance?"

"I don't know, my lady."

"No letters?"

"No letters this morning, my lady."

Dolly Pybus continued to ask questions as she had asked them as a round-eyed and tow-headed little egoist of five. Growth with her had been mere enlargement, a doubling or trebling of the little suburban ego. She had been a very healthy woman, without subtlety or reservation, an enlarged child with the mental make-up of a child who treated her menfolk like dolls. For years she had been full of healthy, human satisfactions, and thoroughly enjoying the climb and the various and expanding vistas it had provided. She had delighted in being Lady Pybus; she had been delighted with Windover; she had been delighted with her boy at Eton.

But life was not what it was. Fiftyish, she had begun to find life less amusing; and having no inward life of her own to compensate for her failing physical reactions, she was growing a little puzzled and querulous. Her doctor had dieted her. She was allowed only one lump of sugar in her tea. French pastry was forbidden, and when she rushed down to Cannes for six weeks in the winter she was supposed to be content with brown bread and butter. No eleven o'clock invasion of the patisserie shop. No cocktails, and she needed cocktails. And modern dancing was not what it was. She had taken Lance with her for three weeks last winter, and for some reason or other her son had refused to dance. He had been moody.

Lady Pybus put the breakfast tray aside and got out of bed. She had become a heavy woman, and heavy in her movements. She went first to her mirror, and then to one of the windows. It was a beautiful morning; but can anything be more boring and suggestive than a beautiful morning, September sunlight, autumn, glimmering trees, youth that is not youth?

Dolly Pybus looked down at the foreshortened Dutch garden. She saw Lance there in an old blue and white blazer and flannel trousers. He was standing by the cistern staring at it, his hands stuffed into his pockets. He had his back to the house. He appeared to be absorbed in watching the goldfish moving among the lily leaves, and the yellow flowers floating on the water.

His figure had a stillness.

His mother watched him. Lance puzzled her, baffled her, He was so "funny" at times. He had so little to say. He was always mooning off somewhere, or shutting himself up in his room. She could remember the time when she had boasted to her friends: "Oh, Lancie tells me everything." He had been such a jolly kid, a boy whom you could take to Gunter's and stuff with food, but now——

She was not a subtle person, and like many mothers when they discover the grown stranger in their sons she was both perplexed and resentful. Vaguely conscious of a sense of loss, she had attempted to grasp at that which was no longer given. She was fussily affectionate. She wanted to be able to feel and to say: "I and my boy are such pals." She took babyish liberties with his young dignity, and was irritated when he treated her with a kind of dark reserve. He would look at her as though he were saying: "Mater, don't be such a fool."

She was always tweaking the hair of her stranger. She could not let him alone. She would not allow him to be silent or thoughtful. She twitted him, and was archly familiar.

"Hallo, solemn face! Who's the girl?"

She was incapable of realizing that she jarred upon her son, and that she was like a distracting, worrying child to a sensitive man. All that he knew intuitively she knew not at all. That little adjective "funny" described him to her. Men were funny about this, or funny about that, or funny about women. But how exasperating, just when a something in her craved inarticulately for the youth in him.

But he was not young. She was the primitive; while he was Paris and London and Trinity and St. Francis of Assisi, and Raphael and Blake, and moonlight on Lake Leman, and Bernard Shaw. She was quite incapable of coping with him.

That orange and black hammock-bed for instance? What was the objection? The thing looked nice and bright in the Dutch garden. Besides—it was comfortable. And he had called it an atrocity.

Child of impulse that she was, incapable of keeping back anything that came into her head, she hailed him:

"Lan-cie—Lan-cie!"

He hated being shouted at, especially by his mother. She was still the common child of the back street, overblown and overgrown. "Mau-die, yer mother wants yer." He did wish that his mother would give up shouting. She shouted at the gardeners, at her menfolk, at waiters, at the girls who came to play tennis. She talked over and through people.

"Lan-cie—Lan-cie!"

After an interval, he turned and looked up at her window. His response was mute.

"Lan-cie—I want to go into Aylesbury."

Which meant that she intended him to drive her into Aylesbury, and he was wanting to go to Castle Craven. All the urge of his swift complex, and yet simple self, was setting more and more towards Castle Craven.

3

That extraordinary old man!

How had his grandfather contrived to become what he was, both a sage and a bearer of burdens? How wrong it seemed,

and yet how right he made it. For Lance had seen a swollen
person in the Saracen yard, a sort of over-ripe human mulberry
splutter at his grandfather. "Here, where's that soot-case.
Damn it, man, I told you room No. 3." And Lance's blood
had felt on fire, until, in watching the Venerable, he had
realized that the heat in him was natural but unnecessary. His
grandfather, looking with one straight blue glance into that
squashed, mulberry face, had answered with resolute courtesy:
"One suit-case, sir, one kit-bag, one attaché-case. The
suit-case is under that rug, sir. There is no need to damn
anybody."

The swollen person had oozed more purple, and Lance,
standing by the Talbot, and rattling the money in his trouser
pockets, had seen the dignity of his grandfather cut like a knife
into that human pulp.

How was it that the Venerable understood the inwardness
of the thing you were saying almost before you had completed
the saying of it? And the delight in being understood without explainings, while catching the gleam in those resolute
blue eyes, and in hearing the right echo, come back to you!
What was the subtle nexus between them? How was it that
in the presence of his grandfather he felt himself both man and
child, and able to reveal his innermost thoughts with a confidence that was perfect? His grandfather was so young, yet
not young like the young things. He could chuckle. He had
a sudden sense of humour. You felt so near to him in that
little brown room, or when idling under the castle ash trees, or
sitting in the oriel of the Bayard Tower and looking down at
the Brent below.

His grandfather had a peculiar dignity. You forgot the
smallness of him in contemplating that massive head. The
more you talked to him the larger he seemed to grow, until
the mere physical outlines ceased to matter, or became a
familiar cloak hanging about a soul of understanding.

Did the Venerable suspect?

For Lance had not told him. There had been a sensitive
courtesy in the younger man's approach to the elder one.
Lance had felt that he wanted his grandfather to know Lance

the man before he knew him as Lance—the grandson. For
there was such a surprising sympathy between them, and yet
—somehow—it seemed to have an inevitableness. Perhaps
it had.

4

Sally Summerscales, coming in to scrub the Venerable's
kitchen floor for him, while the Venerable shaved himself
before a little mirror hung by the garden window, made
conversation through the doorway. Sally on her knees was
the Sally of symbolism.

"Your young gentleman been to see you again, Mr.
Pybus?"

No, he hadn't, not since last Thursday, but Mr. Pybus
was expecting him. Sally, flopping down a wet cloth on
the red tiles, straightened on her knees.

"He's got such lovely eyes."

Lovely eyes indeed! Sally was incorrigible. And Mr.
Pybus nicked his chin with his razor.

"What do you know about his eyes?"

"Only just passed him in the yard, that's all. What's his
name, Mr. Pybus?"

"I don't know."

"What! You don't know his name?"

"I don't."

"Well—I'm blowed. You're kidding!"

"I'm telling you the truth."

"Where's he come from, Mr. Pybus?"

"I haven't the faintest idea."

"Go on; you can't tell me you don't know his name or
where he comes from. And he's been here four times."

"Counted them, have you?"

"No—I haven't. I was told."

"Well—you can take it from me, Sally, that I have told you
the truth—though it is no business of yours, my dear."

There were splashings and scrubbings, and the Venerable,
having washed the remains of the lather from his face, was

applying a small pad of cotton-wool to the cut on his chin. He made allowances for Sally, for when a young woman comes in of her own free will to scrub your floor—and more especially so in these days when service is called slavery—she is entitled to her graciousness.

"Mr. Pybus——"

"Hallo——"

"I've just had a sort of idea."

"Splendid. What's the idea, Sally?"

"You haven't noticed it—I suppose?"

"I haven't seen it yet."

"What?"

"Your idea."

"Oh, don't be such a quizz, Mr. Pybus. I suppose you haven't noticed that the young gentleman's eyes are awful like yours."

The Venerable was looking at himself in the mirror. Sally heard him give a queer little laugh.

"I gather that's a compliment, Sally."

"It's a fact, Mr. Pybus. You look at him next time."

"I will."

John Pybus was putting on his collar; he was very particular about his collars. As for his young friend's eyes, of course he had noticed them; you could not exchange a dozen words with Lance without being aware of those eyes and of the spirit behind them. And old Pybus had thought—"Now, if I had had a son like that!"

CHAPTER VII

I

LANCE had left his car in the Saracen yard and had walked down to the cottage in search of his grandfather. It was half past four and the Venerable's tea-time, and the pigeons waiting upon the gutters and the ridge-tiles were on the watch for the Venerable's white head. A few of them fluttered down to Lance as he stood on his grandfather's doorstep.

Getting no reply to his knock he walked back to the main yard, where Sally Summerscales, sitting idly at a window, smiled out upon him.

"Are you looking for Mr. Pybus, sir?"

"Yes. He's not at the cottage."

"He's busy, sir. Put off his tea a quarter of an hour. A 'sharry' has just come in. Thirty of 'em. We call them 'one-nighters'."

Sally thought his smile as lovely as his eyes.

"Thank you so much. I suppose he's in the hotel."

"Looking after the luggage, sir."

Lance entered. Sally's "one-nighters" and their luggage were collected in the hall. They were very much in charge of a brisk and bald-headed man, who, standing on the third step of the stairs with a list in his right hand, was assigning his sheep to their pens. He knew his party. He was a humorist in the English manner. He drew little twitters of laughter from the women. "No. 12, Mr. and Mrs. Bibster—please. No. 13—Miss Soames. No, as you were. That wouldn't be gallant. Can't put a lady in No. 13, can we? Mr. Brown, perhaps—you will take No. 13? Thank you, sir. Turn your pyjamas inside out for luck, sir. Supposed to be infallible—they tell me. No. 14, Mr. and Mrs. Lovejoy, and good luck to them. It's a long time since I had a honeymoon." Lance saw his grandfather standing in the centre of a circle of suit-cases and bags. The strong lad who helped with the luggage was having his half-day off, and old Pybus had the whole of it to deal with.

"Luggage for No. 12."

The Venerable was about to ascend the stairs with a suit-case in either hand when Lance, pushing through the crowd, waylaid his grandfather.

"All right—I'll do the carrying. Show me No. 12."

Old Pybus gave him a queer, smiling look.

"You here, sir! Not one of the party? I can manage quite well."

He climbed the first three steps, but Lance wilfully got in front of him.

"I'm serious. I've done it before. I was a porter at Southampton during the General Strike."

His grandfather climbed two more steps.

"There's no strike here, sir, thank you all the same."

"You'll let me carry that luggage. I ask you to let me."

"You can't do it here, sir."

"But I can."

"It's not your job."

They were alone on the stairs, Lance holding out his hands for the luggage, the Venerable looking up at his grandson, and refusing to surrender the burden.

"If you please, sir. Can't allow it."

Lance was smiling, but there was much behind that smile.

"I suppose I can help my own grandfather——"

He saw the Venerable's figure stiffen where it stood. The old man's face had a kind of staring pallor. He looked straight up at his grandson. He seemed to be asking himself and Lance some momentous question.

"Probyn's boy?"

"Yes."

"Does he know——?"

"No."

Something happened to old John Pybus's face. A sudden strange softness overflowed it. The blue stare went out of his eyes. He allowed his grandson to take the luggage from him.

"All right. Bit of a shock. Turn to the right when you reach the landing."

Lance went up with a heart that was beating more rapidly. His grandfather followed him.

"Second door along the corridor—on the left."

"Right, sir."

"Don't call me 'sir'."

"Of course," said Lance, glancing over a shoulder, "you won't do that to me any more, sir."

"I shall—unless——"

"Grandfather," said Lance, pausing outside the door of No. 12, "isn't this a rather great occasion?"

Old Pybus's white head seemed a little bent. Lance put down a suit-case, opened the door of No. 12, went in, and placed the suit-case he was carrying on the luggage-stand.

"Why didn't you tell me before, boy?"

"I—I wanted you to know me a little."

"Ah!" said his grandfather—"I see."

He carried the other suit-case into the room and placed it on a chair.

"Did they tell you about me?"

"No."

They did not look at each other.

"Then—how——?"

"I heard something."

"Made you feel inquisitive?"

"More than that. I think I had to come. I wanted to come. And—of course—now——"

The sunlight striking through the window fell upon the Venerable's head and face.

"We had better clear up the rest of that luggage, Lance. Then—we'll have tea."

2

At the door of his cottage John Pybus paused and looked up at his grandson. He was carrying a plate of bread and butter, with two slices of plum cake laid to one side.

"Just one moment. It's rather important. Are you going to tell them at home?"

"No—I'm not."

"Ought you to tell them?"

"They did not tell me."

His grandfather appeared to consider the question before opening the door.

"Ashamed of me—of course. Quite natural. I dare say they did not want you to know. And you are up at Cambridge. It is conceivable that most young men——"

Said Lance with a kind of smiling seriousness:

"I have a friend at Trinity whose father was doing what you are doing, grandfather."

"Oh, cleaning boots and fetching and carrying——"

"Yes—chap named Sorrell. Great man. Rather a peculiar coincidence—though."

John Pybus opened the door.

"I haven't quite made my mind up—yet."

"About my people?"

"That's it. There was a time when I was bitter, my lad, but bitterness comes back to you. That's done with. I want to be fair."

Lance, following him into the cottage, and closing the door, stood looking at the two photos on the mantelpiece. Old Pybus, putting the plate down on the oak table, went towards the kitchen to light the oil-stove on which he boiled his water, and to fetch a cup and plate for Lance. They talked through the doorway.

"Grandfather."

"Hallo——"

"Why do you keep those photos there?"

He heard the Venerable strike a match.

"All sorts of reasons, mixed reasons. I call them the photos of my sons who were killed in the war."

"They weren't in the war."

"No."

"Is that—why——?"

"We never got on very well together. There seemed to be

nothing of me in them, and nothing of them in me. Queer, but it's a fact. They liked their mother, but I don't think they ever liked me. I have often tried to work out how and where—I was to blame. Too strict, perhaps. Expected too much."

"But they are not like you."

"Not much——"

"Conrad's a perfect swine—Sorry, sir, I oughtn't to have used that word."

His grandfather was measuring tea into the teapot.

"I am more shy of using hard words than I was, lad. Because—we can't always help ourselves. When a man was born a pig, it doesn't help to call him a pig. It's not piggery, it's nature. I'm coming to believe that we carry our fate with us."

"You're a determinist, grandpater?"

"Suppose I am. Though it's not all Mendelism. I have a feeling that something's put in, or not put in. The divine spark. Anyway—it's all mystery—mystery. That's why that church tower is right to go on calling with its bells."

There was a short silence. Then Lance said:

"Grandpater—my father and I have never exchanged a single word on anything that really matters."

"To you?"

"Yes—I suppose I'm looking at it—like an egoist."

"How else can you begin to look at it?"

"We're strangers. It's rather terrible—in its way."

"They and I—were just such strangers. There are old souls and young souls. That's how I look at it. And you can't mix your souls. Different planes. The big soul, and the little greedy soul. Amazing rot—all this blather about equality. I'll have the kettle boiling in a minute."

Lance strolled to the mantelpiece, and having looked steadily at the portraits of his father and his uncle, he saw them as strangers, people to whom he would never have anything to say. Also, with all deference to the Venerable—Conrad was a perfect swine. No other two words fitted him as those two words did. As for his father——? Poor old pater, such a sedulous and flamboyant snob! Extraordinary world! People ashamed of their jobs, and ashamed of their own people for doing particular jobs. Blind as bats—too! And he himself was ashamed of his father's snobbery, and his mother's loud and florid nature.

He crossed to the window where the Venerable's flowers were blooming—without taking thought. Good old Solomon! And from the kitchen came the sound of a purring kettle.

"Grandpater——"

"Yes."

"Don't you get very tired?"

"No, not very. There's not too much for me."

"You're a wonder."

"Simple living, my lad."

"More than that. You are mediæval."

"What?"

"You make me think of Sir Isumbras, and St. Christopher, and people who did simple and beautiful things. Service, you know. I've watched shepherds, and they seem to me to be about the only people in these days—who carry you back. Yes; sailors, too, in a way, and fishermen."

"I get tips," said his grandfather.

"Do people tip you?"

"Of course."

"How perfectly—scandalous and splendid."

"I take 'em, too. Bank balance and books. Besides—you never know. England isn't India. You can't be a sage—in England—on twopence-halfpenny."

"Climate?"

"Call it that. I admit that I respect good blankets and a fire. Now for tea."

He arrived with a little brown teapot, and looking with new affection at his grandson, put down the teapot, and stood to say grace.

"For what we receive—let us be thankful."

Lance sat down at the table with the air of a young man preparing to break some solemn fast.

3

Said Lance to his grandfather:

"Tell me all about yourself, grandfather."

The Venerable's eyes laughed gently under the bushy white eyebrows.

"Once upon a time there was a little old fellow who kept a bookshop."

"So you did keep a bookshop?"

"For thirty years or so. What was the family tradition?"

"If you don't mind, I'd rather not talk about it at present. The reality is so much better than the make-believe."

"Well—I kept a bookshop in London, and then—another bookshop in a Dorsetshire town. Then we had the war as an interlude, and my books remained on the shelves. I ceased to be a bookseller, and conducted a tram. I have been in this billet for about seven years."

Lance stirred his tea. His face had a clouded look.

"Didn't they know?"

"We had passed out of each other's lives."

"But was there no—no effort?"

"Your father did make an effort."

"I'm glad of that."

"But—he did not like my job. Quite natural. It did not inspire credit. Very kindly—he offered to pension me, to turn me into an old fellow pottering about a parade. But I did not see it—as he saw it."

"And you told him——?"

"I'm afraid I told him to go to hell."

Lance flushed up.

"Splendid! That's just like—these people, they always want you to do what suits them."

His grandfather gave him a shrewd look.

"You, too?"

"Yes. It has all been arranged. I'm to be a business man. I'm to be the expert specialist. Everything is taken for granted. I'm to be a little second edition of my father. Of course—I know—that he has never grudged me anything. Parents don't; but when it comes to the crisis——"

"Yes."

"They grudge you the one big thing."

"And that?"

"The right to be yourself."

Old Pybus appeared to be counting the currants in one of the slices of cake.

"Yes, we are all guilty of that, more or less. We like to retain control. I let my boys go; but I kept the right of telling them what I thought——"

"Did it do any good, grandpater?"

"Not a shred. It made them dislike me—a little more. They meant to go their way, and I went mine. And you——?"

Lance looked out of the window.

"My way's different, too. At least—I think so. I want to be myself."

4

At the end of the meal John Pybus piled the crockery neatly on a tray and carried it into the kitchen. He came back to join Lance in the lighting of pipes. The talk between them had turned aside into one of those silences which resemble a halt under the shadow of a tree before the next march forward. They went out to feed the pigeons.

"About this being yourself," said the Venerable, scattering crumbs; "it's easier to be a pigeon than a man."

"How do you mean?"

"A complete man. Being yourself is being a complete man, isn't it? Crowds, and still more crowds. Peas packed in a pod. How many men can be themselves? Can't afford it; haven't time, isn't enough room. Besides—what is myself?"

"I see you very clearly, grandpater."

"It's easier—perhaps—to see someone else. What am I to see in you?"

"A free man—body and soul."

"No one—is wholly free. Even the desert island idea has its limitations. What you are asking for is free self-expression."

"Yes—that's it—that's it. I want to interpret things; I want to write."

His grandfather watched the birds feeding at Lance's feet.

"Yes, if you are big enough, people will come and feed at your feet. But, meanwhile——"

"One has to live."

"Exactly. Being yourself may mean doing without."

"I've thought of that."

"Standing aside from the scramble. Teeth set—stomach empty, alone, the woman passing you by, the successful young tripe-merchants calling you—'That fool!'"

"Need it be—like that?"

"Take it for granted that it may be like that. What's your plan?"

"It's in the making, grandpater."

"A top-floor room in London, or a labourer's cottage in the country? Sending up manuscripts and having them sent back again? There's bound to be some of that. Unless—of course—your father——"

He glanced at his grandson's set face.

"I don't want help."

"That's unusual."

"I'm as good as other men who have had to go into the dog-fight without a collar."

"Money helps, my lad."

"Does it?"

"Unless it saps your fierceness."

"My father made his own success."

"Business is easier than the writing of books. And books have to sell. I'm not a commercialist. But youth asks for things. It feeds on its own heart. I'm old; I have ceased to ask for certain things; I have the few simple things I want. For me—there is no—woman."

Lance was leaning against the wall with the air of a man with his back very much to it.

"Yes, I think I understand. You have to begin with the hair-shirt idea."

"Somewhat," said his grandfather; "come and look at life, modern life. You get it—samples of it—even in Castle Craven."

5

Standing in the Saracen yard with his back to a big blue "saloon" which had come in for the night, John Pybus pointed with the stem of his pipe at Lance's little "Talbot."

"There won't be any of that, Lance."

"No, I suppose not, grandpater."

"Not to begin with. Books don't—as a rule—produce motor-cars. But—of course—you have thought——"

He looked with a courageous kindness into his grandson's serious face. He was being braver than Lance knew. It is so much pleasanter to utter comfortable words; and this new and human relationship had suddenly become precious to him.

"Criticism is one of the most difficult drugs to swallow. You'll be thinking me a platitudinous old devil——"

Lance's smile came back.

"He—whom the Lord chastens—grandpater——"

"You've got it. Don't we all want to wave flags and shout hooray. But I won't—my lad—to you."

"No, I don't think you could."

"But I can shout hooray at the right moment. We are flesh and blood—remember. And then—— Well, there's something to look at."

A long, white two-seater, a de luxe machine, had glided in through the archway. A very tall man, brown as to face and clothes, climbed out of it, and turned to smile in a particular way at a very decorative young woman in a velvet and fur coat.

"Puss staying on the cushion?"

She was a pretty thing with oblique dark eyes, and a slow, sophisticated smile.

"Need I get out?"

"Need you do anything? Just going across to the gun-smith's, that's all. Snuggle up."

The Venerable, after looking admiringly at the little lady in the black and white chariot, glanced up at his grandson.

"Interested—in that sort of thing?"

Lance looked a little fierce. He was more interested in—that sort of thing—than his grandfather suspected.

"Oh—yes—sometimes. It hasn't lasted long—yet."

"Expensive hobby in these days. Say you sell fifteen hundred copies of a novel. A hundred pounds, more or less; probably less. How far would that go? There is a sort of celibacy——"

And suddenly he took his grandson by the arm.

"Let us go and look at the river. You haven't to pay to look at the river."

6

A moon, as big and yellow as a harvest moon, raised its face over Castle Craven, and the whiteness of the Venerable's head was like the sheen of a helmet. The shadows of the ash trees lay like the shadows of clouds upon the broken walls of the castle, and the castle field was a goblin ground pocketed with darkness between folds of silver. John Pybus had finished his supper. He had come out with a pipe and his own thoughts. He took the path to the swinging gate in the stone wall, and passing across the grass-grown courtyard, climbed the three steps to one of the windows. The stone mullion cut the sky into halves. A hundred feet below, the dark river slid beneath the droop of beech boughs, and into the moonlight rose the soft thunder of the abbey weir.

John Pybus—of course—was thinking of his grandson, for, in Lance's own words, the day had been a great occasion. And if it is possible for an old man to succumb to flattery, Lance's grandfather should have succumbed to it; but flattery floats on shallow water, and old Pybus was deep.

He had been touched. He could think of nothing but the grandson in the place of the father; Lance coming to help him with that luggage. What an ironical reversion to type! If Probyn! Ought Probyn to know? But there was no spirit of malicious exultation in old Pybus. Did one gloat over the strange unexpectedness of human kinship, that sacred something in the blood?

He felt accountable to youth, and for it. He had overcome temptation. In this little kitchen, with the brown teapot in his hand, and Lance's voice coming to him from the other room, he had confronted and frowned down facility. No Agag easiness. Rather would he be Samuel to the young David.

Watching the smoke blow from his pipe drifting into the moonlight he reviewed his resolution.

"I'll not try to bribe him. If there is to be anything between us that will last it shall be worth lasting. Not the easy thing. It is so pleasant to prophesy the easy thing. He is asking for the most difficult thing that a man can desire."

Looking at the moon, old Pybus went back to his cottage. His head had a radiance, and in the face of the moon he seemed to see the ardent, questioning face of his grandson.

CHAPTER VIII

I

LANCE was looking at the same moon, and seeing it through the branches of the Bosquet. He, too, was reviewing the great occasion, his back turned towards the marble figure of the nymph, into whose white bosom the moon threw a handful of light. Her head was in the shadow, and out of this shadow she seemed to gaze with a gentle and wondering disdain at this man thing who came to such a place and at such an hour to meditate upon a grandfather.

But if the nymph was of stone, and could not move from her pedestal, there were other nymphs and matrons. Parental conjectures may seem self-justified, especially if you have been playing tennis—the last game of the year perhaps—and dinner has caught you unchanged and you are still wearing tennis shoes. There were no pebbles in the path for the moon to shine upon. Striking through the foliage of the yews and hollies, it spread upon the path and upon the paved space of the Bosquet, a flowered carpet in which the flowers were moonlight upon a groundwork of shadow.

The mother saw the son standing there. He made no movement. He was watching the moon climbing through the branches of the trees. His face and figure were covered with patches of light. And to his mother he was a figure of interrogation, a human question-mark. She answered the question as she was made to answer it. Obviously Lance was waiting for someone or something; she could not imagine a young man stealing out to such a place and at such an hour without a purpose. Being the woman she was, she postulated "woman."

But who? One of the maids? She passed them in review. Yes, it might be Florrie, the under-housemaid, a sly, smoky-eyed little thing. Or could it be a girl from outside? Lady Pybus was as suburban in her suspicion as she was in her other attitudes toward life.

But suddenly Lance moved, and she was caught.   He came upon her in the narrowing path where the shadows were more closely woven.

"Lan-cie!"

"Mater!"

"What are you doing here?"

How was it he knew that he had been spied upon?—for know it he did.   He stood looking at the large, dim whiteness that was his mother.   He was conscious of feeling shocked, repelled, humiliated.   Had she so little inward dignity that she could so offend against his own young dignity?

"I came here to think."

His voice was as cold as the moonlight.   He knew, even while he was uttering the words, that she would not believe him.   But why should he not reply to her challenge?   Did she not understand solitude, moonlight, those moods of aloofness?   But how could she understand them?   He had a feeling of helplessness in her presence.   This vulgar, possessive prying.

"One—has—to—think—sometimes, you know, mater."

She laughed.

"You funny boy."

Insensitive though she was, she was aware of his discomfort. Essentially a woman of the people, she understood neither irony nor the finer shades of courtesy.   She resented contact with anything that she did not understand, and like a child sought to make the contact crudely physical.   Posed—she became familiar.

"Well—it should have been a girl.   I believe it was."

He stood apart, head up, looking at her.

"Mater——"

"Well—and why not?"

"And if it had been?"

Again that discordant, voluminous laugh.

"Don't be silly.   You're so touchy."

He was silent, with a kind of lamentable, fierce silence.   The vulgarity of it!   Had she no feeling of reverence for things, no reticence, no delicacy?   And this silence of his was like a hand laid resolutely over her mouth.

She bridled.

"Well—I suppose I've got feelings. You're so funny. Always mooching off, and shutting yourself up. Always scribbling——"

"Am I?"

"Are you—indeed! Why don't you tell me—things? We used to be such pals—Lancie——"

"I'm sorry, mater."

His voice sounded tired. Yes, that was part of the pity of it. A kind of weariness would come over him during these hopeless arguments with his mother. They were intimate without intimacy. She was like a woman picking at a tangled skein without being able to find the ends of it, and she made him feel more tangled, and more knotted, and more tied up within himself.

"I suppose it's the funny age, isn't it?"

She reverted to a sudden and ingratiating cheerfulness. She caught his arm, imprisoned it, and turning him made him walk with her down the shadowy path.

"Why don't you tell me, Lance?"

"What am I to tell you?"

"Who—it is?"

She had a glimpse of his patient, frozen profile outlined against the moon.

"Nobody, mater. There isn't anybody—in that way."

2

Lance was both angry with his mother and sorry for her. He had made himself kiss her when they had reached the house.

"We're at cross purposes, mater."

She had talked to him and at him all the way through the gardens in a voice that was unhushed. She had the naked soul of a common child. She did not shrink from, or hurry by, those too public occasions. Like a common woman, she would have exposed all her domestic disharmonies on her doorstep before a group of interested neighbours.

"If I don't understand you—who does? It's absurd."

Yes, it was absurd, pathetically absurd! But why should she assume——?

"I wish you would try and let me alone, mater."

"I think you are a perfect pig."

Perhaps he was. He was ready to grant her her sense of injury and of injustice. But if only she would not assume——He had let her go into the house, and had turned away along the terrace and across the gravel, to find himself at the end of the avenue of beeches pillared under the moonlight like some great gallery leading to mysterious sanctuaries. He stood there very still. He saw the splashed trunks, the black sweep of the foliage, the moonlight in streaks and star-spaces, light and shadow clasped and intermingled. There was a great stillness, the freshness of dew, an indefinable suggestion of mystery of other presences, other worlds.

"Beauty!"

Yes, beauty, and more than beauty! Why was he so made that he could tremble at some sound that his mother would not hear? The "Ah!" of the woods in the arms of the west wind, the voice of a bird solitary at dawn, the flutter of aspen leaves, the sighing of the grasses! For beauty and his awareness of it had come to him so suddenly a year ago. It had seemed as though a blindness had fallen from him. He could remember moments of awe and of wonder, sunsets, light under a thundercloud, a world wetly and passionately green, tears in his own eyes, a voice singing, a sudden drift of perfume.

It seemed to him that life should be beauty, and that without beauty life was as nothing. Yet, how could you define beauty, or explain it? It was so instant, so inevitable. It came to you full of a poignant, sweet strangeness in a word or a sound, or a gleam of the eyes. It leapt upon you out of the pages of a book. "And the last sunset cry of conquered kings." He had seen it in the Venerable's white head with its background of gold.

Could anything be more wonderful than these old beech trees under the full moon? And then he remembered that these trees belonged to his father. His father had bought them, and all the other beauties of Windover with the profits of big business, yet he had never surprised his father in a moment of gazing. How much did his father see, and how little? And his mother?

How extraordinary it was! For he was very sure that the secret and exquisite moods of the gardens and the woods were hidden from his people. Pan and his satellites remained in the deep glooms; the fairies danced unseen. And his mother would rush off to Brooklands, and get her eyes full of sand, and her nostrils full of the stink of burnt oil, and climb on the roof of her car, and shout, and see nothing sinister and ugly in that most strange crowd.

Wandering down the avenue until the round face of the moon gazed at him over the iron gates, he felt himself confronted by reality. There was the reality of beauty, the reality of an ideal, the reality of a world's materialism. He was still full of his grandfather's forewarnings.

To get certain things you might have to give up certain things. Self-expression might entail self-martyrdom. He had been shown himself as a young man scribbling in some top-floor room, high above the world of motor-cars and women, detached from it, despised by it. There was still the wilderness for the world's failures.

But what was failure? According to the material standard his grandfather was a failure, and his father a supreme success, and yet in the world of spiritual realities how subtly the position was reversed. Lance had no doubts as to which was the more impressive figure. His father had made money; his grandfather had made a man.

Yes, his urge was to follow his grandfather. The Venerable appeared to him as an unconquerable figure, a shining veteran on a hilltop, sword aloft, calling him on. Was he to lack the courage? Was he to choose the easy thing? His grandfather had spoken hard words, but did you ask to see honey drop from the lips of an old Roman who was captain of his own soul?

"Be yourself, to the uttermost and to the end."

He turned back.   He came again into the beautiful, mellow presence of the old house.   In the moonlight the brickwork had a blurred softness.   It was solid and yet not solid.   Its texture had the quality of old velvet.   And he remembered that his father had been complaining that the place looked shabby, and that he thought of having the walls re-pointed and the mortar painted white.

"Good God!"

A week ago he had been reading that very significant book of Chesterton's—"The Everlasting Man," and there was a little sentence in it that, no doubt, he did not remember, but which expressed this moment when he stood there looking up at this most English house.   "Such men realize the real truth that enormous things do often turn upon tiny things."

His father proposed to deface that old façade.   In the same way his father proposed to deface the soul of the son.   It was his father's notion of self-expression; it was life; it was one of those inevitable personal urges.   It need not need consideration, but it did need defiance.

He would go in and talk things out with his father.

3

Sir Probyn Pybus was a philatelist, but with Sir Probyn philately was rather the hobby of a man who had spent his life in acquiring material things, and who was nearing the end of his possibilities.   Certainly he was the possessor of some very rare specimens, and he could say that he could show every stamp that had been issued by the Republic of South America. His collection was insured for a considerable sum.

He had made a purchase that day from a dealer, and when Lance looked in through the open french window of the library he saw his father seated at his desk, with one of his albums open before him.   He was examining a stamp through a lens mounted on a silver handle.   The desk lamp showed an incipient baldness as he bent forward, and on his face there was a little self-satisfied smile.

Lance had come to the window feeling a little sorry for his father, but there was something in that smile which checked the flow of this feeling. At the age of fifteen Lance had collected stamps, and had given his collection away at the end of eighteen months. Rotten bad business! His father, jokingly had told him so at the time. And here was his father, fiftyish where the son had been fifteen, but giving nothing away without a swivel-eye on the profit or the "advert." Sir Probyn still spoke of "adverts." It irritated his son.

Lance stood there a moment looking through the lens of his own sensitive nature at his father who was scrutinizing a postage-stamp. The son was trying to see some resemblance between that other father and his other son, but to Lance they appeared as unlike as two men could be. Three generations of Pybi, and the middle one a warehouse built between a cathedral and a castle! Extraordinary!

"Pater, can I come in for a minute?"

Probyn had not heard his son's footsteps; he had been absorbed in squinting at that stamp. He looked up with bland, civic expression. It seemed to him that his son's figure set in the white frame of the window looked taller than usual.

"Come in, Lance. Look at this Honduras. What do you think of it?"

Lance, moving to a position behind his father, looked at the stamp, and also at that patch of baldness on Sir Probyn's head.

"Nice issue. I want to talk about—things, pater. It's—it's inevitable."

Sir Probyn placed the magnifying glass between the leaves of the stamp album. He pushed back his chair six inches. He was deliberate, for deliberation seemed to be the right response to so flustering a word. Inevitable! Was anything inevitable save death and one's dinner? Had the boy got himself into some mess, an affair with a woman?

"What is the trouble? Sit down, Lance."

Lance remained standing behind his father's chair.

"There's no trouble, pater—but I don't want to go into business."

So that was it! Probyn, looking over his shoulder, with

a shrewd and facetious finger stroking his polished chin, prepared to receive his son as he would have received a deputation.

"What's the matter with business?"

"Nothing, pater. But I have reasons. I'm not made for business."

"Haven't tried it, my lad, have you?"

"I want to do something else."

Probyn was no fool. His shrewdness cast a wide circle, but it was a circle described on a flat surface. Youth's urges, and its impossible enthusiasms were all very well, but they were like the tantrums of a child, ebullitions of unadvised emotion. You had to be patient with children and young people; they could be very exasperating. But the trouble was that Lance did not appear to be an ordinary young person with a healthy appetite for the good things of life and a sensible determination towards the getting of them.

"Well—what do you want to do?"

"Write."

Probyn could understand a lad wanting to be a racing motorist or a wireless expert, something that was virile and adventurous—but literature!

"Novels?"

Lance's eyes were on his father's stamp-album.

"Books. They may be novels."

"Ah!" said his father—"want to be an Arnold Bennet or an H. G. Wells, do you? That's quite all right if you are an Arnold Bennet or a Wells."

He was bland and tolerant, and Lance understood the implication.

"I don't know what I can do yet, pater. Writing's a great craft. You have to work at it."

"Quite so. Have you tried anything with the publishers?"

"Not yet."

"And how long do you think it will be?"

"I can't say. I'm working on a novel."

"That's very interesting. But—meanwhile—how do you propose to live?"

His tolerance had a gaiety. He made that point because it was worth making, and all fathers have made it, but it was no more than a point, a suggestion.

Lance seemed to reflect. He stood with his hands in his pockets, his eyes looking over his father's head and through the open window.

"As best I could."

"How could that be?"

"Odd articles and short stories—while I was getting going. Or—I might take on a secretarial job."

His father smiled, much as he had smiled over that new postage-stamp.

"My dear lad!"

He turned his chair, and looked up obliquely into his son's face.

"I suppose you realize that you are my son. I have always tried—— The best education—and all that. Because—you know—his son does matter to a man."

"You have been very generous to me, pater."

"Well—well——"

"I want you to be generous to me—in this other way, not with money."

"You mean—you want your chance?"

"Yes."

Sir Probyn got up, and walked to the window. He stood there at gaze, rattling a bunch of keys in a trouser pocket. He was shaping an attitude. Every situation has its key.

"Supposing I made you an allowance—say for two years. You are twenty next month."

"Would it be fair, pater?"

"To whom?"

"To you."

His father faced about, still rattling those keys.

"To me! Well—now. Why—to me?"

"Because I should be doing what I wanted to do, and not what you want me to do."

Sir Probyn looked blank for a moment. The boy was so

unexpected. He was always skipping out of the nice little circle you had drawn about him.

"Oh—I don't know about that. I might make it quite a moderate allowance. Feeling on your dignity about it?"

"In a way."

"Quite right. Supposing I allowed you two hundred a year. When you had taken your degree—I suppose you would go up to London. Or you could live here and work. Why not?"

"I should have to see things, pater."

"Life—eh! Get your copy. Well, you could go into rooms—I might even find you a part-time post—secretarial work—as you say."

"It's very good of you, pater. I——"

But his father had turned a sudden back on him. He walked across to a cabinet in which he kept his cigars. He opened two or three different boxes; he appeared to deliberate.

"That's the son's point of view, Lance. Ever considered the father's?"

Lance, watching his father rolling a cigar between thumb and fingers, let his thoughts revert to that other father.

"I'd like to hear it, pater."

"You shall. Ever occurred to you that I must have worked pretty hard?"

"It has."

"Watched you grow up, made plans, felt proud of you. And a time comes, my lad, when a man's responsibilities—get —rather heavy. He finds himself wanting to sit in a chair and potter round his garden. And that's the time when he begins to think—'Here's youth coming along. It will take something off my shoulders. And it will be good to watch it growing big.' Not unnatural—that—eh? It's a point of view. Hasn't occurred to you—perhaps—that I had hoped——?"

He threw a quick glance at his son's face. It was immensely grave and resolute and silent, for Lance was remembering that his father had not behaved to the Venerable as he expected his own son to behave to him.

"I know—pater. I'm not saying to you that I did not ask

to be born—because it's just as possible that you did not ask for me to be born."

"As a matter of fact—I did. But aren't there other considerations?"

"There must be good fellows in the firm who would be of much more use to you than I should be. I'm perfectly honest. I should not be any use in business."

"If you made an effort——?"

"My heart's not in it. All this may sound very foolish and selfish, but oughtn't one to try and do the thing—the big thing, that calls you? After all—you did, sir."

He watched a queer little shimmer of a smile flit across his father's face.

"That's true. But I made money. I set out to make money. I don't think you know yet, Lance, how important money is."

"Perhaps I do—and perhaps I don't, pater. But I want to follow my own craft. I'm not talking high-brow tosh. After all—it seems to me that his craft should matter to a man, and that if it doesn't he might just as well be dead. I know men up at Cambridge——"

"Is that where——?"

"No—I try and work things out for myself. I haven't thought much of making money."

"You haven't!"

"Perhaps it doesn't seem so enormously important when your head and your heart are full of other things."

His father put in one of his sly touches.

"I dare say—that is so. I did not have your advantages. I had to scramble for myself. My money has made things pretty easy for you."

Lance's head went up.

"Yes. But you ought not to taunt me with it, pater."

"My dear boy——!"

"That's one of the reasons why I want—well, perhaps you don't understand——"

Sir Probyn, bland and affectionate, crossed over and patted his son's shoulder.

D

"More than you think, perhaps.   Well—we'll see about it.
You have got another year at Trinity."

4

Probyn was unpinning his tie.   It was his habit to leave his
dressing-room door open, for his wife liked to talk while she
was in the process of going to bed, and had he left the door
closed she would most certainly have opened it.   Ever since
Probyn had attained to the dignity and the culture of a dressing-room they had discussed night by night their own private
affairs, their son, their friends, or their servants.

Said the mother, dabbing at her face with a piece of cotton-
wool—"There's something funny about Lance."

Probyn was removing his collar, and uncovering a rather
prominent Adam's apple—

"Funny !   Oh, yes—I think I know all about that.   It's the
hot-air-season."

He smiled at himself in the mirror.   Yes, he had every
right to think that he had handled Lance very well.   It did not
do to jerk the reins.   A soft hand was the thing.

"The boy wants to be an author."

"Well—why can't he be an author?"

"But he doesn't want to go into the business."

"Told you that—seriously."

"Might have been telling me he had had a call.   Going out
as a missionary to China."

Lance's mother turned in her chair.   She could see a part of
her husband.   He was getting into a blue silk dressing-
gown.

"What did you say?"

"Said we would see about it.   Fact is—the boy has had
things made too easy.   My fault perhaps——"

"But—you can't let him——"

"Might be the best way, mother.   Let him go and find
things out, the things that matter.   I'm not so sure that I
shan't give him a small allowance, and let him try the scribbling
game for two years.   That's to say—if the obsession lasts."

"But—authors—don't make much money, do they—unless they happen to be best sellers?"

"That's my point. If the lad's got any sense he'll soon realize the limitations of that sort of life. He doesn't know what life is. It would be an experience. Teach him values. Besides——"

He came to the door, and stood with his hands tucked into the pockets of his dressing-gown.

"Things happen—women—and all that. Bound to happen some day, mother. That'll teach him. He's a good lad, a nice lad, bless him. He's the sort that will take falling in love damned seriously. Expensive game these days, marrying the modern girl. She'll soon knock the nonsense out of him. Nothing like responsibilities for bringing a lad down to bedrock."

Lady Pybus picked up a hairbrush.

"That's rather clever of you, Byn. Poor old Lancie. He's so dreamy—dear old thing."

"He'll get over it. The thing is—to let him—find things out. I bet you that in a couple of years he'd be turning to with me—like a Trojan. Art—and all that's a mug's game."

"But there have to be artists and authors, Byn."

"I know. But it's we who keep 'em. We're the people who make all that — possible. Mark me — Lance will find that out—if he has to find it out. He'll want to do the keeping, hire fellows to write and paint for him. That's the idea."

CHAPTER IX

I

JOHN PYBUS had learnt to say—"Don't expect too much from people. The world's full of children."

Nor did he blame children for being greedy when there is a scramble for cake and jam; but from his grandson the Venerable was daring to expect higher forms of hunger. For to some the Apples of the Hesperides hang on mystical trees, and while most snouts are in the fleshpots, other eyes look over the edge of the world.

Old Pybus was a mystic, though there might be a touch of the Puritan in his mysticism. He insisted upon mysticism. He would tell you that mere cleverness is so much camel-dung, but that mysticism sets it alight. You smell a flower—but—who—is it that smells it, and what is it that you smell? The perfume of an essential oil? But lose your mysticism and life loses its odour.

For a week he did not see his grandson.

"Hard words."

Yes, he had spoken hard words to Lance. How to be yourself with everything and nothing! A diamond in your head and twopence in your pocket. A scribbler's income—unless you were one of the lucky scribblers—cheap clothes, new soles to your boots a problem, soap a consideration, flat food and perhaps flat feet, your mouth full of bad teeth, a third-class ticket to Brighton, your wife's head indifferently shingled—if you could afford a wife; no scent on the dressing-table, cotton pyjamas, grey flannel trousers at twelve shillings a pair, the barber once in two months, the doctor not at all—save as a disaster! The eternal chasing of sixpences in a climate that demands beer and beef; days when the soul of the world looks like a boiled potato! Yes, that was what your mysticism might have to contend with. London and an empty belly, and a red winter sun setting over the trees of Hyde Park.

But at the end of a week Lance reappeared.

He found the Venerable at his post in front of the brass gong.

"Sorry, grandpater—but the car has been laid up."

John Pybus's very blue eyes filled with little glimmers of light.

"Thought I'd frightened you."

"No. You gave me something to think about. Shall I wait here?"

Old Pybus pulled out his watch.

"A quarter past four. I shall be free in five minutes. Go down to the cottage and start the kettle."

"Right, grandpater."

Miss Vallence was leaning forward over her desk with her head half-through the office window. She had heard Lance call John Pybus grandfather. She intended Lance to look at her, and look he did.

"Good afternoon, Miss Vallence."

"Good afternoon, sir."

She smiled upon him. She wanted to ask him if his name was Pybus, for if old Pybus owned such a grandson—well—the situation—would be unusual and interesting. Miss Vallence spent so much of her life in a glass case that she was thrilled if a mouse ran across the hall.

"We thought you had forgotten us, sir. Lovely weather for the time of year."

Lance paused by the office window. Miss Vallence was a friend of his grandfather's, and Lance had often noticed her tired face suspended over her books. She made him think of a little, pathetic, yellow-haired monkey, full of amiable chatterings and characteristic phrases. He could see himself offering Miss Vallence a red apple or a banana, but he never could think of anything to say to her. What did you say to that sort of girl? Lance had his limitations.

"Had your holiday, Miss Vallence?"

"Me!—I—don't—think! I've forgotten all about it."

"You haven't had one?"

"I had a week at Torquay in May. Do you know Torquay, sir?"

"I've been there once."

"Lovely place—don't you think? And Dartmoor? I went in a 'sharry' to Chagford. We—were—gay. You ought to tell Mr. Pybus to take a holiday, sir."

"Doesn't he take a holiday?"

"He's never had one since I've been here."

Lance glanced towards the figure of his grandfather, and found the Venerable's eyes fixed on him with a kind of gentle and amused shrewdness, for John Pybus saw many men—young and old—approach Miss Vallence's window, goggle-eyed men, bright boys, bagmen away from home. Lance was the unusual male outside the glass cage. He exhibited a shy, serious courtesy.

Lance smiled at his grandfather.

"I had better see to that kettle."

He nodded to Miss Vallence and went down the passage, and Miss Vallence, passing a hand over her shingled head, addressed Mr. Pybus.

"Nice boy, your grandson—such nice manners."

"That's so," said the Venerable.

"Comes in his own car, doesn't he?"

"Yes, his own car."

"My word! His people——"

But the Venerable was not to be tempted. He glanced at his watch, and decided that he could follow his grandson. But he did pause momentarily outside the office window to give Miss Vallence something to satisfy her.

"Pots of money, my dear. Between you and me, family differences. You keep that to yourself—if you can!"

But his face had a softness as he went out into the Saracen yard and saw the familiar redness of the old walls and the brown-grey cobbles, and the grey and russet roofs, and pigeons wheeling and waiting. One white bird flew down and settled upon his right shoulder, and the Venerable was made to think of the Holy Spirit descending. He smiled and, putting up a hand, caressed the bird. He walked on past Lance's little blue Talbot, and in the cobbled breadth of the passage leading to his cottage, he paused as a man pauses to look at life and his thoughts, as through an open window. The Castle ash trees were hung with golden keys. Creepers were reddening on the walls. Autumn was here. And he thought—"How many more autumns shall I see? Not so many. But if—in the winter of my years I am to have a son—may it please God to give me ten more years." The pigeon was still upon his shoulder, and taking it gently into his hands he threw it upwards into the air as though sending up a living prayer.

2

When old Pybus came to the door of his cottage he heard two voices, and one of them was a woman's.

"That will save you five minutes, sir. I'll turn it up full."

"Thank you."

"Mr. Pybus likes his tea fresh and strong. One spoonful for him, one for you, and one for the pot."

Woman—everlasting woman, that irresponsible, petticoat fluttering on his grandson's heels! The Venerable stood and listened, not as a mere eavesdropper, but as a man bending to catch the voice of youth. Sally was incorrigible, and yet as natural as a fluttering pigeon swooping down upon his grandson.

"Thank you. I can manage now."

That was Lance's voice, pleasant but a little shy, and suggesting that he did not quite know what to do with Sally. "Confound the young minx!" was the Venerable's reflection. But he remained there for a moment looking through other windows, and remembering how a kind of brightness had come to Millie Vallence's face, and how Sally had spoken of "lovely eyes." Damn it! He supposed that Lance might have that fatal something which draws women like the piping of the Pied Piper. His very shyness in the presence of certain petticoats was a lure. Sex and its vexings and its disharmonies! Paris and the fatal apple, and those three goddesses! Were women going to trouble his grandson, and were their tempestuous petticoats storm signals? Sex was both a necessity and a sacrament, but it got in a man's way. It was like a pair of retarding arms clasping his knees.

John Pybus turned to the door just as Sally came out with one of the hotel kettles. Her dark eyes had a little glimmer of mischief and defiance. She held up the kettle.

"Brought you some hot water, Mr. Pybus. I put it in your kettle for the young gentleman."

"Yes, hot water!" said the Venerable.

She sidled past him with an air of mystery and archness, but she made herself meet his blue eyes.

"Don't be cross with me, Mr. Pybus."

"Am I looking cross, my dear?"

"I did think you'd like your tea—quick."

She ran away and up the passage with one shy, backward glance at him perched there like a little old eagle. The Venerable nodded his head at her with consenting kindness, for, after all—the Sallies of the world cannot help themselves. Birds fly down to the corn.

Entering, he found Lance in the kitchen, standing by the oilstove, and holding the brown teapot ready, and undisturbed by Sally's flutterings. He met the Venerable's eyes without a flicker of self-consciousness.

"Nearly ready. That girl brought us some hot water."

"Very thoughtful of her."

"I have put in three spoonfuls of tea. Is that right?"

"Yes."

A smile passed between them. They stood side by side watching the kettle and waiting for its voice to be raised.

"We shouldn't be doing this—I suppose, grandpater?"

"Quite wrong, according to popular superstition. Shows that one's estimate of time is purely relative!"

"I say, ought I to have put some hot water in the teapot?"

"Never mind to-day."

"Sins of omission! Tell me, grandpater, was that true——?"

"What?"

"That you haven't had a holiday for years?"

"What is a holiday?"

"Then you haven't."

"I have not removed my body to some place by the seaside, or into Wales or the Lake District. But the other part of me has travelled."

The kettle was boiling, and Lance lifted it from the stove.

"Do I fill it full?"

"Yes, for two."

"Have you ever been to Cambridge, grandpater?"

"No."

Lance's face was very serious.

"I'm going up again next Tuesday. My last year. Would you come up for a few days this term, and stay with me? I can get you a room outside, and you could feed with me."

Old Pybus looked hard at him and was silent.

"I'd love you to come up, grandpater. I want you to meet two or three fellows, Sorrell and Frensham. And we should be able to talk. I shouldn't have to rush off."

Having filled the teapot, he glanced at his grandfather, who was holding the lid of it.

"Will you?"

"My son," said old Pybus—"I will."

3

When they were seated at the Venerable's oak table, John Pybus, because of the emotion that was in him, and because the spout of the teapot had somehow managed to develop an obstruction, appeared to be twitching his white eyebrows. Feeling his heart like a bag of blood and water, he looked fierce.

"I make one condition, Lance."

"Yes, grandpater."

"I pay. Do you understand me?"

"But you will be my guest."

"Not exactly—yours. God forgive both our prides."

Lance looked at his grandfather with a flushed seriousness.

"Yes, I understand. I'm sorry. Of course——"

"There's no need for you to be sorry," said old Pybus.

"The 'boots' of the Saracen's Head visits his grandson at Trinity. I take off my hat to my grandson, and I take off my hat to myself."

Lance helped himself to strawberry jam. If the moment was rich in emotion, it had other inferences and little jarrings of the memory. Was the mood of the moment ever of one texture, simple and continuous, like a red or yellow jelly? You saw people like figures in a landscape. The very "I" of yourself was a complex of seeming contradictions. The Venerable walking round the Great Court of Trinity would seem a part of the mysterious reality of things. Whereas— his father——! Lance had heard men say, "Awful bore, but the gov'nor's coming up for the week-end," though some of them were not ashamed of their fathers, and may have felt for them a tolerant affection. What was snobbery? If your father made the intimate inward self of you wince, was that snobbery? And yet how queer it was that he should be conscious of pride at the thought of walking about Cambridge with his grandfather, a little old fellow in a bowler hat. Was it affection, or a mere flush of egotism, or defiance? Was there not some deep and rather sacred bond between them——? But how ironical! The Venerable had been the despised and the rejected of his sons, and the son of one of the sons was reversing the process, not as a prig, but rather as a disciple.

But he ought to be fair to his father. Sir Probyn might be what you called a materialist, but his father's materialism had given the son Eton and the Great Court at Trinity. And what was materialism? Was there not a revolt against the social cataloguing and labelling of life's reactions? Were not the impudent young moderns a little more subtle than their fathers? They were more conscious of what really did go on inside them, and were ready to think about it and act upon it. Their seeming impudence was the aliveness of the urchin who had climbed a wall and, seeing top hats passing solemnly to and fro in a stuffy lane, felt moved to shy green apples at all that solemn headgear.

But youth has its reverences. It might desire to make a holy relic of Hobbs's bat. It respects accomplishment, and especially physical accomplishment. Lance would not have been the lad he was had he not known what it was to row himself blind in the Long Reach.

With his elbows on the table, and his eyes fixed on his grandfather's plate, he made his confession.

"The pater has been rather decent. I told him. He has offered me two years."

"An allowance?"

"Two hundred a year for two years—when I go down. I'm wondering whether I ought to take it."

"You have taken—it—for twenty years."

"I know. But this is different. I'm self-conscious."

"More tea, Lance?"

"Yes, another cup. I want you to tell me something, grandpater."

"Well?"

"Did you ever feel—an enemy—in your own father?"

"Yes, and no. We clashed—sometimes. What else can you expect? Two live personalities. Just as Probyn and Conrad clashed with me. But my father had a sense of justice. In these days you'd call him a sportsman."

"But you had a sense of justice?"

"Generations differ in their ideas of justice. What's to happen at the end of these two years?"

Lance took the cup from his grandfather's outstretched hand. He looked at the cup and not at the Venerable's face, but he seemed to be aware of the Venerable's eyes looking at him and into him. His grandfather had asked the one inevitable and pregnant question, just as Lance had realized that he might be expected to ask it.

"Yes. It's beastly. Do you ever remember a time, grandpater, when you suddenly seemed to see people—naked—people you'd lived with for years——?"

"I do. Something in you—strips them. All the conventional clothes come off."

"It's rather horrible."

He stirred his tea, and his face expressed suffering, the shrinking of youth from certain nudities.

"Caricatures—of what people had seemed to be—when you were a kid. Even your mother. You feel in a sort of bog. Horrible sense of things being squashy and insecure under your feet. You've lost faith. You seem to see people's real motives coming out of their mouths—like the puffy old labels the cartoonists used to draw—like visible breath from the mouths of those Georgian folk. All coarse and crude and vulgar. Because—one does ask to believe—in people. My God!—one does ask——"

The Venerable's white eyebrows were twitching.

"Go on asking. But perhaps one learns to choose one's people. There's a lot that's wonderfully decent in human nature. Decent. That's a modern word turned upside down. But what happens after those two years?"

Lance looked suddenly and with a kind of flashing straightness into his grandfather's face.

"He wants to see me fail. He's letting me make a fool of myself. He's quite kind about it—but I'm to be the silly prodigal back from the husks. I shall go like a sheep into the shearing-pen."

They looked at each other.

"Did that come to you?"

"Yes, how—I don't know. Like catching someone grinning in a mirror—when you were not supposed to be looking. It's damnable—to feel——"

His grandfather got up and reached for his tobacco tin.

"Prove people wrong. That's the only way. Remove that grin. It comes off like a mask—when they see you yourself—not the little manufactured self they'd like to make you. That's the only alternative—that—or slavery—soul slavery. It may be a bloody business—like the war, but it's worth it."

4

When they walked up the Saracen yard, Lance had a hand tucked under his grandfather's arm.

"I shan't see you again till Cambridge. You—will—come?"

"Oh, yes; I shall come."

"I'll write and let you know. Or perhaps you would like to fix it. The end of the month?"

Summer-time had passed, and the sun was setting.

"I shall have thirty miles with the lights on," said Lance, turning the switch. "I expect they wonder——"

"You haven't told them yet?"

"No."

Just before getting into the car he remembered something. He drew a long envelope from an inner breast-pocket.

"I want you to read some of my stuff, grandpater, will you?"

"What's that? Manuscript?"

"A short story. You may think it a bit intimate."

"I'll read it."

"I want you to tell me. No humbug. Of course—I think it rather good—but I dare say that in five years I shall think it tosh."

"No humbug."

"Not from you."

5

The Venerable had lit his lamp, and tilted the green lamp-shade so that the light shone over his left shoulder. His grandson's manuscript, neatly folded down the middle, lay on the oak table. It had been lying there untouched for quite a quarter of an hour, while Old Pybus sat very straight in his Windsor chair, and pulled hard at his pipe. Twice he had put out a hand to pick up those sheets of paper, and each time his courage had failed him.

Because if the boy wrote rubbish, or expressed himself with a conventional and uninspired facility! If he expected praise? If he were to resent criticism? Because it is human to resent criticism, and youth flares quickly, or looks sullen and hurt when challenged. No humbug! Yes, that was all very well. But in asking for sincerity from those we love, we ask for a sword and a courage that does not flinch. We ask them to

stand up and wound, and in wounding—to be wounded.
Just how candid can a friend be, and is candour a poison or a
purge?

Old Pybus's pipe became plugged, and he removed the
mouthpiece and blew down it with fierceness, but the trouble
was in the bowl, and he got up to look for a pipe-cleaner.
He wandered to the fire-place, and came back to the table.
He spread the manuscript, and holding down the folded halves
with two fingers read the title.

"The Green Mirror."

Yes, there was something arrestive and unlikely about the
title—but how did Lance manage to get his mirror green?
The Venerable's curiosity rallied his courage. He turned
over the title-page and read the first paragraph. It was made
up of short, crisp sentences. It had a vividness—though there
were crude streaks in it. It had been written by a young man
who had vision, and who saw things with so sensitive a clearness that sometimes the words had a raw poignancy.

"The still water was her mirror, and the mirror was green
because the willows dyed it with their green reflections . . . .
She was very thin, so pale and thin that she looked like an
altar candle, and the flame of it was her hair. Her lips seemed
to have bitten deep into red fruit——"

The Venerable put his pipe down on the table, gathered the
manuscript, and returned to his chair. He read quickly,
turning over the pages with a fierce deftness. Now and again
his white eyebrows twitched.

He came to the end. He sat with the manuscript on his
knees. His face expressed relief. There were little tremblings
as of an exultant smile.

"It's there. He's got it. Extravagant—of course, young,
too much colour. But it's there. I can tell him so. I
can——"

He got up and relit his pipe.

CHAPTER X

I

ONE of the Trinity porters was handling Lance's luggage. "Had a good vac., sir?"

"Very, thanks."

Lance looked neither at the man nor at his luggage. He was standing under the span of the gateway, facing the Great Court. Hundreds of times he had passed through this gateway, and the court—with its grey buildings, its brown cobbles and flagstones, its fountain and its grass—had become so familiar that his eyes had accepted it without wonder. But on this October afternoon it had a strangeness. He seemed to be looking at it with other eyes. The red geraniums in the beds round the fountain were like flowers in some mystical picture, blood-red stigmata. The day was very still. The sunlight lay softly upon the very vivid grass. The air had a crispness. And Lance Pybus felt out of his body, and floating in a beautiful autumn sadness. Life was as plaintive as some of the modern music.

He spoke to the porter who was loading luggage on to a handcart.

"Mr. Sorrell up yet?"

"Yes, sir. I think so, sir."

"Same rooms?"

"Yes."

The porter trundled the luggage away, but Lance walked slowly across the Great Court to the hall, still full of that most strange feeling of being out of himself. He did not meet any men of his year; he did not want to meet them at this particular moment. He climbed the stone steps of the hall, passed through the dark "screens," and down into the cloister court. Taking the right arcade he saw suddenly before him the open space of the gate under the library. He walked on a few steps and stood still.

Within him a voice was saying—"How is it that I never saw it like this before?"

The picture, framed in the warm stone, was both soft and brilliant, an infinite greenness of grass and trees, and scattered sunlight, and still black water flecked over by the incipient gold of autumn. Yes, everything was very still. He had come in out of the mechanical clatter of the K.P., away from the odour of progress emitted by taxis and motor-bikes, to pause in front of this live picture. It had a sadness, an exquisite glow, a dignity. It seemed to be an expression in sunlight and water and grass and trees of that which was in him, a yearning, a poignancy, an unexpressed and almost inexpressible something.

He found himself thinking "The Venerable will understand this."

Yes, he could see the Venerable's white head passing out through the gateway, and the Venerable's blue eyes taking in all that beauty, and the repose and the rightness of it. What an atmosphere! He remembered bringing his father to see the library, and his father's bland progress past the books. Almost —he had bowed to them like a superior sort of shop-walker.

"Oh, damn! What a beast one is!"

He turned quickly and retraced his steps. He made for the doorway in the Great Court where Kit Sorrell had his rooms. He saw the familiar name in white over the doorway. Sorrell's "oak" was unsported.

Lance opened the keeping-room door. He saw his friend stooping in front of a bookcase with his hands full of books. He felt something in his throat.

"Hallo!—Kit."

"Hallo! Pybie—old man."

Lance's arm went out and back.

"Mind if I shut you in?"

"Rather not——"

Lance pulled the outer door to with a crash and, strolling into his friend's room, sat down on the blue sofa in front of the fire. He took out his cigarette-case, extracted a cigarette and lit it. He felt most strangely near to tears.

2

Sorrell slipped the books one by one into their appointed places, for, like his father, he had an orderly mind. Also, he was deliberate. He did not rush at people, or ask them to rush at him, but for Lance Pybus he was ready to make allowances.

"What a hulk you're growing. They'll be putting you in one of the Trials."

"Not rowing this year."

"What rot! Nor am I."

Kit turned about to collect more books from a trunk behind the door. He looked for a moment at his friend who was looking at a photograph of the elder Sorrell.

"Mind if I finish the books?"

"No, go ahead. How's your pater?"

"Oh—all right."

"So's mine. It's not supposed to be decent to reverence your parents."

"I don't find that a trouble."

"Sentimental old idiot."

Kit crossed the room and collected more books. He was more solid than Lance, rounder in the face and head, but he was as quick in his feeling of things. And he was wondering what was the matter, for there was something the matter with Lance Pybus. His friend's voice had the casual tone of a fellow who had been afraid of blubbing, and when Lance was flippant you might know that he was on fire inside.

"A girl—I suppose," thought Kit. "He was like this—after that Christmas vac. Met a flapper at a dance."

He crossed again to the bookcase.

"Been reading anything?"

"Not much. I did come across one funny thing about our stinking generation."

"Do we stink?"

"The young man of the day, no manners, no reverence, no ideals, all petrol and jazz. We're a filthy crowd, Kittums."

"We always were. But the old fusters were glad of us in the Great Strike."

"Your pater's not a fuster."

"He's a great man."

Kit Sorrell had a smile in his eyes. He was thinking for the moment of his father, and also of Lance's father, whom he had met last May Week, and how he had not felt himself comfortable in the presence of Sir Probyn Pybus. And what a baffling creature was this "self." There were times when it shivered like a very small boy afraid of his first swimming lesson. Fellows were afraid of such different things. Pentreath was afraid of being himself; Lance was too much afraid of being anything but himself. Then there was that poisonous little fellow upstairs, Cornlees—who did nothing but talk about syphilis, because he was dreadfully afraid of it. Christopher Sorrell knew his own particular fear to be a dread of disappointing his father. But Lance took himself too seriously, and was inclined to exact too much from other shelves.

"Yes, my pater's a great man. I'm quite out of fashion, Pybie——"

"I'd like you to drop that name."

"Right-o."

"I'm in the height of fashion. If you are able to think of your father as a snob and a cad——"

Young Sorrell, squatting on his heels in front of his bookcase, looked round over his shoulder, and then became very intent upon the proper and nice grouping of his text-books. Embryology, physiology, anatomy, pharmacology, chemistry. But the self in him understood that something had happened to Lance Pybus, and that his friend was full to the lips with what old Ponsonby, their tutor, would have called "the quintessence of emotion." Lance had something to let out. He was in a stammering mood. He was both closing a fist and trying to open it.

"You take your people rather seriously. What's happened?"

"Several things. The angel of the Lord and Balaam's

ass. Supposing your pater had insisted on your going into business."

"But he didn't."

"I know—but supposing——"

Christopher rose and leant against the bookcase.

"It doesn't follow. My pater gave me my choice. Being what he is—I suppose it was bound to happen like that."

"And being what you are."

"Oh—I don't know about that. What line did your pater——?"

"Offered me two years' board and lodging, and a chance to prove myself an idiot."

"Sure?"

"Pretty well. But—damn it—I know—and I feel——"

Leaning forward and picking up Kit's poker, he prodded at the fire.

"I want to write. I can write. I've got it in me, just as you have surgery in you. You want to cut up people—I want to cut up life."

"Is it quite like that?"

Lance turned quickly on the sofa. He looked up into Christopher's fresh, brown face with the firelight playing upon it.

"What does one want? Isn't it self-expression? I don't want to be my pater's pup. I want to be myself—here and now—and to-morrow—and to the end of things. I'm not asking for a comfortable job. And I want to see and to know. What do I know? One ought to be dirty and hungry—one of the slave crowd, get your guts twisted——"

"You will," said Sorrell's son—"if you don't make money. You see—I know. My pater had to——"

"Oh, money be damned!"

"You'll be damned without it."

"Rot!"

"Unless you are a saint, my lad, or so smitten with your job. But if you begin to want things, all the things people scramble for? I want certain things, and I mean to get them if I can."

"What things?"

"Well—freedom. No boots to be licked. You see, comes a time when you want things for other people, for a girl or a kid. My pater wanted things—for me."

Lance stared at the fire.

"You're a good chap, Kit. I'm not quite so beastly selfish as I sound. I've got something else to tell you. Rather astonishing. I've discovered a grandfather, John Julian Apostasius Pybus. He is coming up to stay with me."

Sorrell came and sat on the end of the sofa.

"How do you mean, discovered him?"

"I always supposed he was dead. And so he was—so far as my people were concerned. Rather awkward for a Sir Somebody to have a little old hotel 'boots' for father."

Christopher's face grew very grave.

"I told you about my pater——"

"Yes, old chap—that's why I am telling you. Extraordinary coincidence. I found it out by chance. My people don't know—that I know. It's rather a filthy business."

The lift of his head was ironical. His nostrils were shadowed with scorn.

"Strange, isn't it? My pater and my uncle despised their father, and now it's my turn. It's difficult to tell you just how I felt. Rotten. But I have reverted. It's as though the Venerable—my grandpater—was my real father. I used to go over and see him—but he did not know to begin with who I was. He is really rather extraordinary. Makes me think of Seneca or Marcus Aurelius. You see, I'm the third generation."

He gave Kit Sorrell a sudden, upward smile.

"I've been through things—somewhat—I'm the son of an old bookseller who has evolved a beautiful philosophy out of cleaning boots. I have shed the Golden Fleece. In fact—I have shed—my father."

Sorrell's son was staring at the fire.

"Isn't that rather hard on him?"

Lance was silent. Then he said—"I haven't seen enough of life—yet—to know."

3

Lance Pybus stood in the doorway of his sitting-room. He had not seen the room for four months, and seeing it now after that intimate half-hour with Christopher Sorrell he discovered in it a garishness. Everything was too pink, and there were too many cushions.

In front of a very bright fire his bedmaker spread a breadth suggestive of innumerable petticoats, bending forward with a pair of tongs in her right hand. As Frensham would have it—"Mrs. Cardew had a Dutch exterior." A pink quilt folded over the back of a chair was receiving an airing.

"Hallo!—Mrs. Cardew."

The claws of the tongs released the lump of coal.

"That you, Mr. Pybus! Well—I'm glad to see you up again, sir."

Her breadth seemed to rise like a great black bubble. Mrs. Cardew still wore her hat with an air of jauntiness, a woman whose hair had been very black and abundant. She looked hot, and the light of the fire lingered in her jocund eyes. It had never occurred to Lance that once upon a time Mrs. Cardew had been a saucy girl and a merry one. If he considered her at all it was as a good-natured, red-faced bundle of a woman, rather too noisy and talkative, and threatening to be familiar.

"That's some fire."

"Always like my young gentlemen to feel like 'ome, sir."

Because of her motherliness her glance was not quite an ogle.

"Had a good vac., sir?"

"Not bad."

"Any more pictures of nice young ladies?"

"No—Mrs. Cardew."

"What a pity! I just 'ad the quilt out t'air. I'll unpack for you, sir, if you like."

Lance gave her a casual and absent smile.

"Yes—please. Any letters?"

"One or two, sir. I put 'em in front of 'er ladyship's photo on the mantelpiece, sir."

Lance went for his letters, consciously avoiding looking at his mother's photograph. He found the envelope that he had hoped and expected to find, a longish envelope which contained the manuscript of "The Green Mirror," posted from Castle Craven by his grandfather.

"I 'ad to buy you a new teapot, sir."

"All right, Mrs. Cardew."

"The young gentleman who 'ad your rooms when 'e was up for 'is examination——"

But Lance did not appear to hear her. He had walked off into another world. He was opening the long envelope and drawing out the manuscript and the Venerable's letter. Mrs. Cardew gathered the pink quilt to her bosom. She looked at her young gentleman—her favourite young gentleman—with a droll and chagrined tolerance. She went out with the quilt.

She thought—"'im and 'is poetry! Don't seem to see you—sometimes; don't seem to know you're there. Shut up with 'imself. Too much so—I should say. Someone will do a bit of screaming—someday. These young women can be 'ot stuff. Poor dear!"

Lance was reading his grandfather's letter, and his eyes lit up as he read it. Of course he could write. Things were so vivid in him. The Venerable understood.

4

The youngest of the "Pybi" kept a chapel. The place seemed to him dimmer, and the high roof more full of vague distances and the soaring of the boys' voices. There was a full choir. Dr. Parry's fine and venerable head made Lance think of his grandfather.

Out in the Great Court night had fallen, and the sky was full of stars. The windows of the hall were all yellow. Other young men went to and fro, and their voices were the voices of youth eager to open life's shell—"But we won't be sloppy about it, thank you." Lance lounged through the Great Gate and looked at the shops in Trinity Street. He stood in front of the window of a bookshop; he saw some of the books of the moment—novels, essays, travels—and the hunger of youth moved in him. He felt a swelling arrogance. In two years, in three years, in five years, he would have books in that window.

5

In the hall he sat with Sorrell and Frensham and Pentreath—the sensitive Pentreath. The same dons, as of old, sat at the high tables. Hanging on the dais panellings, Henry VIII, superb and brutal and human, seemed to swell and swagger in the light, looking down at all these young men.

"Come to France with me. Come and see the French women."

Afterwards they went to Sorrell's rooms, and five of them sat on his sofa, and two in each easy-chair, and they shouted their Babes Ballad. Frensham was its author:

> "We have no manners, we have no sense,
>   We hang our noses over Brookland's fence;
>   We criticize our paters' ties,
>   We think our aunts and cousins guys.
>   Vile children, sons of stink;
>   Oxford bags and ruddy ink.
> Accurséd generation!
> The decadent of the nation!
> We toil not, neither do we spin.
> We play the game and never win.
>   Say bo, say bo,
>   To old Man Jericho.
> What ho! What ho!! What ho!!!"

6

When all the clocks were striking ten, and the stars up above seemed to quiver with their chimings, Sorrell's son and

Probyn Pybus's son wandered round the Great Court arm in arm. They debated solemnly of life with that almost innocent seriousness that persuades an older man to smile very kindly and to regret the dimming of his own desires. For him the apple has lost its polish, or there is no apple left; but to Kit and Lance the apple was mysterious fruit, both sweet and bitter.

Said Christohper—"I wonder how we shall feel about this—place—ten years hence?"

"Does one ever know—how one is going to feel about things?"

"No—that's true. You get such surprises."

Christopher was thinking of his father and of his father's face when a certain old portmanteau had burst open on a railway platform and exposed—pathos.

"Seems to me—you have to be a bit selfish," said Lance—"insist on yourself."

He looked up at the stars, but young Sorrell's glance was level and at the height of another man's face. His eyes would always be more level than Lance Pybus's. The stars and the gutter! For Kit had some of his roots in the heart of another man, and Lance's roots were all his own—for the present. He was a syndicate of one.

"You'll bore people, you know," said his friend.

"Not if you insist—successfully, old solemn face."

"You ought to have won the Diamond Sculls."

"Irony!"

"A seat in a May boat isn't a bad ideal."

"What about the pairs?"

"That's a funny ship to row in. Who sets the pace?"

They laughed, but young Sorrell's laughter was deeper than his friend's. The simple people laugh more easily. You can subtilize laughter until nothing appears but a sardonic grin.

"When is your grandpater coming up?"

"The beginning of next month. I think I'm rather red—old Kit."

"Rot! You're the most utter individualist. You'll bring

your grandpater round to breakfast with me.   My pater may be up for a week-end."

"Thanks, old thing.   You might tell that dirty little swine, Cornlees, that my grandpater's an hotel 'boots.'   Ask the little brute to breakfast."

"Shut up," said Sorrell's son; "things like Cornlees don't matter."

CHAPTER XI

I

O N account of his small stature John Pybus always had
had trouble with his clothes. A ready-made suit would
be passable as to the coat—but when it came to the question of
trousers—it was indeed a question of bags and frills. As a rule
Mr. Pybus had solved the problem by buying boy's breeches
and a man's coat. In the matter of hats he leapt to the other
extreme, needing the biggest in the shop.

But on this notable occasion he visited Potter's in the High
Street and was measured. Mr. Potter made for him a black
coat and vest, and a pair of black trousers with a faint white
line in them. Mr. Potter's "fitter" was politely inquisitive.

"Is it for a wedding, sir?"

"No, for a funeral," said old Pybus.

"Sorry to hear that, sir. Just a leetle bit off the sleeve, I
think. These things will happen."

"Nothing you can do will prevent them."

"That's right, sir," said the young man very cheerfully.

"Your parents can prevent you being born, but they can't
prevent you dying."

Mr. Potter's young man began a snigger, but meeting the
Venerable's blue eyes, thought better of it.

"Yes, children are a problem, sir."

"Worse. They're a necessity."

The Venerable also purchased a new felt hat, three collars
that were not ten years out of date, and a ready-made pepper-
and-salt bow tie. He hunted out from somewhere a little
accessory that he had not used since his bookshop days, a
monocle set in tortoise-shell, with a handle like that of a
miniature lorgnette. It had been his custom to wear it
dangling on a black ribbon fastened under his coat collar, and
to use it for reading small print. He took it up to Cambridge
with him, and that piece of black ribbon gave to him a touch

of Roman distinction. The Venerable was not without finesse. A little piece of black ribbon, and something which glittered!

Creepers were reddening the walls, and the Castle ash trees scattered yellow leaves. The Venerable, listening to the gaillard singing of a robin, saw in the fall of the leaf no lowering of a flag. He was driven down to Castle Craven station in the Saracen bus. No one had objected to his taking a week's holiday.

At Cambridge station Lance met him. They shook hands. If either of them betrayed any shyness that one was the younger Pybus, who had experienced a moment of surprise—and perhaps of relief—in reacting to the atmosphere of the outer man. The Venerable was far more presentable than the majority of "fellows". But "presentable" was a base word.

"I have been lucky about rooms, grandpater."

"That's good."

"I'm afraid they are across the river, and about a quarter of a mile away from Trinity."

"There is a discretion in distance," said his grandfather; "and I like to go to bed at ten."

Lance had taken the Venerable's fibre suit-case, and they got into a taxi, and were driven up the straight and ugly road from the station. Old Pybus's blue eyes looked at everything, but he looked at them like a little old emperor, a veteran who had a right to his opinions.

"How abominably the Victorians did some things."

"Pretty poisonous, grandpater."

"Perhaps—they were staging a contrast," said his grandfather. "The man who first baked a yellow brick should have been frizzled in his own kiln."

But this drive through Cambridge was the beginning of a new intimacy, because it was associated with the ripening of their confidence in each other. Both age and youth registered swift impressions. Passing St. Catherines and Corpus Christi, the Venerable's blue eyes took to themselves a gentleness. He sat in silence, but he was thinking that it is possible for men and buildings to grow old beautifully.

He was at his ease.   With his suit-case left in the bedroom of a little house across the Cam, he walked back with Lance, pausing on the bridge in Bridge Street to look up and down the river.   He had paid for the taxi; he had insisted on paying for it.

"That's 'John's' up there, grandpater."

"Just—'John's'."

They smiled at each other.

Under the arch of the Great Gate of Trinity the Venerable was constrained to stand very still and to survey the Great Court.   He said nothing at all.   He remained thus for half a minute.   At the end of this period of silence and stillness he raised his new hat and kept it raised for a few seconds.

"That's all—that's needed—I think."

Said Lance: "Some people are so full of the superfluous. Can't forget themselves."

"Do you ever—forget—yourself?"

The Venerable's blue eyes quizzed him.

"Oh, sometimes.   But one is so—damned self-conscious. What about tea?"

2

It was borne in upon Lance that his grandfather was somehow a man of the world.   The Venerable could dominate his environment.   He was as much at his ease in the Great Court of Trinity as he was in the hall of the Saracen's Head at Castle Craven.

Crossing the court they met Lance's tutor, always in a hurry as to legs and arms, but never in a hurry as to his inward soul. Lance capped him, and Mr. Ponsonby paused.

"My grandfather, sir."

The Venerable and the Don shook hands.   Mr. Ponsonby, being a very subtle person who could talk to you all night on "conditional reflexes," or multiple personality, or scribble Gilbertian verse and sing it to you with a vamped accompaniment, could say everything that was apposite while saying nothing. He just bent to you and smiled down through beneficent spectacles. He was admirable with parents. He had a wicked way of making mothers feel that they were even more interesting than their sons. He had the fine qualities of an Aldine and of Audit Ale.

Said Mr. Ponsonby to the Venerable:

"I always apologize to visitors—for our grass."

"It is very good grass," said the Venerable.

"Sacred to solemn feet. I dare say—Pybus—will be in a position, if he chooses."

Old Pybus's eyes twinkled.

"I approve. Something—should be sacred to age!"

Mr. Ponsonby's face appeared to grow more round and beneficent.

"Do you eat breakfast, sir?"

"I do."

"I—likewise—and a very large one. To-morrow, say, at half-past eight. Pybus, is your grandfather a porridge man?"

"I think he is, sir," said Lance.

The three of them smiled upon each other, and Mr. Ponsonby passed on, arming his way along like a swimmer.

Upon Lance's stairs they met Mrs. Cardew busy with kettles, and ready to flatten as much of herself as was possible against the wall. She looked boldly into the faces of grandfather and grandson, and "Good afternooned" the Venerable, whose response was scholastic and bland. She followed them into Lance's sitting-room, where old Pybus—sitting in the middle of a pink and purple sofa, and looking like an old Stoic over whose shoulders someone was about to throw a superfluous garland—was listening to Lance's apologetics.

"My mater—you know. When I first came into college—she would furnish for me."

"I see—you—over there, my lad."

His blue eyes were turned towards Lance's oak bureau, which suggested the late activities of a burglar in search of paper money. Note-books, and odd pieces of manuscript and envelopes, and an Italian dictionary, and publishers' catalogues, and old letters made a vast untidiness.

"Yes, that's—me!"

"Very much the throes of composition."

Mrs. Cardew rolled in with a kettle. She found self-effacement difficult. Moreover, she thought Mr. Pybus's rooms "heaven," a paradise of pinkness and "artiness." Her ladyship had inspired enthusiasm by presenting Mrs. Cardew with a pair of cast silk stockings and a five-pound note.

"Shall I make your tea, sir?"

"Please."

"Ain't it a lovely room, sir? Her ladyship 'as such taste."

The Venerable produced his miniature lorgnette, and examined Mrs. Cardew through it.

"Exquisite taste—undoubtedly."

There was a silence, that male silence which patiently awaits some feminine departure, and Mrs. Cardew, knowing something of her world, cushioned herself respectfully to that silence, and left them alone.

"I wish she wouldn't clatter cans," said Lance.

"A form of self-expression, my son."

"Just when you are——"

"In the thick of self-expression. You'll never get a hawker to understand that you don't like him shouting under your window. One-half the world's a nuisance, the other half's fussy."

Lance went to pour out tea.

"I say, grandpater, it's good to have you here."

"It is good to be here."

"I want you to dine in hall with me to-night."

"I shall love to."

"Afterwards we'll talk. We'll shut ourselves in."

"And let ourselves out."

"That's it."

3

During those autumn days young men observed that singular figure wandering through the colleges with something of the air of an old man returning to gaze upon the scenes of his youth. The big hat and the big head had an unexpectedness on that boyish body. The blue eyes were so very much alive. They looked at towers and windows, and gateways and chimneys, and at the faces of men, with the same interested intentness. The Venerable had no apologetics. College porters were polite to him. Had he chosen to walk on the sacred grass it is possible that he would have escaped unchallenged.

Because—he was at one with the spirit of the place. Never having visited its courts before, he yet came to them like a scholar and a sage, young man and old in one, nor was he a mere creature of chapels and of libraries. Nothing pleased him better than to wander about the streets and watch the young faces. He felt very kindly towards all this youth, these lads with their smooth cheeks, so exquisitely old in the body of their newness. He liked to walk briskly down Jesus Lane and across the green space to the river, and watch the life of the boat-houses, and all that stir upon the water, "freshers" being tubbed, fours shooting past, eights labouring less gracefully on flashing feet down towards the gas-works.

He disapproved of the gas-works. Who has not?

Lance had lectures to attend, and sundry hours with a coach, nor was the Venerable afraid of solitude, for solitude is precious even in the midst of a new comradeship. Violets should not be vexed. The weather was fine and not too cold, and each morning he would cross Trinity bridge into the "backs," where all was drifting autumn gold. Sometimes he would stand on the bridge, and look up towards Clare or down towards St. John's. The weeping willows dropped their leaves into the water with a gentle stealth, and the water itself was very still in that windless weather. Great elms were towers of gold beyond the green spaces where the autumn leaves lay scattered.

The Venerable's favourite seat looked towards the library across the river; and when sitting there he was conscious of a gentle spaciousness, of a world's wealth transmuted into spiritual values, and of the murmuring of Tennyson's elms. What a world within a world! He liked to utter the names

"Newton," "Milton," "Thackeray." Here—time was not, and life's plaintiveness tuned to a robin's singing.

He would utter the word—"progress!" and smile.

But youth's voice was everywhere, and it was the voice of youth as it should be, undiscordant, purged of loutishness, both serious and gaillard. Everywhere the Venerable seemed to see the swift and eager and impatient face of his grandson. How impatient youth could be, how generous, and how ruthless!

4

Lance's three intimates, Sorrell, Frensham and Pentreath, accepted the Venerable and were accepted by him, but young Sorrell was the Venerable's favourite.

They took to each other from the first. They liked each other's looks and each other's voices. The Venerable's resolute, blue-eyed naturalness found its counterpart in the quiet, square-faced, wholesome determination of Sorrell's son.

His heart went out to Christopher, as it had gone out to Lance. He was attracted by the essential cleanness of the lad, his wise simplicity, that sudden smile, his air of oldness in youth. They went out and walked together. Kit found the Venerable very easy to talk to.

He talked to him about his father. The impersonal is founded upon the personal, and the struggles and the braveries of Sorrell's father, as seen by the son, were understood by old Pybus as few men would have understood them. Here was a live reaction. They were under the elms, with a light breeze bringing down leaves like amber rain. The Venerable's black bowler did not rise much higher than Christopher's shoulder.

"Seeing people hurt," said the Venerable.

Kit's eyes had a softness.

"I've seen—my father suffer. Oh, yes; kids do see things, sir. I think that some kids see them more clearly than grown-ups do. I remember. His face used to be pale, with something knotted in the middle of his forehead."

The Venerable's voice was gentle.

"You did see that?"

"Oh, yes."

"Then—you have seen—what shall we say—the great mystery—the eternal—what—Christ on the Cross? That's it."

"Suffering?"

"It's not my theory, Christopher. These mysteries aren't theories. They are as real as the blood. Mystic blood. They are as sure as the fact that if you butt your head against a wall—it will hurt you. Being hurt is one of the necessities. It's an inception. It's the first."

"And the second, sir?"

"There are just two. You begin by being hurt for yourself. The next—and sacred state is being hurt for some other person, feeling in pain because that other person is in pain. So simple—isn't it? But on that hangs all the law and the prophets, and all that we call civilization."

Young Sorrell was silent for a while. His face had an inward look, the flush of a mystical tenderness.

"What the psychologists would call sin——"

"It doesn't matter what the psychologists call it. It does not matter a damn. The thing is to experience it."

"What would you call it?"

"Reaction—is a great word in these days. I'd call it the reaction of tenderness, or say—the crystallization of emotion about a certain person—or figure. Or simply—in the older —more human sort of language—compassion. That's a live word."

"So many words seem dead, sir."

"Turning language into a sort of dissecting knife! I prefer it as a flame, my son, a tongue of fire."

On one occasion they talked of Lance and of Lance's future. It began with young Sorrell's visualizing of London as a place to live and work in and to be vexed in. For certain aspects of modern life did vex you, its ostentation, its hurry, its red lips, its many perfumes. And Christopher believed that his friend could do big things.

E

"He's got it in him. You have read some of his stuff, sir? Don't you think——?"

Old Pybus's white eyebrows seemed to come closer together under the brim of his hat. He did believe with Kit that his grandson had the big thing in him, but one or two of the big and simpler things that had become part of the mystic consciousness of Sorrell's son were still below the surface with Lance. Lance had the wildness and the fire, the generosity and the selfishness of the child. He was a child, a brilliant and lovable child. He had not become man quite as young Sorrell was man. One lad had suffered more than the other.

Said the Venerable:

"It may be better for someone if he does not find things too easy."

"Have to struggle a bit, sir?"

"That's it. The easy thing can be so fatal. Besides, he has had things made rather easy for him. It doesn't do."

Christopher looked at a yellow elm leaf that had settled on the Venerable's hat.

"I have—and I haven't. What I mean is—my pater is such a sportsman, he's so——"

"Ah," said John Pybus, "I'll tell you what has always seemed to me to be—the ideal situation. To begin with— I mean. That one person should believe in you solidly, while the rest of the world should think nothing of you at all. There's an urge for you."

Kit gave him one of his sudden smiles.

"Yes, I should think that's rather a sound idea, sir. But you have to believe in yourself."

"Assuredly. Lance does. The rub comes when you find other people hard to convince. Not even taking you for granted. Business men. Excellent fellow—the business man. He eliminates the rotter—but he is also apt to eliminate the genius. Lance has to prove that he is not going to be eliminated."

"I think he'll do it," said Christopher; "he's got a lot of character, you know."

5

The Venerable was less sure. For Probyn's plan for the production of the prodigal son had a sophisticated and commercial shrewdness.

Moreover, there was an up and downess in Lance. He was swift, but he might tire. And he was sensitive, almost absurdly sensitive. Nor is it always a question of what you make of life, but what life makes of you.

The Venerable had open eyes, though they were eyes of supreme affection.

"He will want to be understood. He will want to be flattered. He will be apt to resent criticism. He has to learn to take knocks, and to shake his head, and go on. He will be tempted. He will have days of fury, and perhaps days of disgust. He will have to learn to push people aside, or be so big that he will have no need to use his elbows. And, God forgive me—but he will have to be hurt."

On the last evening of the Venerable's holiday they went to chapel together, and afterwards there came to old Pybus a vision of life as it is. Lance wanted some tobacco. The Great Court was hung with autumn vapour, and as they passed from it out into the town new lamps were changed for old. Modernity suggested to old Pybus Bruges plastered with American electric signs. A shop window glared. The Venerable stood with his back to it, and the blare of the various windows met in the market-place and were sobered. Lance had gone in to buy four ounces of his particular mixture.

As he came out a group of young wenches went by, looking to old Pybus like so many pairs of legs and hats joined by flat strings of colour. They were full of giggles and loud talk. They appeared to flow past Lance and round him. The Venerable saw one of them look with a kind of inviting defiance into Lance's face.

"Sorry to keep you, grandpater."

A wench's voice mocked him.

"So sorry to detain you—haw—grand—fawther. So—sorry."

There were little screams of laughter.

Lance's right hand grasped the Venerable's arm. They crossed the market-place and came out on to King's Parade. Lance was looking up at the dim outline of King's Chapel.

"Distractions," he said. "Is it the vulgarity of ugliness—or the ugliness of vulgarity—that makes you scorn."

He stood still a moment, still holding his grandfather's arm.

"I suppose you have to bolt yourself down."

"But not in," said the grandfather, "not in."

CHAPTER XII

I

THE girl stood at an upper window of No. 7 Parham Crescent. The lower sash was raised, and by leaning forward she was able to see the curve of the crescent and the little white houses with their green area railings and their green, blue and brown front doors. The houses were not so white as in Victorian days, nor were the railings so green. Vaguely north-west of Baker Street, Parham Crescent was in a position to welcome artificial silk, and to feel peeved when a new stocking "laddered."

The girl was dressed for going out, though on a warm May evening all that was required for out-of-doorness was a little black hat with a black aigrette cocked over the left ear. She was a pretty thing, and much more than pretty. Someone had described her type as both hot and hard. Her smartness was relative, sufficiently sleek to catch the eye of a man, and it was all that she could afford. But she had youth, and youth's skin, and a dewiness of the eyes.

The girl was watching for a young man who presently emerged from the doorway of No. 17. He turned to the left along the curve of the crescent, and having assured herself of his direction the girl scurried out of her bed-sitting-room and down the stairs. The green front door closed on her with a crisp thud, and for a moment she stood poised on the steps, her dark and rather oblique eyes going in search of the desired one. He had passed some ten yards beyond No. 7, and was about to cross the road to gain the path that skirted the railings of Parham Gardens, where the young green of the lilacs made the trunks of the planes and acacias look more sootily black. The grass had that curious unrealness of London grass. You could fancy it taken up at night and put down again in the morning. Even the lilacs had a sophisticated air in such a place, an exotic vividness, like a London girl's face. They woke up tired in the morning, and tinted their hot lips with green stick while the young moderns were using red.

Lance walked fast. He was very much a young man with a purpose. What the girl saw of him was youthfully modern, a soft brown hat with a rather flat brim, a cigarette jutting out from a long holder, a brown jacket slightly pinched at the waist, ample grey trousers. She knew as much about him as Mrs. Gasson, her landlady, could tell her, for Parham Crescent was Mrs. Gasson's Zoo, full of monkeys and snakes and parakeets, and laughing jackasses. Mr. Pybus was what they used to call a "literary gent." It appeared that he had some money. He was an odd young man who was always scribbling and walking. On occasions a big car would stand for an hour outside No. 17. His mother visited him; at least— they supposed that it was his mother. She was a somewhat pink and yellow lady.

The girl followed Lance into the Marylebone Road, along it, down Harley Street, and along New Cavendish Street into Portland Place. She did not know where he was going. He crossed to the Queen's Hall and, dodging a taxi, she saw him enter the hall. The bills told her that Thibaud and Cortot were giving a concert. Obviously No. 17 was in search of nothing more adventurous than sweet sounds.

The girl hung about for ten minutes, and then strolled away up Portland Place. She had sat out a Queen's Hall Concert once or twice in her life, and had been interested in watching the conductor of the orchestra playing at what she had called —"swatting flies." His active and almost vicious handling of the baton had struck her as very funny. She had been sure that he had not succeeded in hitting a single fly. Meanwhile, on this warm May evening, with the London dusk beginning to dim her face, she strolled, and supposed that the Pybus boy would be safely seated for some hours. She had gone out as the butterfly; she would return as the moth.

2

To Lance music was coloured sound. It gave him pictures, moonlight on southern seas, old forests at sunset, or perhaps the face of a girl looking out from some high window. There was sex in it, and the sublimations of sex, and all the colour and the plaintiveness and the unrest of his years. Youth's music is personal. The impersonal ear listens when the urge of life loses some of its fierceness.

He came out full of the colour weavings of Thibaud's violin. He made his way through the crowd without realizing the crowd as a collection of fellow humans. He would have made his way through the hazels of a coppice wood in just the same fashion. He had all the artist's intense self-absorption. If he saw the moon he saw it as his moon.

Walking along Portland Place he may or may not have realized that a girl was walking some ten yards in front of him. He was thinking of a particular scene in a novel that he was writing, and how he had been unable to see the characters in it clearly until Thibaud's violin had given him the movement and the colour. He was wondering, also, what Richmond of Blair and Donnisthorpe's would think of his novel. Great man, Richmond! It was something to have interested John Richmond in his work. Meanwhile the figure in front of him was keeping its distance. Working upon probabilities it turned into New Cavendish Street. So did Lance Pybus.

Suddenly he was challenged. He was aware of a girl standing under a street lamp and looking up into his face. He had the impression of anger.

"What do you mean by following me?"

"I beg your pardon?"

Lance's hand went to his hat.

"It's abominable. One can't walk along a street—without—this sort of thing——"

"I wasn't. I assure you——"

"Oh, men say that."

"But I assure you——"

Her anger seemed to him very genuine. She spoke with the voice of a gentlewoman, and he could see her face clearly in the light of the street lamp. It was one of those faces which are sleekly thin, and illusively sensitive. It had a dusky pallor. Its eyes seemed darkly defiant.

"Oh, yes—I know. It's perfectly disgusting."

Something in the movement of her lips stung him to the retort.

"It's nothing of the kind. If you want to argue the question——"

"So you—were—following me."

"No—I was not."

He was aware of a sudden flickering of her very dark eyelashes. She appeared to look at him both more attentively and with a less confident resentment. Her lips opened to a quickly-drawn breath.

"I say—I'm sorry——"

She smiled faintly.

"I really am awfully sorry. I believe—I've made a mistake——"

He looked at her steadily.

"It might be rather awkward——"

"Well—make allowances. A girl does feel—— When you have been working all day—you do like—to get out and walk. He followed me—three evenings. Such beastly—cheek. And I thought——"

Her candour had an appeasing softness. Her face looked less thin, and her lips seemed to ripen. She gazed up at him with an assumption of half-amused shyness.

"He was just your height, and wore a hat like yours—I'm sorry."

She saw the beginnings of a smile.

"I suppose I ought to apologize for resembling—the cad. If he is a cad——?"

"Surely."

"Well, he might not be. It doesn't follow—does it?"

"Oh—that depends. On the way——"

"It is done."

"Well, doesn't it? Besides—when a girl has to scrap along for herself."

"And a man——?"

"Oh—a man—can——"

"But can he? He might be most damnably lonely. London is—sometimes. You can't go and ask the nearest policeman to introduce you."

She laughed. She had an attractive laugh. That rather curious mouth of hers showed the sudden whiteness of her teeth. It gave Lance an impression of softness, and also of two very red lips which protruded slightly, as in the act of biting. He was looking at her mouth without quite realizing what his looking meant.

"Well—this lamp-post seems to have introduced us. I hope you don't bear any malice?"

"None."

"I'll be going—now. Good-night——"

He looked at her inquiringly.

"Look here—oughtn't I to—see that other fellow doesn't bother you? Mere matter of form—if you like."

Her eyes puzzled him a little.

"Oh, perhaps. I think—I don't know. I live in Parham Crescent. It's not far."

"So do I," said he. "Let's be sensible."

3

Walking beside her, he was aware of her slimness, the swift and easy movement of her young body. There was something vivid about her, a sleek thinness, little—subtle swayings of the hips and the shoulders. He could imagine her dancing very well, and those slim legs of hers swift as glimmering silk. She wore black, and it suited her and the London night; so did her little hat with its dark aigrette. Her dusky eyes and her pallor and her vivid and slightly voracious mouth had all that modern provocation which provokes without satisfying. She carried her head with the chin lifted so that her face had something upward and piquant in its expression as of a face raised to be kissed, but ready to laugh at kisses.

He said: "Your home is in Parham Crescent."

She gave him an oblique glimmer of the eyes.

"If you call a bed-sitting-room a home. I work."

He wondered what sort of work she did, and did not quite like to ask her. Probably she was a secretary, or a typist, or something of that kind; but she was smart, and no common wench. Lance had come to know his London as few men know it; for London was part of his self-expression as rendered in his craft. London had captured him with all its richness and its movement, its baseness and its beauty, its blood-red mouths and its little trinket shops, its perfumes and its sophistications. As Mrs. Gasson had said—he was a young gentleman who was always scribbling or walking. He wanted life, life for his word-pictures, for those strangely ruthless and flamboyant sketches which had so startled John Richmond.

Here was a young man of three and twenty who could see and enjoy and render a handsome young Jewess in Aldgate, or some Covent Garden fruit porter with a face like the squashed fruit in the gutter. How much enthusiasm is required for a wet night spent on the Thames Embankment, or for some perfectly innocent visit to a professional's flat, where you sat on her bed and smoked cigarettes and talked of the women police? He knew his Bond Street, and he knew the Borough. He did not let a day pass without explorings. He lounged in pubs, and loitered in warehouse yards. He would talk to anybody and everybody. With perfectly clean fingers he would—so to speak—pick up rubbish out of the street, examine it carefully, and toss it back to its rightful home.

He talked to the girl as they walked up Harley Street. He talked to her as he would have talked to a man, and yet behind his almost casual frankness there was an appreciation of her as a woman. Thin girls attracted him, but only when they were dark and vivid and lissom, and full of a sparkle of restlessness. And particularly was he affected by this girl's

mouth. It was his business to estimate the significance of a
thing.

"Always lived in London?"

No, she had not.

"Southsea. Know it?"

"Never been there."

"Don't."

He smiled.

"As bad as that?"

She reacted to this frankness of his. It gave her a pleasant
little feeling of intimacy. She thought him very modern;
his frankness passed with her for that easy impertinence which
allows a girl to know just where she is and where she might
be. She thought it a pose, when it wasn't. London and his
craft had developed in Lance an almost terrible frankness. He
could be so sincere that you could be blinded by it as by a
bright light. The glare of his young and ruthless ardour was
understood perhaps by one solitary observer, an old man who
carried suit-cases up and down the stairs of a provincial hotel.

"We were service people. That's Southsea."

"Is it?"

"Which also may mean—a glorious independence. My
father left my mother five kids and a naval pension. A
Commander—you know. Pretty rotten."

"Why should it be?"

"You are not sympathetic."

"Do you want sympathy?"

"That might depend——"

"One's always giving sympathy where it's not needed, you
know. Like the old lady who saw a dirty youngster sucking
a squashed orange in Soho—and said, 'You poor little dear'
to him—'I'll buy you a clean orange.' She was off the mark,
you know."

"How?"

"The squashed orange he had found for himself was—the—
orange. More to be envied than some old fellow trying to
get ready for dinner on a gin and bitters. We always go and
pity the wrong people."

They turned into the Marylebone Road and she seemed to draw a little away from him.   He could see her profile better. Besides—the finesse of such a walk with a young man who was supposed to be a stranger—was the perfume in the little bag of her pleasure.

"Very sure of yourself, aren't you?"

"You have to be—or pretend to be."

"Part of your job, is it.   What is your job?"

"I'm what they used to call a literary man."

"Books."

"Oh—books are nothing, as mere books.   It's life I'm after—life as you see it, and try to get it down on paper. What do you do?"

She gave him an ironical look.

"Does it matter?   I help to sell frocks.   Also I give dancing lessons to the fat and fifty who want to feel gay.   O, my God—and they are gay!"

"Gayer than we are?"

"Much.   We're not gay."

"Then—what are we?"

"Greedy."

He gave a characteristic toss of the head.

"You've got it.   Greedy—for self-expression.   We young things!   What about crossing the road?"

"Right."

They crossed it in the glare of a car's headlights, and he saw her flesh-coloured legs lit up, and a knot of green silk on the front of her frock.

"My name's Pybus," he said, as they reached the kerb.

"Mine's Gadsden, Olive G.   They might have called me Gadabout.   That's a joke, please."

But he did not laugh.

She appeared inclined towards silence for the rest of their walk, for silence can be like a veil, and though a woman does not veil her face she can make play with her "atmosphere." He had talked to her sufficiently for one London night.   You could be a mannequin in your moods as well as in the showing off of a frock.   Moreover, she was confronting a peculiar coincidence, that his name should be Pybus, and that he appeared to be the very Pybus whom another Pybus had referred to as a "Damned young fool."

They came to the steps of No. 7 Parham Crescent. She held out a hand to him. The light from a street lamp was on her face.

"Good night. Thanks for your—protection."

He seemed to look at her intently for a moment. His grasp of her hand was firm, but impartial.

"Good night. I belong to No. 17."

She nodded and smiled, and he raised his hat as she ran up the steps, and brought out her latch-key.

"Good night."

"Good night."

He was walking away towards No. 17 before she had closed the door of No. 7.

4

Lance threw up the lower sash of his window. He lit a cigarette, and straddling a chair with his elbows resting on the back of it, he looked at the trees in the gardens of Parham Crescent.

He interrogated. He had come suddenly against his self and his self's orientation, against that London night and a girl's mouth, and his work and its fascinations. Thibaud's violin—too! He had felt a certain artificiality drop from him while he had listened to the Frenchman's music. But what did he mean by artificiality? A London mood? The soul of Rimmel and Lafayette, and the picture shops in St. James's, and a girl running into you suddenly, and a red mouth and a perfume, and the luxury of Bond Street, and the fat and flamboyant tulips in the Park. Yesterday he had lunched with somebody at Claridge's.

What was artifice? Assuredly London did change you. It persuaded you to accept with smoothness that which in your more exalted academic days you would have shrugged aside. What a child he had been two years ago! But what mattered was your work, the fever and the urge of it. Were any lips as hot and as alluring as the lips of your imagination?

He had accepted his father's allowance. He had had great qualms about it, but the Venerable had helped to allay those qualms. "It's a bet, my lad. Take it up—and win the wager. Even parents gamble with their children.". And now he had no qualms, but only a slight feeling of resentment, as though his father had provided him with an artificial leg which might refuse to function.

Would it? He had but three months of the two years left. Was it possible that his father would foreclose on the mortgage? Was it possible that all the blandness concealed the business man's determination to have his way?

And if so—where was he? He was earning about five pounds a month. His acceptances included two short stories, for which he had been paid three guineas apiece. Richmond had paid him eight guineas for each of his London sketches. He had managed to place a few desultory articles, but his soul abhorred hack work. There was his novel—"Rust"—half completed, an intoxication, a panache.

He sat and considered the situation. Not that he had the slightest intention of going into business—no, not the slightest. That bounder Conrad might go on calling him a damned young fool. He was far less of a fool than he had been. More sophisticated? Yes, he supposed so. He had his eyes wide open. He was not an art for art's sake young man. His art was going to get the world—that is to say, England and America. He might shock people a little. His business was to splash life down as he saw it, and as he had made John Richmond see it, through the rather merciless eyes of a young man who stood and stared. There was to be no pretty-pretty business, but he meant to get his public. Incidentally, they would throw money at him. He had come to agree with young Sorrell as to the virtues of money.

Besides, was there any money like your own money, the feel of that first cheque?

He threw the cigarette end into the roadway. The situation seemed completely clear. If his father had allowed him two years' rope with the idea of pulling hard on the rope at the end of the period, well, he would have to cut adrift. He would take a cheaper room somewhere, and just go on working.

But—somehow—he could not bring himself to believe that his father had so much phlegm.

5

Lance was unfastening his collar when he remembered the girl's face. It seemed to rise within him with a sudden personal vividness. It—was—within him. And that queer, provocative mouth of hers. It was the sort of mouth that made you feel——

And then the stud fell out of his shirt and rolled away under a chest of drawers, and he had to go down and grope for it.

CHAPTER XIII

I

THERE were times—too—when the Venerable also did some groping, for Lance was a different Lance. Once a month or so he travelled third class to Castle Craven, and was driven up in the Saracen bus, to spend a week-end with his grandfather. He stayed at the cottage, and slept in the little bedroom which looked out on the Castle Field.

Lance had changed, but people saw differently the change in him. Sally Summerscales would have said that he looked at you differently, and as though none of the points of a woman escaped him. His eyes had a hard, frank friendliness. She thought him less good-looking.

"Well, Sally, how goes it?"

"Very nicely, thank you, Mr. Pybus."

He was so easy and so casual. There was nothing personal in his smile. He talked to you as though you were a kid in short frocks. A woman understands very well when she is not looked at as she may wish to be looked at.

"London ain't done him no good."

She had the audacity to make that statement to the Venerable, who twitched his white eyebrows at her.

"I'll tell him what you say, Sally."

"So you can. Men get spoilt—these days."

"Who spoils them?"

"They spoil themselves. We—don't."

"I agree with you."

The Lance Pybus of the Windover beech woods and Trinity Great Court and the river had gone the way of Lance the child. Our inwardness changes like our clothes, and in the young man who walked down the Saracen yard the Venerable saw youth on its high horse, a figure still loved, but loved with a difference. Old Pybus was one of those rare persons who can remember themselves in the twenties, just as they

were and not as an illusive distance would have them to be.
He could remember his own cocksureness, a young arrogance
that had been both aggressive and diffident. He had known
just what books people ought to read and would read; he had
known it so much better than his father.

For Lance was in the flush of those years when the will to
power comes to a young man, when he has discovered the
power that is in him. If he was inclined towards intellectual
insolence, he had a right to it. He was as determined as young
Sorrell was to impress himself upon the world, and to do it
with a smiling ruthlessness. He had not young Sorrell's
strain of courageous humility.

All the shyness had gone from him. He was bold; but
even his boldness had a charm. You could never quite con-
vict him of being a prig, for he was too swift and subtle for so
starched an attitude. His swift face and his swift imagination
were in sympathy.

He knew what he had written. The world had come to
life in him; the world as he saw it, with all its colour and artifice, its exquisite blackguardism, its beauty, and its ravishing
ugliness. He neither scorned nor admired at this period of
life. He saw. He took. He had discovered the mystery of
words, their mordant and perhaps merciless power. To put
a harlot on paper—just as she was! To paint a city father.
To take Piccadilly Circus at night, and render it with all its
lights and shadows, its frenzies and its faces. He was in the
midst of doing it; he was in the midst of the exultation of
doing it.

To some people—no doubt—he appeared as a very impertinent and self-sure young fellow-my-lad. His Uncle
Conrad thought of him as a particularly offensive and swollen-
headed "Damned young cub!" Not that they met very
often. His father, bland and deliberate, felt more and more
uncomfortable in his son's presence, and was preparing to
rid himself of that feeling of discomfort. His mother remained completely bewildered, but without realizing her
bewilderment.

Nor did Lance realize that he was completely alone in the

world—save for that one friend and spiritual father. He was so full of himself that the world was no more than a picture-gallery. He judged and priced things as he pleased.

Meanwhile, old John Pybus observed him with eyes of trouble and affection. The boy was brilliant, almost damnably brilliant.

That was the danger.

2

Lance unfastened the lid of his leather suit-case. He had placed the suit-case on one of the Windsor chairs. His grand-father was in the kitchen attending to the kettle.

"I have brought you six more chapters to read, grand-pater."

"That's the half-way house, isn't it?"

"The end of a phase. I got rather stuck over Stilton's marriage."

"I don't like the name. What's your reason?"

"If a fellow is called Stilton—it gives you the kind of flavour you want about him in the book."

"Gorgonzola or cream?"

"Oh, Gorgonzola at its rankest."

"I seem to recognize your Stilton."

"One of the family—grandpater. Uncle Conrad, with green spots on him, and beginning to crawl."

The Venerable heard the crackling of brown paper. Lance was unfastening the parcel that contained the six chapters of "Rust"; the parcel would be tied up with a boot-lace or a woollen golf-stocking garter, anything that came handy. But John Pybus's thoughts were not so much with the book as with the author of the book. After each of Lance's visits he would ask himself, "Will he come down next month? Or will a month slip into three months? How much does an old fellow like me matter to him—and why? If he lasts with me through this second phase—he may last with me till the end." For this was the Venerable's last adventure, and per-haps the greatest adventure of his life, the vicarious sailing with this young Argonaut towards Medea and the Golden Fleece.

Old Pybus filled the teapot.

"Seen Probyn lately?"

"I was down there last week-end, grandpater. The mater had produced two choice flappers."

"A Medea?"

"Hardly."

The brown teapot was carried in, and Lance brought his grandfather's chair forward. The Venerable noticed the act and was touched by it, for whatever Lance might be to the world he was never anything but gentle to this little old man.

They sat down to bread and butter, and raspberry jam.

"Extraordinary crude ideas people have."

"Our people?"

"My mother thinks—that a pretty flapper might make me diverge."

"It's natural. You might. Jason—even——"

"Didn't he drop Medea in the Euxine, grandpater?"

"A most ungentlemanly act, my lad. Because—he had got the fleece, and Medea had helped him to get it."

"You mean—she had a claim. I suppose a woman might have. But the avoiding of Medea. Then there is my pater. I know he is watching me—just a sly old dog waiting for the rat to come out of its hole. He thinks if he spreads enough garbage——"

The Venerable's blue eyes stared.

"I don't like cheap similes. Cut them out. The trouble with cleverness——"

"Oh, I know. It's apt to be cheap. The margin between wit and cheapness is very fine. I have written stuff I thought clever, and next day—one was nauseated."

"But about your father?"

"He is quite sure that I shall want to play with dollars instead of with words. It's not his fault. It's simply that I'm an absolute stranger to him. I'm wondering what he'll do."

"At the end of the two years. You've no idea?"

"Has one ever—a safe idea? Probably he will let me go on. But in some ways——"

"You would rather he——?"

"I should. What he doesn't realize is—that I'm going on, even if I have to live on porridge and jam. He doesn't realize how inevitable the job is."

He helped himself to more jam.

"You are about the only person who does understand that, grandpater. I wonder why you do."

"Because I do."

"Is that an explanation?"

"Think it over. We are—and must be. I suppose Windover is still blind—as to my—being——?"

"Absolutely. I'd rather they remained so—until I've stuffed it into the world—that I can write."

That he could write there was no question. For a young man of twenty-three, "Rust" was an extraordinary book, vivid and fresh as a cold May morning, naïvely crude in places, but perhaps all the more vivid because of its crudities. It had the tang of unripe fruit. It was audacious and modern to its finger-tips. The Venerable, who had read novels for fifty years, and who had passed through William Black, Meredith and Hardy, Stanley Weyman and Anthony Hope, Mrs. Humphry Ward and Joseph Conrad, to Wells and Bennet, and so to the young old men of the moment, was finding "Rust" peculiarly fascinating. And not only because of the book, but because of the writer of the book, and his reactions to life. For there is no question but that age can be intensely curious as to youth's outlook, while pretending to think youth callow. How do the old problems appear to the young things? Or have they ceased to be problems? Or what are the new problems?

"Rust" had astonished John Pybus not a little. How the devil did the boy know what the writing part of him appeared to know? Did he know? And then his women! They puzzled the Venerable, did Lance's women. They were all legs and little hats joined by a thread of sexual cynicism. They seemed to do things without knowing why they did them, and yet without obvious impulse. Yet everything was arranged, your attitude towards your parents, marriage or an affair, the advent or the non-advent of babies, the apartness of the sexes, the antagonisms, the disharmonies. Nothing of life was taken for granted; everything was questioned.

When tea was over they went out and fed the pigeons. Lance's sophistications, whatever they might be, had not taken away his pleasure in the feeding of the Venerable's flock. He was "Hallo—old fellow" to any dog, and he could not resist the amber eyes and the silky ears of the spaniel who lived in a kennel in the Saracen yard. Seeing him so gentle to dogs and birds, the Venerable would wonder at his impartial ruthlessness towards the men and women in his book. Self-centred he was and had to be, for youth in its earlier adventures must travel alone. He talked more about himself and his work, more than was necessary; but he did not talk to the world as he talked to his grandfather. And John Pybus forgave him. A spiritual father should listen to his spiritual son.

"One has to bolt oneself down, grandpater. There is a sort of selfishness in a craft."

The Venerable retorted as he had retorted once before.

"Yes, that's all right. But don't bolt yourself in."

3

On that particular week-end in May, Lance stayed with his grandfather over the Monday, for he could work in his bedroom, and the mood happened to be much with him. He would get up at six and make early tea, and write for an hour, with the dew still on the grass of the Castle Field. On these occasions old Pybus would dress himself very quietly, and descend the stairs in his socked feet. His grandson's inspiration was a delicate egg, and to see that old Roman going softly about the cottage was to glimpse something humorous and beautiful.

Lance's breakfast was sent across from the hotel—and what

the hotel thought of the pair of them can be inferred—but on this particular Monday morning, Lance's breakfast was late, and going up the yard with the idea of meeting it, and of saying good morning to Floss, the spaniel, he chanced upon a very ordinary situation. A shabby little old two-seater car had been driven into the yard. The radiator was tarnished, the wings dented and rusty. One back tyre was flat, and from the dicky, cluttered up with egg baskets and boxes, a young woman was extracting a jack and a wheel-brace.

Lance stood for a moment and observed her and her activities. She wore a kind of loose holland coat, breeches, brogues, and neat fawn-coloured stockings. He could not see her face. She was jacking up the rear wheel. She looked very workmanlike, and slim, and capable. He noticed that she had a pretty back to her neck, in spite of her shingle, for it was only a half-shingle, and her crisp, dark hair covered the white curve with soft shadows.

But apparently the hub bolts were too tightly home for her to turn them with the brace. Maybe they were rusted up like the rest of the car, or some over-energetic mechanic had put his beef into them. She straightened up, gave her head a shake, and tried again, but the bolt would not be persuaded.

"May I try?"

Still stooping, she turned her head and looked up at Lance. His first impression of her face was that it was rather plain. It had a kind of austerity. The little blunt nose and square chin, and the firm, fine-lipped mouth were neither soft nor hard. She had the air of a young woman with a job on her hands, and not too easy a job, perhaps, but then—she was not made for easy things.

"Thanks. You might."

Her eyes had an apparent coldness. They were unusually fine eyes under vivid black eyebrows, and of that quality of brown that is neither soft nor sensual. She looked at Lance just as she would have looked at a garage attendant.

"Some idiot had smashed a bottle in the road. I saw it just too late. Thanks—if you would."

She made way for him and handed him the brace.

"What Kipling calls one of the 'Too Many People'."

Her face and eyes retained their aloof seriousness. A punctured tyre was just an annoying delay in the hurry of her day's affairs. She was not a talker. She had that in her life which made for silence.

Lance conquered the bolts.

"I may as well finish the job."

"Thanks—I can manage now."

She was unshipping the spare wheel. There was something in her voice and attitude which suggested that she would prefer to manage for herself, and that she was used to it, and had come to regard it as her right. She did not encourage interference.

"Sure?"

"Quite, thanks."

Lance supposed, if he troubled to suppose anything, that she was just as casual a modern as he was, and he was moving away when his grandfather came up the yard and stood beside the grey car.

"Trouble, Miss Merris?"

She smiled at John Pybus, and when she smiled her face seemed to become the face of another woman.

"Oh, yes—trouble."

She implied that trouble was the most obvious of life's accessories, and that if you had a spare wheel you were lucky.

"This sort of thing always happens."

"Just when you are busiest."

"Yes."

"I may as well be of some use."

She allowed him to be of some use, and Lance, watching them from across the yard, was a little intrigued by her change of attitude, though his interest was the casual and desultory curiosity of a young man waiting for his breakfast. She and the Venerable appeared to be very good friends. Her pleasant voice had lost its impersonal abruptness. Her gloved hands became the hands of a woman. And Lance was sufficiently interested to remember her, and to remark upon her to his grandfather, though she was no more than a figure in his picture show. He collected types, but not as his father collected postage-stamps. The watermark corresponded to a personality.

"Who's the young woman with the car?"

The Venerable told Lance that he—Lance—had to thank her for the morning egg that he ate with his bacon. There were occasions when his grandson's flippancies drew from old Pybus a puckish reply.

"Independent young person."

"Possibly. She earns a living."

"Chicken farming?"

"Yes. Rents a little place from Hargreaves over at Woolshot. She supplies us and the White Hart."

Lance was lighting a pipe.

"Not much romance in chicken farming."

"Better ask her, my dear. Possibly she doesn't ask to be romantic. She has her job. I know a little more about it than you do."

It was one of those rare occasions when Lance felt that the Venerable had snubbed him.

4

Mrs. Carver, Lance's landlady, opened the door to Lance's mother. Lance was away at Castle Craven upon one of those mysterious week-end visits, but Mrs. Carver knew nothing of Castle Craven, or of her young gentleman's adventures.

But Mrs. Carver had the eyes and the heart of a hare. She was *timidus lepus*, and having been chased by little sordid tragedies for the best part of thirty years, she had a soul that crouched and trembled. She was afraid of everything and nothing; she was afraid of things happening or of failing to happen. Her little, anxious whimpering face was rather like the face of a marmoset.

She truckled to people and to life; she would be immensely polite to a police constable and servile to the dustman. And with this golden and glorious creature on her doorstep she felt tremulous, and a little excited and proud, and ready to abase herself.

"Mr. Pybus is out of town, your ladyship."

Lance's mother sailed in. She had had previous interviews with Mrs. Carver. Almost they were a Musical Comedy couple, and their understanding of each other was as obvious as their contrasts.

"What—again?"

"Yes, your ladyship."

"I think I'll go upstairs and rest."

Mrs. Carver preceded her. She supposed that Lady Pybus had reasons for everything she did and said, and that you might allow yourself anything and everything when you travelled through life so expensively. You could ask any sort of question and expect an answer. Besides, her ladyship was a mother.

"Could I get you a cup of tea, your ladyship?"

Dolly Pybus, arriving in her son's sitting-room, sat down upon the situation.

"Yes, I will take a cup of tea. But shut the door, please, for a moment."

Mrs. Carver closed it. She expected questions, and was ready for them as woman to woman.

"Mr. Lance goes away every week-end?"

"Oh, no, your ladyship. Just now and again. He really does work very hard. I've never had a young gentleman who gave less trouble—like——"

Lady Pybus looked at Mrs. Carver, and Mrs. Carver blinked back at her consentingly.

"Nothing that you know of?"

"Nothing, your ladyship."

"Not women?"

"He's had young gentlemen here, your ladyship—but never a girl. I don't hold with girls in my house. Besides—he's such a little gentleman."

Lance's mother opened her handbag and extracted something that crackled.

"Yes, I would like a cup of your tea, and perhaps you would

send a cup out to the chauffeur. I'm sure you look after my son like a mother."

Mrs. Carver's thin fingers accepted the note. She looked almost tearful.

"I shall never forget your kindness, your ladyship. I had a son of my own once, poor lamb. Of course—if I ever thought—Mr. Lance—was in trouble—like—I'd say so. There always will be women—your ladyship. But then—as I say— Mr. Lance is such a gentleman. Never gives me any trouble. And I have had young gentlemen and old gentlemen."

Lady Pybus made a gracious movement.

"Of course. You're a woman of the world, Mrs. Carver. You'd let me know—as one mother to another. Now, I really should enjoy a cup of tea."

5

Dolly Pybus returned to Windover without having seen her son. She discovered nothing but his absence. She was not a woman who rationalized her motives, for surely a mother need not worry about motives, and she had searched her son's rooms, and gone through his drawers and his papers. Lance appeared to be of an unsuspicious nature; none of his drawers was locked, and his mother had been able to rummage among his manuscripts and letters. She had found the first twelve chapters of "Rust" put aside by themselves, but her son's work did not interest her. She had discovered another drawer half-full of old letters, and had read quite a number of them, but she had been unable to find a letter from a woman. Nor had she lighted upon any of the Venerable's letters to his grandson, for they were stowed away in a locked attaché-case on the top tier of Lance's bookshelves.

It was difficult for a woman of Dolly Pybus's mentality to deny herself the right of interference. She talked at her men, not to them. She did not so much disapprove of Lance's profession as she disapproved of his environment. She disliked Parham Place. It was seedy and shabby. The houses smirked at you. They had that back-street secretiveness which suggested pretty ladies. For—after all—there was no need for this shabbiness. It was not inevitable that Lance should go into business. It was a mere gesture of Probyn's. Of course, a man liked to get in his gesture. The whole business was rather absurd. She would prefer to see Lance with a thousand a year, and in a flat somewhere near Sloane Square, and publishing nice little volumes of verse. It was not a question of money, for money abounded, and Probyn had only to write cheques.

She took it up with her husband that evening after dinner. She followed him to the library, and sat down by his fire, for the evening was chilly, and she watched him select a cigar and light it.

"It isn't as though he was going to be any use to you in the business. Besides—there's no need."

Probyn prevaricated. His attitude towards Lance's career had changed during the last twelve months, but he was not going to tell his wife so. You should never be completely frank with women. Business was all very well, and to Probyn business had meant profits, not the service of making the goods that the multitude needed. He was the financier, not the creator; he manipulated things. And with the present attitude of organized labour and the state of trade he was thinking less and less of creation and more and more of capital. In fact he had disposed of large packets of "Jason" shares. He had money in the Argentine, in the States, and in rubber. His swivel-eye saw a good distance.

"You want him to be a young gentleman at large."

"Well, he's going off for week-ends with someone."

Probyn squinted at the end of his cigar. He had plenty of good nature, but he liked his slice out of the cake of possession.

"How do you know?"

"The woman told me."

"Ah," said her husband, "but did she say——?"

"No. But I'm not a fool. Living in a seedy place like that! What are you going to do about it?"

"About what, my dear?"

"His allowance. You know—you agreed——"

Probyn smiled at and over her.

"Haven't quite made up my mind yet. It wouldn't be a bad thing for him to try and stand on his own legs for a year."

"But how could he? His writing——! Don't be absurd."

"I—had to stand on my own legs. If you throw a pup into the river——"

"Don't be mean."

"Have I ever been mean?"

"No, to do you justice, old lad, you haven't."

Probyn went across and patted her shoulder.

"You leave it to me, Dolly. I wasn't born yesterday. I think I know how to handle the lad."

CHAPTER XIV

I

THE front door of No. 7 opened two seconds after the door of No. 17 had closed.

It was May, and sunny. The sooty lilacs in the railed garden across the way had produced a few pale flower-spikes, and the chestnut tree opposite No. 7 was set with wax candles. No. 7 was wearing a new pair of flesh-coloured silk stockings, and her hair was very much in wave.

They met. Lance's eyes were amused as he raised his hat.

"Not working to-day?"

"What about you?"

"I work when I walk."

"So do I—in a sense. But there is no walking to be done this morning. Clothes aren't walking well."

"How's that?"

"Ask the public. There are four of us at 'Mirabeau's.' Instead of sacking two of the four they have let us arrange to take alternate weeks."

"Decent of them."

"Oh, Mirabeau's not a bad old blighter. His real name is Odgers."

They stood surveying each other, two young things temporizing, and conscious of having nothing very definite to do.

"Well, what's to-day's good deed?"

"Buying a pair of shoes."

"Serious business?"

"Very. I have out half the shop."

"I'd like to see it."

"All right, why not! You'll have a long way to walk."

"Splendid! Where to?"

"Shaftesbury Avenue."

"I adore Shaftesbury Avenue."

"It's good enough—at a price."

So, on that May morning they sailed off together like a couple of birds on the wing, and turned into "Jake's" in the Avenue, and sat side by side on two chairs. It was amusing and intimate. Shoes and more shoes were unboxed by a patient little slave in spectacles. Lance could not help watching a slim foot crinkling up its toes under the crepitant silk. He was fascinated by those restless toes, veiled and yet visible. They had the feverish and provoking aliveness of their mistress. She used those very red lips of hers almost like a French woman; they seemed to curl outwards and to grow plumper and more sensuous when she talked and smiled.

"Now—what exactly do you want? That poor devil——!"

"I want what I want. It's his job, too."

She glimmered her eyes slantwise at him.

"Evening shoes?"

"Yes, really. I've got a dance on to-night."

"Then why try walking shoes?"

"Silly—don't you understand—that a woman enjoys——?"

"Like buying a pipe!"

"Something like it—perhaps. Don't you ever let yourself go over silk pyjamas?"

"I have done."

She laughed, and made a movement of the shoulders. She was thinking of this ironical position, that the nephew should be helping her to buy the shoes in which she would dance with the uncle. Yes, she had found that out. Old Conrad was quite silly about her. He had arrived suddenly at that age when an elderly fribbler becomes frightened and sentimental, and desperately eager to make sure of one woman by marrying her before the whole sex found out his fatness. Conrad Pybus had been taking dancing-lessons, and Olive Gadsden had happened to be his instructress at the "Curzon Rooms," off Bond Street.

Finally she selected a pair of shoes, honey-coloured satin, and size three, for she had smallish feet for a girl of her height. Lance did not offer to pay for the shoes; his petty cash was none too abundant, and he was a little surprised that she should be able to afford three guineas; but he supposed that by combining the professions of mannequin at "Mirabeau's," and that of dancing instructress at the Curzon Rooms, she did not do so badly. Probably she earned more money than he did. Nor had he arrived at that state of intimacy with her when a man buys a woman shoes or stockings. A lunch was allowable. He suggested it, and they went off to one of the little places in Soho where for half a crown you could run through five courses. They shared a half-bottle of Burgundy.

Her sleek pallor warmed to him. She was in teasing, mischievous mood. How shallow or deep she was he had no means of knowing, nor did it matter. What did matter was her mouth, and her rogue's eyes, and the cream of her skin, and the scent she used, and all those provoking little flicks and gestures and shruggings of the shoulders. She cultivated a frankness, the candour of a girl who worked for her living. She let him feel that she could be smart without being exactly raffish. Oh, yes, she had a goodness of her own, younger sisters who had to be helped occasionally.

Leaning forward, smoking a cigarette and stirring her coffee, she looked him straight in the eyes.

"I'd love to be able to write. Besides—if you make a boom. But then—I don't suppose——"

"My ambition is ninepence a word. I believe Arnold Bennett gets a shilling."

"Well—well——!"

"Not for the mere money, mark you, but because my stuff is worth ninepence a word."

"That's rather clever of you. You want to catch the high-brows and make the low-brows pay. After all, the high-brows are a rather useless crowd. They wear slippers and talk psychoanalysis to an audience of three."

He laughed.

"That's about it. I belong to a little high-brow club. Both sexes. None of them will ever do much."

"Freud on the brain."

"The men—aren't—so bad. But the women——"

"What's the matter with women?"

"You can't kick a woman."

She protruded her lips at him.

"Not me—at any rate. I'm tough—to a point."

"Oh, no—I shouldn't put it like that."

"No?"

"Hardly. You are half Piccadilly and half the daughter of Commander Gadsden, R.N."

"I don't think I like that. When a girl has to scrap for herself—she has to have a scrapping surface. You don't know the real me."

"May I?"

"Perhaps. The fact is—you haven't had to scrap. I shouldn't, unless you're obliged."

"You mean to say——?"

"Sir Probyn Pybus. Only and beloved son. You have only to sit down and write what you please."

He looked at her with challenging intentness.

"You think so! Let me tell you—writing—may be bloody sweat. You've got to be nailed to a tree."

She allowed herself a sudden gentleness.

"Yes, laddie—I know. You are the serious sort. I was only teasing. Scrapping doesn't make you noble. You have to learn to scrap back."

"Ought a woman to scrap?" he asked, looking at her mouth.

2

Lance was due at Windover for the week-end. His mother had arranged a house-party, two or three girls—pretty ones, of course —Mr. Adolphus Send, a young old gadabout whom she had met at Monte Carlo; young Rowbottom—one of Probyn's bright young men; a Mrs. Verity, who was asked because of her bridge; and Uncle Conrad, to complete a third couple. Probyn and his wife had been in council together. They had decided to dress the house with people, so that if he or she should find anything serious to say to their son it should have no air of premeditation.

But the inviting of Conrad was a mistake. He had a fit of bouncing youngness upon him. He would play tennis and he would dance. He could not help trying to boss a party, and to appear your witty, masterful fellow before the young things. He had grown absurdly sensitive and touchy, and was apt to sulk like a fat boy deprived of the prize plum.

Also, Pamela Fish was a mistake. She had no parents, and money, and was supposed to be clever. She was one of those very fair women with a complexion like whey, eyelids that were red in the morning, and the old scar of a scrofulous gland in her neck. She had a peevish voice, opinions upon everything, a sharpish tongue, and a cold and consuming vanity. She treated men with great casualness; yet she would go very far with a man, if he wished it, without the slightest intention of letting herself go as far as was natural.

She talked books. And Lance loathed anybody who talked books, because he was one of those who wrote them, and the person who talks pertly about the thing you do and doesn't do it—is apt to be an eternal offence to the creator. Lady Pybus thought Miss Fish bookish and smart and amusing, quite the right sort of girl to put next to Lance. They ought to understand each other.

Lance arrived for lunch. He found Conrad there in flannels, and was displeased.

"Hallo, my lad; how's the great work?"

Lance gave his uncle one of those curious, homicidal smiles, and was silent; and Conrad, being a loud fellow, was always annoyed by his nephew's silence. "Damned young fool!" But on this particular week-end Conrad treated his nephew with a jocund and pallid condescension. In fact, Conrad Pybus was in great form.

He fired genial shots at Lance across the table.

"Now—if you could write a book like 'The Green Hat,' my lad. What's the title of yours?"

Lance looked bored.

"Not made yet."

"You want something striking, you know, something that hits you in the face."

F

"And as obvious—as some faces."

At the end of the meal his mother purloined him. She wanted cushions, and there were chairs to be carried out, and she had a new racket to try. Lance could knock balls over the net to her before the others arrived.

"Lan-cie."

"Yes, mater."

"You'll find a box of new balls—in the morning-room."

Suddenly, while they were adjusting the tennis-net, she shot her arrow. Lance was turning the winch-handle.

"Another inch. Where—were you last week-end?"

He gave the handle a final turn.

"How's that?"

"Just right—I wanted to send you a wire—and you'd left no address at Parham Crescent."

Lance threw the balls on to the court.

"I went down to stay with a friend. You don't know him. Shall I knock you a few over?"

He retired to the side of the court facing the great cedar of Lebanon, and with an air of tense casualness lobbed balls at his mother.

"What time do you expect the others?"

"The cars are going to the station. Don't send them so fast, Lancie. So—it's a man! Did you meet him up at Cambridge?"

"Yes—when I was up."

"Where's he live?"

"In the country. He's keen on books. That's one of the reasons."

"Is that where you go—when you don't come here?"

Lance, with a kind of controlled fierceness, smashed a lob into the stop netting.

"Mater, do you expect me to provide you with a time-table and a map reference?"

"Don't be so touchy. After all—your father——"

"Yes——"

"He does make you—an allowance."

Lance walked up to the net to recover a couple of balls.

"Mater—you always drive me into saying beastly things. When will you stop thinking of me as a pup tied to a string?"

She flared up at him.

"Well—really! You young things! Aren't we to be allowed——"

"Here's somebody's car."

It was the Fish girl driving her own little de luxe saloon, languid and sour, and observing everything. Lady Pybus had to go across to greet her, and then the Windover cars arrived from the station with Mr. Send and Mrs. Verity and two young things in white tennis kit. Rowbottom turned up five minutes later in a two-seater. The party was in being, with Conrad rotundly feverish to get up a game at once. Lance, after collecting the balls, had strolled off into the gardens.

He found himself among the azaleas. Their strange perfume filled the air, and he lingered among them, walking up and down, suddenly and poignantly conscious of the young year's beauty, of the green of the beech woods on the hillsides, of all the secret and exultant life. Beauty! How amazing it was that his mother should live here and be what she was. And yet—in a way—how natural. You could not alter people. As the Venerable put it—the world was full of children—and of very raw children; and to most children a garden was nothing but a place to play hide-and-seek in. They tore through it; they trampled. But how he had been tempted to say to his mother: "Yes, I go to stay with my grandfather in his cottage at Castle Craven."

He heard his mother's voice calling him.

"Lan-cie—Lan-cie!"

But he was in a stubborn and non-consenting mood. He idled as far as the Bosquet and sat down on the stone seat. Windover, as Windover, was all that it had ever been to him, but he felt more and more a stranger with his people and with their people. What had possessed them to ask Conrad over for the week-end? He loathed the man. He had to hold himself in lest he should say impossible things to Conrad.

Wandering back at last, and looking through one of the squared openings in a yew hedge, he saw them at tennis. Conrad and one of the Minchin girls were playing young Rowbottom and Pamela Fish. Lance saw his uncle in profile. Conrad protruded in both directions; he ran about with a kind of clumsy fierceness; he had no idea of the game; he was full of patter. Conrad's paunch should have been supported by a broad red sash; he should have worn rings in his ears, and had his black hair oiled.

Later, Lance had to play against his uncle. He partnered his mother against his uncle and the younger Minchin girl. It was a futile game, for Conrad would come up to the net and smite wildly at any ball within reach, and usually he missed it. He was fat and fierce and talkative and complacent.

Lance found himself driving and smashing balls at his uncle. That belted protuberance seemed to offer a target. And then—suddenly—the crude, human malice went out of him. He felt a kind of hatred of himself for loathing the other man as he did. It was just a ridiculous game played by ridiculous people.

His mother, very hot and active, ran about and shouted.

"Yours—Lan-cie. Buck up—you lazy thing!"

3

After dinner they danced in the hall. A young Prue had arrived from the local parsonage, and Conrad took possession of her and tried to teach her Charleston. Lance was running the gramophone, and watching his uncle's fat legs wobbling. Conrad danced like a jelly. Lady Pybus, too, was trying to Charleston with young Rowbottom.

It was absurd and it was damnable. Also it was damnable that he should see it as he did, and feel himself humiliated—because his own seeing of it was vulgar. How could you see or render such things without being vulgar? Where was the subtlety?

Pamela Fish had come to sit on the oak settle beside the

gramophone cabinet—and she was watching Lance's face. They had got on very well together during dinner. Her rather acid cleverness had appealed to Lance. He would have liked her to have spilled some of her accumulated cleverness over his uncle.

Observing the ditherings of Conrad's fat legs, and observed in turn by Miss Fish, he turned suddenly and met her eyes and the unpleasant wiseness of them.

"Don't you dance this?"

"Sometimes."

Her cold glance fastened upon Conrad Pybus, and then passed to Lance's mother.

"When a man looks wrong—he is wrong."

"Always?"

"Infallibly. Whereas—when a woman looks wrong—it may only be the fashion."

"I'll remember that," said Lance, "unless you want to copyright it."

"You can use it—with pleasure."

4

Probyn had never been so near to winning his son's confidence as when they found themselves on the terrace on that Sunday morning, after Conrad had driven them from the breakfast-table. The Fish woman, dangling a hook, had caught Conrad at the first cast.

"I'm not a narrow-minded man—but I am an old-fashioned man. It's the woman's business——"

His voice still oiled its way out of the breakfast-room window, Poo-Baaing Miss Fish, who gave the line a tweak whenever his flounderings showed signs of flagging. Probyn was lighting a cigar.

"I'm going to look at the new plantation. Care to come?"

"Yes—I'd like to."

"It won't take us half an hour—Conrad talks too much. Always did."

They went through the gardens and across the park and past the big fish-pond where yellow water-flags were in bloom. Probyn had had red, rose and yellow lilies planted in the pool, and he stopped to look for the growth of the young leaves which should be spearing up to spread and float in the still water.

"Ought to be rather good when they are all in full bloom."

The son gave the father's figure one of those quick and considering glances which betray a reaching out towards some unexpected impression. Was it possible that he did not know the real Probyn, and that his father was as much a stranger to him as he was to his father? They walked on up the slope to the beech woods, and under all that young greenness lay the sheeted blueness of wild hyacinths, touched here and there with fingers of light. The elder Pybus paused, his cigar forgotten for the moment.

"By Jove!" he said—"by Jove! Fine that, isn't it?"

And Lance was moved. He felt more near to his father as to a man walking out on a May morning with all the green of the young year dewy and fresh and innocent. If the father could feel this innocence, and the beauty of all that sheeted blueness, had they not something in common?

"For what more could one ask?"

"Just so," said his father; "what more!"

They followed a little winding path ascending through the beech wood, and the greenish light under the trees made the blueness of the flowers more mystical. The air was scented and very still. There was a silence between them as of mutual questionings, and had the elder Pybus renewed himself in that silence—and forgotten the ulterior purpose behind the morning's ramble, he would have come very near to knowing the man who was his son.

"How are you getting on, Lance?"

"Not so badly."

"What are you making? Are you making anything?"

There was a kind of closing up of Lance's face. It was as though all those blue flowers withered, and the unseen presences withdrew.

"Yes—I am getting stuff placed. Richmond of 'Blair's' is interested. They're big people."

Probyn had resumed his cigar.

"Good. I've been thinking. These two years. Nearly up—what about——?"

"I'm going on, pater."

"I see. Nothing like responsibility, your own legs. Supposing you try a year—on your own?"

"That's my plan."

He glanced quickly at his father, who was looking straight ahead and smiling faintly to himself.

"Of course—you've got me to come to, my lad."

"You have given me these two years."

"Oh—that's all right. If you find—that you can't do——"

"I shall manage."

The illusion of that nearness had gone. His father's voice—tuned to authority through all the years—had that fatal tinge of patronage. Its inflections condescended to youth. It talked down, even in its attempted and shrewd kindness; it betrayed that something behind the man. And Lance's head was up. He was seeing the sky through the young green of the foliage, his father's foliage. He was wondering whether there was not something inherent in the reaction of most parents upon most children which rendered real intimacy between them impossible. It was one of those fatal and pathetic disillusionments, shared by both fathers and sons, mothers and daughters; the illusion of a beautiful friendship that is rarely realized, because one assumes the possession—and the other refuses to be possessed.

Yet Probyn was blind. He thought that he held a kindly, world-wise noose dangling over his son's dead.

"Well—try a year on your own, old lad. You can always come to me."

And the son—in silence—was saying——

"I shall never come to you."

CHAPTER XV

I

WITHIN three miles of Castle Craven there were other beech woods, and other blackbirds that sang in the Spring of the year, but to Mary Merris the voice of her brother was the voice of every day.

"Mary—I'm bored."

He could put such varying expression into those few words. Sometimes the cry would be whimsical, sometimes peevish, sometimes the whimpering of a little boy, and always she would answer it with patience, and mostly with compassion, though she was not patient by nature, and when one is over-tired compassion may falter.

On that May morning she saw him coming up out of the green glooms to the rail fence that ran east and west under the beech trees. The path was safe and he knew every foot of it, but he did not know that she was up above there looking down at him. He paused by the stile, testing it with his foot as he tested everything, and, throwing a leg over the upper rail, he felt in his pocket for his pipe.

The silence was supreme. It associated itself with pale greenish light under the trees so typical of beeches in young leaf, and with last year's leaves following the slope of the little valley and making the floor of the wood all bronze. The sky was effaced. Not a patch of blue was to be seen.

She stood watching her brother. He had not gone on with the filling of his pipe; he smoked too much, and tobacco at a shilling an ounce added to her problems. He sat there perched on the fence, and looking as much a part of the wood as a man could, and had he been stripped of his clothes he would have resembled nothing so much as a lean brown faun. Always he had an air of listening intently, and a habit of turning his head from side to side. He turned his face towards her at this moment, and she felt the strangeness of being looked at and not seen. His sightless eyes had that effect upon her, and never had she grown quite hardened to their emptiness.

For to Mary Merris he was like a child, and perhaps the saddest thing in all the world—a blind child. He had been blind now for five years, and she had taken his blindness to her, not because she had wanted to, but because human necessity and that something which was in her had made her feel responsible. She had had to give things up, her beloved craft, her paints and brushes, though in the beginning she had proposed to find time for it; but somehow her brother's blindness had become like a hungry and insatiable mouth. Mary this—and Mary that! The strangest thing in her life was her compassion for him. He might wound her, but there was that in her which accepted wounds, and made a business of them. It was just—life. You might have chosen it otherwise but when it happened as it did you took it as it was—yes, in spite of the impulse to run away or the urge towards self-pity. She worked. She rented the little place called "Marions" below Woolshot Wood, with its garden and orchard, and seven acres of meadow. She had a girl in for three hours a day; she could not afford more. Gilbert had thirty pounds a year—she—a hundred and fifty. She was making another seventy pounds a year with her poultry, her eggs and her honey. She had not touched her brushes for a year.

Yes, that was the strangest part of the business; she had lost her craft, but he still had his—his piano. But he was so incalculable, so moody, so easily and pathetically bored. Always he had been one of those people who light candles and blow them out. Even before that motor smash and the flying glass in his eyes he had been a wayward creature, blowing hot and cold, lacking her courage and consistency. She had doubted then whether he would make much of his music; and now it was no more than a melancholy or complaining stream running through the world of his darkness.

She had only to rustle her feet in last year's leaves and he was on the alert. His hearing had become extraordinarily acute.

"Who's that?"

Her footsteps answered for her.

"Mary."

His sightless smile was a mere movement of the facial muscles, most horribly like a grin. He seemed to prick his ears. Listening gave to his face an attentive sharpness when he was interested; but there would be days when he was interested in nothing, and his face would be flaccid and listless.

"I say—Mary—my pouch is empty. Did you get that tobacco?"

"I haven't been in this morning."

He looked peeved.

"Oh, it doesn't matter."

"You said you had enough to last."

"I thought I had—If Hargreaves drops in he'll have a pouch full. I don't mind cadging from Hargreaves."

His sister's face was like the rest of the world, a mere blackness to him. She was to Gilbert a voice, a presence felt and divined, a woman cloaked and veiled.

"I shouldn't cadge from Hargreaves."

Her voice was controlled. She had learnt to control it, for he had grown very clever in picking out its inflections, and reacting to its sound-shadings. He was so easily ruffled. She had to think of her voice as a wind playing upon water. Her face could express what it pleased.

"Why on earth not? We pay him sixty pounds a year. Besides——"

She was silent.

"He likes my music. If he sits there for an hour—it should be worth the fill of a pipe. You're peeved with me."

Her voice had a deadness.

"I'm not. I may be able to get in to the village this afternoon. It's nearly lunch-time."

He came down from the fence and was groping for her hand.

"Yes, lunch. Take me home, Donna; I'm hungry."

It was his pet name for her, and he used it when he played the child and snuggled up to her and wheedled her just as a child wheedles a mother. He had always been a little fellow, and it was difficult to say "no" to him, and now he had so little; and, if she feared anything for his sake, she feared those moods of apathy or bored restlessness when he would play the piano like a man in a rage, or refuse to touch it. She felt responsible. Yet why did she feel responsible? And in feeling the pressure of his fingers as they went up the path under the beeches, she knew that her sense of responsibility was like her response to his groping fingers. But she did wish that he would not cadge from Bob Hargreaves. She had her reasons, and they were very good reasons. To-day there are no blackguards, but only gentlemen who are a little irresponsible. It does not matter what you are if you have plenty of money and throw it about, and smile largely at people. Goodwill is on sale for sixpence; but there are some men who believe in barter.

She had to guide her brother through the kissing-gate in the Woolshot fence. He pretended that he could not manage it for himself, but that was part of his childishness; he played games with her. Often she had seen him go tapping along the fence with his stick until he found the gate.

"Do come along. There's a cheese omelette for lunch."

"Poor Gilbert's a greedy boy."

In playful and cajoling moments he would speak of himself as "Poor Gilbert; poor little Gilbert," and yet in spite of his blind egoism he could be so very lovable. After some fractious mood he would put up his face like a child. "Kiss me, Mary. Gilbert's been a bad boy."

Her land lay on the edge of Woolshot Wood. A lane sloped up to "Marions" from the Castle Craven high-road, and beyond the high-road ran the river. "Marions" itself was all that the artist in her might have asked for, a little stone house thatched and well creepered, with two old yews to guard it, and a garden that could be left half wild. Between Woolshot Wood and her orchard the grassland was cut up with wire netting, and dotted with brown chicken-houses. There were Silver Sussex and White Leghorns and Minorcas. And how —at times—she loathed these birds! More than once at feeding time she had to hold herself in lest she should hurl basin and food at those feathered fools! Was there anything

on earth more exasperatingly foolish than a hen! She—
a fastidious woman—when a boy was not available—had to
clean out the houses. But—then—what did it matter? Life
usually had the laugh of you.

2

Mr. Hargreaves had two dogs with him, a black spaniel and
an Airedale, and Castle Craven would not have known him
without a dog at his heels.

"Good morning, Mabel. Well, John; how are the
pigeons?"

He called people by their Christian names after the old
English fashion, though his privilege extended back no
farther than two generations. In his presence Castle Craven
addressed him as Mr. Hargreaves, and in his absence he was
known as Hargreaves, or Bob Hargreaves, or briefly as Bob.
When half a county knows a man as Bob he wears the boots
of an English worthy.

"I'll have something, John. Mac, come here—you blackguard."

"What can I get you, sir?"

"What I always have. Miss Vallence, how many gin and
bitters have I had since you've been in that glass box?"

Miss Vallence simpered at him.

"That would be telling, Mr. Hargreaves."

"By Jove! it would."

Bending down he pulled the spaniel's ears. Dogs were
devoted to him, though he was ready with stick and voice,
and the women who had pleased him—and there had been
many of them—had behaved like dogs. He had a ruddiness,
a round and yellow head, blue eyes that stared, broad nostrils.
His breadth of nostril suggested that life to him was full of
interesting appetites and odours. The Venerable, who liked
him not at all, could picture Robert Hargreaves as a tawny
savage smelling a bone before putting it between his big teeth.

The Venerable was never anything but the debonair angel

of the Lord with this big, buxom, overbearing, genial man of forty.

"Will you take it in the lounge, sir?"

"Yes—John, in the lounge."

He walked into the lounge with the two dogs following him, and they remained standing, watching him until their lord sat down. Then they lay at his feet. He had a way of staring at strangers, and his stare could be very disconcerting.

"Put it there, John."

"Yes, sir."

"Local paper about anywhere?"

"I'll get you a copy, sir."

As a philosopher the Venerable had often contemplated the popularity of Mr. Hargreaves of Woolshot Hall. He typified something. He was—perhaps—to certain Englishmen—what the wild English in them acclaimed and envied, and longed to imitate. He did what he pleased. He was full of a sort of large good-nature, always provided that he was not thwarted. He rode well, shot well, and could make a speech that—with a thick mixture of crude humour and sentimentality—captured the working-class mind. He was a man of property, a Justice of the Peace, a generous subscriber to all the local clubs and charities. His public gestures were free and lavish. He had done many kind things on his own estate. Though he was not quite a Sir Roger de Coverley, he had a sufficiency of those qualities which impress a gamekeeper and farmer-tenants and grooms and chauffeurs. He did what he pleased, and as much of it as the world would allow him, and the world allowed him a good deal. Probably he was the unregenerate man's ideal of what a gentleman should be; large and comely and debonair; easily familiar, yet keeping his height, full of strong language and strong appetites; casual with money, and still more casual in his adventures; the sort of man who never asked for his change, and could use his fists. Mr. Bob had been a bit of a lad, and he was still very much of a lad, a gay bachelor. The morals of Woolshot Hall did not matter, save, perhaps, to one or two men who had been made to look cruelly foolish.

When the Venerable took Mr. Hargreaves his local paper, Mr. Hargreaves gave him a shilling.

"Something for bird-seed, John."

"Thank you, sir."

The shilling did not go into the Venerable's pocket. He dropped it into a collecting-box for the Castle Craven cottage hospital which stood beside the office window. He resumed his place with his back to the brass gong. It occurred to him to wonder how Lance would render Bob Hargreaves in a book. He would not be easy to render. Besides, the behaviour of the essential animal in man is apt to be boring, and if the description is too vivid it has the crudeness of caricature.

"A man with protruding blue eyes and broad nostrils and much money," thought the Venerable; "perhaps one might as well leave it at that."

3

Lance Pybus walked along Park Lane. He had been dining at the Ermyn Club, and it had been one of the club's literary evenings, and in the smoking-room he had been made known to an amazing little woman—one Lola Kentish—who, with the face and clothes of a country schoolmistress, had sat drinking cups of black coffee while talking to him upon literary methods. He had got himself becalmed in one of those stagnant phases when a book refuses to move, and loses its sense of sincerity. He had torn up one whole chapter. He had gone to dine at the club, feeling baffled and impatient, and by good luck had found Miss Kentish seated next to him. As a novelist she had arrived, while he was unknown.

Extraordinary little woman, looking mild as milk, yet exuding the most flamboyant language! But she knew. He had found himself listening to her, arguing a little at first, but in the end he had surrendered to her rather flat and undistinguished voice.

He had said to her—"Do you ever find a character running away with you—and getting you into a sort of cheap back street; and do what you please you can't escape from it?"

Of course she had had that experience.

"Nothing is cheap. It's all behaviour. If you treat it as behaviour—it comes out as what it is."

Her words retained for him all their vividness as he walked slowly along beside the railings. Somehow—she had put him right, and he saw his formless and cheap chapter reconstructed and simplified. She had said: "What matters is what people do, not what they look like or what they say. You may describe a man through a whole page, whereas you would have got the inwardness of him in a flash if you recorded what he did and looked like when he cut himself while shaving. Keep your people doing things, see them doing things. That's the only way to keep cheapness out of your work, for behaviour is never cheap if you treat it as behaviour. If a man blows his nose without a handkerchief—he just blows it without a handkerchief. Start to meddle with the act on moral or æsthetic lines and you are on the edge of the cheap and the vulgar. An incident—simply described—can be far more subtle than pages of psycho-analysis. Cut it out. Stick to behaviour."

He paused and stood with his back to the railings. He looked at the windows of the Park Lane houses; he saw red buses and taxis going by. The London night was a dim mirror into which he gazed and saw happenings and the simple significance of things as they happen. Nothing was adjectival. You just did what you had to do. You wrote about the things that people did—because there was a kind of inevitableness in their doing of them.

He strolled on to the Marble Arch and stood on the pavement and watched the traffic and the lights, and the figures which were alternately dim and bright like moths flying through a garden lit by fairy-lights. He felt tranquillized, reassured. After all—the whole business of life was movement —or behaviour—as Lola Kentish had said it was. But then— if your book—and your own intimate self were just behaviour, what became of the Venerable's mysticism? Was life an affair of miracles or of muscles?

4

But behaviourism as expressed in a book and behaviourism as it is expressed in intimate personal happenings are very different propositions, and Lance Pybus in Portman Square on a May evening was very much the young theorist. The lights of the square spread a soft canopy supported by the dim tops of the trees. There were the lights of the houses and the faint silver of the stars. And it occurred to him to wonder how beauty arrived, that impersonal beauty which does not seem to depend on muscle and nerve cells and glandular secretions.

Yes, life and your consciousness were problems, but in Parham Crescent he returned to realities. A taxi had left a girl at the other end of the crescent, and half-way between No. 7 and No. 17 these two young things met.

"Olive——!"

"Hallo, laddie."

They stood facing each other under a lamp, very close together, and mutually glad of their nearness.

"Where have you been?"

"Oh, my dear, where haven't I been? On duty at a dance, being gay with a gay old thing of fifty. I had to go. He's a posh patron of ours. And my poor feet!"

Her face looked very live and sensitive to him in the lamp-light, with its big bright eyes and mobile mouth.

"Bad luck! Did he tread——?"

"Oh—those new shoes of mine we bought. One ought to have steel shoes when one dances with an elephant. I'm sure the skin's off one toe."

"Poor Olive."

"Not a bit of it. I told him off, my dear. And where have you been?"

"At a literary dinner."

"High-brow?"

"Oh, very."

"Poor Laddie."

Her little quick movements and the dim flashings of her face seemed part of the May night. He wanted to touch her clothes. She was all soft and perfumed, and exquisite reality, and he felt towards her a sudden tremulous tenderness. How alone they were together !

"Had any supper?"

"Oh—yes. I did expect that—and I got it. But one does get—rather bored."

"Just bored——?"

She looked up at him, and then away.

"A little more than that. Life's tantalizing. Giving your youth to old idiots. Part of my job—I know. One has to live."

"Yes, it's beastly."

"Oh, not quite that; rather humiliating sometimes. Laddie, who tied your tie for you?"

"I did."

"It's all crooked."

She put up her hands, and with her head slightly on one side, gave his tie little tugs and touches.

"There. You want—somebody——"

He was looking at her mouth, and her hands still seemed to linger under his chin. And suddenly—in the emptiness of the crescent—he had his arms round her. Her mouth seemed to lift to his, and he was kissing it, that eager, warm, voracious mouth.

CHAPTER XVI

I

AT breakfast Lance opened and read a letter from his father. Sir Probyn's letters were rather like himself, buttoned up in a conventional and stilted good-nature, and reminiscent of a commercial phrase-book. It was as though Probyn sat down self-consciously at his desk, shot his cuffs, and with a clearing of the throat announced to himself that he was about to produce "Letters from a Merchant to his Son." Probyn's kindness had not quite been able to get into country tweeds. It had remained frock-coated, civic, authoritative.

"My DEAR LANCE,

"In continuance of our talk, I should like to say that I have decided to let your allowance run to the end of September. I hope you will not accuse me of any lack of generosity. I think we agreed that a young man should try to stand on his own feet, and if I remember rightly you said that you would prefer to have things thus.

"I appreciate your desire for independence. Need I say that you can appeal to me at any time. Your mother and I are solicitous for your success."

Lance put the letter away in a drawer in which there were scores of other letters. He rang for Mrs. Carver to come and clear away his breakfast, for it was his habit to write from nine till eleven. Being young, noise did not distract or irritate him as probably it would do when he was forty, and while Mrs. Carver was collecting the breakfast things on a tray, he stood at the open window and took stock of the situation. So the paternal siege would begin on the first of October. But just how serious was his father? And did his father's seriousness matter? for it was his own seriousness that mattered. Possibly he might have to move into cheaper rooms. Anyway he would push on with the novel. He would go and see Richmond and ask for suggestions from that most irritable, kind, and understanding of men. It was probable that some pot-boiling would be necessary, but if the Blair and Donnisthorpe magazines would take from him two short stories a month he would be in a position to hang on until "Rust" was published. He had no doubt that "Rust" would be published and that it would be a success. He was sanguine even to the point of arrogance.

So—to the book! Mrs. Carver had sidled out backwards, carrying the tray, and giving him one of those anxious and propitiatory glances that she gave to all her lodgers. Lance filled a pipe, and lit it and pushed his table into the window. He made a practice of reading through the work of the previous day, so as to reinsert himself into the atmosphere of yesterday's inspiration; but this morning there was no inspiration. He sat and fidgeted, and let his pipe go out, and scribbled fragments of sentences upon an odd sheet of notepaper.

Nothing would come. The mirror of his imagination remained clouded, for there was a restlessness working in him, a distracting curiosity. He had said to himself that he would not look across the curve of the crescent towards the door of No. 7, nor to that upper window, and yet—in a little while he found himself looking. Her window was open, and the opening appeared to him as a narrow oblong of darkness in the pale brickwork. He found himself watching it.

But he had work to do. He relit his pipe, and prepared to bolt himself down in front of the white foolscap that waited for the functioning of his pen, but the white sheet became a face. Yes, her lips would be just there. And how did a woman look when she was kissed? He had heard that she closed her eyes, a sign of shy or of sacred surrender. He had not noticed Olive Gadsden's eyes. He had been too absorbed in feeling the warm texture of her eager lips. She had come to the surface after that emotional submergence with a catching of the breath—and a little gloating laugh.

"Oh, my dear, you've made me feel all funny."

Funny indeed! He had gone to his door, trembling. Even his latch-key had been tremulous.

He looked up and across at her window.   Had she gone out yet?   Would he have to wait a whole day before seeing her again?

Something showed at her window.   It was the crown of a little rose-coloured hat.   She was looking down into the crescent; he could see a part of her profile.   A moment later she was looking towards his window.   Could she see him sitting there?   He wanted to be seen.   He pulled out a handkerchief and fluttered it.

Mrs. Carver, having allowed something to crash from the "first floors'" breakfast-tray, heard Mr. Pybus's door open, and Mr. Pybus coming down the stairs.   He appeared to be in a hurry, and to Mrs. Carver haste suggested anger.   She had disturbed that blessed work of his, and he was coming down to tell her that he would go elsewhere where women did not drop jam-pots.   But Mr. Pybus had his hat on.   Mrs. Carver stood shrinkingly at the foot of the stairs, blinking her hare's eyes at him.

"Oh, I'm afraid I've disturbed you, sir."

He gave a passing and casual glance as he went towards the street door.

"No.   I'm not working to-day."

In Parham Crescent he took up the pursuit.   He saw her rose-coloured hat and her black frock and those slim, febrile, flesh-coloured legs ahead of him.   She was walking fast, as though she had not expected him to follow her, and when he overtook her at the end of the crescent she turned her head as though startled.

"Laddie—you ought to be working."

His face had a white swiftness.

"I'm walking with you to Chalfont Street."

"Do you think you ought to?"

"I'm going to."

She gave him a little subtle and almost soundless laugh, and an oblique glance.

"Cave man!   Well—perhaps.   You look tired, my dear. Sat up writing, I suppose?"

"No, not exactly."

"I heard two o'clock strike."

She hid her eyes from him for a moment under that sensuous little hat.

"You ought not to have done—that, you know."

He said, looking at her steadily :

"I couldn't help it.   You can be angry with me if you like —but I simply couldn't help it."

At the Marylebone Road crossing he held her arm, and she did not resist him.   She had a wise, sleek look.   They made a dash like a couple of children in front of a red bus, and on the farther pavement she betrayed a laughing breathlessness.

"Quick work !   And to think that I shall have to loaf all day, or mince about showing off frocks.   Like this—my dear. Imagine yourself 'Moddom'."

She walked ahead of him for a few paces, giving him an exhibition of the mannequin's walk with its little, gliding swiggerswag of the hips, and its exotic gestures of the hands. But he caught her up.

"You can stop that, Olive."

"Don't you approve ?"

"I say—are you going to be shut up all day ?"

"Till half-past five."

"And to-night ?   Dancing ?"

"No, not to-night."

"Let's go somewhere.   I'll wait for you."

"Perhaps."

"You simply—must."

"Indeed !"

"Please——"

She looked straight ahead down Baker Street.

"Very well.   We'll be good and just sit in Regent's Park and listen to the seals in the Zoo.   I shall be outside the Baker Street tube at six."

"That's great of you."

"Don't keep me waiting.   I don't wait."

"Do you think I shall ?"

But at the corner of Chalfont Street she told him to turn back.   She was very determined about it.

"I don't allow men to hang about my place of business, laddie.   It isn't done.   So—remember."

He stood looking at her with a kind of smiling yet serious ardour.

"All right.   I think I approve."

2

When he had left her he did not know what to do with himself.   In fact there seemed to be nothing worth doing until he saw her again.   Life marked time, and he—alone in these hurrying streets—wondered at the haste of these people on a day in May when the sun was shining.   He kept his promise to her about Chalfont Street, and finding himself in Regent Street, he idled down it, looking in the shop windows.   He found himself suddenly absorbed in the fascination of feminine things, dresses, coats, precious stones, perfumes, shoes, all those exquisite and provoking veilings of the flesh.   In one window he saw a particular dress of black and jade-green which seemed to associate itself with the body of the girl whom he had left twenty minutes ago.   He would like to see Olive in that dress.   But how?   He—an unknown young scribbler, who was to be marooned by a shrewd and Roman father !

He was spurred.

He quickened his pace.   It occurred to him that he had good cause to go and see John Richmond, and to put his case into Richmond's hands.   Richmond would help him.   The May sunshine had a new urgency; the scattered gold, the goblin gold for which a young man's hands might begin to grope.

He found himself in the yard of Blair and Donnisthorpe's historic "House."   Vans were delivering paper, or removing packages of books and periodicals.   A porter, with the face of a sot, blundered into Lance on the narrow sidewalk, and glared at him with bleary hostility.

"'Ere—mind yerself !"

Lance made a movement as of dusting his sleeve.   Demos, handling its parcels and packages, received more money for its brainless job than did many of the authors. The commission-aire in charge of the door had known discipline and gentle-men. Lance's card was handed to a flapper.

"Will you take a chair in the waiting-room, sir."

Lance sat down in the little tank of a room. He glanced at the magazines on the table with the names of popular authors announced upon their bright covers. The "House" of Blair and Donnisthorpe had a vastness. He could hear the pulsing of machines, while he felt rather like a stockfish in a tank waiting for someone to fish him out of his obscurity. But what did it matter? At six o'clock he was meeting Olive Gadsden.

The flapper returned.

"Mr. Richmond'll see you. Come upstairs."

No "sir" or "please," but were not such frills superfluous? He was led up stone stairs and along corridors into which people popped through glazed doors. The flapper, with an air of stodgy boredom, passed him in to Richmond's secretary.

Lance smiled at her.

"Good morning, Miss Vincent."

His smile was returned, and it was the smile of a woman who worked. Miss Vincent was big and fair and deliberate, with a face that was wide open to you, and eyes that were not to be beguiled. Richmond always said of her that she was the best secretary in London, and the only being who knew when he was angry and when he was pretending.

"Mr. Richmond's engaged for a minute. Please come in and wait."

"It's good of him to see me. I won't keep him five minutes."

Miss Vincent, returning to her desk and her labours, gave him a kind of mother's look, much the look she would some-times lay upon the crown of Richmond's big head.

"You won't mind if I go on working?"

"I should feel wrong here if you didn't."

At the end of two minutes Richmond's bell rang, and Lance was allowed into the great man's inner room. For John Richmond was a great man. You would find him as Lance found him, sitting squarely and heavily behind his desk, and ready to look at you with curt, blue eyes from behind rimmed spectacles. You would—perhaps—think him a plain man; he had not a feature that was as it should be, but when you knew him, when he had talked to you, the whole man became transfigured. His very plainness was lovable; it had a sort of beautiful rightness, a Cromwellian vigour. He talked very fast—in swift, forcible bursts, or he said very little. If he was silent you might take up your hat and go. He had moments of explosive energy. At times he might appear intensely irritable, because he was intensely sensitive, and became fiercely impatient in the presence of humbugs, and prigs, and obstructionists. No man at any time had done more kind things and forgotten them. If he troubled to curse you it meant that you were worth cursing.

He said: "Sit down, Pybus. What's the matter?"

Lance had the sense not to waste Richmond's time. He could forgive you anything but prosiness or false modesty.

"Nothing's the matter, sir. I think I told you once that my father was financing me for two years."

"Are the two years up?"

"At the end of September. I was wondering if I wrote a series of short stories."

Richmond got up out of his chair. He liked to walk about the big room when he was talking to particular people. He held himself very stiffly; head and shoulders seemed to have been carved out of one solid block. He would look at a photo, take a book from the shelves, and then turn suddenly upon a person with one of his curt, blue stares.

He did this to Lance.

"Finished your novel?"

"Not yet."

"You had better let me see it."

"If you don't mind, sir, I would rather finish it before you see it. You see——"

"Quite. What's the matter with your father?"

"Paternal curiosity, I think. I'm to find my own feet, or go into business."

Richmond paused in his paradings to raise the lid of a silver cigarette box.

"Have one. It's a pity——"

"What, sir?"

"Pot boiling."

"Need it be?"

"No, not necessarily. Of course you're young, but youth doesn't matter. Look at Arlen and Margaret Kennedy. It's youth's day. What's your idea?"

"To live on short stories and articles until my novel——"

"You believe in it, do you?"

"I do, sir. It's not conceit—I believe I have the stuff in me."

Richmond returned to his chair.

"Look here, Pybus—you must promise me that I shall see the whole of that novel—say—by the end of September."

"I think I can do it. It's very good of you."

"Rot! It's my business. And write me three short stories. If I like them I'll start you with an order for two a month, at eight guineas apiece. Our magazines eat up stories by the hundred."

"It really is awfully good of you, sir."

"Hold on. Wait till you see whether I like your tales, my lad. If they turn out as good as those London sketches of yours, you'll like me."

It was the moment to go, and Lance, touched and a little flushed, stood in front of Richmond's desk.

"I shan't forget this, sir."

The curt eyes looked up at him kindly.

"Don't forget—the end of September. Get those three tales done as soon as you can."

When Lance had gone, Richmond rang for Miss Vincent.

"Make a note—please. Mr. Pybus's novel to be seen by the end of September. Three short stories to be submitted. If satisfactory—an offer of two a month at eight guineas——each. Got it!"

"Yes, sir."

"Nice lad—that. It is so much pleasanter to do things for

the right people.   Now, what the blazes are we to do about
that buccaneering blackguard, Corthrow?"

Lance was descending the stairs.   He had been offered a
chance such as few young men receive.   He had but to keep
his word, and Richmond would be to him a literary godfather.
But Lance did not yet know his John Richmond as he was
destined to know him, as a man who had no use for delays,
prevarications, and excuses.   A generous gesture was a generous gesture; let it be responded to.

3

Mr. Conrad Pybus emerged from a taxi in Chalfont Street,
a very glossy Pybus on this May morning; the complete man
about town, silk hatted, be-spatted, sleeked into his black
morning coat.   He tipped the taxi-driver a shilling, and was
saluted.   With his malacca cane under his left arm he walked
towards the glass doors of "Mirabeau's," and the doors opened
before him as before the breath of a god.

A woman with magnificent white hair, and wearing black
silk, came down the showroom to meet him.

"Good morning, sir."

Conrad removed his hat.   He was feeling at home with
himself and with all the world.

"Good morning.   Suppose you can show me some
frocks?"

"Certainly, sir."

"Want to buy one—a bet—you know, lost it.   That's the
position."

"Will you please take a seat, sir.   What kind of frock?"

"A thing that'll do for afternoon—or evening—at a pinch.
Well, let's say—Ascot.   But it's got to be—it."

"I quite understand, sir," said the white-haired woman
with a gracious and imperturbable face.

Mr. Conrad Pybus sat down on a black satin sofa.   He
placed his hat and stick on a white table.   The showroom was
all white, with a black pile carpet.   It was plastered with

mirrors. The door of every cupboard seemed to have a mirror attached to it. On Mr. Conrad's right were a series of white boxes in which the mysteries of fitting were observed. Directly in front of him two black curtains looped back from a white doorway suggested a stage.

The white-haired woman had disappeared. Conrad, pulling off his yellow gloves, felt the need of slow music. The first mannequin appeared, a red-haired girl in a purple and green printed chiffon, mincing in between the black curtains. She postured towards Mr. Conrad, her defiant blue eyes looking over the top of his head. She walked to the right and to the left, revolved, and passed away with undulations of the hips.

Mr. Conrad smirked. Not a word had been uttered. Not a word would be uttered; that was part of the ritual.

A second mannequin appeared. Ha!—this was it, both the dress and the girl—Olive Gadsden in a kind of tomato-coloured thing, superbly simple and superbly expensive. The frock had that indefinable French manner. It both floated and clung. Yes, Conrad knew a smart frock when he saw it.

Olive's face appeared as expressionless as the wax face of a model in a window, but she fixed her eyes on the man's face, and did not look over the top of his head. He was smiling; he nodded his head. He winked at her.

Her right eye flicked out a response.

"Thank you. Will you tell madame—I'm pleased."

He watched her walk back towards the doorway. His heavy white face had an oily sheen. He was thinking.

"The clever young devil! She knew what she wanted, and which one to put on. And, by Jove!—she's a peach."

Madame reappeared. Conrad was extracting a cheque-book.

"I'll take that frock. How much?"

"Forty guineas, sir."

"Right you are. I'll write a cheque."

"You will have the dress sent, sir?"

"No, taking it with me. Your porter can get me a taxi. My cheque's as good as the Bank."

"Of course, sir.   May I have your name and address?"
"Pybus.   Conrad Pybus, Esq., Chlois Court, Bucks."
"Can we show you anything else, sir?"
Conrad gave her a sly look.
"Another day—probably—yes—very probably."

4

At the rendezvous outside Baker Street station, Olive Gadsden was twenty minutes late, but that was a young woman's privilege.   She had dashed back to No. 7 Parham Crescent at twenty minutes to six to try on the frock that had been delivered by a special messenger.   Conrad had been too tactful and too cautious to drive up to No. 7 in a taxi and deposit a parcel in the hands of Mrs. Gasson.   Conrad was a man of the world.   He might have matrimonial inclinations, but, since that pup of Probyn's happened to be most inconveniently lodged in Parham Crescent, his uncle exercised discrimination.

"I'm afraid I'm a little late.   We had a wretched woman in who kept us parading till half-past five."

She looked up into his intent face.

"You're not cross with me, laddie?"

"Cross!   I was just a little frightened—that's all."

"What of?"

"That you might not be coming."

"Oh, I wanted to come."

"Really?"

"Rather.   What do you think?   Oh, let's get away from this damned noise.   Aren't people fools?"

"I sometimes stand here and watch them stampede into the Tube."

"Funny form of amusement.   Half of us should never have been born."

"Which half?"

"Oh, the sploshy-faced, spoilt in the baking sort, and the sickly sort.   Come along, my dear.   Let's find something green to look at."

He walked very close to her, as close as was possible.

"I feel I have such a lot to say to you, Olive. I want you to understand——"

"Oh—serious laddie! Let's be ''Arry' and ''Arriet,' or Chloe and Strephon. We'll sit under a tree, and then I'll take you out to dinner in Soho. It's my turn——"

"My dear, you can't——"

"Oh, yes, I can. I'm in funds at present. And have you been working hard, my dear?"

"Not a stroke. You wouldn't let me.

"Poor laddie!"

CHAPTER XVII

I

THE Venerable's after-breakfast pipe refused to draw. Absorbed in reflecting upon other matters he had plugged the tobacco too tightly into the bowl, and since the flight feather of a pigeon failed to clear the stoppage, he was constrained to employ the blade of a pocket-knife. Having come out into the Saracen yard he made use of the window-sill of the billiard-room. After scraping out the tobacco into a little brown heap, he blew vigorously through the pipe, and proceeded to replace the tobacco.

"Beautiful morning, Mr. Pybus," said a voice.

The Venerable agreed that the morning was beautiful, but he had the air of not appreciating its beauty. His eyebrows had a constrained bushiness. Lance had not written to him for ten days, and the Venerable had grown accustomed to a weekly letter. Moreover, that last letter of Lance's had bothered him a little, because it had suggested haste and perfunctoriness.

"Getting exacting—are you?"

He addressed the inward remark both to himself and to his pipe.

"Getting like an old woman! Drop it. The boy has enough writing to do."

He relit his pipe, gazed at the sky and saw that it was very blue. Also, he became aware of Miss Merris's car standing in the yard, and looking as dusty and as deplorable as a car could look. She was bending over the open dicky; she was lifting something out; old Pybus saw her face, and his attention was arrested by its sadness, the sadness as of some inward pain suppressed and resisted.

He said to himself: "That girl's not well. She works too hard," but in a moment he was correcting his reflection. Hard work hurts nobody, not even a miner; and most certainly it would not hurt a strong young woman who spent half her life in the open air. But there was no question about her sadness. You could not cleverly get rid of it as Shaw might do by putting it down to the effects of insufficient food, or the wrong sort of food. There are other and more complex disharmonies, especially in this most unhappy age when toys are too plentiful and too easily discarded.

Observed, she became conscious of it. Some faces are very sensitive—especially some women's faces. Her eyelids flickered; her self-absorbed melancholy was disturbed; she raised her head to see who it was who stood watching her. She was impatient, resentful.

But it was only old Mr. Pybus, and the hardness went out of her eyes. She did not mind old Pybus. Her rather brusque manner relented. There was that in her which ceased to resist, or to defy the man in him, because it was not necessary.

She lifted out a wooden box.

"I'm loaded up this morning. Shopping day."

Old Pybus laid his pipe aside on the window-sill.

"I'll carry that in."

"Will you? There's another."

"I'll carry both of them in."

Her brown eyes seemed to regain their depth and their secret courage. She was so very much alone; she had no one to go to, no one whom she wished to go to; she had to carry two lives on her shoulders. And sometimes the heart of her courage felt so hard and strained that she would wonder whether there was any softness left in it. Also, she did not dare to be soft. There were times when she could have thrown up her hands and wailed, or broken into a storm of furious and bitter words. She had to cherish her gentleness, and, paradoxical though it may seem, the exaggeration of an attitude of gentleness and forbearance seemed to be creating in her an inward hardness. She was starved of contrasts. No one was gentle to her; men wanted things from her, selfishly, brutally. There were moments when she felt a wild impulse driving her to be brutal towards men. But old Pybus——!

"Thank you so much."

He took the egg-box from her hands.

"They keep you busy."

"It's best to be busy.   There is a box for the White Hart."

"I'll carry it up to them.   You go and do your shopping."

Courageous she might be, and self-restrained to the point of severity, but she was hungry for kindness.   People called her a hard young woman; she was judged by the surface she showed to the world.

"But that's not part of your job, Mr. Pybus."

"It's my job, if I choose to do it."

Her brown eyes softened to his blue ones.

"You're kind.   Most people are in too much of a hurry."

"It's a pity."

"I dare say I'm the same.   I'm always in a hurry."

She was smiling at him.

"It's when you feel rushed and flurried—inside——"

"Yes—that's it.   Try and take deep breaths.   I don't allow people—now—to make me hurry.   But then your blood is younger than mine."

She turned to go, but pausing, looked back over her shoulder.

"How peaceful to be old.   I should like to be seventy."

He shook his head at her.

"Mustn't say that.   That's not you."

2

The Venerable had asked that every other Sunday should be made free to him, and since the autocrat of Castle Cottage and the autocrat who owned the Saracen's Head were cronies, John Pybus had his way.   It was a June Sunday, and June as it should be, and on the Saturday morning a letter had come from Lance, a jerky, rambling, disconnected letter.   It suggested some inward restlessness, or that Lance was trying to talk on paper to his grandfather while thinking of something else.   It made old Pybus feel vaguely uneasy and insecure.

"What's wrong with the lad?"

He decided that he would go out and walk. Unlike the majority of old men he had not become dulled by age; he would never be a dodderer, moving the young men to impatience or a kind of scornful tolerance. If he dreaded anything, that was the thing he dreaded.

Old Pybus retained his sensitiveness. It is possible that he had grown more sensitive, and as he took the path below the Castle and saw the river sliding its swift silver below the young green of the beeches he was conscious of emotion. Always he had understood those lines of Tennyson's—"Tears, idle tears —I know not what they mean." There were tears that are never wept; laughter that is never laughed, save in secret, or on some autumn morning when the yellow leaves fall slowly or on some evening in the spring of the year when birds sing. Oh, that singing of birds in the green and chilly twilight, and the dead faces that were remembered, and dead springs! How poignant a thing was beauty, the beauty of this green valley, and of this England that was ceasing!

"I'm growing old," he thought.

And, as though defying the thought, he struck a stone post sharply with his ash stick.

"Nonsense. Don't fuss. Nothing's so boring as fussiness. Old idiot, don't young men fall in love!"

But was that it? He paused on the footbridge over the Brent and watched the swirl of the water. The last week of May had been wet. Youth chafed like that, and fretted itself, and was driven by its own swollen swiftness.

Old Pybus raised his hat to the river.

"Find the sea, my lad; find the sea."

He regained his tranquillity. He had a feeling for landscape, an old man's feeling for it, for he saw it as it was; and not as a youth sees it, as a mere setting for its desires and dreams; nor as a man sees it in the force of his acquisitive years, as a building site or as a possible golf course or a test hill. Here was a green valley in early June, and the river, and Castle Craven on its hill. He loitered. The path brought him to the main road, but it was Sunday and car day, and being

G

offered the lane that ran up past "Marions" to the Woolshot beech woods he accepted it.

Coming to the hedge of "Marions" he had heard a piano being played. The Venerable did not know the name of the piece—it was Cyril Scott's "Pierrot," but the richness and the depth of the rolling chords were irresistible. Old Pybus went a little way along the hedge and past Mary Merris's white gate, and happening to find a stump where a young oak had been felled, he sat down there. The music went on. It had what the Venerable called "a human cry." It yearned, and was baffled. It was full of life's—"Whence, and Why Whither?" It was blind and beautiful and sad, and it had the cry of a man who was blind.

The music ceased suddenly. It was replaced by another sound, the clatter of a light mowing machine being pushed over a piece of grass. The Venerable heard voices.

"Mary."

"Hallo!"

"Must you make that damned noise?"

"Sorry—dear—but I must get this done."

"Oh—what a fuss——! If the grass is too long—I can't see it. But I can hear. I'm playing."

"I thought you'd finished."

"Well, I haven't!"

"All right. I'll mow the grass later."

The piano playing commenced, but it was angry and egotistical playing, an outburst of childish impatience. In the garden there was silence, and the Venerable was intrigued by that silence. He could picture the girl on her knees, with a set face, pulling up weeds. He seemed to get a sudden understanding of her life here, with that poor, spoilt blind child of a man. The devotion of some women, the patience of them! The Castle Craven bells began to ring out across the valley, and they had been at it for a minute when John Pybus heard another voice.

"Hallo—working on Sunday?"

The Venerable's eyebrows bristled. He knew the voice and its owner, and he recognized the quality of both. He heard the girl's voice reply to it, and he could still picture her, on her knees, determinedly busy.

"As you see."

It was both a parry and a thrust.

"Quite wrong to work on Sunday."

"Is it!"

"Listen to those bells. Know what they are saying?"

"Many things."

"The damned fools! the damned fools! the damned fools!"

There was a moment of silence, a stressed silence.

"Where's Gil?"

"If you listen——"

"Oh, plastering the ivories. This is a soulful little place."

"Do you mind telling me how you arrived here?"

"Through your orchard gate."

"I'd prefer you to use——"

"Don't be silly. I use any gate."

The piano playing ceased abruptly, and the third voice joined in.

"Mary, I'm bored. Confound those beastly bells!"

"Hallo, Gil! Here's your good sister breaking the Sabbath."

"Bob—that you—old chap?"

"Large as life. Come and fill a pipe."

John Pybus left his tree stump and walked slowly towards the Woolshot beeches. He felt that the virtue had gone out of the morning, for in some ways he was still as fastidious as a sensitive boy, and as quick as Lance was with his qualms and aversions. Hargreaves, with his complacent, well-oiled voice, and his air of "Come hither—my lass—when I call you," was the sort of man who gave him qualms. Yes, a voice was a subtle revealer. John Pybus trudged up the hill, rapping at the oak fence of Woolshot with his stick, conscious of himself as an old fellow who had been skulking behind a hedge while two dogs were driving a brown-eyed creature into a corner to worry it.

"Mary, I'm bored."

"Hallo, young woman, I want you. What about it?"

Yes, the blind, and the broad of nostril! Troublesome people, greedy children! The Venerable reached the shade of the Woolshot beeches, Hargreaves beeches, purchased fifty years ago by the original Hargreaves, who had kicked his way up to wealth in a pair of weaver's clogs. Again— three generations! Old Jock Hargreaves had been a stout, surly, useful old curmudgeon. His grandson was just a gentlemanly cad.

The big bell of Castle Craven sent a tremor across the valley, and old Pybus sat down on a dry bank in the shade. Rather hard luck on the girl down there. Was the fellow after her? And that poor, blind, petulant brother, bored and fractious! What a situation!

Old Pybus prodded the ground with his stick. He found himself wondering what his grandson was doing on this morning in June.

3

As it happened, Lance was attempting to harmonize a situation, and to drive two selves in double harness. At half-past ten he was to meet Olive Gadsden at the Baker Street tube station en route for Waterloo, Hampton Court, and the river. Meanwhile, he was trying to bolt himself down in his chair and to complete the last five hundred words of a short story, the second of the three John Richmond was to read. But he could not see things clearly, or rather he saw certain things too clearly, a mouth, a pair of eyes, a summer frock, cushions, a punt on the river. His vision as an interpreter was confused and clouded by his vision as a man.

At half-past nine the word-master in him surrendered. The sun was shining, the trees were green, and his own restlessness fluttered at the window. He got up, and without looking at his manuscript, put a book upon the sheets so that they should not blow away.

He was before her at the station, and that was as it should be. The first he saw of her was her little rose-coloured hat. She

came towards him on those swift, feverish legs. Her eyes
were mischievous and intimate, and challenging.

"Well, we've choused the snooky people."

He looked at her eyes and mouth, and the olive in her skin.
"No need for ostentation."

She laughed. Everything about her was a little exaggerated,
as though the rhythm of life had been quickened; her flickering
movements, the rogue's brightness in her eyes, her colour, her
chatter. She touched his arm as they went down the steps,
and her fingers exercised a caressing pressure.

"It's our day. Got enough money?"

"Plenty."

"Because I have. Share and share alike."

"Not for a moment."

"Oh—all right. Pity we haven't a car. You've got a
car?"

"I had."

"At home?"

"That's it."

"So there are three cars?"

"Yes."

"Borrow one?"

"Can't afford to keep it."

Her eyes teased him.

"Oh, yes, you could."

At Waterloo the crowdedness of life began to assert itself.
Everybody seemed to be going on the river, and everybody
looked more or less alike; there were hatless young men with
floppy hair, and girls with standardized hats. All trousers
were white, and all stockings flesh-coloured. There were
gramophones and tea-baskets and cushions and children. The
carriage to Hampton was crowded; Lance had taken first-
class tickets, but five blatant "thirds" pushed in without
attempting to find a third-class compartment. A very hot
and obstreperous small boy kept wiping his shoes on Lance's
white trousers.

"Sit still, Eddie, will yer."

"I want t'look out of the winder."

"Sit still or I'll smack you. Mind the gentleman's trousers."

Hampton Court was a larger replica of the railway carriage. Humanity was spilt about it like confetti after a wedding. The bridge was a jam of cars and pedestrians, and the road space opposite the entrance to the palace adventurous with trams and buses and dawdling crowds. Lance's eyes had a restiveness. Crowds were very well when you came out to study them—but to be one of a holiday crowd—with a girl at your elbow . . . !

He said: "Damn all these people."

She was far less sensitive than he was.

"What about that car?"

"We'll have one next time. Or we'll go fifty miles out. I want to get away."

"That's why money's worth while, my lad. Hot Sabbath humanity! Me no likee."

It took them an hour to get a punt. Punts were at a premium, and while they waited, the river grew more and more crowded. A steamer went by, and the jazz band upon it ceased its syncopations to refresh itself with bottled beer.

Lance's face grew stiffer.

"Damn all these people!"

She knew her world better than he did. She produced a half-crown, and waylaid a harassed boatman.

"We want a punt. See——"

"Right, miss, right; I'll do my best."

They got their punt—and curled up on the cushions, and looking up at him wickedly, she made her point.

"Money, see? Money all the time!"

4

She had brought lunch for two in an attaché-case; sandwiches, pastry, cherries, and a bottle of cider. They lunched under the shade of a vast plane tree which grew inside the wall of a private garden, and threw its shade on the earth and water beyond the wall. The yellowness of the Palm Beach buildings on Karno's Island gleamed through the trees like an artificial after-glow.

"Rum world, isn't it? Have another raspberry tart, old thing?"

"No, thanks. I say—I wonder if these people like going about in crowds?"

"Does it matter whether they do or don't? You're much too self-conscious, laddie. Give me a cigarette and come and lie down here."

"Is there room?"

"Try."

They lay side by side in the stern of the punt, he looking up into the green shadowiness of the plane tree, she resting on her side and watching his face. She blew smoke at him.

"Penny."

"Not worth three farthings."

"Sure?"

"Quite."

"Then it's not about me!"

He turned towards her. She had taken off her hat, and her dark hair stood out in black and shadowy cloud. It was soft and scented, and suddenly he felt tempted to take that soft head in his arms and to bury his face in her hair.

Her eyes glimmered at him.

"Mustn't—not now."

"Why not?"

"Don't you know that the Conservancy people won't allow you to kiss on the river?"

"What rot!"

"It's true. Besides—too many people——"

He looked into her eyes.

"That's true. Always—too many people. Do you know, we never have a chance to be alone. There is no aloneness—in these days."

She patted his chin with the tip of a finger.

"Oh—yes—there is. But it means money. A big car, a place in the country."

"My God!" he said, "just listen to those gramophones! There must be half a dozen of them all going at once.   Look here—Olive."

"Well?"

"Let's go right away somewhere—next week-end.   Will you?"

Her head made a little consenting movement on the cushion.

CHAPTER XVIII

I

RICHMOND, having read the third of Lance's short stories, asked himself the obvious question.

"What's wrong with young Pybus?"

For when the work is wrong something must be amiss with the workman, and Richmond, who had written and read for twenty years, had somehow contrived to keep himself fresh to the perfume or the rankness of the product. And here was a lad who could when he chose command an exquisite and remorseless intensity, writing aggressive and succulent tosh!

Richmond was annoyed. There was nothing he misliked so much as mere cleverness, and especially cheap cleverness. Also, it is annoying to open a door to a young man, only to find that he has lost his literary manners.

But why?

You could assume some distraction, or that fatal lapse from virtue, when an ulterior motive edges in between life and the interpreter. Richmond knew that when you take to kissing your craft on the mouth for money—your craft becomes a harlot. Extraordinary—but it is so, and exasperatingly so, and John Richmond had had to experience many such exasperations. He had found that he had debauched people by trying to help them, and so often had this happened to him that he had developed a distaste for helping people.

"I'm not so sure," he reflected. "Better if the young beggar had been polite to his father. Give them a fence to climb—make an obstacle race of it. You should have to get at your craft like a boy breaking into somebody's orchard after school hours."

He sent one of the short stories back to Lance, with a curt, kind note. "This won't do, my lad. You can do better than this. I want the better."

To himself he said: "This young man will have to be

watched. London's got him, or a wench, or perhaps both of them. This tendency to write for glitter!"

At Castle Craven the Venerable was at work upon the same problem. Lance, arriving for a belated week-end, had brought with him five more chapters of the novel, and a face which suggested to old Pybus the simile of a window filled with frosted glass. His grandfather had to read both the book and the face, and he read those five chapters in bed. He blew out the candle. In summer he liked to sleep with the blind up and the curtains undrawn, and he lay in the soft June darkness and considered his problem.

Obviously a change had come over Lance and over Lance's work. You could not dissociate one from the other. As to those five chapters, they suggested the workings of an imagination whose temperature was raised, and whose sense of perspective had been given an oblique twist. It was cubist stuff, all jagged and angular and raw as to colour, and the people had blue faces and green hair. Like the late "cubists", Lance had sat down in a cold frenzy to emphasize consciousness, and that feature was sex.

The stuff had the face of a woman.

So clearly did the Venerable see that dominant face that he could not conjure sleep, and when the Castle Craven clock sent out twelve deep notes old Pybus got out of bed and relit the candle. He was wakeful and restless. He went downstairs and rummaged for a pipe, and in the stillness he fancied that he could hear his grandson's confident and almost aggressive voice crowing like Peter Pan. "The best five chapters. The best work I've done."

Inadvertently, old Pybus trod on the cat. Pussy should not have been there on the rug in front of the fire-place; she should have been out hunting or being hunted. The Venerable said "Damn," echoing poor pussy's squawk.

He bent down to make amends.

"Well—you shouldn't have been there, you silly."

While stroking Sarah's head he heard the door of Lance's bedroom open.

"Hallo! What's that?"

"I trod on the cat—my son."

"Anything wrong, grandpater?"

"No. I thought I had forgotten to lock the door. I'm just making it up with Sarah."

Lance's door closed, and his grandfather, having filled a pipe, and held the mouth of the bowl to the flame of the candle, made his way back to his room. He was thinking—"Is it my business to tread on those five chapters as I trod on the cat? Is it my business? And also—is this how youth sees things? The eyes of the young generation? Am I an old stuffer?" He slipped into an ancient blue dressing-gown, effaced the candle, and with his crossed arms on the window-sill, smoked his pipe. He did not see the dim, jagged bulk of the Castle, or the tops of the ash trees, or the star-dust scattered above them. His consciousness was all within.

He was thinking of Lance and of Lance's work. He was confronted and antagonized by some of the crude, flashing sentences.

"Mallinson's teeth looked like a stick of celery stuffed between two great tomatoes."—"Her hot lips dissembled."— "Everything in life is as you happen to smell it, cabbage or face-powder."

Old Pybus blew smoke, much smoke. If this was not what he called—"Impertinent art," what was it? An inflammation, youth seeing red, and especially a redness of hair and lips. Arrogant stuff! And he swore softly to the June night.

"Damn it—what a pity! Self-expression, self-expression!"

For you might liken a man's power of self-expression to the water in a conduit which serves to work a fountain or to flush a drain. Turn on the drain-cock and the flow is downwards, and your fountain will not play. All the pressure that the heart of man's consciousness can give is needed for the raising of that mystical plume. Lance had opened the lower cock of life's conduit. Maybe it was gushing red wine, blood, adventure. But the "jet d'eau" was out of action.

Also, the Venerable was persuaded to remember two volumes of English plays that had been sent down to him six months ago by his London library. "Hindle Wakes"—

"Mary Broome," and others of that sort of industrial dismalness, had set John Pybus contrasting the pre-war with the post-war. He had not liked any of the young men in these plays; he had not wanted to like them. Leonard Timbrell in Alan Monkhouse's "Mary Broome"; impertinent, ineffectual, unpleasantly clever, selfish as hell, had set the Venerable handling an imaginary strap. How admirable to be able to despise your father, to treat him with easy insolence, and at the same time to be content to sponge on him! The cult of the temperamental young rotter! And why should the son, who worked, and stuck at things, be represented on all occasions as a crass prig and a bourgeois fool?

He remembered his own sons, Probyn and Conrad. H'm—yes! Rather unsubtle souls—certainly. But if your interesting pre-war young rotter had been portrayed as an insolently inefficient young person—the war had produced a useful reaction. You might be a rotter, but there was something to suggest that the post-war rotter had developed an efficiency.

Besides, words, words, labels, fatuous generalizations! The whole point was that Lance had a face like clouded glass, and that he had written those five chapters. Sexual stuff, and sexual stuff unrelieved by other urges, can be so horribly boring. Young wenches loosening their garters!

The Venerable was troubled—not so much by those five chapters, as by his grandson's clouded and taciturn face. The candour had gone from the eyes. Lance was shut up with himself in some inner chamber—a stuffy, cheaply scented, tumbled apartment—where certain things happened. He was secretive about it; he had locked the door.

And old Pybus realized himself as being outside that locked door, and desiring nothing so much as to be able to rush in and throw up the window.

But there you were! Half of life's doors are always locked, and some of them are never opened. We have closed cupboards within our inmost selves.

The Venerable's pipe went out—and he stood breathing the night air.

"Oh, he'll come back to breathing this. Sex stuffiness can't last. But—meanwhile——? Spiritual inflections, Damn it."

He went back to bed.

2

When John Pybus looked out of his bedroom window the distant country was very blue and clear, and in the south-west clouds were smudging up. Rain was coming, but not yet, and it was the Venerable's own Sunday, and therefore he would make Lance walk.

At breakfast, Lance ate less than usual, and had silent periods. He was expecting his grandfather to say something about those five chapters, and the Venerable was aware of being expected to say something. But what? He had not seen Lance for a month, and to play the Roman at breakfast and before the first tranquillizing pipe, was not humanly easy. Therefore they talked disjointed nothings to each other, and became self-conscious—though old Pybus did not betray himself as Lance did.

"How's your egg?"

"Quite—excellent."

"So it should be. Game for a walk?"

"Yes; let's walk."

"Woolshot way; get away from the cars."

"Splendid," said Lance, with that clouded but half-expectant face of his.

He had a second cup of tea. He got up and looked out of the window. He remembered that the first thought that had come to him on waking was that Olive was going up the river with a party in somebody's launch. And he had wished. No, he hadn't—not actually. And then he had gone on to remember that Richmond had flung back one of his stories. The memory rankled.

"Going to rain."

"Not before five o'clock," said his grandfather. "I know that horizon almost as well as I know my own chin. Both things that I look at early in the morning."

Lance failed to respond. He stood by the window, rather moodily filing a pipe.

"What time shall we start?"

"Ten o'clcok suit you?"

"Yes."

They went out by way of the Castle Field, and down the path through the hanging beech wood to the river. Lance appeared preoccupied; but to the Venerable this air of preoccupation took the guise of a veiled expectancy. He was right. Youth may be exacting, but had he not helped to create an appetite for praise in this beloved child? Also youth is nothing when it is not egotistical. Even its valour is not that of the veteran. It must advance, wave a flag, hear a cry. It loathes negation, retreat, stillness. And there had been a kind of deliberate candour between them. Old Pybus's white eyebrows seemed to hang heavy.

Said Lance, loitering on the bridge, and looking at the water, where it lay a brownish green under the beeches:

"Richmond threw one of my tales back at me. Should like you to look at it—I can't see much wrong with it— myself."

"Did he say why?"

"Said I could do better, and he wanted the best."

They passed on over the crown of the high and narrow old bridge, and met the first batch of Sunday cars fuming up the road from Abbey Mill.

"Let's get out of this."

"I'm with you, my lad."

He glanced at that restive, impatient head.

"How old is Richmond?"

To Lance the question appeared irrelevant.

"Oh, quite oldish; forty-five—I suppose."

"Just old enough. I read somewhere the other day that a man is a hog until he reaches forty."

"Isn't that a rather crude generalization—grandpater? I say—confound these cars!"

The Venerable gave him one of those blue glances.

"All under forty—I should say—my dear. Cars and men

in the force of their years, in a hurry to get there or to get something.   After forty a man's latent period lengthens."

"What's that?"

"The little interval or pause between the stimulus and the response.   A divine pause, selection, choice, restraint.   You don't hog it; you give yourself and the other fellow a chance. We get off the main road here."

The Venerable's taking of the "Marions" lane may have had premeditation, or it may not.   But on this blue, June day, with the smell of rain in the west, and the green of the year still vivid, he had a feeling of sensitive aliveness.   It was a vivid day.   He saw the high woods, and the clouds, and his grandson's face, as a man sees them where there is no haste behind his eyes, with a tenderness and a deep delight.   Troubled he might be, but there is a tang in trouble; it had a pungency. Heavy midsummer is for the material mood.   The plaintiveness of spring, and the sharp, sweet sadness of autumn are for those who have wept inward tears.

Said the Venerable as they passed along by the hedge of "Marions":

"A blind man lives in there."

"Does he," said Lance absently.

He was both blind and deaf to all poignancies save his own, and yet when the sudden sound of a piano being played came to them as they passed the gate he could not but heed it, for it was music that had to be heard.   It was Debussy's "L'après Midi"—and Lance loitered.

"Who's that playing?   Rather unexpected here."

"Young Merris—You remember his sister?"

"No."

"You changed a wheel for her."

"Oh—that girl."

"Her brother is blind."

"He can play.   Was it the war?"

"No—a motor smash.   Rather hard on the girl.   She gave up her job to look after him."

They moved along beside the hedge.   It was like a high green wall shutting in those two young people, but if the

Venerable's sympathy could leap over the hedge, his grandson's could not. Sympathy is not youth's strong point; though it may have a facility for discovering a grievance. It did not occur to Lance to wonder what the Merris girl's job had been; her present occupations were breeding chickens and looking after a derelict brother. A quite reasonable occupation for a woman. Lance did not say so. It is probable that he was too self-absorbed at the present to register impressions as expressing other people's troubles.

"I want you to read that tale, grandpater."

"Richmond's rejected?"

"Peevish people, editors."

The Venerable's eyebrows seemed to bush out.

"Richmond may be right, you know. I'll tell you if I agree with him."

"Of course——"

"Like those five chapters, my son. They don't please me."

He was aware of the swift lift of Lance's head.

"Oh! Why?"

"There is a smell of cheap scent."

Lance was startled and compelled to take notice, not so much by the blunt impact of his grandfather's words upon his young self-love as by a something in old Pybus's voice. Almost—the Venerable's voice had sounded impatient and angry.

"Cheap scent? I don't quite get you."

"If one is shut up in a fuggy room, Lance, one gets accustomed. One doesn't notice the atmosphere."

"I say—grandpater, that's rather—severe."

"Sorry—my son; I can't help it. If I were you I should put those chapters aside, and read them at seven o'clock in the morning some time next month."

3

Lance had been hurt, but he was not going to show that he had been hurt, and he met the Woolshot beech woods with a face of constrained cheerfulness. He was quite sure that he was right, and that Richmond and the Venerable were wrong. It was a question of three generations, and his grandfather might be a wonderful man, but it was asking too much of him to expect him to understand London in 1927. Whereas Lance had a feeling that in those five chapters he had reduced London 1927 to paper as no other fellow had done it.

"You think it rather too vivid, grandpater."

Old Pybus had a set face. It seemed that he was treading on those five chapters as he had trodden upon Sarah the cat—but this was deliberate, and he hated doing it.

"Whom the Lord loveth He chasteneth. But I haven't that sort of meddlesome mind that loves rubbing things in."

"But just how and where—do you quarrel with me?"

"That's the difficulty. The work's damned clever, too damned clever. Supposing I say that you had set out to paint an impression of Piccadilly, and that what you produced turned out to be the Marylebone Road."

Lance's head went up.

"Good Lord!"

After that he was silent for quite a long while, and in the silence of the beech woods old Pybus experienced a personal breathlessness. It may be easier to quarrel with a young man's virility than to quarrel with his work. The Venerable had fired a shot at the craftsman's self-esteem. He was conscious of a moody and disquieted face drifting beside him in the greenish light under the great trees. Youth can be so sympathetic to itself, yet down there at "Marions" a girl was cleaning out chicken-houses, while little tubes of colour remained untouched.

"You'll have to try and forgive me, my son."

"Grandpater!"

There was a swift change. Lance's right hand got hold of the Venerable's left arm. His mouth winced.

"You—of course—I'm a cub."

Old Pybus's right hand came across and pressed his grandson's wrist.

"No—that's great of you, my dear. No humbug, no humbug."

4

Returning by the same way, after going as far as King's Standing, they sat down on a dry bank under the Woolshot park fence. Castle Craven looked at them across the valley. The blueness of the landscape was changing to grey, and the occasional stirring of the tops of the beech trees gave to the day those rustlings of sadness and unrest that come with the west wind and its rain. The mood of the weather was very English, and so, too, was the figure moving about the chicken runs in the meadow between the beech wood and the "Marions" orchard.

The Venerable had his eyes and his thoughts on Mary Merris. He saw her in her tawny-coloured jumper and rust-coloured skirt moving in and about the little brown houses, and he had a feeling that she was affected by a blurred sky, and wet windows, and English sludge, and that if she accepted those grey days and their sadness she accepted them because life was sad. They blended. The Venerable accepted them because age sits down in its chair to confront the inevitable. But youth——?

He glanced at his grandson.

"What of the pastoral age?"

Lance smiled, emerged from his meditation to reply, and relapsed into meditation.

"Arcady is dead—grandpater."

The Arcady of the moment was the music of Debussy. Lance had seen the Russian dancers, the faun and the nymphs, translate that music into a movement that was queer and archaic, and yet supremely modern. If he happened to be aware of Mary Merris in her tawny and russet, she was no part of the picture. She would have seemed too prosiac, too practical, too cumbered with her affairs. She belonged to the stodginess of England—not to Arcady. Something more artificial and Sohoish was needed, a pair of febrile legs, and a young woman who knew not mud, performing a pseudo-classic dance in a frock of vine leaves. Lance, like the rest of his generation, had no eyes for Barbizon, and turnip fields, and cloddy peasants leaning upon rakes in the centre of flat, melancholy spaces. His estimate of beauty had changed, but no estimate is permanent, especially at four and twenty.

"Ever indulge in whimsies—grandpater?"

"How and when?"

"An idea—a vast glass roof over England, and orange trees growing instead of turnips."

"Try it—my dear. You would want to blow the roof off in six months. England gives us contrasts."

He pulled at his old silver watch.

"Time to trudge."

As they passed along the "Marions" hedge they heard a man's voice plaintive and aggrieved.

"Mary—I've lost my pipe."

The Venerable's bushy eyebrows twitched expressively.

"The pain of losing is the joy of finding."

Said Lance: "That practical young woman ought to tie it round his neck.

5

Lance walked from Paddington station, carrying his brown leather suit-case, glad of London because he himself was London, and especially so on this summer evening when even the smoky foliage of Parham Crescent was sensuously sufficient. He had a window looking down upon this world of splashed legs and artificial silk, and on all the hurry and vast impatience, the huge, anonymous, greedy, thundering streets. As an artist he would not have had it altered. He saw it as the eternal scramble between the Haves and the Have-nots, inevitable and ironical, hiding itself behind pomps and ceremonies and religions and associations of this and that. Even the modern "Red" had his uses; he was something to be scorned and roasted. Moreover, there is a pungency in unlikeness; ugliness can be exquisite. The pimply face shows up the face with the glowing skin. Supposing faces were all the same, like the faces of millions of identical children scrubbed and polished for some smug civic occasion?

Lance had the ruthlessness of the young observer, but unlike most youths he had no wish to tear the clothes off civilization. He liked the contrasts as they were, the clean old boys in Pall Mall, and the sweating fellow—complacently unclean—whom you edged away from in the "Tube." No doubt the whole business was a huge and ironical mess, but it was an interesting mess. Like a child beside a dubious pond, he rather delighted in stirring it up with a stick.

Moreover, if he had a window overlooking the show, he also looked up at a particular window, for at half-past six on a Monday evening beauty should have ceased to pander to the beast.

The lower sash of her window was up. He had said to her before going away: "See you on Monday. Make it my evening." He let himself into No. 17, and met Mrs. Carver carrying up the "first-floors'" dinner-tea, a chop, fried tomatoes, two wedges of jam sandwich—shop produced—and the teapot and its accessories.

"Evening, Mrs. Carver. Anybody called?"

She blinked at him. The china jiggled on the tray. She was never anything else but agitated.

"Oh, my pore nerves! A young lady left a note for you. Will you be ready for your dinner at seven, sir?"

"I shall."

He hurried upstairs to find the note lying on his desk. He opened it and read:

"Boy—So sorry. Puss has got to be good and sociable to-night. The dibs. Dancing with old elephas—another elephas. Dance and dine for fifteen and six. Fizz-bang! Put on paper caps. What fools they do look in caps! Jumbo wearing a pink paper crown!

"Oh, my poor toes! But I'll be all aboard with Boy on Tuesday. Let's be Hyde Parkers.

"Thine, Olive."

He felt balked and angry, and he looked it. Of course she had to go out with these old fools who paid her to dance with them at "Clubs" and night-shows. But what right had some bald-headed idiot, whose business should be domesticity at Surbiton or Woking, to get in youth's way? It was youth's way and its right of way. He stuffed the letter into his pocket.

And at midnight, with his back to the garden railings, he confronted a full moon which was contriving to shine on him between smoky clouds. If it was raining at Castle Craven it was not yet raining in London, though rain did not matter in London as it did in the country. He was the tempestuous lover. He waited there, not so much for a woman as for a mouth. He was in the savage stage. He craved without the sacred compassion of the playfulness of an older and happier tendresse.

He waited till a quarter to one, with the iron bars digging into his back. A passing police constable crossed the road and investigated his crucified stillness.

"What's your game, young fellah?"

Said Lance—"I'm not a young fellah. I'm a gentleman. Will that for do you?"

It did.

At one o'clock he heard a taxi pull up at the end of the crescent. He heard the bang of a door and the tapping of her shoes. He went to meet her. He saw her as a slim, sleek, sinuous streak of blackness below the whiteness of her floating face. Her very movements were exotic, jaunty, feverish. Country wenches did not move like that.

"Oh—Boy——!"

"I had to wait—I——"

He felt both the silk of her cloak and the satin of her face.

6

At the top of the stairs Mrs. Gasson appeared in her night-dress, large and white and properly solicitous.

"All right—dearie?"

"Quite."

"You do look a peach"—and Mrs. Gasson's very sophisticated blue eyes touched her with a gloating and envious approval—"Pity it was an old one. But, then—the old fools have the money."

Olive showed her teeth.

"But I've said good night to a young one."

Mrs. Gasson chuckled.

"That's better, dearie; that's something to go to bed on."

CHAPTER XIX

I

LYING in the hammock, slung between two old apple trees
in a far corner of the orchard, and looking up at the burrs
of sunlight shining through the foliage, Mary Merris would
sometimes wonder at life and at herself. She would take a
book with her to the hammock, but there were days when the
book would fail to hold her, either because life was too un-
avoidable, or the book itself too empty of life.

She insisted upon this hour in the hammock after lunch
each day, and even when it was raining she would put on a
mackintosh, and taking an old ground-sheet with her, snuggle
up under the dripping leaves. It was her one hour of relaxation, of escape from the interminable trifles of the day's
routine. It meant solitude, an hour's relief from the pressure
of that other personality, the one hour when she was soft to
herself and hard to her brother. At first he had refused to
understand or to respect this withdrawal of hers into that green
corner. He had complained that deliberately she had eluded
him; which was true.

For, with a little secret, guilty exultation she had realized
that he could not find his way to her among those orchard
trees.

"I must have my one hour, Gil."

Twice he had come blundering and groping into the
orchard, calling to her like a peevish child.

"Mary—Mary!"

She had raged, but in silence. She had remained perfectly
still, and allowed him to exhaust his persuasive egotism. For
in this hour she refused to pity him; she was hard for one hour;
she knew that she had to be hard. She owed it to herself, to
the sweetening of her sanity, to the very patience of her pity.
She had given up so much to him, and he would have taken
that one hour from her had she suffered him to do it.

He was such a child.

Lying there in an hour of sunlight after rain, she wondered at herself. Why did one do the things one did? She had no religion as her forbears had understood it; only urges, impulses, prejudices, restraints which seemed part of her individual make-up. That her pity went out to this blind and exacting creature as it did was a source of wonder to her. It was as natural and effortless as the gushing of water. And yet—all the while——her individual intimate self somehow stood apart; calm, austere, with set face, conscious of the emotional moments and sometimes angry with them. She—Mary the artist—could be furiously impatient—while Mary the mother spoke gently and felt gently. She knew that he played upon this gentleness. He had a kind of innocent, childish cunning.

Why did one do these things? Was it due to some age-old instinct, a habit of soul that woman—a woman such as she was—could not eradicate? Also—she had a feeling that these things had to be done. Compassion flows. All the things that she had loved to do she had ceased to do. Her hands gave themselves to pots and pans, and garden tools, and sheets and blankets, and fluffy yellow chicks, and eggs, and whitewash brushes. She loathed the details, while kneeling before the inspiration.

So long as she could say—"It is worth while."

She had a book with her that day, but she was not reading it. She lay and looked at the leaves and at the background of blueness beyond. The grass of the orchard stood high about the tree trunks, and it was full of red sorrel and white daisies, and when the wind stirred it all those silver and purple panicles and plumes made obeisance. The track which her feet had trodden wound down from the hammock to the lower gate of the orchard.

She lay in the hammock, but unrelaxed. She took with her now into this green retreat a secret fear, a doubting of the whole business, for she had begun to doubt whether her devotion was worth while. In the early days she had said to herself—"My poor paints and brushes will be put away, but he will have his music"; and he had had his music, but it had not satisfied him

She had moments of panic when she wondered whether anything would satisfy him, and whether she might go on stripping herself of everything that was hers in a hopeless effort to keep him even passably happy and amused.

"Poor, blind, restless, temperamental child."

But if only he would refrain from being mean! She could forgive him a querulous unrest, the turning of the wheel in the cage of his blindness; but this other thing, this kind of human dry-rot.

She had begun to suspect and to watch, and to hate her suspicions and her watchings, feeling her sacrifice being cheapened, debased, and twisted into a caricature of itself. She was the suspicious nurse observing the tricks of a perverted child.

Oh, and there was more than that—and in that green corner of the orchard she would feel herself cowering under the foliage, alert, listening, unable to lose herself in nature or in a book. She asked in that hour of solitude for impersonal things, and life had become a face obtruding itself with a gluttonous gallantry through the foliage.

Half-past two! The clock of Castle Craven's tower sent down the message from the hill. She swung her legs out of the hammock, but remained there for a minute, swaying gently to and fro like a girl in a swing. How long was it since she had been a girl, or had felt like a girl?

But she had work to do. The little wench who came in daily from a cottage on the Castle Craven road to scrub and wash and polish had arrived that morning wearing a pair of black silk stockings, and Mary had set her to scrub the kitchen floor.

"Can't I do it to-morrow, miss?"

"Because of the stockings, Nelly? If you are such a little idiot as to come to work in such things—go back and change them."

So Nelly would be in one of her sulky moods when she smeared everything, and advertised a maddening and wilful incapacity, because Rudolph Valentino was to be seen at the Castle Craven picture-house that evening, and Nellie's urge towards romance and sheikishness was symbolized by silk

stockings.   Mary got out of the hammock, and took the trodden path through the long grass, but half-way through the
orchard she paused.   She seemed to stand like Lot's wife.

"Hallo, young fellah my lad—what about it?"

"Bob—old man!   Come in."

"I will."

"There's a deck-chair somewhere.   Can't find it for you.
Mary's having her siesta."

"Lazy young woman.   Where?"

"Oh, in the orchard.   She's got a hammock."

"I'll go and wake her."

"Shouldn't, old man.   She's a bit touchy about it.   Where's
that girl?   Nelly—Nelly, we want another chair."

Nelly had ears for a man's voice.

"Yes, Mr. Gilbert.   I'll bring it out."

Mary, standing wide-eyed under the orchard trees, fled suddenly through the long grass to the rough hedge separating the
orchard from the garden.   An old and unkempt elder tree
straggled here, and she pressed in and under the screen of
branches.   She saw Hargreaves come into the orchard and
stand looking about him.   He made her think of a dog sniffing
the air.   He followed the trampled path to the hammock and,
finding it empty, came back towards the garden gate.   He did
not see her.   He disappeared.

"Bird's flown, young fellah."

"Oh, don't bother about Mary; she's always got some job or
other.   Nelly has brought out a chair."

"Try one of these?"

"What is it?"

"Cheroot.   Smell.   It's good."

"Thanks, old man.   I say—you know, it's fine to hear your
voice.   One gets so sick of women's voices."

Mary had emerged from the droop of the elder branches.
Her face looked pinched.   Something seemed to stifle in her,
an angry anguish, a passionate resentment.   Was nothing
sacred to man?   Had she no sure corner of her own that was
not to be betrayed or violated?   This shameful blindness of
eyes and soul.

She fled along the hedge to the far corner. There was a gate here giving into the meadow, and she went through it, and up between the wire runs. Her face seemed to wince. Oh, those two men, the blind and exacting child, and that great tawny creature who seemed to sniff at you like a complacent, confident mastiff. They had her alone here between them. To them she was not a fastidious, self-created, individual woman, but a thing in petticoats, a pair of hands, a pair of legs. She was full of a frozen and inarticulate disgust. She carried her fastidious shrinking self away with her like a woman running away with a child at the breast.

She went up and into the Woolshot beech woods, into their solitude, which was also the solitude of her sacrificial self.

2

The Venerable, having watered a bed of lobelia, rose petunias and purple asters, and taken a look at the sunset which was trailing like a double banner from the tower of Castle Craven church, entered in and shut the door upon the world. He had had a heavy day, and he was tired after humping things up and humping things down, with the strong lad away on a week's holiday, and Mr. Pounds fussing politely and unpolitely—here—there—and everywhere.

Old Pybus was about to pull down the blind, but seeing a crimson streak turning to smoky pink under an arch of jade-green and primrose, he left the blind up and stood watching the sky. It occurred to him to wonder whether London was enjoying such a sky? But did anyone in London ever look at the sky? Also, how was it that he knew that Lance's trouble was "woman"?—for know it he did.

Though not a word had been spoken, and that was the queer part of it, that he should somehow have sensed that other presence in Lance's life like a hot wind ruffling the surface of his grandson's self-consciousness. They had been just a little shy of each other, but the shyness had not been due to the Venerable's literary condemnations, or to anything that had

been said, or that had not been said. It was as though John
Pybus had been looking at his grandson through a little cloud
of steam, and so had seen the familiar face and figure dimmed
and slightly distorted.

The sky grew grey, and old Pybus pulled down the blind.
His own marriage had been so unromantic an affair that he
might have been expected to have had views upon the interplay of the sexes, but he was not a man of views. When the
light died out of the sky you pulled down the blind. You had
to pull down the blind upon most problems. Views were no
more than squinting through a hole in a fence. You observed
human and earthly happenings for three score years and ten,
and at the end of that time you knew everything and you
knew nothing, which is to know everything. You returned
—somewhat—to the mysticism of the child. And in knowing
the things that you felt you knew—you yet did not know how
you knew them.

John Pybus lit his lamp. He got out the little black account-
book in which his financial position was recorded. He
glanced through the figures, seventy-three pounds—five shillings and twopence in his current account, fifty pounds on
deposit, six hundred and sixty pounds invested in New
Zealand and Canadian Government stock. Not that he had
any need to refresh his memory, but there are occasions when
the contemplation of figures is pleasant and soothing. Those
written symbols did not tail off into fractions, but spread into
possibilities.

But—woman! What sort of woman! Which of Adam's
wives? And was it an adventure, or was it the great occasion
when Nature drapes the beloved with that mystic veil?

The Venerable slapped to his book.

"Much too young. He can't afford it—unless—— Besides—if it were—mysticism—I think he would have told me.
Yes—I think he would have told me. I suppose it is the other
sort of savagery—damn it!"

There came a knocking at the door, and the Venerable,
supposing that he was wanted for something at the hotel,
went resentfully to open it. He was tired and bothered,

and at half-past nine at night excursions and alarums are an impertinence. He opened the door, and against the black panel of the night he saw a woman's face.

"Miss Merris——"

Her voice seemed to come to him like a whisper.

"Mr. Pybus—may I come in—a moment?"

He held the door open, and she stepped in. Her face had a strange, still look, the eyes very wide, the nostrils faintly quivering. He got the impression that she had been running, and that she had come to his door breathless, and that she was smothering the tumult of her heart beats. She was a woman who would resent panic, disorder, fear, and try to conceal them.

He pushed a chair forward.

"Sit down."

"May I?"

She was carrying a wooden egg-box. She placed it on his table, and he noticed that her movements had a kind of rigidity. She managed to smile.

"I was short of eggs this morning. I promised to make up the number, but some things—hens—won't be hurried."

He had closed the door. He was very careful not to look at her too closely, for he seemed to know that the soul of her was raw and asked to be shielded. He went and unfastened the clasp of the box, raised the lid, looked in, and reclosed the box. Three of the eggs in the upper tray were broken.

"Supposing—I take these up?"

"Will you?"

He allowed himself a glance at her white, set face.

"It's a longish way to come—at this hour. You stay there. I make myself a cup of tea—sometimes. You'll have one?"

"I—think I will."

It seemed to him that her air of breathlessness was eased. He nodded his big white head at her, and picking up the box, went out into the broad passage. It was dark here with the darkness of a summer night, and screened from the Saracen windows by outjutting roofs and buildings. He closed the door, and stood a moment to listen. He had a feeling that someone was there against the wall, and deliberately he walked close to it, nor had he taken four steps when he was aware of a vague shape sheering off into the darkness towards the gate of the Castle Field. The Venerable trembled like a dog; his hair was bristling.

"Get out—you swine."

There was no reply to those soft, swift words. He stood, staring into the darkness, gripping the handle of that box with its broken eggs. He went quickly up the passage and across the yard and, leaving the box inside the kitchen door, hurried back to the cottage.

But he showed no haste when he closed the door. She was still sitting there, but she had taken off her hat, and her eyes had a narrowed softness. She made him think of a woman glad to sit still after the passing of a spasm of pain. He smiled at her.

"Contract kept—all right. You and I—feel the same about that sort of thing."

Her eyelids seemed to flicker under his smile.

"How kind—of you. I——"

"What's that—my dear! Kind—and at seventy odd! That's the only success worth having at my age. Now then, what about that tea?"

She offered to help him make the tea, but old Pybus would not hear of it; she was to sit there or to look at his books, and when he came back from lighting the oil-stove and putting the kettle on it, she was standing by his book-case. Hitherto their intimacy had not extended beyond the little friendlinesses of the Saracen yard, but on this summer evening when she had fled to him like some big-eyed, panting thing, he thought of her as Mary, and not as Miss Mary Merris. He joined her in front of the book-case. He took out a book.

"Read that?"

She took it from him, and looking at her clear, strong profile he was made to realize that it would not be easy to make her afraid. Obviously, she had very good reasons for her breathlessness, and, old man though he was, he felt a generous rage in him. That sort of swinishness! Almost one forgot that life produced such savagery.

"No. What a queer title."

"'Shepherd's Bane.' Take it back with you. You'll like it."

She turned the pages. He was giving her time to get her breath, and she wondered if he knew just how grateful she was to him for his gentle and prosaic quietism. A little, old hotel porter! Yes; but he was more than that, unquestionably much more than that.

"It's about the country?"

"Yes. You'll understand. Some books don't make one feel worse—about life. I ask for a philosophy or some sort of mystical act of living. When a book gives me that——"

She let him see her eyes.

"I buy it—if I can afford it. You see—I used to make my living by selling books, and now—I buy—well—perhaps about six a year. I had better go and look at that kettle."

When he returned with the teapot, milk, sugar, and two cups, she was sitting in his chair with the book lying in her lap. A kind of instant smile came into her eyes directly he entered the room, as though he was one of those rare and mystical persons to whom she could hold up a mirror. She did not think of it in that way; she was not thinking at all. She may not have known that her face opened itself to him as it did, or that this old fellow with a tea-tray felt to her as she looked.

"Disgraceful habit—tea drinking. Is it milk and sugar for you?"

"Please."

She noticed how clean the hand was which held the sugar-tongs. So—he had been a bookseller.

She said: "Do you ever walk as far as our cottage?"

"Often. Every other Sunday, perhaps. From the high beech woods over your way Castle Craven looks like an old wood-cut."

"Just. An illustration from Albrecht Dürer. Next time—won't you have tea with us?"

He made her a little bow.

"With very great pleasure."

She drank her tea, and he foraged out a tin of biscuits—
Bath Olivers—a luxury he kept for Lance, and she took one
and broke it almost as though she were breaking a sacramental
wafer. His white head shining in the lamp-light surprised
her sense of the beauty and the dignity of things. She felt
soothed and reassured in this little room of his. She thought
and was sure that she had never met anyone quite like him.
He was unique.

She finished her tea. He had finished his before her, and she
saw him go to the door and open it, and stand looking up and
out.

"Stars shining now. Lovely night. When you are ready
I'll get my hat."

She put her cup down on the table.

"Oh, please—you mustn't."

"I often go for a walk before turning in. I'm going for one
now. The honeysuckle will be smelling in the hedges."

"It's nearly two miles," she said.

"I can take the short way home. Know every inch of it.
Supposing we go by the town?"

He took his hat from a peg behind the door, and turned to
find her standing and looking at him with full, wide eyes.

"I had better turn the lamp out, and leave a candle here.
I'm a man of method. Now—my dear."

Her lips quivered. How droll to be called "my dear" by
him, and yet how right and natural! She moved to the door
so that he could turn out the light.

"I've got the book," she said.

"That's right. Come in here and choose one any time you
want to." She was out under the stars, and the Venerable was
locking the door.

3

In the darkness she felt herself nearer to him. In the empty
High Street he took the outside of the narrow pavement, and

though he was an old man, and two inches shorter than she was, he gave her the impression of being as big and solid as the tower of the church. But "solid" was not the inspired word. She was thinking of his clean old hands, and those very blue eyes, and his air of infinite and wise kindness. She had that exquisite sense of being understood, of being able to lay her hand in his, and that anything that she wished to say could be said.

"How empty!" she said as they descended the steep darkness of the old street.

"It's the town's hour—I always have a feeling that the churches and the houses and the inns stroll about and talk to each other when people have gone to bed."

"What a fancy! You see things like that?"

"Yes."

"So do I."

At the end of Bridge Street she paused on the crown of the bridge and looked over and down at the water. The river was very still on this summer night, with the stars blinking in it, and the piers of the bridge and the passing water making a soft, wet whispering.

She said: "Mr. Pybus, have you ever thought what it means to be blind?"

He—too—was looking at the water.

"Have I? Yes. But can one think oneself—into that? Like living in a black tunnel that roars and whispers. Every sound exaggerated."

She was very still.

"Oh—a kind of purgatory, in which you blunder against things."

"And people."

"Yes, and people."

"And hurt them."

She made a little sound as of drawing in her breath.

"And hurt them! How do you understand that?"

"I don't quite know, but I do. Also, my dear, living with a soul that is blind."

"Soul or eyes?"

H

"Both. There's a likeness, isn't there? Both sorts of blindness blunder against you and hurt."

"I wonder how you know these things?"

"I have lived a long time. Besides—how does one know things? How is it one can feel quite sure about something you've never seen?"

"And that something?"

"What we used to call—God."

Her stillness was like a silent reaching out to the realities that are divined but not seen.

"Tell me."

He had taken off his hat.

"Why does one do things and go on doing them—things against oneself. I mean—what are supposed to be unselfish things. Is there unselfishness? Say there's a splinter, and you push your finger against it, knowing that it will hurt. And you go on doing this—not because you want to—but because there seems to be something in you——"

"They used to say it was God in you."

"Yes—yes; but now—in these days—when people are decently selfish and selfishly decent—some of them."

"Most of them. Fact is—we are looking round for a new word, a nice, scientific, high-brow word to paste over the obsolete divine. Why does anything happen?"

"I don't know."

"Does anybody know?"

"We know a great deal."

"Know! We observe. We see and feel things happening. When a tree falls you explain it. When the milk boils over— you explain it. You allow for these things. But when you feel some beautiful mystical urge towards beauty of thought or behaviour—when you feel lifted up—immediately you say: 'This can't be so. It doesn't happen. It's self-suggestion—or something. Let's look in the psychology book.' But—it does happen. It's a reality. It's the one reality that's worth while. But we are all shy and self-conscious these days in the presence of the thing we used to call our soul. We are afraid of the people in spectacles, of the horn-eyed high-brows.

Talking of walking with God, well—I've walked with Him. I don't know how or why—but I have."

She said:

"Perhaps you have walked with yourself. I'm glad you have talked like this."

4

He went with her as far as the white gate in the "Marions" hedge, and there she gave him her hand. The stillness of the summer night had descended upon her; she felt soothed and reassured.

"Thank you—ever so much. I'm afraid you will be very tired."

He held her hand.

"I was tired—when you came, but not now. Whenever you are in Castle Craven—and feel that you want to rest or to get away from the world——"

She seemed to be thinking; her glance was upward.

"If I brought my brother, would you—would you talk to him——? I mean—I could bring him in the car with me, and leave him in it. You might have time. He's so shut up inside himself."

"Yes, bring him."

"That's good of you, Mr. Pybus. Good night."

"Good night, my dear."

She went up the path to the cottage, and he saw a slip of light as the door opened. Also he heard a voice.

"That you, Mary?"

"Yes."

"What a time you've been. Where's Bob?"

Then the door closed, leaving the Venerable standing by the white gate, and thinking how strange it was that neither of them should have spoken of the thing that had brought her to his door. But he knew, and he was sure that she knew that he knew, and that she had been grateful to him. Hers was a fine and a fastidious reticence.

"Yes," thought the Venerable, "some of us don't want

to talk about such things when they happen to us, not like the Maria woman in 'Mrs. Cheyney.' I wonder how much of the world is Maria and how much is not? Of course, it's the fashion to regard all women as Marias—more or less. But I wonder——"

He walked home.

CHAPTER XX

I

SAID Mrs. Gasson of No. 17, when she heard of the river expedition: "Well, if the young things haven't some cheek these days!" And going on to argue the case, with a loaf of bread against her immense bosom, so that it resembled the head of some monstrous infant taking sustenance: "No morals. Not as I'm criticizing. They do just what they want to do. Course, people always did that—in a sense, but more sneaky like."

For Lance Pybus's world had much to say of him during those six months, and undoubtedly he deserved it. He had arrived suddenly at one of those periods of youthful inflation when everything youthful in him was emphasized and exaggerated—his trousers, his ties, his cigarette-holder, his adjectives, his appreciation of woman as woman.

John Richmond, having read two more of Lance's short stories, and laid one of them aside for rejection, reminded himself that he had responsibilities, and asked Lance to lunch. They met at the "Reform," Lance wearing a hat very broad in the brim, and a floppy tie. Richmond, dressed much as everybody dresses at the "Reform," noted these exuberances.

Swelled head!

They went in to lunch. Richmond had reserved a little table for two at the end of the dining-room, and while he was scribbling down the dishes on the yellow slip, Lance observed his neighbours. He did not look at the plane trees in the Carlton Terrace gardens; six months ago they would have been very noticeable to his eyes.

"Well, that's that. What will you drink? Draught ale, or some white wine?"

"I think—white wine."

His inflation was not literary but amatory, yet how was

Richmond to know that? Having settled the wine, he fired at Lance point blank across the table.

"Say, my lad, those tales of yours are damned clever; also—they are damned cheap."

Lance's eyes seemed to widen. He accepted bread from the bread-basket proffered by the waiter.

"Is that so? I'm sorry. You've got a really—exquisite crowd here, Richmond. They may be very eminent men, but—my Harry—their clothes!"

Richmond's curt eyes gleamed.

"Quits," he said. "All square. I suppose you thought I was rude to you."

"Not a bit. Those tales may be a little fresh."

The soup arrived, and with his eyes on his plate, Richmond went further.

"Two points of view, Pybus. Mine—at forty-five, yours at four and twenty. You may be a brilliant young beggar. My feeling is—you've lost your sense of landscape. I asked you here to tell you so. It's an opinion; that's all."

Lance smiled at him.

"Thanks, sir. I'm sorry. I don't think I'm a landscape man—any longer. I can't help it."

Richmond looked up at him over his soup spoon.

"Tell me, lad, haven't you young things any reverence?"

Lance appeared to reflect.

"I suppose—that has always seemed so. There are things. But you don't remember, sir, being full of red blood?"

"Red bunkum! Oh, I know the phase. I had it, and I came to the conclusion that it was a pity. Take Conrad. As a writer—he escaped that phase—perhaps, because he picked up the pen rather late. There's reverence in Conrad. There must be——"

"Quite. But one sees—what one has to see."

"Your little totties, and your fat stockbrokers, and your people with squashed faces! Oh, come now! A year ago —you were seeing quite different things. I want you to see those things again. I'm not a city father."

There was a slight flush on Lance's face. He swallowed a rather large piece of bread.

"Yes, those other things. I know. You're quite right, and I'm quite right. All the same, it's awfully decent of you to take the trouble. Oh, yes—I mean it."

After that there was peace, or rather—a truce between them, and over coffee and cigars in the smoking-room, Richmond extended a big, inward hand.

"Finished the novel—yet?"

"Another ten chapters or so."

"Don't forget—the end of September. If it's what I have every right to hope it. Spring publication."

Lance's eyes lit up.

"It's awfully decent of you, sir."

Meanwhile, at Windover, Dolly Pybus was worrying her husband. Hadn't he observed that Lance was "funny?" Had he appreciated the fact that their son had not been to Windover for quite six weeks?—while she happened to know that Lance had been absent from Parham Crescent for three week-ends. And where did he spend those week-ends? As for Parham Crescent, didn't Probyn know his way about the world—and if Parham Crescent wasn't full of little totties——?

Probyn squinted.

"Same for everybody—no use in fussing a lad like Lance. Better leave him alone."

"Why—only six months ago——! You never did know your own mind, Byn, for three months together."

"Adaptation, my dear."

"And what about his allowance?"

"Well, what about it?"

"You're not going to cut it?"

"Probably."

"That's mean."

"He can come to me if he wants to. I told him so. I'm not so sure I don't respect the lad all the more for wanting his own way."

"I never knew any man so inconsistent. You started off with the idea——"

"I did. Adaptation, Dolly. I haven't more than half a foot left in the business. I took a man's tip. He said to me: 'Pybus, don't you put a penny into any concern that's dependent on British labour. The British working-man's an awkward beast, and he's going to stay awkward for years.' I came to the conclusion that that man was right."

"After the last strike?"

"Yes."

"Who was the man?"

"An American."

"Don't they have strikes in America?"

"Plenty. But they work in between. Half my money's over the other side of the water, old girl."

"So you've changed your mind about Lance and the business?"

"That's about it."

"Surely you're not going to back him up in his scribbling."

Probyn twiddled a waistcoat button.

"If he shows he has the guts for it."

"Don't be so vulgar."

"Sorry, old girl. But if the lad's got it in him to make a name—like some of these other fellows—Bennet—and that Galsworthy chap—and the fellow who writes plays—what's his name—Noel Coward—why not? That chap Richmond's taken him up. He's got a big pull. If Lance makes a hit over here, and spills over into America, I'd like to see him get some of those dollars."

His wife breathed heavily.

"Well, you men are funny! Why don't you let the allowance go on?"

Said Probyn:

"I'm not quite a fool, Doll. Most men have to be driven. I guess Lance is one of the other sort. Got his own engine inside him."

2

It so happened that the Berkshire Pybus was visiting the Buckinghamshire Pybus on the very Saturday when Lance and Olive allowed themselves the adventure upon the river that shocked Mrs. Gasson to admiration. In fact Conrad drove his car over Marlow bridge five minutes after the adventurous punt had passed beneath it, equipped with green canvas cover, cooking-stove, camp bedding, and a hamper. Parham Crescent had gone on the river for the week-end. Lance had arranged for the punt and the outfit with a boat-house keeper who supplied camping equipment. At the boat-house Olive Gadsden, addressed as "M'am," had rippled over with mischief.

"Don't put the hamper there, dear. Aren't husbands terrors?"

That they were quite irresponsible goes without saying; yet had Conrad Pybus been able to look down into that punt as it glided under Marlow bridge he would not, with his usual facility, have thought of his nephew as "That damned young fool." Mr. Conrad would have been considerably piqued and annoyed. There are varying hierarchies of fools, and follies of graded dimensions. Always Conrad had been cautious; he was no buccaneer, and no Jason; nor—on that July day—did Lance remember the mythical Argo and the black billows of the Euxine.

It was the climax of Lance's obsession. The gliding water, the Bisham beech woods, heavily green in the July heat, the willows, that fervent blue sky, were but tapestries hung upon the walls of his consciousness. To begin with they reclined at opposite ends of the punt, with their gear piled between them, lazily paddling. The mood of the day was youth's —"I will," a challenge to all the pedagogic, "Thou shalt nots."

Said she—sleek as a cat on her orange and blue cushions:

"How are you liking it—boy?"

With the paddle laid across the punt he looked at her and continued to look.

"The Golden Apples of the Hesperides! The sun on your skin is wonderful—a kind of glow——"

She made a little grimace.

"What about a sunshade? But I don't freckle or scorch."

They made tea under the flickering shade of a big poplar. The Primus stove showed itself possessed of a sense of humour, and in persuading it to burn, their hands touched. Her short dark hair, crisp and scented, brushed his forehead. He kissed one of her ears.

"Olive——"

"Dear old thing."

She ran the tip of a first finger down his cheek.

"You've got a skin like a girl's."

"I haven't. Try my chin."

"Lordy—you'll have to shave to-morrow morning. Won't it be funny? Can you manage with Thames water?"

He rubbed his cheek against her hair.

"Hot water—all right. The place I know of where we can lay to for the night—fits you out with eggs and hot water. All the advantages of civilization."

"What's it like?"

"An ex-officer man and his wife run a bungalow and a garden. Give teas and lunches. There is a little backwater where they let you tie up."

"Won't there be a crowd?"

"Plenty of room. I've arranged——"

"And can I go in and powder my nose?"

"Once an hour—if you want to."

It was as he said. That accommodating rest-house stood on a little island separated from the mainland by a narrow backwater that was like a green and silent tunnel. You could land; you could take a walk across the fields to a village and buy cigarettes and picture postcards. The day was full of good fortune, but bad for trade. Lance pushed the punt in the backwater under an alder tree. He went ashore and had a few friendly words with the ex-officer man, who was a little depressed over the solitude of the surroundings. Lance was not.

"We can rig you out with a little dinner in the garden. Quite simple—you know—but Chinese lanterns. I suppose you've brought your own cellar?"

"Splendid," said Lance.

"If your lady wants anything, my wife——"

"I'll go and tell her."

Later, three more punts arrived, but they contained people of discretion who showed a nice delicacy in mooring themselves at a considerable distance from their fellows, and the only offence was that one of them carried a young man who played very badly upon the ukulele. There was to be a moon. Lance, preparing to spread the green canvas cover, told Olive that he had arranged specially for that moon; also, that they were to dine by the light of Chinese lanterns.

"Boy," said she—busy with a suit-case, "did you think to bring any candles?"

He had forgotten the candles.

"A man would."

"Well—make allowances. Our great-grandfathers—who were poetical jossers, would have sworn that beauty's eyes would be sufficient."

"Thanks so much. What candle-power are my eyes? Also, what are we to do?"

"I'll buy a candle. The ex-warrior up above is sure to stock them. Or we'll borrow a Chinese lantern. Give me a hand, my love, with this contraption, will you! Did you ever read 'Three Men in a Boat'?"

"No. Never heard of it, darling. How very dull! It must have been written years and years ago."

"It was. But it had a dog in it."

"And no petticoat?"

"Not one—if I remember."

"Or they didn't mention it. That's much more likely."

They dined in the garden of the bungalow under what appeared to be a very young and precocious apple tree which had gone all to leg, with two Chinese lanterns dangling up above in a haze of green gloom. There was a table-cloth, but they had to drink the red wine which Lance had brought with him out of sixpenny tumblers. As the ex-officer had prophesied, the dinner was simple: the savoury being sardines on toast, and the sweet, tinned apricots with dabs of cream. But they finished the bottle of wine between them, and laughed, and looked at each other consentingly, and became aware of the moon unfurling a silver ribbon across the blackness of the river. Coffee was provided. They lit cigarettes from the same match.

A white footbridge spanned the backwater, and they took their cigarettes with them, and wandered along a field path, with the moon looking impertinently over the hedge-top. They had achieved the unusual; they had escaped from the crowd, from the splurge of humanity.

Said Lance:

"Has it occurred to you that this is about the first occasion on which we have managed to be alone?"

"Seems so. What's your arm doing?"

"But isn't it a tragedy! Ever been to Newlands Corner, or Runnymede, or a place like that—on a bank holiday?"

"Can't say I have."

"Humanity like flies crawling on meat."

"But they like it."

"Think so?"

"Of course they like it. Take the crowd away from modern life—my dear—and where are you?"

"That's true. Our culture's a crowd culture."

"Say, we are getting pompous."

At ten o'clock they prepared to turn in. Lance had procured a candle from the ex-officer, and he attached it to the top of a tin on the hamper in the centre of the punt. The young gentleman in one of the other punts was still playing the ukulele. There were little bursts of laughter, and scufflings, and an unravelling of rugs and cushions. The queer little mattresses provided by the boat-house keeper emitted creakings which suggested straw.

"What's yours like, boy?"

"A little bit—intolerant."

"Oh, I say, you must hold up something."

"All right. You get settled first."

He spread a towel over the handle of a paddle, and smoked a cigarette behind this screen. He heard rustlings; the punt rocked slightly.

"All right, boy."

He lowered the towel, and saw her sitting there on the rugs in a pair of cerise-coloured pyjamas, her black hair fluffed out, her eyes very bright.

"Your turn. Shall I hold up something?"

He looked at her steadily.

"That's some colour. I shan't be a second. The thing is to make sure of your collar-studs."

She held up a rug.

"Get busy."

"I say, is that bold fellow going to scratch at that little boy's thing all night?"

"Slow music—darling."

"Collar-studs in one's pocket; that's it."

"Got everything?"

"Everything."

"Quite sure?"

"Quite. All serene."

She lowered the rug.

"Who's going to blow out the candle?"

"I will."

"If you like—you can come across and tuck me up."

CHAPTER XXI

I

IN a whimsical moment Mary Merris had referred to her little old car as "Jude the Obscure," though whether she thought of the book and the chariot as being equally pathetic and dusty were not points that she elaborated. But on those crowded August days she insinuated her decrepit two-seater into the broad passage leading from the Saracen's yard to the Venerable's cottage. She brought her brother with her. He remained in the car while she disposed of her produce and did her shopping. Wearing no hat, and dressed in an old black and gold blazer, a boating sweater and grey flannel trousers, he sat there with a peculiar rigidity of head and shoulders.

"Gil, this is Mr. Pybus."

On that first occasion the Venerable was conscious of feeling the distinct shock of Gilbert Merris's strangeness. The closed eyelids were the eyelids of a man asleep, and yet the face had a peculiar and attentive wakefulness. It was a handsome head and a weak head, the upper lip and chin covered with a dark dapple of soft hair like the virgin hair on the face of a Greek youth in marble. The closed eyelids produced an effect that was curious and slightly sinister. Sometimes a supercilious smirk seemed to hover over the still face. It had both a placidity and a mobile peevishness.

The stillness of him as he sat there was his most noticeable feature—that and the droop of his closed eyelids. No part of him moved. He suggested a statue listening attentively, and with a slightly sardonic expression. At times there would be a twitching of the nostrils or a tremor of the lips. He sat with his arms tightly pressed to his body, the closed hands resting on his thighs. The figure had an extraordinary stillness, but it was the stillness of tension.

When old Pybus spoke to him the change was instant and

vivid. The head turned with a little jerk, and the eyelids confronted the voice and its owner.

"Oh, you're the porter here. Quite a bookish person— I hear."

His voice was affected, his animation strangely lacking the light of his eyes. He gave the Venerable the impression of being shaken by his own breathing.

Mr. Pybus rested his arms on the side of the car.

"Not quite a bookish person."

His voice was gentle, for he was conscious of pity; but, also, he was conscious of a slight feeling of repulsion. He tried to get the impression of what that face would be like with the eyes alive in it. He thought the sensous mouth above the little dark Assyrian beard too much like soft red fruit.

The Saracen yard was full of cars and chauffeurs, and of people who were packing luggage away, and the Venerable —between his comings and goings—remained beside Mary Merris's car.

"Very busy to-day, sir."

Said her brother, with a curious little twisted smile:

"You don't know how silly—all that sounds to me."

"Silly?"

"Silly and interesting. I suppose most things are silly and interesting."

"The voices?"

"Ugly."

"I suppose your sense of hearing is very quick—sir?"

"Oh, too much so; too much so."

His self-pity betrayed itself in a kind of whisper.

"Most modern sounds are ugly."

"Are they?"

"Your culture—Mr. Pybus, is that of a boy kicking an empty tin along the street. Horrid disharmonies."

There were white pigeons on the roof above, and old Pybus gave a characteristic whistle and the birds—poised on white wings—came floating down.

"Can your hear them?"

"Wings. I can feel the wind of them."

The Venerable had a bird perched on either wrist.

"If you are gentle, sir, they'll let you stroke them."

But when Merris put out a hand the birds flew away, leaving behind them on his blind face a look of vacancy and of annoyance. His fingers came into contact with the Venerable's right arm.

"Gone?"

"You put out your hand too quickly."

"Just like humans. They run away from you—if you are deaf or blind."

The tragedy of his blindness was also the tragedy of his self-pity. Theoretically his music should have sufficed him, filling his dark world with luminous sound; but he was not sufficiently the impersonal artist to lose himself in the rendering and the giving. He was older than his sister, yet, when they were together, she was the mother and he the child. Coming down through the crowded yard she would look anxiously at his somnolent face. Even her smiling glance at old Mr. Pybus was an appeal to one who understood.

"Have I been a long time, Gil?"

"I'm used to sitting."

His manner to her could be shallow and casual. She took it as she took his blindness. She was amazing, and yet she made mistakes. She would bring him sweets, or a new brand of tobacco, and his acceptance of her little presents was tacit— and slightly sullen.

Old Pybus, watching them from day to day, and having perhaps more understanding of the unregenerate male in every man, began to wonder and to doubt. Wasn't the whole devotional business a mistake? Was she not giving too much, and he—in his blindness—sick and satiated with her giving? The relationship was too exacting. Both of them were growing irritable under the strain of it—though while she was able to repress her ego, the man—her brother —could not.

Often she would go into the Venerable's cottage to borrow a book, and if he happened to be free he would follow her. He began to question her taste in books, not openly, but to himself. It seemed that she asked to discover in a book those sad disharmonies which were her own, perhaps without realizing that her appetite was tending towards bitter fruit. She did not crave for and seek out the conventional contrasts.

Now, there is in life a necessary and a wholesome grossness, a hearty animalism which some women—and the most sensitive and fastidious of women—may fail to understand. Old Pybus would wonder whether Mary understood it. She had accepted self-repression. She was like a woman who, when a natural hunger clamoured in her, ate less and less in order to chasten her inward self. She was making a cult of devotion, scourging herself to it, like some wilful saint in a nunnery; and the pity of it was that she was not made for such celibacies. That was the Venerable's impression. She had put away her colours. As for the brother, he made old Pybus think of the child who was tired of being good.

2

The Venerable had some understanding of the child who is tired of being good, and of the sudden tantrums which shock those people who, having locked life up in a dark cupboard, are indignant and a little frightened when they hear the hammering of its fists.

On a very hot day in August, with chauffeurs trying to find shade for their cars and hanging rugs over the mud-guards to screen the tyres, old Pybus saw Merris struggling with the hood of his sister's car. He was kneeling on the seat and trying to raise the hood, but it was one of those cussed contraptions which might be expected to play tricks on a blind man. It would come so far and no farther. At the critical moment it collapsed with a kind of wooden laugh; and Merris, overbalancing, lay doubled up over the back of the car.

Someone guffawed, someone who may have not realized the other man's blindness. The sprawling figure regained its knees. Merris had heard that laugh, and his face flamed to it.

"It's easy to laugh—you swine."

He got on his feet, holding to the screen of the car, and the man who had laughed was laughing no longer.

"Who's a swine?"

"That cackling fool——"

"Am I? I'm not taking lip from a bloody toff in a broken-down pram."

The Venerable intervened.

"Can't you see the man's blind? You might have helped him—instead of——"

There was peace. He who had laughed—a little chauffeur in a smart green livery—fell over himself with that inherent English decency.

"Sorry—sir. I wasn't meaning——"

The Venerable patted his shoulder.

"That's all right, my lad. Let's get that hood up."

They got it up over a figure which had relapsed into the shabby seat, and was sitting there tense and rigid with its arms pressed to its sides. The man in green was awkwardly and regretfully cheerful.

"It is hot, and no mistake. I had the sun in my eyes, or I shouldn't have mugged it."

He looked appeasingly at Merris, who sat there like a man in a stark trance, and took no notice of either of them.

He continued in that state, while the little chauffeur with a quirk of the head and a "Well, I suppose he's funny" glance at the Venerable, sheered off. Pybus remained by the car, under whose patched brown hood that blind face seemed to hang like a bubble that was about to burst.

Should he speak, or should he leave, Merris alone? There was something in that explosive yet rigid quietude. He was about to slip away when he saw a kind of spasm pass up Gilbert Merris's arms.

"Anybody—there?"

"I'm here."

"Mr. Pybus. He—he called me—a bloody toff in a broken-down pram!"

"He was sorry afterwards."

Merris's fists began to drum upon his knees.

"A bloody kid in a pram! That's it. A silly, squalling, helpless brute. By God—he's about right. Get me something to drink, will you?"

"A glass of water?"

"No, get me my bottle, the babe's bloody bottle. Here—something to drink—something stiff."

He stuffed a hand into a trouser pocket.

"I'm allowed five bob a week. What's this—a shilling or a halfpenny?"

"A shilling."

"Get me something stiff, yes, for the pity of God. I've got to have something stiff."

And the Venerable went for it. There are times when the stormy child in a man has to be humoured—but as he returned with that glass of grog he wondered how far such a child should be humoured.

A week later, on another such August day, John Pybus observed further happenings. He had been helping an owner-driver to fasten his luggage on the luggage grid, and had pocketed a two-shilling piece, when a voice hailed him in passing.

"Well, Pybus, plucking the pigeons?"

The Venerable followed him with his eyes. Much raw spirit may come from Glasgow, and also a raw sense of humour which is essentially Scotch, a kind of dry and blurting rudeness which resembles the gruffness of a little terrier, but Hargreaves was not Scotch. The brown bigness of him held on towards the Merris car.

"Hallo, my lad."

"That you, old chap?"

"Come in and have a drink."

Merris fumbled his way out of the car with a smile on his blind face, and Hargreaves, taking him by the arm, piloted him across the yard and in by the Saracen's side door, the surreptitious door that was used by the gay fellows of the town.

Old Pybus followed them in, and watched them into the lounge. He stood by his brass gong, able to see and to hear.

"Couple of double whiskies, George."

"Right, sir. Very hot to-day, sir."

Ten minutes later the Venerable was listening to the brother's facile and foolish laughter, while he waited for his sister. Now, just how would she appear? He had his own picture of her coming in at that side door and up the rather dark passage, inwardly flinching, but refusing to let herself flinch. And it happened as he had foreseen. She came in with a kind of swiftness, her face asking to be left unlooked at. She passed the door of the private bar, and the office window.

"Mr. Pybus——"

He inclined his head slightly in the direction of the lounge. She passed on. He saw her go straight towards the two men in the far corner. She looked at her brother; never once did she look at Hargreaves.

"Gil, I'm ready."

Hargreaves stood up. He stared at her. There was a kind of brutal playfulness in his full eyes. Merris remained in his chair.

"I'm coming back with Bob."

She stood a moment, looking down at her brother.

"Are you coming with me, dear?"

"No," he said. "I'm not," and his defiance ended in a kind of foolish giggle.

She turned and walked straight out of the lounge. She was very white. She paused for a moment by old Pybus.

"I'm leaving him. You will be here?"

"I shall," said he.

3

At "Mirabeau's" on idle occasions, Olive Gadsden and the other young women dealt with life as though they were disposing of French pastry in a tea-shop.

"Oh, my dear, he's a nice kid, quite a nice kid, but a bit difficult."

In the affair between Lance Pybus and Olive Gadsden, there

were no suppositions and no arrogations. Youth is very wise these days, yet however modern you may be, there is always the danger of your reverting to the archaic outlook of your parents. But Olive had put on and off a series of these affairs, as she put on and took off the frocks at Chalfont Street. Marriage was the sort of dress you had to wear until it was shabby, and marriage—according to her own observations—wears very badly in the nineteen-twenties. She was quite without cynicism, for cynicism is an obsolete negation. She was just a sophisticated, practical, and hard-eyed young woman, who handled life's affairs as she would have handled bargains at a sales counter. She had a fallacious softness, a perfect complexion, and she was as hard as nails. She desired certain things, and if they were to be got she got them.

But is there a woman living who is completely unconventional?

Mrs. Gasson asked that question, though she did not use those very words.

"Don't we all come to hanker after the smell of the orange blossom, dearie?"

She could have pointed out that even the oldest of the professions has its code. If your skirt is knee-high, and your stockings of a particular colour, you are still one of a crowd. A crowd must have its conventions. And Olive had her own peculiar conventions. She had an open mind as to a possible marriage with Lance, but she intended him to suggest marriage. In the minds of all women that little gold circle retains its symbolism.

But as yet Lance had not produced that conventional and gentlemanly gesture. He was absorbed in the sex of her, and she knew it. It might be said that he was behaving as the Victorian cad was supposed to behave; but the margin between caddishness and naturalism is a very narrow one, and Lance was being ruthlessly yet impulsively natural. That is modernity, and Olive understood it.

Because there was in their relationship none of that mysticism, that over-mastering and beautiful tenderness which raises woman above the leopardess. Moreover, the leopardess is justified by her instinct. They were not lovers as lovers should be, and she knew it. She knew it, because, once in her life—and in spite of her hardness, she had experienced that tenderness, and it had turned to bitterness in her mouth. It may be that she knew that every woman—somehow and at some time—has been ready to give of herself utterly and completely, consumed by that ridiculous and saving compassion which is the blood in the body of her love.

But then every woman—as a woman—has a kind of professional pride.

Again, Mrs. Gasson could describe it.

"We do like to be asked, dearie, don't we? I must say as I do like a gentleman to take off his hat. It mayn't mean much, you know, but it's manners—manners!"

4

Lance was not happy.

He was smoking too much, and his work was indifferently done. Also, he was conscious of its indifference, and was both bothered and baffled by it, yet nothing he could do seemed able to mend it. He had lost both his touch and his vision.

Also, in six weeks' time, Richmond was expecting to read the novel.

Also, he was beginning to wonder whether the Venerable had not been right in misliking those five chapters.

Also, at the end of September, the cheques from Windover would cease to arrive.

Problems, and very serious problems, but the essential problem was his own intimate self and its sex escapade, and its merging into sense-impressions that were symbolized by Olive Gadsden's mouth. He was not happy about Olive, and he was not happy about himself. If words only conceal the truth, then romanticism and realism are but terms invented for the justification of a phase or of a physical tendency. There is no romance and no realism, nothing but our own reactions and the sublimation of our own sensations.

Yet, during those August days, Lance was made to remember his grandfather's mysticism. It hung there like the light beyond the hills; it was the other world, that eternally other world, the bourne of our inmost urges, the home of the thing which is somehow better than the thing of the moment. There was nothing mystical about Olive Gadsden. He had reclined with her at a little pagan feast; they had halved the apple, and emptied the same cup. Curious—that now there should be no apple and no wine!

Unable to write, afraid of the pen and the paper, he would sit at his window at night with the lights out, thinking. His thoughts seemed to go groping down those restless streets. Had this city infected him with its infernal restlessness? The faces seemed to have changed, or was it that he saw them differently? The strained, set faces of some of the bus drivers, the faces of hurrying and worried women! What was the matter with him? Why the devil couldn't he get life down on paper as he had been getting it three months ago?

Olive? Yes, but he and Olive had only done what thousands of people did, the supremely natural thing. Was he becoming emotionally self-conscious, sexually diffident? He knew lots of men who were boastful and exultant in the successful swelling of their youth. They told a tale, laughed, and passed on.

What was the matter with him?

Rushing out on one of these evenings of ineffectual restlessness he felt that he must talk to somebody, a man, a man of his own age. There was Sorrell; he had not seen Kit Sorrell for some months. The urge was instant. He climbed on to a bus and went eastwards, and getting off at King's Cross, cut into Bloomsbury. He found himself on Sorrell's doorstep, looking at the London greenness of the Bloomsbury Square, and hearing voices. Girls were playing tennis.

Into his head—suddenly—came the word—"Marriage." It shocked him; it brought with it a kind of frightened silence. Unless you were a cad, a mere animal, you married a girl when she had given you intimate and unforgettable moments.

The door opened. He was aware of a face, plain and tired.

"Is Mr. Sorrell in?"

Yes, Mr. Sorrell was in.

He found Kit at work, sitting at a table by the window, the same old Kit, but a little slower of speech, and more observant of men and of things.

"Hallo, old chap—clear me out if I'm in the way."

"No, sit down. I'm always a little ahead."

"You old devil—you always were. No distractions."

"Oh, I don't know," said Kit, going to the mantelpiece for a pipe.

"Seen anything of Pentreath?"

Young Sorrell opened a tobacco tin.

"Yes, some. He's had rather a rotten time, poor old thing. Got married. The girl turned out—oh—well—you know what."

"No!"

"Yes, the very last chap you'd expect——"

"Poor old Pent. What on earth! You are not out on the marriage market, boy?"

"A mug's game at my age," said Sorrell, applying a match to the tobacco in his pipe.

Lance sat and stared. If he had come to Kit for inward counsel he could not have obtained it more aptly and without less prejudice, for Christopher had always been such a sound beggar, even in his rowing. There was nothing of the "sugarer" about young Sorrell. But just how did Kit manage——? And then Lance happened to notice that the lower sash of the window was closed, and that a muslin blind screened it.

"You work with your window down, old thing."

"Yes."

"I like mine up."

"Oh, I dare say. Distractions—you know. Girls playing tennis out there. Should find myself watching them."

Lance got up, and lifting the edge of the muslin blind, looked out of the window.

"M'yes. Your job keeps you bolted down. Oh, damn sex, my lad, damn it! I sometimes wish——"

"I've wished that too, Pybie, but one's got to put up with it. Apparently—the trouble is—that nice women don't or won't understand. So, the alternative——"

"I don't believe it," said Lance with sudden passion; "the alternative isn't always a totty—surely?"

"No, that's true. But—for me—old lad, nothing or everything. Oh, yes, there are women who make you feel humble."

CHAPTER XXII

I

LANCE was Sir Yea and Nay for a week, and then, because his indecision vexed him, he rushed headlong upon finality. Olive and he set out to spend a second week-end on the river, but the pagan materialism had gone from the adventure, and two young moderns looked at each other with sophisticated self-consciousness.

Moreover, the weather was English and threatening, and Lance had packed five chapters of "Rust" into his suit-case, and he took with him to the Thames the reborn spirit of mysticism.

"How deeply do you see into me? Beyond the skin, the mere glass of the eye, and the redness of the lips? What am I—the man—to you?"

Conversely, what was she to him, eyes, lips, a body whose tricks had inflamed him? Could he see more in her than that, or was she but the product of Chalfont Street and Parham Crescent, a displayer of dresses, a dancer, a pretty piece of physical expression?

The sky was leaden; so was the water; and from the other end of the punt he was aware of her eyes watching him. They made him think of two eyes looking at him through the slits in a mask. The beech woods on the hills had a heavy melancholy, like the foreheads of solemn city fathers frowning over a forward generation.

She was teasing and flippant.

"Don't look so bored, dearie."

"I'm not bored, Olive. And I'm not dearie."

"My landlady calls everybody dearie."

"Let her—by all means. It's going to rain like blazes."

"What fun! A little green tent for two. I wonder if the ukulele boy will be there? Chinese lanterns should be a wash out."

She jangled.   He found himself looking at her critically, as he might have looked at a stranger, and realizing as he looked at her that in spite of their intimacy—they were strangers. It struck him as being rather deplorable, though the fault was as much his as hers; for had he desired to see more in her than the mannequin, or a dancing girl on a stage appealing to him with legs and arms?   They had lost themselves in the physical, and in emerging from things physical he seemed to become aware of her meretricious smartness, the thinness of her, both physically and spiritually.   Yet, could she help it?   Had he asked her to be anything else?   Could she be anything else?

They sighted their Island of the Hesperides.   The white bungalow looked rather soiled and shabby on this grey August day.   Almost it was as shabby and unmystical as an anonymous room in some anonymous back street hotel. Lance conceived distaste for the place as he looked at it, and he was moved to wonder whether it affected Olive in the same way.

She gave a sudden little laugh.

"Dearie, he's taking down the lanterns!"

The owner of the bungalow, looking swollen in a white sweater and flannel trousers, was standing on a garden chair unfastening the Chinese lanterns.   A few heavy rain-drops were making little circles on the dead surface of the river.

"Poor devil!" said Lance.

She jerked a sudden glance at him.   Was her lover feeling like that?   Or just how was he feeling?

"I don't see the 'poor devil.'   He's a careful old thing."

Lance's face was strangely overcast.

"He's a symbolist, the eternal symbolist."

Inevitably the rain came down.   They had to pole hurriedly into the backwater, and spread the canvas cover, and make tea, with the rain dripping from the willows and the alders. English weather, river weather, reality and not romance. After tea, Lance lit a pipe and, with a preoccupied expression, explored the interior of his suit-case.   He had brought with him those five chapters that the Venerable had disapproved of; it was his intention to re-read them.

"What's that, boy?"

"Manuscript. Care to read some?"

He got the impression that her attitude was full of watchfulness and suspicion.

"We're quite domesticated—aren't we? I ought to have brought some sewing."

"Not a bad idea."

He passed her the last of the five chapters.

"Read it. You can give me an opinion."

She asked him for a cigarette, and having lit it, she sat considering him. The pages of MS. lay in her lap.

"Think my opinion's worth anything?"

"It might be. What do you read?"

"Not much, Edgar Garland—and Isaac Gildenstein."

"Edgar Garland?" said Lance. "Good Lord!"

She made a face at him.

"You —do—take yourself seriously. Who's going to wash up the tea things?"

"Woman's department."

"Thanks. We'll do it presently, together. Meanwhile—I'll go and visit Clara."

"Who's Clara?"

"The lady of the bungalow. She's rather amusing. No dinner under the lanterns, dearie, to-night."

He gave her the enigma of a smile.

"Smelly paraffin lamp—probably. Tomato soup, tongue and salad, prunes and tinned milk."

"Pessimist."

"Well—go and see."

She lifted up the flap of the canvas, and uncovered the wet grass bank, and the slimy black stem of an alder. The rain was coming down. She looked a little pathetic.

"Oh—boy—I'll get wet."

He glanced at her flimsy shoes and silk stockings, and suddenly he realized the pathos of her, but not as she would have wished him to realize it. He was aware of her pretty flimsiness, of all her little expedients and ingenuities, her oneness against the world, the finality of her appeal. She had just that face, and that mouth, and her mannerisms, and a kind of cheap defiance. He felt sorry.

"Stay here—I'll go presently."

She looked at him for a moment, and her eyes puzzled him. He did not know how quick a woman can be picking out the threads of a man's moods towards her.

"Thanks—awfully—dear Edgar."

She was out of the punt and up the bank like a cat with wet fur, and he sat and pulled at his pipe, and looked at the grass bank, and tried to sort out the situation. Was it that she suspected? Or could a woman be jealous of a few pieces of paper pinned together with brass clips? Vaguely irritated, he settled himself to read those five chapters.

2

At the end of ten minutes he was relighting a pipe that had gone out. His face was very serious. He was thinking "How did I come to write this stuff?"

He was feeling disturbed and perplexed, for a few weeks ago he had been so sure that he had written something that was both vivid and very clever, but on this wet August evening he saw his impressions hanging like chunks of red meat in a butcher's shop. It was all glare and crude flesh, a butcherly business, and he was conscious of being shocked by it because it was his. The stuff was unpleasant—yes, and more than unpleasant, and vividly was he reminded of the Venerable's simile of the Marylebone Road. Yes, but it was far more unfragrantly suggestive than the Marylebone Road. His imagination, pushed suddenly into the glare of a Saturday night street, seemed to see and to smell its surroundings. Life was uncovered, that part of life which is vulgar and cheap and unclean, the stale sweat in the clothes, the grossness beneath the skin, feet that would not bear looking at when the stockings were peeled off. What had he been doing? For somehow, he had a suspicion that the lapse had been in himself, and in his manner of seeing things. A fact is a fact; but butcher's meat is butcher's meat—but—in this work of his he saw a hand turning over odds and ends of flesh and offals in a tray.

But how was it that he had written the stuff, and thought it good? Had he been obsessed? Had he been seeing too many painted faces, and sploshed faces? It was not that the work was sinister; you can be fastidious and very sinister—but these chapters were vulgar, and vulgarity is a personal product. The thing in itself need not be vulgar; it is the way in which you treat it. And he had given those chapters to the Venerable. He felt hot.

But was it all bad, mere cayenne and tripe? He read on. He was able to assure himself that the rest of it was almost as unpardonable, and that it produced in him a sense of anger and of heat. What muck! Though there was nothing moral—so called—in his gesture of scorn, but the impatience of the craftsman who has caught himself perpetrating baseness. Away with it! The stuff might just as well go into the river.

But he held his hand. Olive came slithering down the bank and into the punt, and she returned with the happy animation of a woman who has thought things over. She sat down amongst her cushions at the far end, and made a whimsical face at him.

"Oh, boy, why didn't we bring gum-boots? Clara, poor dear, won't be able to cook us any dinner."

"Oh, how?"

"Pain in her poor tummy. I'm going to be cook. Say, I want to read some of boy's story."

"You do?"

"Please."

His glance was deliberate and thoughtful. He tossed the chapters across to her.

"Right, you shall. My writing's pretty awful."

"Why don't you have it typed?"

"Economy—and caution. I'm not going to have it photographed until the picture is complete. The critic in the punt. You can say just what you jolly well think."

"And supposing——?"

"Call it tripe. I've only got three cigarettes left; forgot to fill my case. Shall put on a mac and stroll up to the village."

"Leave me one of the three. Thanks, old thing. Now I'm going to be awfully studious."

After slipping off her shoes, she curled up among the cushions, and Lance, getting into his mackintosh, scrambled out and up the bank.

In crossing those wet fields under the grey sky and the dripping elms he seemed to be walking with a lost self that had been recovered; and the fierce chagrin of the craftsman became a sadness. Yes, bad work hurt; it hurt you more than did bad living; for bad work, unless you were ruthless in destruction, remained like some cast mistress exacting blackmail. And the virtue went out of you. The fine mirrror of your consciousness became blurred and tarnished; the girdle of your restraint was loosened. Pausing by a field gate under an old beech tree, he listened to the drippings from leaves, while the soul of him reached out to life's essential mysticism. He began to feel things understandingly, for mysticism is knowing by feeling, and life is recreated and carried on by every man feeling things afresh. The great simplicities recur and are eternal.

Lance felt cooled and calmed by the rain. The grey landscape regained its beauty. He looked up into the green heart of the tree under which he was sheltering, and seemed to absorb its strength and its steadfastness. You had to root yourself like this tree in order to spread your branches. Flounderings among the flesh-pots made you assume the likeness of a human flesh-pot, big-bellied, gross and heavy. To pull your weight in a boat you trained and chastened your body; for the greater and more exacting crafts you had to train and chasten your soul. Had not your craftsman to be something of the ascetic?

He walked on to the village, bought his cigarettes, and returned to the island with a wet head and a secret serenity. He felt strangely gentle towards life, and to that piece of life under the green canopy of the punt. Poor Olive! He had become conscious of the futile crudeness of the affair, and of the damage such an affair inflicted. It cut away your ideals, it blurred your vision; it tricked you into accepting easy, casual things. Was it not true that his splurgings into a false realism had begun with this sex adventure?

He hesitated for a moment on the top of the bank. The ending of such an intimacy was no easy matter, and with this sudden feeling of gentleness possessing him he even doubted for a moment how you ended such an affair. Or did it end itself? Yet there was a ruthlessness in him which cried out that it would have to be ended. He wanted to get back to work, the real work. He was in a growing fever to efface that butcherly phase. The mood of his gentleness would change into impatience and haste. It cost him an effort to slither down the bank and raise the canvas flap.

She met him with her actress's smile.

"Oh, boy, you—are—clever."

She waved a white flag that was his manuscript.

"Wet and clever. What a mop of a head! But I say—this is one of the funniest things I've ever read. It's a yell."

He climbed in with a very serious and unsmiling face.

"Like it?"

"It's lovely. But you're cruel. You do take people off. I'm really—awful—scared of you."

Extracting the box of cigarettes from a mackintosh pocket, he tossed it to her, but without looking at her face.

"So—it strikes you—as good?"

"Topping. Of course—it's a bit so-so—but that's just what people like. Even the old ladies love being shocked, the old humbugs. But where did you learn it all?"

"How do you mean?"

"Why, how do you know about such things? If you had asked me I should have said that some priceless person of forty had written it. Some raffish old blighter."

He was searching in his suit-case for a towel, and having found it, he enveloped his wet head in it and began to rub.

"Yes, a seedy old blighter with all the paint worn off him. I get you, my dear. But—the seedy old blighters are apt to be sentimental. Some young thing of three and twenty. Very young stuff. Gemini—but the rain has got right down my back."

3

On that Sunday morning Lance woke very early. The rain had not ceased, for he could hear the drip of it on the canvas from the boughs of the alder tree, and for a while he lay and listened to it. But presently, being full of the wakefullness of a new inspiration, he slipped a hand under the canvas and raising it until it was clear of the punt's gunwale, he looked at the river. He saw it as a sheet of grey water spreading beyond the green opening of the backwater, with dim beech woods rising beyond it. Everything was smirched by rain. And yet, as he lay on his side and looked long and steadily at the water, and the woods, he knew that—somehow —his old way of seeing things had come back to him.

Meanwhile, he was observed, and was unconscious of it. Olive had raised her head. She was watching his silent contemplation of the river, but when at last he made a movement, she let her head drop back upon the cushion. Her eyes were closed.

4

By mutual consent they returned to town by an afternoon train. They sat at opposite ends of the carriage and looked out of opposite windows, for there was a constraint between them, and the grey chill of the river seemed to linger. They were alone together, yet not alone, while very conscious of each other. If he appeared absorbed in the wet landscape and his own thoughts, she—from her corner—threw an occasional chafed glance at his half-averted profile and his wilful preoccupation.

She was angry. Men were so much of a muchness, so fickle, so inconsistent, and though she was vaguely aware of him as a winged Mercury poised for an upward flight, she

I

still wished to hold him because—in a way—he had been hers. Cold, clean, ruthless, soaring youth! For somehow he reminded her of the poised figure in Piccadilly Circus, so alive though so motionless above the chaotic crowd.

But as the train neared Paddington she slipped across to him, and put her chin upon his shoulder.

"Boy, what's the matter?"

She felt his irresponsive rigidity.

"Nothing. I was thinking something out."

"Awful serious fellah! What about—to-night?"

His reply was abrupt.

"Work, my dear, much work. It is boiling up in me. I have got just five weeks."

"What for?"

"Oh, for the book. I've promised it—for the end of September. It will have to be done."

She withdrew herself.

"That's the sort of thing, my dear, a man says to his wife."

At No. 7 Parham Crescent a sympathetic and inquisitive Mrs. Gasson brought Olive up her tea. She placed the tray on the table by the window and turned to the girl who, seated on the edge of her bed, was changing her stockings. Olive had come in with a thin, peeved face, and eyes of defiance. Obviously the weather had not been kind to the lovers, but Mrs. Gasson could recall days in her own youth when hailstones and hurricanes would not have mattered.

"Now, you drink your tea, dearie."

Olive tossed the discarded stockings into a corner.

"Filthy weather—I'm not a pair of stockings—either."

"There, dearie, you've been quarrelling. You drink a cup of nice hot tea. Nothin' like it. A cup of tea's saved me from sooicide many a time."

She went to pour it out, added two lumps of sugar, and carried the cup to the girl.

"Such weather! Enough to damp a bloomin' Venus. Wasn't he loving, dearie? Men get such moods."

Said the girl on the bed, sulkily stirring the sugar in the cup:

"I'm not going to let him off."

"Feeling like that, are you dearie?"

"He's got me cussed."

Mrs. Gasson stood with her red hands folded over her bosom.

"That's to say—you'll marry him, dearie?"

"I shall. Perhaps you know what it is to feel cussed about a man?"

"Well," said the lady, "I do and I don't. But I wouldn't spite myself for a man, dearie. Specially—a boy gent like 'im. If I was out for the white satin and the orange blossom I'd take someone older and with a bit of money. Now, you try and eat a piece of plum cake, dearie. I wouldn't get cussed if I were you. Men ain't worth it."

Meanwhile, at No. 17, Lance was writing a letter.

"I have torn up those five chapters, grandpater. I shall be with you next week-end."

He went out to post the letter and, returning to his room, took the first twenty chapters of the manuscript of "Rust" from the drawer in his desk, and sat down to read them. He began with a feeling of curiosity and of distrust, but as he read on the feeling of distrust vanished. His face softened. He smiled, but there was nothing of the smirk in that smile. He was recovering the craftsman's sense of rightness and of happy exultation, the consciousness of being able to interpret life with an understanding that was somehow greater than his smaller self. And when he had finished reading the chapters he sat looking out of the window. The rain had ceased. The cool, wet sky was clearing. It was as though Spring had returned with all its tenderness and mystery.

5

Lance, carrying his suit-case across the Saracen yard, whistled to the pigeons on the red roofs. It was tea-time, and he supposed that he would find his grandfather at the cottage, and feeling in a playful mood he walked softly. The green door was open a few inches, and giving it a noiseless push, he stood looking into the familiar room.

But it contained an unfamiliar spirit, the figure of a girl, who, standing by his grandfather's window with her back towards him, seemed to droop like a tall flower at the end of a sultry day. She had her hands on the window-sill, and her dark head was on a level with the purple and gold heads of the Venerable's dahlias.

Something arrested him and held him still, the poise of the figure, the faint perfume of its sadness, the curve of the neck, the droop of the head. He stared. He was met by a sense of mystery, though the figure was just that of a young woman surprised in a moment of self-revealing anguish.

Suddenly, as though made conscious of his presence by the intentness of his gazing, she turned and faced him, and he saw what he had not been able to see before. He lowered his eyes. He could tell that she wished herself veiled.

"I'm sorry. I thought my grandfather was here."

She answered him in a very still voice.

"Yes; he will be here. He——"

Placing his suit-case on a chair, and his hat on the table, he turned away.

"I'll go and find him. It's all right. I didn't know."

And very gently he closed the green door.

CHAPTER XXIII

I

LANCE went in search of his grandfather, and as he recrossed the Saracen yard it occurred to him that this was the first occasion upon which he had seen a woman in tears. He still was very conscious of a pair of wet, brown eyes, surprised and resenting the surprise. But how sentimental! He had seen young women weep on the "films," and he had wanted to smack them; he had felt uneasy in the presence of those hysterical "close ups" when a young woman goes in for exaggerated emotion, and looks—as he had put it—like "A wet gooseberry." Did anyone weep these days? Surely the lachrymatory glands were superfluous, save as the providers of a physiological eyewash? He had rather believed that tears were an exhibition of temper or of childishness; but the tears of Mary Merris, wept in the Venerable's little room, had fallen before him otherwise. She had resented their discovery. They had stirred in him—somehow—little tremors of tenderness, a mysterious tenderness which was like the trembling of leaves in the rain. So must other women have wept, the women of his dream world, the Iseults, The Medeas, the Beatrice Cencis.

Besides, what was she doing there in the Venerable's room? He pushed in through the Saracen's side door, and discovered his grandfather standing at his post by the brass gong where the passage joined the hall. The Venerable's head was all whiteness, which meant that his grandfather's eyes were turned away towards the Saracen's lounge. He was looking at something or somebody, and as Lance walked up the passage he saw two men coming out of the lounge. The taller man had the other by the arm, and the shorter one was laughing, like a man in his sleep. He was a figure of somnolence that cackled.

They passed from view into the hall, and Lance walked on to

speak to his grandfather, but old Pybus's blue eyes had a fixity. The grandson now saw him in profile. The Venerable was watching those two pass out into Castle Craven market-square, the man of the broad nostrils and the man who laughed with his eyes shut. Lance paused for a moment, arrested by the look upon his grandfather's face. It had a grimness.

Lance approached him silently.

"Hallo, grandpater."

There was a quick movement of old Pybus's head. The blue stare went out of his eyes.

"Hallo, my son. Shan't be five minutes. Go and make tea."

"For two?"

The Venerable looked at his grandson, and then he turned and looked at the clock.

"I may as well come now. The lad's about. Well, well——"

They went down the passage together and out into the yard, and Lance knew that his grandfather had something to think about, and perhaps something to say. You could allow the Venerable the use of all his faculties, and assume that if there was a thing to be seen, he would see it, nor would he look grim without provocation. And in Lance's consciousness those two figures had come together, that of the man with the blind eyes, and that of the girl with the wet ones, and there is always a reason for things, even for secret tears and silly laughter.

Said the Venerable, when they were half-way across the yard:

"You went down to the cottage?"

Yes, Lance had been to the cottage, and had left his hat and suit-case there.

"Found you had a visitor, grandpater."

"Still there—was she?"

"Yes. I thought I'd come up and find you."

His grandfather's blue eyes asked a question.

"She looked—rather—as if she wanted to be left alone, grandpater."

And old Pybus said nothing.

To say nothing and to suggest everything is a great art, and the Venerable was the poet of silence. Lance knew these pauses and reticences, and the little, understanding, observant glance that his grandfather would throw at a person or a pipe. Sometimes old Pybus's eyes would seem to change colour; he would look mischievous, or proud, or thoughtful, but always his silence was like the seeming silence of a deep wood. There were little secret sounds to be heard if you kept very still and listened for them, and Lance felt that something was going on inside his grandfather's head. He was conscious of feeling curious as to what his grandfather would do or say.

The Venerable paused on the doorstep and, looking round and up, pointed to the waiting pigeons.

"Same as ever, my son."

"Same as ever—grandpater."

"Like your letter. Great stuff in it, my dear."

Then, having made known their coming to anyone who might be waiting in the cottage, he opened the door, and Lance understood the inwardness of that considerate loitering. The room was empty; yet neither of them remarked upon its emptiness.

The Venerable closed the door.

"Nearly a month, isn't it? I'm glad to see you. I'll go and get tea."

"I'm glad to be here."

"I do believe you are."

They looked into each other's eyes, and then Lance's right hand went out, and rested on the Venerable's shoulder.

"Seems that I come to you only when I want you, grandpater. No. It isn't quite like that. It's good to be here."

The muscles of old Pybus's face quivered.

"That's good for me to know, my dear. A little old fellow."

"No, not that, grandpater. You're as big as the earth."

"Oh, come now! Tea, my lad, tea."

"I'll make it. You sit down, grandpater, please sit down. I have something to ask you."

Old Pybus sat down.

Lance went into the kitchen and lit the oil-stove under the kettle, and saw that the tray was all ready, the milk in the jug, and the bread and butter cut. The very simplicity of these details seemed part and parcel of the situation, and typical of that simplicity which characterized both the head and the heart of this old Roman. You could not be a neo-this or a neo-that in the presence of the Venerable; there was no pose that was adequate, no sort of cleverness that would carry you past the shoulder of a crisis. You had to stand up square and straight, rather like a frank and fearless child, a creature of sheer simplicity, because the ultimate and serene simplicity is childlike, and all circuitous things squirm at its feet.

"Grandpater——"

"My son."

"Which matters most to a man—his job—or a woman?"

The Venerable sat in silence for some seconds.

"Doesn't that depend on two qualities?"

"Yes?"

"The quality of the job, and the quality of the woman?"

The kettle was on the point of boiling, and Lance reached for the teapot.

"You mean—that the two qualities—should be alike?"

"Gentleness, my dear, understanding."

"In both?"

"Is not great writing—gentle and compassionate?"

"And woman?"

"The same. How we have gone astray with all our little hardnesses, and this freedom complex. Freedom—indeed! What freedom has a mother?"

"The old idea, slave to husband and children."

"The slavery of giving, the slavery of loving, the slavery of being loved! Oh, my lad, what shallow water we paddle in! Unless you can see that something in your woman, that holy glamour, that gentleness which makes you feel on your knees, avoid her, run from her. A man must work, and so must woman, but so much of woman's work is for the man."

Lance filled the teapot.

"Grandpater—you stand—against everything—the tenden-cies—the newness——"

"What is newness? I stand where I stand."

"Like the Angel of the Lord."

"Like an old man who has looked at life. See—the mystical in woman—the sacred flame burning within the body of her flesh. It is there, it is there."

Lance appeared in the other room, carrying the tray with its white cloth. His face had an inward radiance, a tranquillity.

"Grandpater, it is good to be here."

And for a while there was silence between them, but Lance was thinking that—perhaps—Mary Merris had found it good to shed tears in this little, funny old room, wherein an old man who had looked on life had brought into being a beautiful faith in the essential somewhereness of God. Yes, and with-out dogmatism and without a contorted gruffness, but just as though he had grown to it by feeling and seeing and thinking.

Lance looked out of the window.

"I wonder if I ought to tell you, grandpater."

"Something about yourself, my dear?"

Lance's eyes smiled.

"No, that's told and finished. I think you understood that, didn't you? Yes. I have been a cad, but I am not going to be more of a cad by being weak. No; it's about the Merris girl."

"Mary. Why, not Mary?"

"Mary. I found her—crying in here. I couldn't help it. I got out as quickly as I could. ''

"Ah," said the Venerable. "I'm glad."

His grandson's eyes were wide and a little questioning.

"You see, my dear, a woman like Mary must have a room to weep in once or twice in a lifetime. And it happened in here. I'm glad."

Said Lance, reaching for the Venerable's cup to refill it:

"Something's wrong with her life?"

"Just pearls and swine, my dear. We may have more words in our language than the jews did in the time of Christ all sorts of isms and exes and ologies and tivities, but the earth and we are made of the same stuff."

2

Lance went back to work on Monday with the creative impatience big in him, and some fifteen chapters demanding to be written in the course of the next thirty-five days.

His promise to John Richmond had no margin left to it, but Lance was not asking for a margin. After scramblings and flounderings he had climbed back to the craftsman's little isolated hill, and the whole urge in him was to write and to write furiously, and to forget everything but those vivid inward pictures that had to be made to flow into the molten metal. He began work that very Monday night. He had walked past and under the window of No. 7 Parham Crescent, with a small part of himself digressing for a moment like a straggler falling out on the march. Oh, yes, Olive! But Olive could wait. She was no mystical woman, but a creature of that other world in which people had ceased to matter as they mattered in the world of his imagination.

He had walked past Mrs. Carver and her apologetic announcements.

"Her ladyship called on Saturday, sir. And a young lady left a letter."

"Let me have dinner sharp at seven, please."

He had opened Olive's note, and replying to it inwardly as he had read it, had torn it up. No, no distractions. He had unpacked; he had got out his papers. The power of concentration had returned to him. When he had passed across to that other creative world, people could bang doors and taxis could hoot, but these noises would not be heard by him. He was able to put external things beyond or below the threshold of sense-consciousness.

About nine o'clock Mrs. Carver crept up the stairs, and stood on the landing outside his door. He had warned her that he was not to be disturbed, but the young woman who had rung the bell of No. 17, and who was waiting in Mrs. Carver's hall, had assured her that Mr. Pybus expected to be disturbed. Mrs. Carver approached his door, listened, and then rapped gently with her knuckles.

There was no response, and she stood there looking bothered. Her fear of offending people had become a pitiful and
ever-present dread. She shook like an aspen leaf if the first
floor front complained of the tea, or rang the bell with unusual
emphasis.

"Oh, dear, what ought I to do.?"

Her diffident knuckles dared to rap a second time.

"Hallo!"

"There's someone asking for you, sir."

"Who?"

"A young lady, the one who left the note. I'm so sorry to
disturb you, sir, but I thought——"

"Will you please tell her I'm working."

"Yes, sir."

"Thank you."

3

Lance's absorption in his work was characteristic and
inevitable, but a woman of Olive Gadsden's temperament
could not be expected to understand its inevitableness. Your
artist may be a fanatic when the urge is upon him, and to the
observer he may appear the ruthless and impossible egoist,
though, because of the fascination of the work in which he is
absorbed, he may be absolutely selfless. Women have been
jealous of a man's craft, sensing in it an alien and impersonal
force which will neither bend nor be persuaded; but Olive
was jealous without understanding just what Lance's work was
to him. To her it was the enemy. It was an affront. It
had "got her cussed." It made of her a hanger-on to the
coat-tails of his casual leisure, an accessory, a shadow.

She did not see Lance for three days, and she made no
attempt to see him, but her obstinacy hardened.

"Oh, very well, my dear; we'll wait."

She could boast to Mrs. Gasson of knowing something
about men. They were quite childish creatures. When a
man was golf-mad or horse-mad, you had to humour the
obsession, and wait for him to emerge from it. Men did

emerge. They became hungry. They craved a meal or a drink, or money or woman. However angrily patient you might have to be, when the man emerged, you had him by the sleeve.

It was Olive's first experience of the author, artist, poet creature—the creative man in contrast to the mule man. It was not likely that she would be able to foresee the permanence and the steadfastness of the urge to write, or to understand that if she tried to interfere with it she would be pushed aside. Were she to display herself as the wild cat, probably he would pick the creature up and deposit it—gently or ungently— outside his door. The more fuss she might make, the less likely he would be to emerge, and when he did emerge, it would not be according to her expectations.

Meanwhile, she remained upon the fringe of Lance's consciousness, not focused, but there, and between periods of fierce and exultant writing his attention was turned to her. She cast a shadow. He could not but feel a little astonished at the way in which the sensuous glamour of her had decreased; the desired of yesterday had become the faded exotic of to-day. Even her mouth had lost its appeal; he was ready to be irritated by her little physical artifices.

But the problem of her remained.

He would say to himself: "This sort of thing can't go on." Having regained his inward vision, he acknowledged the futility of the affair, while realizing that, however modern and tolerant and natural you may be, the instinct of responsibility still functions. He could say to Olive: "We have had our play, my dear. And now—to work. Good luck to you." He could smile and raise his hat, and do the thing in a gentlemanly way, and yet there was a something in him which would not be satisfied.

For he was not the sort of cur that slinks off round a corner. Also, there is a quality in creative work which—when it is being well done—makes a man better than himself. He is drinking the wine of the gods. Also, self-expression is most subtly associated with the particular atmospheres of people and of places. The renewal of Lance's mysticism was associated

with the Venerable, and the Venerable's little room, and with
that other incident of Mary Merris and her tears. Always a
little memory picture was rising before him of a woman
surprised in the midst of her weeping. He could not call it
sentimentalism; he did not call it anything. He was just
conscious of it as he might have been conscious of an effect
of sunlight and of shadow, or of perfume; it seemed to per-
meate life; it permeated his work. It seemed to associate
itself with a new note of tenderness which had been lacking.

Also, it had a positive and a practical effect. It made him
see in Olive something of that other woman, something that
a man should see in every woman. It moved him to a sensitive gentleness. It was as though that glimpse of a woman's
tears had softened his young ruthlessness.

So, one afternoon, with a pipe smoked after tea, and two
pages of manuscript left serenely behind him, he went out and
along the crescent to No. 7, and calmly rang the bell. Mrs.
Gasson opened the door. He looked into her large, red,
accommodating face.

"Is Miss Gadsden in?"

Mrs. Gasson smiled over him and at him.

"She won't be in till after six, sir."

"Can I leave a message?"

"You can, sir."

"Will you please tell Miss Gadsden that I'll call for her at
half-past six?"

"I will, sir."

Mrs. Gasson smirked and closed the door on him, and was
ready with her message. "He's been round, dearie. He's
coming round to call for you at half-past six. You won't be
feeling cussed, will you?"

Olive loitered on the dark stairs.

"That's his affair."

4

Her upward glance at him was both challenging and
whimsical.

"Been working awful hard, boy?"

He said that he had. He walked beside her with an air of a detachment, approaching the conclusion that no piece of work could be more intricate and harassing than the persuading of a woman that her femininities have become superfluous. How did you begin so ungallant a business? Did you blurt out the confession, and then hasten to apply the necessary and bland unguents? And what if Chloe refused to regard the affair as a poetical incident, a mere *fête galante*, though there had been a tacit acceptance of its incidental nature.

He said: "What about a little dinner? Suppose we taxi down to Soho?"

He was all profile to her for the moment.

"Why not!"

"You're free?"

"Quite."

They had crossed into Baker Street, linked no longer like young things in quest of life, he—a little in front, and hurrying and looking as though he expected her to hurry. He paused on the edge of the pavement, raised head expressing swiftness and impatience. He seemed to have the wind in his eyes. His impatience was personal; he was being abrupt and casual when his purpose had arrived at a reasoned gentleness. His first glance at her in Mrs. Gasson's doorway had been sudden and revealing, as though he had not seen her for many months, and had returned to realize her as a stranger. He had been aware of her hard flimsiness. Also, he had begun to be horribly afraid of talking down to her, and all the more so because he was horribly sure that there was nothing in her that could be talked up to.

"There's a chap. Hi, taxi, taxi?"

When the cab swung round to the pavement he opened the door for her to enter. Almost his impulse was to push her in, and to get himself and her and their mutual involvement hidden inside the cab.

"Fleur de Lys restaurant, Soho. Know it?"

"Yes, sir."

"Right."

He got in and sat down beside her.

"How will the Fleur de Lys do for you?"

"Lovely."

The word jarred on him. He was thinking how strange it was that he could find nothing to say to her. He was feeling as awkward as an overgrown boy, while she sat there in her corner with an air of sleek rightness, watching him. Fleur de Lys! White lilies on a blue shield! And the trees of Portman Square, and the traffic, and a pair of black glacé shoes below two slim, flesh-coloured legs! And what an extraordinary thing it was that she could have lost all her lure for him, and that he should feel cold and rigid and mute, unwilling to touch her or be touched by her.

And what were impressions? He stole an oblique look at her, and was caught in the act. He had to blurt out something.

"How's 'Mirabeaus'?"

"Oh, continuing," said she.

They were held up by a traffic block in Oxford Street, and leaning forward, he appeared absorbed in watching the rear wheels of the vehicle in front of them. The silence—like Mirabeau's—continued. But from her eyes and from the corners of her mouth a little acrid smile began to trickle.

"You are bored with me, boy, aren't you?"

The traffic and their cab moved on.

"My dear," said he, "you and I are strangers. We should never be anything else."

5

Sitting opposite her in a corner of the Fleur de Lys, he ordered a bottle of red wine. The name of it did not matter; the wine-waiter's grubby finger had indicated a Château Something or Other on a page that was spotted. The place was both pretentious and second-rate; the Frenchwoman who waited on them was scented to the eyebrows; three asters in a cracked vase looked—poor things—shabbily ashamed and tired of life.

Olive had produced the inevitable mirror from the inevitable bag, and it occurred to Lance to wonder how many times in a day she peered at herself in that piece of glass. Or was it just part of her restlessness, or the counterpart of a Georgian woman's flirting with a fan? There was too much of the mirror and the shop window. But, poor little devil, she had had to scrap for her living, and even her flimsies were little flutterings of courage.

He said—with a deliberate gentleness: "You look a bit tired. I wanted to talk."

She glanced at him over her mirror. Her face had a frozen and bright friendliness.

"You're just like the rest of them my dear."

"Am I?"

"A cad—though you want to be a sort of high-brow cad."

The soup and the wine arrived. He picked up his soup spoon, and passing the bowl of it to and fro through the brown fluid, found himself wondering how she knew. And the phrase had an aptness. A high-brow cad!

He smiled, but it was a wincing smile.

"Causes and effects. Supposing I married you——?"

"Thanks," said she. "That would be a nice gesture, wouldn't it? You needn't explain."

He paused with poised spoon.

"Then—haven't we both been cads?—I mean—it was supposed——"

"Was it?"

He tried to hold her glance, to compel her to look at him.

"Think."

"Did you?"

"I didn't think—I felt. Don't be *maniérée,* my dear. We were just hard and greedy young people. I grant you now that one ought not to be like that. I suppose London makes one like that. It's all wrong."

"Oh, yes, afterwards," said she; "when you have had what you wanted. But there's a difference."

"How?"

"Between man and woman."

"But—is there? Wasn't there anything in me——?"

She gave him a malicious look.

"Oh, that! Aren't you rather a beast—to hint? Because one happens to be human."

Their soup plates were removed by the waitress, who observed them with cynical but impartial curiosity.

He said: "I'm sorry. I suppose we are not going to have a row here. But since we are down to bedrock, I'll tell you the truth. I'm ashamed of this business."

"Thank you."

"It has taught me one thing, that a man has to choose between a woman and his work. That's the ultimate caddishness, I suppose, but it's a fact."

She did not flinch, but her face gave him the impression of having received a blow. And it hurt him. The memory of it was to hurt him a little for the rest of his life.

She became flippantly calm.

"That's priceless of you. You used the knife quite nicely. Right-o; I'm excised."

CHAPTER XXIV

I

AT that period of the year, when his Michaelmas daisies and his early chrysanthemums were coming into bloom, old Pybus had two matters on his mind—what the potent John Richmond would think of Lance's novel, and how long and thoroughly a woman would sacrifice herself to the blind hunger of things and of men?

The Venerable would not admit worry.. He differed from George, the Saracen's head-waiter, who, in spite of a flat and sophisticated blue eye, suffered from fantastic nauseas and inhibitions. George spent a great part of each day in watching overfed people overeating themselves, until to George the very act of eating became an offence. He would be attacked by a kind of surfeit of disgust, especially during August and its holiday atmosphere, the "Month of the Guzzlers," as he called it, and he would lose weight and maintain himself on apples and toast and water.

"Munching and sucking, John; nothing but munching and sucking. In this hot weather it makes me feel all upset inside. Nothing but mouths, mouths. Now—if they were children it would be sort of natural—but all these fat people."

"Does it worry you, George?"

"Why, just look at the waste of it. I tell you—that by the end of August I don't want to see—ever—another tomato, or a round of beef, or a veal and ham pie. They look like rounds of beef and chunks of pie, John. Some day I shall blow up and go round swishing at 'em with a table-napkin: 'Get out—you pigs'."

The Venerable had to pacify George, holding George's attacks of nausea to be symptomatic of a wholesome mind and not of a disordered liver.

"You want a week on the east coast, George."

"I'm going. Just bread and cheese and a glass of beer for

me, John. And if anybody offers me a second helping of boiled beef and dumplings—there'll be murder."

Cabbages are gross feeders, and continue to be cabbages, but the Venerable's mysticism fed on apples. Someone had discovered this, and from the "Marions" orchard a little basket travelled twice a week in the dicky of Mary Merris's car. Old Pybus liked a good red apple, and she brought him the choicest.

"Very good of you, my dear."

"Just one little thing I can do."

"Tush," said he; "it's fruit from the Hesperides. How's life to-day?"

She would go to his book-case and stand and gaze.

"I survive. Oh, books! Choose me a book."

"With a laugh in it?"

"No, a book with courage in it. Do the makers of books realize how some of us need courage? We, who happen to struggle with sordid things, do not ask for dust-bins."

"I'll choose you a book, my dear. But I do not question your courage."

Who, in these days, speaks of a man or a woman as nailed to a cross?—and yet that was how the Venerable thought of Mary Merris. He approved and he disapproved. If there was one person upon earth whom he mistrusted, it was the good woman—so called, for the mother of his sons had been of that sort of goodness, unripe fruit smothered in sugar. And Mary was sacrificing herself—and for what? He did not ask her whether it was worth her while, but he asked himself that question, and the answer to it varied as the mood of his response to the woman in her varied. Was sottishness worth saving? Should the unfit and the futile be cherished at the expense of the fit and the free? He saw her as a rather tragic figure fiercely absorbed in helping to perpetuate a tragedy. Young Merris was no good. He was not even logically and understandably bad. He was an egotistical young rotter with a temperament, and the very worst sort of temperament. There were moments when old Pybus would have suggested that wise circumstances might make a useful end of the situation by pushing young Merris off the crown of Castle Craven bridge.

But you could not say that to his sister. She was one of those women who persist in following sacrificial courses, because sentiment in them has a fanatical urge. She would have thrust her hand into the fire just to prove that certain things have to be done against the flinchings of the flesh. And the Blond Beast of Woolshot stood and watched and mocked her.

2

Mary might have echoed the words of Mrs. Gasson, who, when challenged by some priestess of progress on the subject of matrimony, had exclaimed: "What's the alternative, dearie; what's the alternative?"

On this September afternoon Mary straightened her back, and looked about her from among the brown chicken houses, and if she saw beauty of woodland and of hill she saw it with a conscious and tense watchfulness. She had the air of a woman who was listening, not for some pleasant sound, but for movements of stealthiness and deceit. Suspicion, most horrible and humiliating of comrades to a nature essentially generous! To have to listen and to watch, and to steal about like a shadow on the edge of another person's consciousness, while knowing that you yourself were watched and listened for!

She opened one of the wire doors and went slowly down towards the orchard. She looked across the valley towards Castle Craven, and seeing it solidly grey and remote upon its hill, she paused as though the old town had some message for her. "Here I stand, my dear. I too have stood a siege, and though they battered at me I did not surrender." She recovered a moment of romance in remembering how a young man on a white charger had ridden up the valley at the head of two thousand "horse," and how the Parliament men had marched away, and Castle Craven had rung its bells and fired off its cannon. A romantic occasion for those gaillard cavaliers prancing up Castle Hill with a flicker of swords in the sunlight, and over yonder eight hundred godly fellows sullenly trailing their pikes eastwards. Yes, such memories stirred her; she had eyes for the colour of them. Her inwardness was irrevocably romantic, in spite of chickens and a motor-car that was all rust, and the deplorable disharmonies, and the starving of her powers of self-expression. Or was it that her essential romanticism expressed itself in the carrying of a flag? And would she, like Castle Craven, desire the coming of a young paladin upon a milk-white horse, and ring her bells and throw flowers? But how old-fashioned! Surely you should lean casually against a gun, and with cigarette in mouth, drawl to your paladin: "Hallo, old thing, bit late— aren't you? That's rather a topping tin hat you've got on. Sorry I can't stay. I'm out of face powder, but now I shall be able to get it. Cheer-i-o."

She walked on, and then another memory arrested her and brought her to a pause by the orchard gate. Had it happened, and only yesterday? Had she surprised Gilbert rummaging at her bureau for the petty cash that she had been compelled to hide! And the sick facility of the smile on his blind face! She had felt a horrible coldness, a humiliation that was both his and her own.

"What is it, Gil?"

"Bob's coming down. You might realize——"

She had been shocked by the stillness of her own voice.

"How much do you owe him?"

Oh, the beastliness of it, the sneaking, shameful, surreptitious game that she was being compelled to play with this poor blind thing! And the beastliness of that other man, his almost incredible meanness! Because she would not play that other sort of game! Because his vanity had been slapped!

She went on and down through the orchard. She found the front door open, and an untenanted deck-chair standing on the little lawn. She hesitated in front of that open door, for the very doorway of her own home had become like a dark cupboard full of childish terrors. She heard the clinking of crockery. The girl Nelly was getting tea ready.

She called to the girl.

"Nelly!"

"Yes, Miss?"

"Where is Mr. Gilbert?"

"Don't know, Miss."

"Haven't you seen him?"

"I saw him go out of the gate, Miss."

"When?"

"Maybe—half an hour ago."

She stood a moment, considering, one hand laid along her cheek.

"You had better keep tea back."

"Yes, Miss."

Going down to the white gate she followed her flair, and her following of it was an act of courage. The lane climbed gradually to the Woolshot park gates, and a blind man tapping with a stick could track his way along the grass bank and the oak fence. That was her conclusion, and confronting it she went up on the winding lane under the shade of the beeches, conscious of an anger which carried her against the tide of circumstance.

3

"Woolshot" had one of those Georgian porticoes which suggest the convential setting for a "shooting party" as the unelect may see it reproduced in a magazine of sport and of fashion. Woolshot was all grey. The portico and its six steps were flanked on either side by a terrace, and upon the terrace wall round box-trees in stone vases punctuated the horizontal scheme like a row of gigantic green plum-puddings. In summer weather Woolshot took its tea here outside the long windows of the gun-room and the library, for the atmosphere of Woolshot was dominantly male. And on this September day Mr. Hargreaves had guests, three hard-bitten men and two women with efficient, weather-beaten faces. They had been shooting over one of the Woolshot farms.

To them—Symes, the Woolshot butler, had brought a blind man, leading him by the arm.

"Mind the step, sir."

"Hullo, young fellah my lad! Run away again from your good sister, have you? This is Mr. Gilbert Merris. Merris, you can't see my crowd, but there are five of 'em. Sit down, here's a pew."

Merris sat where he was placed, and took what was given him. Very sensitive to sounds and more especially to voices, he had no choice but to listen to these strangers who talked of things of which he knew nothing. He sat and smiled that little sinister smile, and held a tea-cup balanced on his knees. He was ignored, and child that he was, he resented it, and felt moved to push his weak voice in among those wooden voices. He was sure that these people had faces of wood. Their talk was all of the killing of things, and of old Somebody's bad shooting and bad temper, and of a poaching scuffle down at Burnt Barn, and of the domestic misadventure of some neighbour. He had a woman beside him, but she smelt of Harris tweed like a man. Hargreaves, straddling a chair, with his arms resting on the back of it, smoked a cigar, and looked at nothing with blue eyes that were sensual and sleepy. The other voices were arguing.

Young Merris heard Hargreaves speaking to him.

"You ought to be pretty good at blind-man's buff, young fellah."

There was a tremor of the closed eyelids.

"That's a game I could play."

"Here, fill up; or will you have a cigarette?"

"I've left my pipe at home."

"Wild lad. Catch hold. Ha——!"

And suddenly Hargreaves was silent, staring with those blue eyes of his over the stone coping of the terrace wall. He had in view a loop of the park road where it curved between two groups of old trees. He saw the tawny slip of a girl's figure, her brown skirt and dove-coloured legs. She had paused there. She was looking up towards the house.

He smiled.

"Supposing your sister comes to fetch you, young fellah?"

"But she won't. Tell me if I'm in the way here."

"Don't be foolish. You'll stay and have some dinner with me. Oh, yes, you will. I'll see you home. This crowd is pushing off before long."

Meanwhile he watched the figure down yonder. It seemed to hesitate, and its hesitation interested him as the falterings of some rather timid creature might interest a big tawny beast couchant upon a rock. Would she have the cheek or the courage to come up to the house? Were his playful pawings of her cub of a brother exercising powers of persuasion? Probably it was only a question of time, for women are temperamental creatures.

He saw her turn back. She retreated down the loop of the road and disappeared behind the trees. So, she had not the courage, or perhaps her courage failed her in the daylight. Yes, women—like cats—were discreet and remote during the day, but when the surreptitious night arrived they behaved differently. He would teach her a thing or two. Meanwhile his people were getting up out of their chairs and preparing to go. Colonel Carstairs and his wife had a forty-mile drive before them.

He laid a hand on Merris's shoulder.

"You stay there."

4

She waited at the gate. It was one of those very still September nights, with a moon coming up to hang poised over the Brent valley. There were the lights of Castle Craven on the hill weaving upwards in a kind of spiral, and a faint glare in the hollow below from the headlights of an occasional car. She heard the clocks striking in Castle Craven, and a murmuring that was like the murmuring heard in a hollow shell, the remote rush of the water over the weir at Abbey Mill. There were other sounds, the hooting of an owl in the Woolshot woods, a faint rustling of some creature in the hedge bottom, the soft thud of an apple falling upon the grass in the orchard. She listened, particularly, to the falling of the apples, because there was a something in the sound that had for her a vague and groping significance. She counted seven such falls, and on this windless night the parting of the fruit and branch seemed strange. So things happened. So your tired heart went on beating. So you stood waiting upon life, and wondering why you waited, when one swift, ruthless act might set you free.

But these sounds were impersonal, and so was the beauty of the September night, with the moonlight splashing upon the tops of the beech trees, and Castle Craven glimmering like some dream town. She stretched out her hands in the moonlight, and pointing her fingers at the moon, looked along them. This was mysticism. This was the passionless, cool, dew-drenched calm of a world purged of its greeds. Oh, to be impersonal; to hear nothing but the birds singing in the woods and the wind in the trees; to hear not the voices of men; to be able to reach up and draw down a spray of apple blossom and inhale the clean pale scent of it; to sit in the sun; to watch the wind stirring the grasses. Peace, that peace within yourself, the delight of innocent seeing and hearing and smelling, and recording. To be able to take colour and play with it like an intent and happy child.

Oh, childishness, dreams, soft breathing!

Leaning upon the gate with her chin on her crossed wrists, she both listened and tried not to listen. Why should she have to listen? Why should she have to wait for the sound of stumbling feet, and for men's flushed voices? How she hated the voices of men!

Why could she not be herself?

If she were old, fiftyish, serenely through with things, the futile and restless things, like old John Pybus. But was one ever through with things? To be purely impersonal is to cease to live. Life's fingers play upon red strings. Your mood may be moonlight, but moonlight passes.

Courage! Was not courage the greatest virtue of them all? Courage in the face of the beast and before the feet of the fool, courage when your heart faltered and your very gentleness stood still.

Another apple fell, but there were other sounds and she

raised her head. She seemed to shrink away from the white gate; she went up the path and into the house, and closing the door, locked it. She stood there feeling breathless.

One of the voices was singing. At the gate there seemed to be some sort of altercation.

"In you go, my lad."

"Don't want t'go in, Bob. I want the moon."

"Oh, no you don't; you want to go to bed. Easy over the stones."

"I'm skidding—Bob. I want the moon; I want Nelly— I want——"

"Shut up—you ass."

"I'm not an ass—won't be called an ass."

"Right, my lad—you're a dear good fellah."

There were scufflings outside the door—thumpings.

"I'm locked out—Bob. Mary—hallo—Mary!"

She waited with her hand on the key.

"Sit down there on the porch seat, my lad. I'll ring the bell like a gentleman and leave you to it. Good night— young fellah my lad."

"Here—stay a bit—she'll be in a hell of——"

"Why, nothing's wrong; no harm done. See you to-morrow."

She heard Hargreaves go down the path, and the thud of the gate as he closed it. So this was his "That's that," his gesture of ironical playfulness! A nice, gentlemanly gesture, the leaving of her brother drunk upon her doorstep! Had such an incident been described to her she would have declared it inconclusive, and quite unlikely. Meanwhile her brother was fumbling at the door handle, and beginning to swear foolishly.

"Mary——"

She unlocked and opened the door, and he blundered forward against her.

"What—locking a man out! I'm—all—right——"

She pushed him past her into the passage, and closed and relocked the door.

CHAPTER XXV

I

LANCE went down to Windover for that week-end, but before going he wrote to John Richmond a letter that had become inevitable, "Rust" would not be finished by the end of September, and Lance asked for another fourteen days. He made no excuses.

"I could rush it—but that would be no compliment to you. I think you were right when you lashed me a little at the 'Reform' that day. My sense of landscape is returning."

Richmond's reply was as inevitable as the tone of Lance's letter:

"MY DEAR PYBUS,

"By all means take your fourteen days. A date can be relative.

"As to your reference to my 'lashings'—I am a little touched by it. Does any man love criticism? Only fools offer criticism—without self-searchings. I am glad of the landscape. Let there be a little of that blueness before rain.

"Ever yours sincerely,

"RICHMOND."

But at Windover Lance experienced a sensation of change. True, it was indefinite and misty, like the stealing on of autumn outside the windows of a house which had grown quieter. He found his mother and father alone, and in looking at his mother he was made to wonder, for it seemed to him that she too had undergone a change, a transmutation that he might have described as a softening and a fading of her colours. She talked less loudly.

So—too—with his father. Probyn had grown more silent, a little more wooden in his movements, less sententious in his son's presence, and yet there was in his silence a something that his civic urbanity had lacked. And there were details in and about the house that Lance should have noticed, and did notice so far as youth pays attention to such things; his rooms kept just as they had been in the old days, the flowers on his writing-table, a kind of tacit acceptance of him and his temperament and his work. Windover was Windover, old brick and freestone, and tile and lead; his father's hands had refrained from daubing a too prosperous newness over the house's face.

Lance wondered. The change made him feel faintly self-conscious and uneasy. At meals he had the impression of two elderly people entertaining a stranger, but a stranger whom they wished to know more intimately. They listened to him. Their attentiveness was just a little pathetic and strained. It was as though a door had been left open and two oldish people were sitting waiting for someone to enter.

On the Sunday Lance and his father wandered out to look at a new plantation. They went up through the beech woods, Probyn stiffly twirling a stick. His very squint had a pre-occupied vagueness.

"How's the book, Lance?"

"Nearly finished."

"That's good. This man Richmond——"

"He's reading it next month."

They paused on the brow of the hill, standing side by side, but a little apart. Lance appeared absorbed in the view.

"Have you got an agreement?"

"Oh—nothing on paper—yet."

"Better let me read it—before it is signed. These publisher chaps—some of them——"

Lance's head went up. His voice was curt, more curt than he realized.

"Richmond's a gentleman."

He did not see the little, wincing look on his father's face.

For Probyn was trying to talk to his son, and to talk to him in a new way, yet now—as always—somehow making a mess of it. But there was a difference, in that Probyn was very conscious of his fumblings, and of the dear and difficult stranger in his son. Though trying to be kind and unsententious, how was it that he managed to say the wrong thing, a thing which should have been right for most men, but seemed wrong for Lance? Was it that his son was more difficult than other sons? Or were all sons difficult? Was the relationship inherently impossible? And what of his own father? Had old John found in him the stranger that he was finding in his son? Yes it was probable. And Probyn, inwardly unhappy, fell back upon a vague and impersonal kindness.

After dinner he did make a second and tentative attack upon Lance's quiet and unconscious aloofness.

"Book coming out in the spring, is it?"

"If Richmond approves."

"I was going to say—that if you find it difficult to manage—feeling a bit poor——"

"Thanks, pater, very good of you, but I shall manage."

To his father, his manner appeared over-confident and a little aggressive. It was final. It seemed to close a door upon which was painted the word—"Private." But there was one remark of his father's—made during the day—that did arrest Lance's attention and remain with him. It referred to his Uncle Conrad, Lance's "Perfect Swine." Sir Probyn had said: "Ah, Conrad doesn't know how to grow old decently," a very apposite and significant remark, and one with which Lance was in cordial sympathy.

As for his mother, she sat and watched, and talked, but not at him as of old. She was both talkative and dumb, or like a woman suddenly careful of her aspirates; and the interrogating puzzlement in her eyes caused him to feel vaguely disturbed.

But if Probyn and his wife could not talk to their son, they could talk to each other, and with a sympathy which sometimes comes when two people realize that they are growing old. Moreover, Dolly was not well and Probyn was worried. He might think of her as "Poor old Dolly," because there were many moments when he thought of himself as "Poor old Probyn," and because he was not a bad sort of man, and mellowing fast now that the business part of him was atrophying.

The conversations carried on through the dressing-room doorway were more human and friendly.

"He just won't talk to me—Byn. He makes me feel a stupid old woman."

Probyn was unbuttoning his braces.

"Funny period, old lady. Suppose there always is. Suppose we had our funny periods——Maybe we've got to wait."

"Yes, p'raps so. Seems rather hard, though. And then—he'll be getting married. Children do hurt."

Her husband hung his braces over the back of a chair. Something in him winced.

"Hope you'll sleep better to-night, Doll. If you get much more of that pain—I'd like you to see—someone in town. Don't like you being in pain."

2

Mrs. Gasson of No. 7, calling upon Mrs. Carver of No. 17, not only delivered a note, but left the impress of a fat and ingenious hand behind her. So, the young gentleman was away, but he would be back on the Monday, and no doubt it would be good and right for him to know that one of Mrs. Gasson's lodgers had been hurried off to a nursing-home.

"Yes, poor dear. The pain came on in the middle of the night. I tried a hot bottle, and some turps on flannel, but it took her something cruel. 'Pendicitis, so the doctor said, and in she went to a nursing-home, toot-sweet. She wouldn't go to a hospital, and I don't blame her—butcher's shops I call 'em; though 'ow she's going to pay's more than I know. Robbers —they are. But before she was taken off she wrote this letter and asked me to see that your young gentleman got it."

So, on the Monday afternoon, Lance stood by the open window and read Olive's letter:

"Boy—I'm in such pain, but I'd like to say good-bye to you before they take me off to this nursing place. The doctor seems to think it will mean an operation. I'm frightened, but I suppose everybody's frightened sometimes. Good luck to the book.

"OLIVE."

He was touched, and touched to self-reproach, as no doubt she had expected he would be, and he went straightway to No. 7, and was met by Mrs. Gasson.

"No, poor dear; she was took away on Saturday. No. 7 Blount Street. Maybe you're a brother of hers, sir."

"No—just a friend."

Mrs. Gasson, with serious and stout movements, inveigled him inside the doorway.

"Well—that's a pity. I wanted her to wire to her mother, but would she? Not she. Said her mother 'ad quite enough worry. She's got pluck. I know, sir, when I 'ad my operation—I was all of a dither. An' then there's the expense. They do charge you something awful at these nursin' 'omes. Coal—sixpence a lump. I'm that upset about it—I've known Miss Gadsden three years."

Lance listened patiently.

"No. 7 Blount Street?"

"Yes, sir. Down Wigmore Street way."

"Thank you; I'll go and inquire."

He went, discovering Blount Street as two rows of flat-faced houses all most respectably alike. No. 7 had a green door, white window-sashes, and pale rose-coloured curtains. Its door furniture was well polished, and its step immaculate. Lance rang the bell. A very tall nurse with straw-coloured hair and a supremely impartial face opened the door to him. He raised his hat.

"Excuse me—but Miss Gadsden's a patient here?"

"Yes."

"I've come to inquire. I believe she has had an operation."

The nurse was deliberate and careful.

"No—no operation—yet. We are not quite sure. Do you wish to leave your name?"

"Yes. Will you say Mr. Pybus called."

"Mr. Pybus?"

"Mr. Lance Pybus. I suppose I couldn't see Miss Gadsden?"

"I'm afraid not. Not to-day. But I'll give your name."

"Thank you."

He raised his hat. The nurse smiled faintly, and the door

was closed, and Lance walked up the length of Blount Street feeling bothered and responsible. It occurred to him—and very forcibly so—that the expenses of an operation and of a nursing-home could not be budgeted for in the financial estimates of a girl who displayed dresses and taught dancing. Poor Olive! Why hadn't she chosen to go into a hospital? But surely that was a rather graceless thought! When you were ill and in pain you allowed yourself to be hustled into any place where you might expect to find skill and kindness. But a nursing-home, and "coal at sixpence a lump," and an operation fee! That slim, feverish body in pain, and cut about! Supposing? Yes, supposing that he and Olive had been pledged in some other way, he would have felt responsible, fiercely responsible.

He arrived—somehow—in Portman Square, and he walked round it twice as though his physical activity corresponded to his mental circling of a problem. Ought he to do something, or try to do something? But what? Help her with money? But how? He might rake up ten pounds; he might ask his father, without giving any reason. No, damn it; he couldn't do that!. For one moment a far more serious solution did suggest itself, but after considering it with set brows, he thrust it aside. Marriage? Good heavens! Could anything be more fatal than to marry out of pity, on impulse, because you felt in a way—that you had taken something without giving? What an alternative! He knew now—as some young men know things—intuitively and ruthlessly—that marriage with a girl like Olive would be a sin against self, against two selves. His work? A frittering away of everything that was difficult and big and splendid in a relationship that would be hopeless and cheap and ephemeral.

He returned to No. 17, but he was unable to work. The problem of Olive lay like a blot upon the page, and in the end he went out and walked and, turning towards Bloomsbury, he sought out Kit Sorrell; but Sorrell was away at Winstonbury, spending a week with his father. The absence of his friend seemed to throw him back upon his own deciding—though it was more a feeling than a reckoning. He ought at least to stretch out a friendly hand to Olive, and with a kind of inevitableness his thoughts went to his grandfather. He could manage ten pounds in cash, and he would write and ask the Venerable to lend him money. And that was what he did. He sat down and wrote the letter that same evening.

"Dear Grandpater,

"This is the first letter of its kind that I have written to you. I am asking you to lend me fifty pounds. The money is not for myself, but for someone I want to help. I will give you a receipt, and repay you by degrees.

"I suppose I ought to say that I hate asking you to do this, but somehow—I don't. If you refuse, I shan't ask you why, or feel hurt.

"The book is going well. Richmond has given me another fortnight. I shall be with you towards the end of the month, and I shall bring the last part of 'Rust' with me. I want you to read it before Richmond sees it."

He posted the letter, and feeling calmed now that he had made this decision, he wandered about the streets for an hour.

3

A part of the irony of language arises from the uses to which words are put, for No. 7 Blount Street was neither home nor a place where you were nursed, as nursing is understood by those upon whom it is practised. Olive had a little back room on the top floor. Its window overlooked the backs of other houses and the Blount Street Mews, where the vigorous children of an aggressive proletariat shouted and played games and kicked tins. Cars returning to the Mews at all hours of the night made pleasant and consoling noises. The kitchen was in the basement, the water piped no higher than the second floor. There were no gas or electric stoves in the bedrooms. Nearly everything had to be carried up and down stairs, and when a bell was rung a nurse had to climb from the ground level. But No. 7 Blount Street did not

K

encourage the ringing of bells, and Olive could not reach hers without getting out of bed, which—in her case—was forbidden. Moreover, the food was flat and indifferent and messily served, and for the privilege of being marooned in this room, with the proletariat noises provided below, the fee was fifteen guineas weekly.

Isolated, and in bed at the top of the house. Olive had leisure to think and to feel, and her thoughts were various and eloquent. Life seemed a topsy-turvy business, and as ironical as the nursing and the home where everything was arranged so that people were in the worst of tempers. Olive herself was frightened and worried and on edge, and in a mood to review life as it had happened to her during the last few years. Life was certainly a precarious business. You scratched about for your seed like a hen. It might all seem very adventurous to begin with, but when you realized the limitations of your own particular "run," conventionalism—a nicely decorated conventionalism—had its advantages.

On that particular morning, not having seen a nurse for an hour and a half, and not being supposed to get up and ring the bell, she lay and fumed. They had been so energetic at six in the morning, washing her like an unwilling cat, and with water which had been none too warm, and at eight something that was called breakfast had arrived. Certainly she had flowers on the table beside her bed, but they had not been provided by the management of the "home." Also, she was in something of a predicament, both financially and emotionally, and desirous of snatching at one possibility while not losing her chance of selecting the alternative. For emotionally she was somewhere at the end of things. That is to say—she was a little desperate.

Her wrist-watch on the table told her that the hour was half past ten, and not being tolerant of any further isolation she scuffled out of bed, and rang the bell.

The nurse found her looking flushed and defiant.

"You got up—against orders."

"Well, no one's been near me for an hour and a half. I want——"

Her want was attended to, and the nurse's face was as cold as the china. There were dissemblings. Your woman of no means must always dissemble.

"Nurse—I'm afraid I'm a lot of trouble."

She appealed against that scolding face and those perfunctory hands.

"I'm so sorry—— You are being so very good to me. What time does the doctor come?"

"About eleven—usually."

"May I see visitors?"

"That will depend."

"Yes—I suppose so. But if Mr. Pybus calls."

The nurse, with lowered eyes, moved towards the door.

"Which Mr. Pybus? "

"The young one. I want to see him—particularly."

"Not the old one?"

"He won't be here to-day."

The nurse left a cold reply trailing behind her as she closed the door, and Olive, sitting up in bed, and clutching the bed-clothes, uttered under her breath the one word—"Beast."

4

The nurse preceded Lance up the stairs, and arriving outside Olive Gadsden's door, opened it, and without entering the room, announced her visitor.

"Mr. Pybus to see you."

She looked at Lance consideringly as he walked past her into the room, and closing the door, remained for a moment or two on the landing. She heard Lance say: "Olive—this is bad luck. I'm sorry."

He was standing in the middle of the room looking at her, and thinking that she looked quite different in bed, with her dark hair hidden under a lace cap, and her eyes curiously watchful and not too welcoming. She was wearing a rose-coloured jacket. The flowers beside the bed were bronze and gold chrysanthemums.

"Sit down, boy."

He felt awkward and self-conscious. When he went for a chair he was aware of her eyes following him across the room. He placed the chair beside the table, so that he was slightly behind her as she lay there on her back.

"Well—what do they say?"

She moved her head.

"I can't see you, boy."

"Do you want to see me?"

"Yes."

He moved his chair and found a smile, but her face was quite smileless.

"Well—what do they say about you?"

"Appendicitis."

"And that means——?"

"Yes, to-morrow."

"Poor Olive—— Frightened?"

"Oh, not much—one gets hard, you know."

She watched his eyes. They avoided hers, and avoided them consciously. He looked at the floor, and the flowers, and out of the window, and she could see him moistening his lips and frowning.

"They said I might stay ten minutes. Look here, Olive. I've got something to say. We are friends still, aren't we? This is rotten luck for you. I want you to let me do a friendly thing."

Her eyes narrowed.

"Oh, how?"

He looked at her two hands lying on the quilt.

"Well, as it might be—man to man. We both have to scrap for a living. And these places must be—pretty ruinous. I can manage something now, and I may be able to manage something more in a few days."

Her eyelids quivered.

"Just what do you mean?"

He slipped a hand into a pocket, and bringing out an envelope laid it on the bed.

"A couple of fivers, my dear. The best I can do for the

moment, but I have asked someone to lend me fifty. You'll take it as a friend——"

She drew in her arms and with one swift movement sat up in bed. Her lips were retracted. He saw the white teeth.

"Cash on delivery! No—thanks. I don't want your beastly money. Here—take it."

She flicked the envelope off the bed.

"And get out, get out quickly, or I'll throw things, you high-minded, magnanimous beast. Get out——"

She was as white as the pillow, and trembling, supporting herself on her arms. And Lance was standing, looking as white as she was, and a little shocked and bewildered.

"My dear girl—I——"

"Get out!"

Her voice had a shrillness.

"And pick up that envelope. You had better get out or they'll hear me telling you things."

He bent down and picked up the envelope, and facing her backed to the door. His colour had come back with a rush.

"I'm sorry. I thought——"

"Get out of my room."

He fumbled his way out of the door, and closing it gently, went slowly down the stiars.

5

Afterwards she wept, and tried to dry her eyes with the frill of her lace cap. It was an emotional storm, compounded of anger and the pain of a mauled self-love, and of mortification born of the consciousness that as a woman somehow she had failed. She was angry with herself, and she was angry with him. She had had no retort save that anger. She had been hurt, and she wanted to hurt back. She told herself that— somehow—she would be even with him. His work—indeed! Swollen-headed and superior young cad! She refused to reason. She would not allow that the relationship had been an experiment in naturalism, irresponsibly begun, and more responsibly ended.

The nurse found her with red eyelids.

"I want to write a letter.   There's a writing-pad in my suit-case."

Said the nurse: "You've got a temperature."

"I'm in a damned bad temper, my dear, if that's what you mean.   Be a dear and get me the paper."

She wrote her letter, using a pencil:

"DEAR CON,

"Poor little Olive is to be cut up to-morrow.   But, dear man, I'm so comfy here, and so full of purrings over somebody's kindness.   I's tryin' hard not to be frightened. Do come and sit downstairs while it's going on.   I shall feel that dear old Wog-wog is there, and it'll help—just lots.

"You're not to worry.   I shall come up smiling.   I've got your flowers beside me.

"OLIVE."

CHAPTER XXVI

I

LANCE met Mrs. Carver on the stairs.
"Any letters for me?"
"No, sir."

He went up and past her as she stood back against the wall.
The Mrs. Carvers of the world were mere shadows to him,
while he walked in the sunlight of his young selfishness, but
on this September day his self had begun to cast a shadow.
He had been made aware of it as of a thing surreptitious and
sly, a something mean which smirked up into his face, and
followed close, and stood beside him as he closed the door of
his room. Two neat white piles of manuscript lay side by side
on the blue cloth of the table. Before starting out on that visit
to Olive he had been reading through the first twenty chapters.

He sat down and looked out of the window. He had
brought away with him from No. 7 Blount Street the memory
of a girl propped up in bed on two quivering arms. She had
screamed at him. Angry? Yes, she had been more than
angry. You might have called it hysteria, and with that redness still lingering about his ears, he had proposed to call it
hysteria. Olive had gone off the deep end—because——?
Yes, just why? And when he had assured himself that he was
doing the generous thing.

But had he been generous? Outside in the street, and
walking fast, he had been conscious of a feeling of relief, yes—
almost of exultation. The business was done with; he could
get back to work; and he had felt himself gloating a little,
youth with the apples in its pocket, and the gardener fooled.
But in that moment of meanness he had—as it were—turned
suddenly about and discovered the face of that other and
smirking self, the male thing naked and unashamed.

Shocked? Yes, he had been shocked. He sat at the
window and stared, and remembered that she had called him a

cad. He had not been aware of his caddishness, but in the open street, with that smirking and cynical self walking daintily bèside him, he had discovered it. He was a cad. And perhaps for the first time in his life he realized the underworld within himself, those shameful crowd faces, the blatant complacency of satisfied sex, the many meannesses which walk at a man's elbow. And he was staggered. While believing himself generous he had behaved like a commercialist; he had gone to her in her moment of blackness, and coolly had closed the account.

But what was to be done? It was she who had closed the account, and given him his dismissal. She had presented him with one of those human records that are put away, but not forgotten, and which, when recurring, as they do recur, reproduce beauty or ugliness, a secret joy or a secret shame.

For, in after years, when confessing to this adventure and describing its anti-climax, he askèd a particular woman a question. "What should I have done?"

And as a woman she had answered his question.

"I think you should have thanked her. You should have said: 'Dear, you have given me a beautiful time, and a beautiful memory. I shall not forget it. You could not have given me more.'"

"But would she have been satisfied?"

"Yes, and no. It would have depended upon how you did it, and upon how you felt when you did it. There are different ways of presenting a bouquet. You should leave the woman the right to feel that the bouquet was not made of artificial flowers. Leave her a perfume. Do you understand me?"

"Now—I think I do."

2

In the morning came the Venerable's letter, and a cheque for fifty pounds.

"My Dear—I'm glad you asked me. Take it and use it as you please."

That letter aroused in Lance deeper self-searchings, and also a more subtle feeling of humiliation. He had gone to this one man in the world, and had borrowed money from him in order to salve his conscience after a sexual escapade. But how had it happened? How was it that the eyes of to-day were so different from the eyes of yesterday? Had he not been sorry for Olive; had he not felt compassion, and the desire to help her? But his compassion had been self-centred, sublimated egotism; it had not spilled itself over into an understanding of that other human self. He had imposed his pity upon her; he had treated her as the Olive of his own wilful conceiving and not as Olive as she was.

But what was to be done?

Should he write a letter, and ask her to take the money, but ask her differently? Or should he go and place the money in the hands of the doctor or the matron, and ask one of them to use it without letting Olive know? He wanted to do something. He wanted to make amends, while dimly realizing that there are some things that cannot be amended.

He remembered that Olive's operation was to be performed at eleven o'clock, and being urged on by the thought of it, he went out and took a taxi to his bank. He presented the Venerable's cheque, and asked for cash. The manager, consulted by the clerk, and seeing a Pybus signature on the cheque, came forward and was gracious to Lance across the counter.

"A family cheque, Mr. Pybus?"

"My grandfather's signature."

"Of course—we shall be very glad to cash it for you. Some names are sufficient security. How will you take it, sir?"

So, Lance walked on to Blount Street with a wad of five-pound notes in his breast pocket, and in his head an idea that was neither quite Quixotic nor quite practical. If he could persuade the matron in charge of the home to take the money on Olive's behalf, and to give him a receipt for it, he would at least have succeeded in freeing her from a part of her dilemma. As for the surgeon's fee it would either be humanely nominal, and so, capable of being dealt with, or the blood money of the

commercialized expert—and therefore to be whistled for.
That was Lance's summing up of the situation.

In Blount Street he felt far less sure of himself and his
inspiration. He walked down it on the side of the even
numbers, glancing across at the green door of No. 7 as he
passed. At the end of the street he was in the act of facing
about when a car swung in from a side turning, a big blue
saloon with a chauffeur at the wheel and a man in the back seat.
Lance had a momentary glimpse of the man's profile. The
car went on up Blount street, and drawing over, stopped
outside No. 7. The man got out, and standing with his back
to the street, and his face to the green door, rang the bell.

Lance stood and stared, for the car was his Uncle Conrad's
car, and it was Conrad himself standing on the doorstep of
No. 7. What the devil was he doing in Blount Street?
Lance saw the green door opened by a nurse, and Conrad's
stout figure entering immediately as though he had been
expected, and had the right of entry. But what an extraordinary coincidence! Obviously, Conrad must be interested
in one of No. 7's patients.

Lance strolled back up the street, but stopped before he came
opposite the windows of No. 7. He looked at the car's rear
number-plate. Yes, there was no doubt about it; the car was
Conrad's, and Conrad's chauffeur knew him, and he did not
think that he wished to be seen by Conrad's chauffeur. He
turned. He was perplexed. He decided to go for a stroll, and
to return in a quarter of an hour, but at the lower end of
Blount Street the coincidence of Conrad and his car linked
itself to two other facts and became associated with them.
Lance suddenly remembered Conrad's passion for dancing, and
those fat legs of his absurdly wobbling in the throes of the
Charleston. And Conrad had been accustomed to talk boast-
fully of his dancing lessons.

Lance stopped dead. Good Lord! Was it possible?
Could Conrad be Olive's elephas, one of the fat fellows who
trod upon her toes? Was he interested in Olive? Had he
turned up to hear the result of the operation?

Lance glanced back up Blount Street. The blue car was

still there, and French—Conrad's chauffeur—had left his seat, and was standing beside the car, smoking a cigarette. Obviously his uncle's visit was not a flying one. Conrad had gone in to wait.

The coincidence seemed almost too significant, and Lance turned into a side street, digesting that most unpleasant supposition, and conscious of a kind of emtional chilliness. It was not unlike the feeling of physical chilliness before an attack of nausea. He was on the edge of seeing life coloured green and yellow.

After twenty minutes of idling in other streets he returned to the lower end of Blount Street, only to find that his Uncle Conrad's car was still in possession of the frontage of No. 7. French was chatting to a maid who had appeared on the steps of No. 9's area. Lance swung round and went off upon another beat. How long did an operation for the removal of an appendix last, and if Conrad was interested in this particular operation, was he staying to hear the result? A rather intimate situation! For, if his Uncle Conrad was interested, it would be interest of a particular kind; for Lance could not visualize Mr. Conrad Pybus as the fatherly altruist and friend. And Lance was beginning to chafe not a little, and to feel that his compassion had flown too high, and might come tumbling. But Conrad!

Once again he looked into Blount Street. The blue car remained, and he went off again with a fiercer action, and a tightness of the lips. Damn Conrad and his car! He must have been hanging about for an hour and a half. But on the next occasion he became the witness of a piece of interplay which added colour to his conjectures. Conrad, minus a hat, was standing on the doorstep of No. 7, and French, half in and half out of the car, was reaching for something, and that something proved to be a big bouquet of red and gold chrysanthemums. French handed the flowers to his master, and Conrad re-entered the house.

Chrysanthemums! Of course!

Lance's head was up, his nostrils looking a little pinched. So—this was the position!

But his youth blew cold in him, and his eyes were like the eyes of his grandfather. Assuredly he was going to see this thing through, and so he hung about the end of Blount Street until Conrad's car had disappeared. He waited for another ten minutes. He was feeling fierce, largely because of the unpleasant qualms that were active within him. He walked very rapidly up Blount Street and rang the bell of No. 7.

A maid opened the door.

Said Lance—looking her straight in the eyes: "My name's Pybus. I want to see the matron, please. If she is busy for the moment I'll come in and wait."

He walked in past the girl and laid his hat down on a table in the narrow hall. The maid had given him a perplexed and protesting look, but when a visitor was in he was in, and Lance made her think of Valentino. She closed the street door.

"Will you go into that room, please."

"This one?"

"Yes. I'll tell Miss Saxby. Mr. Pybus—you said?"

"Yes. Mr. Pybus."

Lance entered the front room, which was the matron's sitting-room and office, and was met by his Uncle Conrad's chrysanthemums standing in a big Doulton vase. He walked to the window, and looked out into Blount Street. He heard voices on the stairs.

"I told you—no more visitors to-day, Kate."

"Yes, but he walked right in, Miss. And he said that if you were busy he would wait."

"Mr. Pybus——? But—Mr. Pybus?"

"It's a young one, Miss."

Lance stood prepared. Hearing someone enter the room, he faced about and smiled at Miss Saxby, but the smile was not returned. She was a woman with limp grey hair, very cold eyes, and a mouth that had no lips. It was like a little sharp slit in her watchful, smooth face.

"Good morning," said Lance. "I'm very sorry to trouble

you, but will you tell me how Miss Gadsden has borne her operation?"

There was a pause.

"Are you a relative?"

"No a friend."

"I see. The operation has been completely successful."

"I'm very glad."

There was a second pause. It was obvious to Lance that Miss Saxby regarded his presence as an intrusion, and, perhaps, as an impertinent intrusion. He had no status. For Miss Saxby had the official mind, and her efficiency extended to the making and observing of social adjustments, and less than twenty minutes ago she had been officially interviewed by Mr. Conrad Pybus. Conrad had status.

She did not ask Lance to sit down. She left the door open, stood by it, and with folded hands and set shoulders, waited for him to go.

Lance had his moment of audacity.

"You will excuse me, but may I ask you to take charge of a sum of money on Miss Gadsden's behalf. May I assume that you would be willing——?"

She stared.

"Money——?"

"Yes."

"Do you mean to say that you owe Miss Gadsden money?"

"No. I wish to be of some assistance."

His impression was that he had never seen a pair of eyes so cold and unfriendly.

"On no account. Besides, Miss Gadsden's stay here has been arranged for by the gentleman to whom she is engaged."

Lance made a little movement of the head and body.

"I see. Thank you for telling me. Of course—it would be quite unnecessary."

"Quite."

"If her fiancé has made himself responsible."

He walked to the door, Miss Saxby revolving like a movable figure on a pedestal, but remaining exquisitely rigid.

"Thank you. Good morning. I am sorry to have troubled you. But—by the way—you had better regard my visit as unofficial."

He gathered up his hat from the hall table.

"Neither Miss Gadsden nor Mr. Conrad Pybus need know of my visit."

4

Lance's closing of the door of No. 7 Blount Street might have been taken by most male creatures for a sober "Well— I'm damned!"

But he was neither damned nor saved, though in the course of a couple of hours he had passed through woods of extreme innocence and of complete sophistication. There was nothing more to be said. He had been pushed over the edge of himself into icy water. He had gulped it. He had emerged with a fierce, cold glow, and a blending of the emotional colours into hard white light. He was neither angry nor ashamed, nor sorry, nor disgusted. True—he had suffered momentarily from an intense nausea. It was as though he had cast off all his emotions, and was walking in spiritual nakedness up Blount Street.

He felt supremely cold and amazingly clear-headed. He viewed the situation as he might have viewed a situation in his own novel, without prejudice, and without pity, merely as an interpreter. Also, he seemed to have a complete and sudden understanding of the affair's human necessities, its justification, its pathos which was not pathetic; though he was not quite sure whether he had the laugh of Conrad, or whether Conrad had the right to chuckle. But did it matter? Did one laugh on such an occasion?

His practical gesture took the form of a second visit to his bank, and a handing back across the counter of those notes.

"Sorry. I find that I shan't want this money till the week-end. Can I leave it with you?"

"You'll have to pay it into your account, Mr. Pybus."

"Oh—all right. I'm afraid I'm giving you a lot of trouble."

"Oh, not at all."

He went out, smiling, and returned to Parham Crescent, sat at his open window, his widely open window, and felt that life had both enlarged itself and grown more particular. Pah, what a business! And yet he was able to understand the pity of it, the jumble of fleshly necessities and foolishness, the sordid little strategies, the bargainings and deceptions. Just because sex should not be a business proposition. Each of the three had been out for sexual self-expression, and he had been eliminated. Thank the Lord! And poor old Conrad was left to pay for and comfort poor little Olive! Oh—well—it had become their affair, and, after all, the Perfect Swine had behaved rather decently.

But Lance felt that he needed clear air and that widely open window. The reaction was upon him, a turning towards the sea and the sky, and music, and work. His sophistication and his simplicity had been ducked in the same pond, and he had some muddy water to get rid of. Poor little Olive, poor Uncle Conrad, but not poor self.

And yet there was a man in him that cried out: "I want to believe in people. I—must—believe in something. I want to get back to mystery."

Yes, mystery! But what was mystery! Moonlight, and Spanish music, and old trees, and eyes that could weep? Was it romantic self-foolery? Had it an esoteric significance? Were all seers and poets fools, and the only wise men your chemistry professor and the porter who opened to you the door of a night-club? What rot! His thoughts flew out of the open window, and soaring like birds—or like those pigeons of the Venerable's—winged their way to Castle Craven.

5

Lance went down to Castle Craven with the tang of September in his blood. The stale season was over, and the year and its enterprise renewed. He had the Venerable's money in his pocket, and "Rust" complete, save for the last three chapters—neatly tied up in brown paper and packed away at the bottom of his suit-case.   He walked up through Castle Craven with the lightness of a young man who had dropped a load of mischief from his shoulders, and to whom the day was a renewal of the great adventure.   For sometimes youth is so sure that the path goes straight forward over the hill, though the path may prove itself to be a circle, and at its best an ascending spiral.   Man's feet are prone to return to the same slough, the same lotus pool, the same house in Queer Street.

"Grandpater!"

"Hallo, my dear."

Lance put his suit-case on a chair.

"I've brought you all sorts of things."

Old Pybus smiled under his white eyebrows, seeing his grandson's face as the face of three years ago.

"Surprises?"

"Well—there's the book.   It's good.   I believe it is better than I thought.   And this——"

He had the money in his hand.

"I didn't need it—after all.   But your sending of it, grandpater——"

"Was nothing, my dear."

"I think it was everything."

CHAPTER XXVII

I

OLD PYBUS sat up till midnight, his white head close to the green shade of the lamp. He had read his grandson's novel from Chapter I to Chapter XXXII, and when he put the book away and lit his candle, his heart was glad in him.

"Good business!"

After turning out the lamp he went slowly up the little steep staircase, the treads of its steps very white on either side of a strip of brown coconut matting. He trod softly, and pausing outside his grandson's door, stood listening. By all the probabilities Lance should be asleep, but the Venerable, full of his own wakefulness, divined a like wakefulness in Lance. He rapped gently at the door.

"Is that you, grandpater?"

"Yes, my dear. Many happy returns of the inspiration."

"You like it?"

"Great stuff—at your age. Had to stop and tell you. Good night."

"Good night, grandpater—I'm glad. You've had a hand in it."

"Nonsense."

"Oh—yes—you have."

"A little stirring with a spoon—on one occasion. Good night, and God bless you."

In Lance's consciousness this little narrow stairway cut a cleft. It was so clean and so steep, not to be taken at a rush either up or down, and you had to be careful of your head or a beam would smite you. They were ascetic stairs, and yet so very intimate, accompanying him up to that bedroom with the muslin curtains and the pink and white wallpaper, where he had a table at the window. The window itself was full of the spacious sky drawn taut across the Brent valley, and the Castle and its ash trees marking the hour in shadow upon the turf of the Castle Field. And somehow the smallness and the simplicity of the room helped him to concentrate. It was very quiet; he was secure against disturbance. It was like a celibate's cell in the midst of the growing complexity of modern life, and he could withdraw into it, and be saved from too much subtlety, and from being too damned clever.

For, as the Venerable would have it—"There's nothing so damning, my dear, as being too damned clever."

On the Sunday, Lance went up to his room directly after breakfast. His craft had its ritual, its little personal predilections; the window had to be open, but not too much so; a box of matches lay handy; the ink-pot stood just where he could dip his pen into it without being conscious of dipping. He preferred an old-fashioned pen. The deal table provided by the Venerable was an eighth of an inch short on one leg, and had to be underpinned with an old envelope folded four times, and if you moved the table the padding came adrift.

Lance sat down. He allowed himself to look at the landscape while he filled a pipe. The Venerable had gone on duty, and from nine o'clock till twelve the cottage would be a box of blessed silence, and silence was to become more sacred to Lance with each year of his living. He would come in his time to marvel at the world's waste of words, and at the vacuous, fool-chatter poured out unceasingly by people who had nothing within them worthy of silence.

At the top of a white page he inked in the heading— Chapter XXXIII. He sat and looked at the Castle trees. There were days when his consciousness would seem too tense and alert, and ready to be distracted by trivial happenings; a fly crawling on the window-pane, a hair caught up in the nib and smudging the letters. There were mornings when your chair creaked, or your pipe refused to draw. He knew this feeling of tension, this fear of the pen, this over-sensitiveness to the externals. Often it preceded a rush of inspiration. But relaxation was necessary, that clairvoyant calm. He would sit back in his chair, and looking at the sky and the tops of the trees, say to himself—"Relax—relax. Let things come."

That mysterious self which lies beneath the conscious self, had to be persuaded to rise to the surface.

He was on the edge of what he described as "Getting off," when he heard the closing of a door, and the sound of two voices, his grandfather's and a woman's. They were in the room below. The sitting-room window was open, and Lance could hear what the two voices said.

"I feel—that—it can't go on much longer."

"Poor child."

"I must talk. Sometimes one must talk."

"I'll shut the window, my dear. My grandson's working upstairs. Don't want to disturb him."

The window was closed, and the murmur of the two voices continued for a couple of minutes, and then it ceased. A door opened and shut, while Lance sat stiffly attentive. His personal consciousness had come back to him. The moment of inward illumination had passed.

Usually he would have felt some impatience, or like a man on the edge of sleep jarred into sudden wakefulness, but on this Sunday morning he accepted the two voices. They were not fool-voices, and his self had been appeased. "I must talk. Sometimes one must talk." Of course! Moreover, the girl's voice had had an inevitableness. And that utterance had had for him the appeal of the first few notes of a violin when some human movement opens. He ceased to feel impersonal. He stood up and looked out of the window, and saw the two figures pass along by the fence at the end of the cottage garden. Mary Merris and his grandfather.

He watched them across the Castle Field. They disappeared behind a grey wall, and he stood holding the curtain aside, very conscious of the memory of a woman surprised in the midst of her weeping. Why had she wept? What was it that could not go on much longer? What had she to say to his grandfather, and he to her?

Lance stood there to interpret, but the interpretation had a sudden, personal significance. It was within himself, and not to be externalized. He sat down in his chair, and smoked his pipe, and watched. He could picture those two standing in the oriel window and looking out over the Brent valley, or sitting on one of the green benches under the ash trees, but the girl's face was misty to him. In imagination he could not see it clearly—the eyes—the mouth, and suddenly he was conscious of wishing to see it clearly. Her voice was not quite like any other voice. But the Venerable, he could see, that massive white head, and the kind and incorruptible blue eyes.

He sat and waited, and presently he saw his grandfather come back alone, and looking rather as he looked when he fed his pigeons. His eyes and face had an upwardness.

2

Lance and his grandfather dined together at half-past twelve. Old Pybus carried the meal down on a tray from the Saracen kitchen, roast beef and Yorkshire pudding, potatoes and kidney beans, and two helpings of cold plum tart. They sat down opposite each other, and the silence between them was sensitive and expectant. For the Venerable had a feeling that Lance was going to ask him a question, and Lance had that question waiting upon his lips.

"Hope we didn't disturb you, my dear?"

Lance, setting to upon that very English dinner, accepted his opportunity.

"No. I was just casting about. Good of you to think about it, grandpater. Besides——"

Old Pybus, knife and fork in hand, cut a potato in half, and waited.

"Some things are importunate."

"Things or people, my dear?"

"Both. I'll confess, that before you shut that window——"

The Venerable gave him a quick look.

"You did."

"I couldn't help it. And I don't know whether I wanted to help it. Some things have a kind of inevitableness. I suppose I could not be allowed to know——?"

"Just what?"

"Yes, just what."

Old Pybus went on with his dinner, but with an air of being less concerned with it than he was with the affairs of his head and heart. Lance had spoken of the importunity of certain things, but the obviousness of them might be equally assertive. Curiosity—as mere curiosity—may be an idle virtue. And yet the Venerable could be influenced by little secret imaginings. He was ending life as a romanticist. A man's outlook and his reactions seem largely a matter of temperament, and dependent upon the heat of his mystical blood. His grandson had that blessed ardour which will persist in discovering beauty where the eyes of the realist can see nothing but dreariness and muck.

"There's an art of living, my dear, as well as an art of writing."

Lance considered the digression. What had beauty of living to do with a woman's tears?

"You mean, grandpater, that what I might try to put on paper——?"

"Beauty, my dear. There's such a thing as beautiful living. The fine gesture, the compassionate gesture. When you come to the end of life such gestures seem worth while. But most of our gestures are muddled gestures. That ought to be obvious, but it isn't."

Lance looked hard at his plate.

"So—you can't tell me——?"

"I'm not at liberty to tell you, my dear. I don't gossip about her, no, not even to you."

"Sorry, grandpater; I did not mean——"

"I know. Physical things and spiritual things muddled up together. And the spiritual—striving to be itself. What's the balance, the balance between body and spirit? Oh— that't the art, balancing of those two."

Lance got up and changed the plates. He had a feeling that his grandfather was talking just to tantalize him, which—of course—was absurd, for all this mystical stuff must have a human core to it. He placed the cold plum tart and a jug of cream on the table.

"You might be setting me a problem, grandpater."

The Venerable handled the cream jug.

"Perhaps. There are live problems, my dear, as well as problems on paper. And the inevitable fly in the cream jug! How to exclude the fly. Or to keep the wasp from gnawing a hole in the fruit! But other people's problems——"

"She's asking you to help her solve it, grandpater."

The Venerable removed the fly with the handle of a spoon.

"Wish I could, my dear, as easily as that. All sorts of ways of solving a problem. Cutting it out—is one of them. Now, if I were a young man! The violence of youth! Violence may be useful——"

He arose to rid himself of a cream-soaked fly.

"Putting certain things and people out of the window. Wish I could do it sometimes. There's an old saying about silk purses and sows' ears. The old people were more downright. We're so subtle, my dear, that sometimes we can't cut an apple in half. Take plenty of cream."

Lance did so. The cream and the plum juice were sensuously pleasing. But why was the Venerable making all this mystery about Mary Merris?

3

Lance turned from the high-road into the lane which led up past "Marions" to the Woolshot woods. He had come down from Castle Craven to stretch his legs and to do some thinking, for if Old Pybus saw certain things as in a glass darkly, Lance saw them not at all. It may be as difficult to tell just when an apple will fall as to say when curiosity merges into interest.

To begin with, the "Marions" lane might be no more to Lance than a green lane in September, the shaggy hedges closing in a steepish ascent, a green cleft which ended in the blue of the sky and the massive foliage of the beech woods. A robin was singing, and Lance idled. He said to himself that this was the lane in which Mary Merris lived, that mysterious Mary Merris into whose wet eyes he had looked for one short

moment. But was any woman mysterious? It was a mere
sex illusion. And yet, as he went on up the lane, she seemed
to be pressing more deeply into a stillness, a secrecy, a sadness.
He was neither a Jefferies nor a Hudson. Green branches were
green branches, and might be monotonously so; his attitude
to nature was very personal; to youth, nature must have an
intimate meaning, some association with a face or a figure or
an event.

Lance came to the white gate, and looking over it saw the
white porch flanked by the two yew trees, the green door
standing open, and someone's brown raincoat hanging on a
peg. The little house seemed to him as shut in by silence as it
was shut in by green leaves. It had for him a curious melancholy.

He went on. He became possessed by a feeling that an
essential something which belonged to that cottage penetrated
the hedges like a drifting perfume, and filled the lane with a
scented sadness. A melancholy place. And suddenly he
paused, becoming aware of a movement on the other side of
the "Marions" hedge. There was a rustling. He saw an
apple-bough shaken.

Someone began to sing, though the murmuring of the
voice was almost inward, suggesting a little moaning, a sound
produced almost unconsciously by someone who was solitarily
busy, and in a lonely mood. But the words and the melody
were recognizable.

"Bend down, bend down to the waters, Melisande."

The music was not of his generation nor of hers, and yet it
belonged to all time. The prongs of a light ladder appeared
in the foliage of the tree. A branch trembled. A dark head
appeared, and then a hand reaching out for a red apple.

The hand plucked the apple, but even in the plucking of it
seemed to hesitate as though the owner of the hand had been
made aware of that other presence. She turned her head, but
very slowly. She saw beyond the hedge Lance's upturned
face and watching eyes.

Neither of them spoke. He gave her a quick and self-conscious lift of the hat, and went on up the lane, while she remained motionless for a moment, her bosom pressed against one of the rungs of the ladder.

4

Early in October, No. 7 Blount Street restored to No. 7 Parham Crescent the person of Olive Gadsden. She was able to walk upstairs, and unhelped, though Conrad was there to encourage and assist, and to close the door on a too officious Mrs. Gasson.

"Get me a cushion, Con."

His fat hands stuffed a cushion into her chair. His largeness, swathed in grey, undulated sympathetically, and a round-eyed survey of her apartment left him puzzled but not displeased.

"Can't think why you wanted to come back here."

"Stuffy little place—but the old woman's rather a good sort. Besides—I don't sponge."

He bent down and pressed his full lips to the back of her shingled neck. He was full of nascent uxoriousness.

"Well—that's all right. There won't be much wrong with Chlois Court, Kid. And what about 'Monte' for the honeymoon?"

She allowed him his fondlings, for obviously they were to be part of the business. She was feeling scratchy, and not in the best of tempers, much as a shop-girl may feel at the end of the January sales. She cherished a sense of bitterness against both her lovers, for one had ceased too easily to care, and the other's caring was too inanely amorous. Infernal predicament! She was not afraid of being fastidiously shocked by his fat finality, but she was afraid of being bored by it.

Mrs. Gasson entered soon after Conrad had left.

"Well, I do 'ope as you are 'appy, dearie. I must say he's a reel affable gent."

Olive's red mouth seemed to writhe.

"He's a fool! A damned slobbering fool! If there were enough girls like me we'd scream the roof off this blasted world."

Mrs. Gasson made soothing noises.

"There—there, you look at the ring on your finger, and think of the car you come here in."

"Like to look?"

She twitched the ring from her finger, and tossed it to Mrs. Gasson, who, with a face of alarm, caught it in a fold of her apron.

"My, it's a marvel! Dimonds and roobies. But you're that reckless, dearie; you always was. Now don't you be for spiting yourself. Marridge is marridge. If you're out for marridge—well—I always says to a gal, do it comfortably."

"I shall. But suppose I didn't?"

"'Mirabeau's,' dearie!"

"No."

"Sure?"

"I've averaged it out. Don't ask me any more silly questions. I'm feeling a bit raw."

"Not hankering after the young one, are you?"

"Oh, shut up! I'm staying on here for a week or two. He wants to take a furnished flat for me till the orange blossom season begins."

Mrs. Gasson, quite imperturbed, handed back the ring.

"I'll get you a cup o' tea, dearie. A cup o' tea 'elps you to get sophical about things. I got sophical long ago. So'll you, dearie. It's just like a moosical comedy, only sometimes you get caught laughin' on the wrong leg."

So Olive sat at her upper window, and realizing life as an affair of bargains, yet felt a grudge against it. She was not fastidious; always—she had been too hard up to allow herself the cult of the fastidious. But she was conscious of the vulgarity and the cheapness of her surroundings, and of her involvement in them. Gossipings with that common, cynical, if kind, old woman! Always—the acceptance of the third-rate and the tarnished. She had had her dreams of little splendours, and now comfort tempted her, a sort of kindness

which was like a large white pillow, money, display, the power
to do things, to order other people about, to walk into
"Mirabeau's" and buy the dresses off the shoulders of other
women.   As for the other half of the bargain—there was—
as Mrs. Gasson had said—the philosophy of getting used to
things.   She was quite sure that she could manage Conrad, for
when a man who was past fifty got silly about a woman he
could be kept silly.   She would have breakfast in bed.   She
would insist on her own car.   The possibilities were varied
and intriguing.

And yet she was conscious of resentment, of a feeling of
rawness.   She would have liked to have combined the properties of youth and the virtues of property.   She had her
grievance.   She might be very old in her sophistications, but
she had a youthfulness of appetite.

Hence this little red blur of resentment which would not
cool—but retained its heat.   She sat at her window, and
looked along the crescent at that other window where Lance
sat at work.   She could not see him at work, but she saw his
goings out and his comings in.   He was the same Lance; he
had the same swift and ardent walk, the same carriage of the
head, that slimness at the hips, and breadth of shoulder.   He
was everything that Conrad was not.   He never looked up at
her window.   He was obviously and cheerfully active about
his own affairs.

The little red blur of anger in her was formed to a fiercer
glow whenever she saw him.   She wanted to be even with
him, to retaliate, to hurt him as he had hurt her.   Her resentment hovered.

She sat and watched.   She had books, flowers, chocolates,
Conrad's daily homage, the croonings of an assiduous and
well-rewarded Mrs. Gasson.   She was able to walk out on
those slim legs of hers and sit in Regent's Park.   She sat there
in the October sunshine, under the yellowing trees, a sulky-
faced young woman with eyes which seemed to be searching
for some particular face or figure.

Her inspiration came to her quite suddenly while she was
walking back one afternoon to Parham Crescent.   She flushed,

her eyes gave a gleam.   Of course!   Why hadn't she thought of it before?

She met Mrs. Gasson on the landing.

"My, dearie, you—do—look better!"

"I feel better!"

"You're the peach blossom—again, I can tell you."

Olive sat down in her chair by the window.   She was able to recapitulate the movements of No. 17.   Lance appeared daily upon the pavement at about half-past eleven and returned to No. 17 in time for lunch.   He went out again about two, and was not seen again till four.   He had his working hours and his walking hours, and they did not appear to vary.

Conrad came to tea with her every day at half-past four.

Her inspiration arranged its time-table.

CHAPTER XXVIII

I

MRS. CARVER opened the door of No. 17. Asked if Mr. Pybus was in, she crinkled up her wizened and perpetually frightened little face as though the persuasive sheen of that other face was too bright for her.

"No, he's out. Went out ten minutes ago, Miss."

"How annoying. How long will he be?"

"I really can't say, Miss. He usually comes back to tea."

Mrs. Carver was one of those women who do not open a door more than nine inches; she had none of Mrs. Gasson's large, free, and welcoming gestures; she looked at Olive with all the suspicion of the plain and put-upon woman for that other sort of woman. Yes, the young person might smile. But Mrs. Carver's caution could be easily coerced; she was no more than a cobweb stretched across the gap.

"How annoying!"

Olive's face had an animated friendliness.

"You see, he has asked me to meet his people to-night. I'll just run up to his room and write a note. Third floor front— I think?"

The assurance of her attack appeared to press Mrs. Carver and the door back against the wall. She gave way even before Olive had made a forward movement, the draught of the other's purpose seemed sufficient.

"I don't know whether I ought to, Miss."

"It's quite all right."

She walked in and past the landlady, reassuring, confident.

"I shan't be three minutes."

Mrs. Carver saw her flying up the stairs like a long-legged girl of fourteen. She was opening Lance's door while the landlady was still prevaricating with herself in the dark little hall. Mouth open and awry, and her breathing tumultuous after that dash up the narrow stairs, she looked about her. Yes, there was a key in the door. She turned it, and with her hand still on the key, she stood with her back to the door, her eyes seeming to consume the room. A fire? Yes, there was a fire. And if she was lucky——?

She was lucky. On Lance's table by the window two neat piles of paper lay side by side, the manuscript and the typed copy of "Rust," completed three days ago, and read through for the last time that very morning. She crossed the room with a swift, gliding rush, and, with her two hands resting on the back of Lance's chair, looked at the two piles of paper.

"RUST"

A Novel

By

LANCELOT PYBUS

Her nostrils dilated. Yes, she was in luck, and able to command a devastating gesture. Her spite hovered and smiled; her fingers curved themselves over the back of the chair like claws. She had no pity; she was telling herself that all this stuff would not be consumed in three minutes.

Her teeth were uncovered, and almost with a little snarl she fell upon the thing that he had created. She carried both manuscript and typescript to the fire, and kneeling down began to tear and to burn. She read never a word of it. She wrenched away a dozen pages at a time, and piling them on edge, saw the flames curl and ascend.

Someone tried the door. Mrs. Carver's footsteps were as surreptitious and as timid as her soul.

"Are you there, Miss?"

"It's all right."

"You've locked the door."

"It's all right."

She tore and tore with a kind of furious and animal haste,

and as though she knew and felt that she was tearing the very man himself. Her face had impressed upon it a curious effect of laughter, but her exultation was silent.

"You oughtn't to have locked the door."

"No need to worry."

"What are you doing?"

"Oh, tearing up a few old things."

Mrs. Carver's voice quavered into consternation.

"Open the door—at once. What will he say?"

"Quite a lot, perhaps."

She tore and burnt. The flames were half up the chimney, and the fender full of flaming paper. When the stuff caked she thrust at it with the poker, heaving it up so that air and fire could penetrate. Her face shone in the glare. And all the while she breathed with a shallow quickness, as though she had a hill to climb, and was breathless in her rage to reach the summit.

Mrs. Carver, after listening to that sound of rending paper, went with a fluttering swiftness down the stairs.

"Annie—Annie——"

A girl appeared frowsily from the depths.

"What's wrong?"

"There's a young woman in Mr. Pybus's room. She's locked the door—she's ——"

"Lawks——!"

"Call the police. Oh—my poor head! No, I don't want any scandal. What'll we do? She's burning things."

Said the girl: "I'd have the police in—if I was you."

But Mrs. Carver preferred to listen on the stairs, while in Lance's room Olive sat back on her heels and contemplated a grate and fender that were full of black and quaking ash. Her face had a malignant serenity. She supposed that she had done the job pretty completely. But had she? Might there not be another copy? She was up and searching, pulling out drawers, turning them out upon the floor, and exploring his empty suit-case and attaché cases. She found no other copy—"Rust" was dead, a thing of smouldering ash, an inspiration which had glowed and been extinguished.

Hunting up a pencil and half-sheet of notepaper, and sitting down in Lance's chair, she allowed herself a last impudence. She drew the profile of a face, and the outline of a hand with its thumb and fingers spread, and scrawled below it: "Quits, my lad! Now go and sneak to somebody."

On her way down the stairs she met Mrs. Carver reascending, and passed by her with an urchin's swagger.

"You can tell Mr. Pybus that I called."

Mrs. Carver, mouth open and eyes blinking, remained irresolutely mute. She hurried on and up and into Mr. Pybus's room, and stood regarding the disorder, and that mass of ash and charred paper. Her face was like the face of a whimpering child.

2

Lance returned at four, and Mrs. Carver, who had been waiting for the sound of his latch-key, dragged herself up the kitchen stairs to meet him. She shook. Her tremulousness discovered a sudden volubility.

"Oh, sir, someone's been in your room; that young woman from No. 7. She said as how you expected a message, and I let her in, not thinking like. She said she'd write a note."

Lance's eyes stared.

"Well——?"

"I'm afraid she's—burnt something; all those papers that were lying on your table."

She saw the sudden wincing of Lance's startled face. "Just as though I'd thrown vitriol at him, poor dear," as she said to the girl afterwards. He went from her with a silent swiftness; he seemed to climb the stairs like a man swarming up a rope. His door banged, and then there was silence.

Mrs. Carver was terrified, but she found the courage—a kind of mother courage—to impel her up the stairs. There was not a sound from the room, and she waited, her body bent towards the door, her hand to her head. After bearing that silence for fully two minutes she knocked.

No one answered, and feeling still more frightened, she put her hand to the handle and opened the door six inches.

She saw Lance sitting on a chair, holding the poker, and staring at that mass of burnt paper. He appeared to be un-aware of the open door or of Mrs. Carver's frightened face. He just sat and stared. And she closed the door very gently, and leaning against the landing hand-rail began to whimper with a kind of surreptitious solemnity.

"Oh, poor dear! How could she have done it?"

3

For more than half an hour Mrs. Carver vacillated between the first-floor landing and the kitchen. She got Mr. Pybus's tea ready, and then was afraid to carry up the tray. She sent the girl up with it, and waited at the foot of the stairs.

The girl returned with the tray.

"Says 'e don't want it."

"Oh, poor young gentleman! What's he doing?"

"Packing 'is suit-case."

"Packing! Why didn't I slam the door in that little slut's face? There's bound to be trouble. What'll I do, Annie?"

"What can you do?" said the girl, who looked sobered and sorry.

But in a little while the two of them heard Lance coming down the stairs. He was carrying his suit-case. His face had a haggard blankness.

"You're not leaving us, sir?"

"I'm going down to a friend, Mrs. Carver."

"Oh, sir—I can't say how sorry——"

He looked at her with a peculiar gentleness.

"Spilt milk. No fault of yours. I'll let you know."

He went towards the door, and she followed, remorseful, deprecating.

"If I'd only known, sir——"

He glanced back at her as he opened the door.

"Who could have known? Who would have thought? That's about all one can say."

4

The Venerable had received a parcel of books from London, and, after looking through them by the light of his lamp, he arranged them in that particular corner of his bookshelf where he kept volumes that might be called acquaintances, but were not yet friends. It occurred to him to think that he would keep a very particular niche for Lance's books, and especially for the first-born, "Rust." He stood with his white head slightly on one side, in a mood of abstraction, until the rubbing of the cat against his legs recalled him to other responsibilities. He bent down to caress Sarah and, opening the door, watched the black shape of her flit out into the darkness. The Castle Craven tower clock boomed nine. A faint drizzle was falling, and the October night had a soft and almost expectant sadness. The stars and the moon were washed out, and somewhere a leaky gutter dripped rhythmically in the wet silence.

Old Pybus, having breathed in the damp savour of the autumn night, was about to close the door, when he heard footsteps crossing the cobbles of the Saracen yard. They came quickly down the broad passage leading to the cottage and the Castle Field. Old Pybus's white eyebrows expressed a surprised alertness. He had been thinking of Lance, and surely these footsteps——!

A figure shaped itself in the drizzling gloom.

"Grandpater."

"My dear!"

And then Old Pybus saw his grandson's face, lit by the lamplight through the doorway. It seemed to come out of the night like the face of one suddenly and strangely sick. It was the face of the unexpected, abrupt and disturbing.

The Venerable reached for the suit-case.

"You're ill, my dear."

But Lance retained his hold of the suit-case. He did not

L

look into his grandfather's face. He seemed to flinch from the blue eyes; he kept his head down.

"No, I'm all right. But—I've been knocked out——"

"What's happened, my dear?"

"I'll tell you in a minute. I'm rather done."

There was a strange, intimate, yet awkward silence between them, while old Pybus closed the door with one hand and held Lance's arm with the other. His blue eyes saw things quickly, for Lance was in the light now, looking strangely thin, and pinched about the nostrils.

"Sit down, child."

He saw Lance lower the suit-case to the floor and sit down in one of the Windsor chairs. It was done with a kind of passivity, as though the physical had been over-stimulated and exhausted by the mental. Lance had burnt himself out.

His grandfather went straight to the little brown cupboard beside the fireplace.

"Had anything to eat lately?"

"No—not since——"

"Put your head down, my dear. Here—drink this. I'll get you some supper."

The glass went to Lance's lips, and as he raised his head to swallow the brandy his eyes had a smudged and vacant look.

"I walked up the hill rather fast. Be all right in a minute. I had to come to you, grandpater."

Inwardly old Pybus was seething, but he pottered off with outward calmness into the kitchen and, feeling for the box of matches in his right-hand pocket, lit a candle that was on the dresser. What had happened? Why had Lance torn the heart out of himself in walking up Castle Craven hill? The Venerable, with a kind of stoical deliberation, opened the kitchen cupboard, and began to lay his hands on what was available, cheese, butter, a couple of eggs, half a loaf of bread.

Suddenly he heard his grandson's voice.

"Grandpater."

"Hallo."

"The book's gone west—my book."

Old Pybus stood still with the milk jug in his hand. It

occurred to him to think how often he and Lance had talked to each other through that doorway.

"Do you mean that Richmond has refused it?"

"No—it's been burnt—type and manuscript—every page."

The Venerable put the milk jug down upon the kitchen table, for his hand was trembling a little.

"Burnt! Good God, my dear! Who?"

"I'll tell you. I've been in a kind of hell these last few hours, grandpater. A girl burnt it."

"A girl? By mistake?"

"No, on purpose. You see, we had had an affair—and I was the first to see—how futile. I'll try and tell you about it sometime. But she got into my room while I was out and made a bonfire—of my book."

There was anguish in his voice, a protest against the thing that had happened.

"Nine months' work. She might have done anything but that. A book's like a child; you've had birth pangs—and the joy. She couldn't have understood. Just spite, a kind of jealousy. It's as though I had seen——"

His voice sank into nothingness, and old Pybus, with white eyebrows twitching, picked up one of the eggs and with a sort of restrained fierceness cracked the shell and emptied the contents into a china bowl.

"It's a damnable thing—a very damnable thing. We have got to get through with it—somehow. You sit still, my dear. I'll make you an omelette. I am rather good at omelettes."

5

The Venerable's white head was wet with the rain. The choice had been Lance's, the wet turf of the Castle Field at eleven o'clock on an October night, and the smudged darkness drawn about them like a curtain. To and fro, to and fro. And in the great stillness of the stagnant night their voices went on and on like the Brent quoting its endless self in the valley below the beeches.

"I can't face it, grandpater."

"You must, my dear."

They had talked for an hour before these particular words were spoken. They would pause and stand still, and Lance, with the rain on his face, would be conscious of his grandfather's white head, and of the wet and gentle darkness. London seemed very far away, and all that monkey world in which you snatched and tore and swallowed at life in a rage of self-gratification.

What a night for old Pybus, a night of exultation and of pain, and of dear and exasperating moments, when the beloved child who had fled to him behaved like a little wailing boy. And the telling of the tale! It was blurted out with a jerky vividness, the phrases snatched out of the darkness and made to flare for a moment. His description of Olive! "All legs and lip-stick. It was her mouth that—somehow— made me mad—grandpater——" He talked endlessly about the burning of the book; for a time he could speak of nothing else, having been appalled by the ruthless reaction of her spite. "She might have done anything to me but that." And sometimes old Pybus would hold him fast by the arm, or let him walk a little apart, wavering from side to side, and always varying his rhythm. Youth in pain, youth writhing, youth burning its lips with the sacred wine of suffering.

Yet something had to be smashed; that illusion of self-satisfaction, that young and ruthless egotism. For a while old Pybus let him talk, for in listening he breathed the atmosphere of the whole affair, and in the drizzle of that October night the thing became so clear. Lance had played the animal game and had got himself clawed, though that other young animal had dug her claws into the artist. She had answered ruthlessness with ruthlessness. Lance must have hurt her; it was action and reaction; few bad things are done out of sheer badness of heart.

"She clawed you, my dear. And why?"

He might be Balaam's ass standing in the path of youth's passionate protestings. He, too, began to talk gently with a kind of naked tenderness. Let life be naked for the moment.

Let the precious and bloody marks be seen and understood. Things have a horrible way of averaging themselves out.

"You broke with her, my lad. Breaking may be a blow. Perhaps she didn't see it as you did. She struck back. Oh— I'm not saying it wasn't damnable."

He, too, was ruthless, the old Roman.

"If you get into a cage, my dear, to play the sex game with naked sex—yes—I know. She clawed the soul of you. What could you expect?"

He wrestled with youth. Youth had to be brought down, made to kneel with humility before man's justice—which might be God's justice. All the old rectitudes, the old wholesome chivalries, the simple tendernesses. Sex—as a mere mouth! Even he could use the whip.

"You've been clawed, my dear—and if I've rubbed in the salt—it's because——"

Something seemed to break in the wet stillness.

"Grandpater."

"My child."

Old Pybus somehow felt the weight of him, the wetness of him.

"Stand up to it. When a flying-lad crashed in the war they sent him up again next day—to conquer the sense of crash. To-morrow, yes—there's always a to-morrow."

"You can't repeat a thing."

"Oh, yes, you can; you've got to. Meanwhile—old lad— it's nearly twelve o'clock, and your coat's wet through, and I've got to put you to bed. No sheets aired. You'll have to manage between blankets."

"I shan't sleep."

He held Lance firmly.

"You'll try to—anyway. Come along."

Watching the kettle on the fire, before which he had hung Lance's wet coat, and listening to Lance moving in the room above, old Pybus realized how mixed are life's emotions. "God forgive me, but I'm glad." Yes, it was possible to curse and to bless, and to see beyond the tangle of such an affair. He had a stone bottle ready on a chair, and as he poured the hot water into it from the kettle's mouth, he smiled and repeated one of his own apothegms—"There's nothing so damning as being just damned clever." Didn't he know? Oh—surely! He screwed in the stopper, and after wrapping the bottle in a piece of flannel, poured the rest of the hot water into a glass containing three ounces of good whisky and a lump of sugar. He ascended the stairs, first with the hot bottle, and then with the good toddy.

"Hallo, my dear, in bed?"

"Yes."

"Nothing like a night-cap. I'm coming in."

The hot bottle wrapped in flannel was slipped into Lance's bed.

"Good for too much blood to the head. You drink this down, child."

Lance lay and looked up at his grandfather almost as a child looks at its nurse. The man-child in him needed comforting.

"You're too good to me, grandpater. I don't know why."

Old Pybus's face had a mischievous tenderness.

"Oh, you are going to find that out."

6

The Venerable sat down in front of the fire. The hour was half-past twelve, but he did not feel like going to bed. Not he, when the most human and wonderful thing that an old fellow could have wished for had happened.

After all what was a burnt book at five and twenty? Better a burnt book at that age than a charred cleverness at five and forty. For if Lance was destined to write the great stuff that touches the heart of the world—then he—Lance—must have the heart to do it. No use being just damned clever. "Rust" had been a little too damned clever.

Old Pybus filled a pipe.

"Too good to him, am I? Being good to someone other than yourself! How very old and simple. Oh, my child, you needed this wound."

He smiled, and leaning forward with his elbows on his knees, gently poked the fire. His old, wise, fearless face warmed to it. His philosophy of life spread its hands. For old Pybus believed that no great and good thing can come out of life without suffering. Youth must have its blow over the heart. It is good and necessary for youth to be floored, and to get up sick and dizzy, and perhaps with a little whimper of shame.

"Too much for self—too much for self."

He smiled.

Would it happen as he wished? He trusted and believed so. Lance would pick himself up, and with a shake of the head, and with that slow smile of his, look life squarely in the eyes. "I have learnt something, grandpater, because I have felt something."

Well, it was time for an old fellow to go to bed, and old Pybus pulled off his slippers, and went softly up the stairs. He paused on the landing to listen.

"Poor old Probyn. The boy came to me. I shall have to see about it—yes—see about it. Full up to the brim—what? Poor old Probyn must be thirsty."

7

Lance was out somewhere in the country, walking—walking, and seeing the world and life as an autumnal scene, for when youth feels old, nothing can be more solemnly decrepit, and Lance was feeling very old. He was sore and stiff with the shedding of a skin. Life seemed a sad and shabby affair. But he was awake to the burning beauty of the beech woods, and in passing down the "Marions" lane he could remember Mary's brother in his blindness, and say within himself— "Poor devil."

Meanwhile the Venerable was active and abroad in Castle Craven. He called at the stationer's shop next the bank and made various purchases. He returned to the cottage with a brown paper parcel and a bunch of bronze and white chrysanthemums. He ascended the narrow stairs.

Lance, returning about twelve o'clock, and mounting to his little room under the tiles, found his table set by the window with ink and a pile of unruled foolscap, and in one corner a vase of flowers. He crossed the room and stood by the table; he picked up the pen that was laid ready and saw that the particular nib he used had been provided.

And suddenly his eyes grew hot. He found himself at the top of the narrow stairs, and listening to his grandfather's footsteps in the room below. He was conscious of turbulent and swift emotion, a rush of something that was creative and generous and splendid.

"Grandpater——"

"Hallo."

"I—I've found—that table. I'll start work—to-morrow."

Old Pybus came to the foot of the stairs.

"No need to worry, my dear. You'll do it again and you'll do it better. Oh, yes—you will. I have got enough for both of us."

He saw Lance's face looking down.

"You mean—I can stay here, till——?"

"Of course. It's an idea—isn't it? Write and tell Richmond what's happened, and that you'll have a new 'Rust' to show him in six months."

"Grandpater——"

Old Pybus's cup of life was brimming over.

CHAPTER XXIX

I

THUS, so far as Lance was concerned, Parham Crescent ceased to be Parham Crescent, but the problem of Windover remained. Lance could take from the Venerable that which he could not take from his own father. Mrs. Carver was paid, and Lance's belongings were packed and sent down to Castle Craven, and Mrs. Carver, deprecating and scared as ever, had wanted to know what Lance's address would be.

"In case of letters, sir."

"Forward them to Windover."

"I'd like to say again, sir—that I shall never forgive myself —somehow—for letting that young wretch. She's left the Crescent, sir."

"It wasn't your fault, Mrs. Carver. One doesn't expect such things to happen."

"Aren't you going to do anything about it—sir, prosecute her?"

"No; nothing."

But the problem of Windover remained, in spite of a fortnight's furious and triumphant work upon the new "Rust," and comings and goings up those narrow stairs, and the applauding blue eyes of his grandfather and a letter from John Richmond that was like the stretching of a big and generous hand.

"If you can rewrite that book and make a better book of it—you will be a great man, my lad. Go to it."

Yes, what of Windover, and this long concealed and singular comradeship? Lance did sit down and write a brief and rather casual letter to his father, in which he said that he had gone down into the country to stay with a friend, and he had contrived to get the letter posted in London, so that the Castle Craven postmark should not appear.

Sir Probyn was posed. Why this secrecy? And nothing
was said about the book and of Richmond's yea or nay.
Probyn, with spectacles on nose—the monocle was less in
evidence—sat long over that letter and was reproached by it.
His son's silences were becoming more and more a matter of
reproach; that they had never understood each other was no
reason for the continuation of a misunderstanding which
disturbed the elder man more and more. Probyn had mellowed. He was beginning to regard things as things and not
as mere possessions.

He sneaked up to town and called at No. 17 Parham
Crescent. Mrs. Carver had on her scared and wincing face.
Oh, yes, Mr. Pybus had left; she had had orders to send letters
to Windover; and didn't Sir Probyn know?

Probyn squinted. He was feeling just a little humiliated
even in the presence of this deprecating little person.

"He told me he had gone into the country, but he gave me
no address."

Mrs. Carver blinked.

"Must be only temporary, sir. But didn't Mr. Pybus tell
you about his book?"

"No. What about the book?"

"Then—I don't think it's any business of mine, sir. I
expect you'll hear."

More mystery, more equivocations! Probyn could not
bring himself to cross-question the lady; but to be cut off in
this way, to be left in the dark feeling rather like a superfluous
old dotard! He went back to Windover, and as his car carried
him up the avenue of beeches under the flaming foliage,
he felt towards Windover as he had never felt before, as to a
house that was pitying and gracious and protective. He was
conscious of its beauty. Also, he was conscious of a sense of
emptiness and of smarting bewilderment. How much had
he carried in his head all these years, too much in his head,
perhaps, and too little in his heart?

But there was Doll to be considered. Should he tell his
wife anything, and, if so, how much? After all, was he not
exaggerating the significance of Lance's silence? The boy had

given Windover as his address, but as yet no letters for Lance had come to Windover. Probyn decided to say nothing. He was worried about poor old Doll; in his good nature he refrained from passing on other worries to her.

But in front of old Pybus's fire, while smoking their pipes after supper, Windover was approached, for the approach to Windover was inevitable. The Venerable could consider the magnanimous gesture, for he was watching his beloved child picking himself up after being given a pair of blooded knees; and perhaps those late October days were the happiest days of old Pybus's life. Somehow he had felt himself sharing in Lance's act of courage. He understood it as few men would have understood it. The rewriting of "Rust" was an act of courage, the going up to recover and to repeat that which had been written and lost; to make the second leap, for the creative spirit is impatient of repetition.

"Read that, grandpater."

And he had been able to say to Lance—"Great stuff, my dear. There's something in this second edition that wasn't in the other."

"You're not humbugging?"

"I'm not."

For with strange suddenness, a something had come into Lance's work which had not been there before, a sympathy, the beginnings of a more complete tenderness, a little tremor that was half-tears, half-laughter. It had—perhaps—less veneer, less of the polished alabaster. It was more raw and more human.

As to Windover, it was the Venerable who made the first approach.

"They ought to know, my dear. Now—that life has become a rather serious business. I'm feeling——"

Lance looked at his grandfather across the light of the fire.

"How?"

"Just a little guilty."

"You?"

"Well—yes. Now, who's to tell them, you or I"

Lance, with his pipe between folded hands and his elbows on his knees, looked steadily at the flames.

"Just when I'm right on the top of the wave. And a pensioner, grandpater! I was so damned touchy."

"No need to feel touchy, my dear. But somehow I think the responsibility's mine."

"Why should it be?"

"The *beau geste*, my dear."

"Yes—that."

"And something more."

Their eyes met, their eyes that were so alike.

"I've been rather a selfish young devil."

"Words of wisdom, child; but a selfish old devil is worse than a young one."

2

It was with Lance's knowledge that the Venerable packed a bag and, assigning to himself a two days' holiday, set out on that great adventure, for a great adventure it was, and as singular as any in which Sancho Panza shared. Old Pybus left the train at Cheam station. A Ford taxi, with windows rattling and mudguards flapping like broken wings, carried him to Windover, and up that soaring and splendid avenue. Old Pybus, sitting well forward on his seat, saw most things that were to be seen, the afternoon sunlight aslant through the autumn trees, the rolling grassland of Probyn's park, the ornamental water and the swans, the soft red stateliness of the old house. So this was Probyn's house, the home of the city father, the sonless fellow who had made a fortune in wool!

The Venerable got out of the taxi, leaving his bag inside it. He proposed to spend the night at the Golden Harp at Cheam.

"Better wait a minute."

The man-servant who came to the door, and who had instructions to discourage the too many penurious persons who came to tout for subscriptions or to sell books, eyed old Pybus, and not knowing him from Adam, waited for the usual question.

"Is Sir Probyn Pybus in?"

All of them asked that question, and if the knight was not at home, they inquired for his lady.

"Any appointment?"

The Venerable had a letter ready.

"No. Take that in to your master. I'll wait here."

The letter was taken in, and old Pybus stood with his back to the door, and looked across the terrace and the gardens to the burning beech woods, and thought of Lance at work in that little upper room. The pomp of life! Certainly Probyn had provided himself with beauty; purchased it, in fact, at that happy moment when the previous possessors of it had been eliminated by the revenue officials. And how would Probyn receive that letter, and the little old fellow who had come to tilt at Windover instead of at Windmills? The Venerable could picture Probyn screwing that monocle into his eye, and squinting at that letter, that very simple letter. Poor old Probyn! He had a very fine property here, and a son who at the moment asked for nothing but to be shabby and quiet while the urge of creation was upon him. For your artist is the eternal child; he will—if he is healthy—prefer to play with the toys of his own creation to having all Gamage's unloaded at his feet.

The servant returned, to find the Venerable surveying the landscape as though it was his for the looking at, and the taxi-man smoking a cigarette.

"Sir Probyn will see you, sir."

Old Pybus faced about with a curious smile.

When the man-servant opened the door of the library old Pybus saw his elder son standing at the french window with his back to the room, a long black silhouette against the gold of an old catalpa which grew on the lower lawn. The door was open, and Probyn must have known that it was open—but he began his confrontation of that awkward occasion with a flat and secret back. It had come upon him very suddenly. Two minutes ago he had been sitting at his desk reading the short and uncompromising letter that had made him remember the blue stare of his father's eyes.

"The gentleman, sir."

Old Pybus walked in, and the man closed the door, and Probyn, as though his shoes were glued to the parquet and the movement cost him no inconsiderable effort, resolved to face his father. He bent slightly, and stiffly at the hips. Old Pybus was a formidable deputation.

"Very surprising. But—I'm glad."

The Venerable standing very still in the middle of the room, and observing his son's face, replied with a movement of the head.

"Astonishing to both of us—no doubt. I came from Cheam. I'm staying the night there. My taxi's waiting."

Probyn responded with a wooden movement of the right arm.

"Sit down—won't you."

"Thanks."

"Care for a cigar?"

"Not in the middle of the afternoon, and not at my age. Fine place—this—of yours, Probyn."

"Yes; nice old place. Still at Castle Craven?"

"Yes; still at Castle Craven."

And Probyn looked at his father, and went to pick up the letter that lay on the desk. His movements were slow and heavy, as though the workings of his consciousness were weighted and delayed—and most uncomfortably so—by that other presence. What was its significance? What the devil did the old boy want? And yet Probyn was aware of a curious sort of throb.

"You said—here—that you had something to tell me."

Almost he had said "Father," and old Pybus, sitting erect in one of the deep chairs and looking rather like a waiting eagle, blinked his eyes momentarily.

"Yes—that's so. About Lance."

Probyn's head seemed to give a jerk.

"Lance? But——"

"Exactly. Keeping a secret too long, Probyn, may sometimes come to smell like a secret sin. Perhaps you won't understand that, perhaps you will. Do you know where Lance is?"

Probyn seemed to draw his breath and hold it.

"No. In the country somewhere. But—what——?"

"Well, I'm here to tell you that he is with me."

"At Cheam?"

"No; Castle Craven—living with me. The boy found me out nearly five years ago," and then he added in a very gentle voice: "He's rather a fine lad, Probyn, finer—perhaps—in his way—than either you or I. You have got to take it—as it is."

Probyn appeared to compel himself to walk to the fire and to stand there with a pretence of warming his hands.

"Don't quite take you. Do you mean that you and the boy——?"

"Four or five years ago, Probyn—if you remember."

Probyn did remember. His face looked hot.

"And after that?"

"Lance turned up one day. He used to drive over; he had found out who I was. I did not know him for my grandson, and he kept his secret for a while. Since—then——"

"I see."

"No—you don't see—yet, Probyn. It's not quite so easy. You and I have something to forgive each other—if we have any sense left in us. You see—in a way—I understood the lad."

Probyn's face seemed to be growing redder. When he spoke his voice had a thickness as though he had developed a sudden cold in the head. The stoop of his shoulders was awkward.

"Are you the friend in the country?"

"I suppose so."

"For years he has been going down to see you?"

"About once a month."

"Suppose you thought—that—you were getting back at me—through the boy."

Old Pybus stood up.

"No; as a matter of fact, I didn't. It just happened that way. The boy came to me; he wanted to come. Somehow we talked the same language."

"You backed him against me."

"No. If you see it—as I see it, Probyn, it is history repeating itself; fathers and sons, fathers and sons. I made rather a mess of being a father."

Watching his son's back the Venerable was moved to feel that Probyn had sore shoulders.

"I think—on the whole—you did much better than I did, my lad. Life's a queer business. Youth has to blaze its trail. I want to say that I wasn't glad. If it had been Conrad——"

"You say you have got him with you now?"

"He came to me. I'll tell you why, and just why he is going to be with me for six months."

Old Pybus had refused a cigar, but he did bring out one of his old pipes and fill and smoke it. He stood by the window, puffing steadily, and looking out over the garden and the park, while Probyn remained by the fire, leaning one elbow on the oak shelf. He had a very tired look; his eyes watched the fire. For he was listening to the very human story of his son and his son's book and a woman, and seeing the message beneath, a palimpsest, the mystic inwardness and meaning of it all. For Lance, when life had dealt him that first wound, had gone to the old man—his grandfather, had fled to him to be comforted and healed and to have his feet planted once more upon the upward and creative path. The father was aware of a dull sense of humiliation and of failure. The thing twinged in him.

"Supposing you were in my place?"

Old Pybus appeared to consider that question.

"Suppose I was, Probyn, if a little differently. Neither you nor I appear to have understood our sons. Isn't that common ground? Can't we meet on it? If Lance has children, I don't suppose I shall see them, but you will. Meanwhile——"

His pipe had gone out and he relit it.

"Let Lance alone. Let him alone—and he'll come back. I can see him on the way to it. If only people would not clutch. He's as proud as hell. He wants to fight his own fight. So did you. Let him alone, Probyn. He's learning—learning fast."

And suddenly he crossed over and stood near his son.

"I'm only a finger-post, or an old fellow who is keeping a quiet corner for him while he fights it out with himself. He's the most lovable creature. Be wiser than I was. Don't meddle. He'll come over to see you——"

He laid a hand on his son's arm.

"I'm a very old man, and you are not so young as you were. We can afford to be a little big. That's all I have to say."

3

On the night when the Venerable was sleeping at Cheam, Lance had drawn the curtains across the window of his upper room, and lit the lamp. He was in the mood for work; he had been working well all day, and the urge was still on him. He could not say why or how. All that he could say was that he was seeing things very clearly, and seeing life with more depth to it, as though the particular pool into which he gazed was clearer than it had been. The new "Rust" was coming to him differently, it had more volume; and already he was realizing that in the earlier edition he had missed his opportunities. Previously the characters had been scored in like clever caricatures in carbon, flat figures; but now they seemed to separate themselves from the surface of the paper. He felt himself all round them. They were more understandable, more human.

He had been working for twenty minutes when something occurred to disturb him. There was an impatient lifting of the head. The hand that held the pen rested tentatively on the edge of the table.

"Let them knock."

The stillness of the cottage seemed to resent the interruption as much as he did. It closed over the sound and smoothed itself out like water. The pen poised itself over the paper.

The knocking was repeated.

"Damn!"

He pushed his chair back. The picture that had been spread before his inward eyes had furled itself up, and he knew by experience that it might not unfurl itself again that night. Balked in your leap, you had to crouch and steady yourself for the second effort. And then it occurred to him that he had locked the cottage door, and that the Venerable might have returned unexpectedly from Windover.

He got up and opened the bedroom door. The stairs and the lower part of the cottage were in darkness, but at the foot of the stairs a candlestick was always kept on a little bracket, and Lance lit this candle. It was a still and windless night, and when he unlocked and opened the cottage door, the flame of the candle swayed slightly, but gave out its full light.

He saw the whiteness of a face, and the dark outline of a figure, and the unexpectedness of both made him mute for the moment. He just stood there holding the candle.

It was she who spoke.

"I wanted to see—Mr. Pybus."

Her voice and its quality were as unexpected as her presence. There was something about it that moved him to feel the presence of her as something mysterious and strange and emotional. He thought of her most curiously as a bird blown against a window, and crouching close to it. That was to say—it was the spirit of her, the personal—intimate—feminine essence of her.

"I'm sorry. My grandfather's away—to-night."

"Oh——"

He raised the candle. The movement was unconscious, prompted no doubt by the desire that was in him, the desire to see her face more clearly. He saw her eyes. They appeared to be gazing at the flame; the pupils were dilated— which should not have been so. The light seemed to blur itself on the dark and swimming circles. And those widely open eyes of hers affected him most curiously. He felt that never before had he looked into such eyes, nor in the same way, nor seen in any human eyes such a strangeness of an inarticulate and stricken something.

"I'm sorry. Can I——?"

He lowered the candle. She stood very still, but he had a sudden fear that she was going away, that she would melt abruptly into the darkness, and there was that in him which did not want her to go. At least—not yet. He moved back slightly into the room.

"Will you come in a moment? I'll light the lamp."

Still looking towards the candle flame and not at his face, she answered him with the same dull and inward voice.

"Please don't bother. It's not worth while. But if I might sit down for a minute."

He made way. He half-closed the door after her, and placing the candlestick on the table, glanced at the fire.

"I'm afraid—it's nearly out."

Having entered the room, she remained standing by the table, giving him a sort of impression that she was incapable of further movement. It was not that she was embarrassed. He would have said that she was almost unconscious of his presence, and that he was without any significance for her, and yet he did not resent her attitude. In some curious way he felt that he understood it as he understood the people in his book; but she was alive and capable of making him feel naïvely shy and full of an exquisite and sudden muteness. He wanted her to come out of that strange, staring stupor and speak to him—to tell him. . . .

"Won't you try this chair? My grandfather will be back to-morrow. If I can take any message."

She looked at the Venerable's arm-chair as though it was the first thing of its kind she had seen, and then sank into it with a kind of gliding movement.

"Thank you. I'm sorry he's not here. No—perhaps to-morrow."

She sat there, straight and unrelaxed, staring at the remnants of a fire—and suddenly she shivered. He had left the door half-open, and yet that little shiver of hers was more spiritual than physical.

"Sorry. Silly of me."

He went and closed the door and, turning to look at her, was confronted by the unknown woman in her, the mystery of her. She was sitting there perfectly motionless, and the very stillness of her had mystery. That she was feeling sick and dumb with some inward torture he was sure. Though the room was so still he could feel a kind of stifled flutter of wings.

"Nothing that I can do?"

He watched her intently, almost appealingly.

"Nothing. I wanted to ask your grandfather——"

"Yes, I see. Would you care to write a letter?"

She put a hand to her forehead.

"A letter. I might. No. Perhaps you will tell him."

"Yes."

"That I should like to see him—soon."

"I'll tell him directly he comes back."

"Thank you."

He did not sit down in her presence, but lit the lamp, standing on one side of the fireplace and leaning against the mantelshelf, watched her stealthily. Her face had the charm of irregularity, as though each feature had its own individual motive, a dark irregularity, with the eyes set wide, and the nose short and broad, and the mouth sensuous and expressive. Ordinarily he would have called it a mischievous face, full of the mystery of elusive moods. But now—— She had made him forget his work; he was more conscious of her than he was of himself. He stood there wondering.

"Wonderful old man—my grandfather."

She raised her head quickly; for the first time she appeared to look at him as though she saw him as Lance the man.

"Yes. There are some people—very rare——"

"A kind of sage."

She reflected.

"He has a strange effect. Like some books. Do you ever find——?"

"I have done."

"There are some books, Hudson—when he writes about birds—and moors, and woods, or Tagoe's prose, which makes me feel—a kind of infinite calmness—something beautifully impersonal, the wind in the trees, or bees among the flowers. What is it?"

He was smiling down at her, but he was not conscious of his smile or of its significance.

"The awareness of mystery. The Venerable is a mystic."

"You call him the Venerable?"

"Yes."

"He is. He's——"

And suddenly she rose with one quick movement, and glancing at the clock on the mantelpiece, allowed herself to look at him momentarily with a quiet fullness of the eyes.

"I must be going. You'll tell him?"

He did not answer her for a moment. Something had happened. He closed his eyes for a second, and looked at her again, and then went to open the door.

"I'll tell him. I wish I could have been of use."

She went out like a woman passing up towards the altar of a church.

"Good night."

"Good night."

He stood at the door, and the darkness seemed to close about her like a cloak.

4

But for him that was not the end of the night; he was thinking suddenly of beginnings, not of endings. Deliberately he watched the hand of the clock mark out five minutes. He turned out the lamp, and locking the cottage door behind him, went after her.

But not to overtake her, only to shadow. He had had that instant impression of her as of a woman who was not to be followed with a light curiosity, and as he passed down through Castle Craven and out into the dark country she made the night mysterious for him. Amazing reality, but he did not question it. He had had a glimpse of her crossing the Brent bridge, under the lamp on the bridge's crown, and after that he went with a swift carefulness, ears and eyes alert.

But just why was he following her? Because he wanted to? Yes, in a way, for he belonged to a generation which follows the light of its own torch—but his wanting was different from what it would have been six months ago, for she was different. Surely! She did not belong to the leg and the lip-stick brigade. Good God, no! And in him there was almost the exultation of silent laughter, but not the laughter that the unmystical understand. It was part of a sudden tremor—lyrical, tender.

How the clouds smoked over the thin moon! Had he indeed damned her—the unknown—for knocking on the Venerable's door? But what was her tragedy? Yes, he called it a tragedy to himself as he followed between the dim hedges, keeping to the grass or the edge of the path. Those eyes of hers, and their look of desperate emptiness when he had told her. He could hear her footsteps now and again, and realized that she was walking in the road and he wondered why, for every little act of hers had become significant and absorbing.

The lane up to "Marions" showed as a grey gap in the southern hedge, and he paused here a moment, and then went on in time to hear the soft jarring of the gate as she closed it. He found himself standing outside the gate looking at a lighted window whose brown blind was criss-crossed by the branches of a young fruit tree—and suddenly the light went out, and everything was dark.

How undramatic, and how quiet! That was his feeling for the moment, though he would come to know that the poignant breaths of life are drawn very quietly. A hand pulls down a blind, or turns out a light, and there is silence.

He stood there for a while, very conscious of the little house's silence, and of a sense of stillness within himself, and presently he saw an upper window lit up, and the momentary flicker of a shadow upon the blind. Her window. And what was she thinking and feeling, and what was the expression of her eyes? And what was it that troubled her so desperately—that poor blind devil of a brother?

He was still there when that other window grew dark, and with a little feeling of wonder at himself he turned back towards Castle Craven.

CHAPTER XXX

I

THE Venerable, wearing a serenity that was like the laurel wreath of an emperor, climbed Castle Craven hill, carrying his bag and the "Pax Romana."

"It is peace, my child."

He sat down in his own arm-chair and in front of his own fire, and Lance listened to him with his mind full of other matters, while hiding his impatience, for Windover seemed far away, and "Marions" so very near. Lance's consciousness was full of Mary Merris and her message, though his father held the stage.

"We shook hands. Things are to go as they are. I'm very glad, my dear."

Looking up into Lance's face he was a little puzzled by its waiting seriousness, as though its attention was focused upon a point beyond the rendezvous of sires and grandsires.

"I made a promise for you."

"Yes."

"That you would go and see them regularly."

"Of course."

His glance was fixed on the crown of his grandfather's white head.

"I think someone wants you even more than I do. Mary was here last night."

Old Pybus's blue eyes cocked themselves momentarily under their white eyebrows. Mary, indeed! It was not Lance's calling of her "Mary," but the manner of Lance's doing of it, that something in the voice which made the Venerable take one long leap from Windover to "Marions." He said: "Give me a spill, my dear, I'll smoke," and spent the next thirty seconds in filling a pipe and lighting it. Youth and its problems! His two young things! And Lance was calling her Mary.

"Last night, was it?"

He felt rather than saw Lance go to the window, and stand there.

"I was working.   Someone knocked.   I thought it might be you.   She wanted you."

"Did she say——?"

The little room seemed tense with Lance's self-consciousness.

"No.   I asked her in.   She sat in your chair for five minutes. Grandfather, I want you to tell me—if you can tell me."

Old Pybus bit hard on the stem of his pipe.

"In trouble—was she?"

There was a pause, and a pause between these two could be eloquent.

"She looked as though——"

"Just how, my dear?"

"Difficult to describe.   At the end of herself.   At first she didn't seem to see me.   It made me feel—— So, you don't think you can tell me?"

Old Pybus bent forward towards the fire.

"If you saw her—like that—I might."

"I saw her—like something I have never seen before.   She wants you, grandpater—now."

"I'll go.   They'll have to do without me till to-morrow. Care to walk with me?"

"As far as her gate."

"No farther?"

He was aware of Lance as a figure that moved.

"No right to go farther—have I?   All right; I'll ask no more questions.   It's not mere damned curiosity."

"It couldn't be, my dear."

They went down by way of the Brent under the flutter of falling beech leaves, and across the valley the Woolshot woods were domes of gold and of bronze.   The valley was a great green trough between these autumn splendours, and on the crown of the bridge the Venerable paused to gaze and to remember.   For in remembering we realize both the past and the present, and with Lance beside him leaning against the grey parapet he was conscious of the immanence of youth and its urgencies.   What may seem an insoluble problem to the old may appear as a destined adventure to the young, for some problems give way to an inspired violence and to passion. And the Venerable was thinking: "Most of my river has run under the bridge—but his is in full flood. What will be—will be."

Perhaps he was a little tired; he walked more slowly than usual, and Lance noticed it. To him the Venerable would never be a troublesome old fellow.

"We ought to have had tea, grandpater."

"Not a bit of it, dear. She'll give me tea. But you."

"I can wait in the lane. She'll want to talk to you."

"It will be tea for all of us—before we go."

They turned into the Woolshot lane, and here, too, the leaves were falling, trickling down through the hedgerows. The bracken, turning gold, laced itself amid the stems and the shaggy branches of thorn and oak and maple. The brambles were loops of scarlet and maroon. Here and there a furze bush or a holly were darkly green for contrast.

Lance opened the white gate for old Pybus.

"I'll hang about here."

And watching the Venerable passing up the brick path to the porch, he felt rather like a dog left leashed to the gatepost. He was outside the affair, and wanting to be in the midst of it, and yet he was nearer to his crisis than he knew.

2

Having nothing else to do, Lance walked up and down the lane, but when he heard their low voices in the orchard he went farther up towards Woolshot so that he could not accuse himself of eavesdropping. But what were they saying to each other—those two——? He turned where the lane flung a curve, and standing on a bank where two or three yards of chestnut fencing guarded a weak place in the hedge, he found that he could look down into Mary's secret orchard. The leaves had thinned, and between two rows of apple trees he could see Mary and the Venerable walking. They went to and fro together over the rough grass, the little, dark, solid figure of his grandfather, and the slighter and taller figure of the girl. She was wearing a tawny-coloured woollen coat which seemed to match the yellow in the apple trees. And it occurred to him to think that the Venerable's best black boots were rather too thin for stodging about in that rank, wet grass.

But presently they disappeared from view.

"Do you mind if I sit, my dear?"

"There, you see how horribly self-absorbed one becomes."

They had diverged to an old, green bench under the hedge, and were screened by an apple tree, and the Venerable bent down to turn up the bottoms of his wet trousers.

"Something has got to be done about this."

She gave a little tragic laugh.

"Oh, yes; I'll put you in front of the fire and find you a pair of slippers."

His smile had a gentle drollness.

"I wasn't referring to—these. You will have to break this vicious circle. The thing's killing you—the real essential you."

"But what can I do?"

"Come down off your cross."

Sitting there she let her shoulders droop, and her eyes had the look of not focusing any definite object.

"I'm so tired. And sometimes when one is tired one gets so horribly impatient. I have thought of all sorts of things. Of course—there is always the obvious solution. One can give in."

He looked startled.

"My dear—" he said—"my dear!"

"You're shocked."

"Not shocked. Only—for you—the thing's impossible somehow; that sort of giving in, a throwing of yourself to the beasts. Let's think."

She let her hands lie on her knees, and her thinking became a kind of toneless monologue.

"It's the consciousness of failure—that—somehow—drives me on. Day after day. I tried everything. I've tried to think myself into his place, and to understand what the eternal

blackness means, the utter boredom of it. But when people
—are—poisoned—you know, and nothing that you can do.
He—poisoned poor Gil. It seemed to him nothing but a
sort of huge—animal jest—the retort physical—because I——
But would you believe such beastliness possible, and the way
he still gloats at me over it. I've felt like a creature in a cage ;
one gets bewildered, mesmerized by the way things happen.
There seems to be a kind of horrible inevitableness about them
all. You can't cry out or make an effort. You find yourself
just standing and staring and trembling. When he comes
down here now I feel as though some big, strong animal were
looking at me gloatingly, knowing that I was becoming
paralysed——"

She ceased, and old Pybus's white brows twitched.

"He still comes ?"

"Nearly every day. It seems so absurd and monstrous,
doesn't it ? As though I couldn't put an end——"

"You are too tired."

"Yes, too tired—somehow—to make any effort. Of course
one could appeal to people ; but would they believe ?"

"The doctor and the lawyers ? Rather useless people—
sometimes—my dear. Throw up your lease—and get out.
Pack the boy into some—'Home.' Isn't that obvious ?"

Obvious it was, but somehow not to her. She was in that
queer, overstrung state when there are a dozen emotional pro-
tests against the obvious. It was as though she clung blindly to
her cross, as some women will. She was still possessed by an
overmastering and elemental pity. She fought against
failure.

"But this can't go on, Mary."

"Some things do."

"But this thing can't and mustn't. It's a little hell in an
age of reason, though reason doesn't carry us very far sometimes. I've got to think—if you're past thinking."

She stood up suddenly.

"Your poor wet feet ! Let's go in. A good fire—and
some tea. And—your grandson ?"

"I'll call him in," said old Pybus.

3

So Lance was called in and, entering that house for the first time, found the Venerable sitting in front of Mary's fire and taking off his wet boots. "Orders, my dear. She has gone to get us tea."

It was a long, low room with two windows, and a larger room than you would have expected to find in so small a house; its floor boards stained and covered with rugs, and drawn up in front of the fire a large old sofa upholstered in faded red damask. The Venerable was sitting on the sofa, but Lance went across to one of the windows, and looking out into the garden, was aware of its sad untidiness, though someone had made an attempt to tie up a row of chrysanthemums.

There were chrysanthemums, too, in a big brown jar on the table, and mingling with the scent of them was a perfume of herbs. A big bundle of lavender hung from a beam, and the scent of it became associated in Lance's mind with the girl who was away there in the kitchen. He turned and looked at his grandfather, who was toasting a pair of grey socks in front of the fire. The Venerable had an air of preoccupation.

There were footsteps, and the man in Lance grew tense and vibrant. She came in carrying a tray, and he looked at her and she at him. It seemed just a look—and no more.

"Can I do anything?"

He made a movement as though to take the tray from her.

"Oh—I can manage, thank you. We shall have to boil the kettle in here."

"Can I get the kettle?"

"The kitchen's down the passage on the right. The black kettle, not the enamelled one. It's full."

He had reached the door, when there came a sound of knocking on the floor of the room above, as though someone was rapping with the heel of a boot or with a stick; and an impulse made him pause and glance back. He saw a hand poised holding a white tea-cup; it seemed to hesitate for a second, and then the cup was placed quietly upon its destined saucer. Also he had observed a movement of the Venerable's head, but a moment later old Pybus had resumed his meditations over the fire.

Lance went down the passage and into the kitchen, and as he went he heard these two speaking to each other, but he could not catch what was said.

"He's awake now."

"Better leave him alone—Mary."

"But he may—— You would understand—but Lance? Sometime he's so violent."

"Let Lance hear it—if it has to be."

She stood erect, with an air of breathlessness.

"Have you told him?"

"No."

"I'd rather——"

"Just as you please."

"I'd rather he knew."

When Lance returned with the kettle Mary took it from him and, placing it on the fire, she seated herself on an old velvet tuffet at one end of the brass curb, leaving the sofa to the men. But Lance was still on his feet, with a "Let me sit on that thing," while she—stretching out her hands to the fire, was not to be shifted. "No, it's my favourite perch, except when I have my feet up, which isn't often." So Lance had to join the Venerable, with his grandfather's grey-socked feet to be looked at as well as a woman's profile, and feeling himself suspended between the intimate and brooding silence of the other two. The three of them watched the kettle until a little cloud of vapour showed at the spout and the lid began to chatter.

Mary bent forward, but Lance was before her.

"All right. Let me——"

The handle was hot and he had to use his handkerchief, and while Mary was holding the teapot for him to fill it, the knocking in the room above was repeated with more urgency. The hand holding the teapot made a slight movement, and the pipe of boiling water from the kettle's spout striking momentarily upon the glazed surface of the pot, splashed a few hot drops upon her hand.

Lance winced.

"I say—I've scalded you.   I'm——"

But she did not flinch.

"Only a drop or two.   It was my fault."

"But I have.   You ought to——   Let me take the thing."

"No, fill it; it's nearly full."

He did as she wished, but when she had placed the teapot on the tray he wanted to see her hand, and when he would not be denied, she showed it to him though there was nothing to be seen.   Both their heads were bent and rather close together, and the Venerable on his sofa watched them over a motionless shoulder.

"You ought to put something on it—some cream."

But she wouldn't, though a kind of softness had touched her face.   She drew up a chair and sat down, and began to put sugar into the three cups, and then remembered; that she did not know whether Lance took sugar.   He was hovering; his glance seemed to envelop without touching.   Yes, he took sugar.   But where was she going to sit?   Not on that chair away from the fire while he and the Venerable occupied the sofa.   No, it could not be allowed.   And she looked up at him for a moment, and eyes held eyes, he bending to her, she with upturned face vaguely questioning and gently grave.

"No; but I——"

She was aware of the sudden smile in his eyes.

"Let's appeal to Cæsar.   Grandfather—who's to sit with you on the sofa?"

"Mary," said a voice.

And she rose, and without looking at him, went to sit on the sofa; but not before she had filled the three cups.

"I'm outvoted."

The Venerable, drawing in his grey socks and tucking them away as though gently repressing two furry little creatures which had presumed too freely upon the rights of the hearth-rug, looked up at Lance who had come to the sofa with a cup in either hand.

"Are we counting heads or cups, my dear?   And like those altruists—the socialists—are we with noble gestures—voting to ourselves—other people's money?"

Lance just smiled at him.

"I am offering Mary—her rights as a woman, to sit and be served."

"Ah, just so," said old Pybus, "when she has done most of the serving. That's our nice male gesture, but it is better than nothing. And what does Mary say?"

Neither of them looked at her. There are moments when a woman is felt—and not looked at.

"Isn't it the drop of sugar in the cup?"

"Ah," said the Venerable again, "that little piece of sugar, the celestial—something! Without it——! My dear, pass me the bread and butter. I'm getting too much like a pontiff."

4

But out in the lane, with the dusk coming down, and the sere foliage of the hedgerows dimly yellow above the grey-blue gloom, both Lance and his grandfather fell into a conscious silence, a silence that would be broken deliberately by one of them. And probably it was old Pybus's wish that Lance should break it, which he did, and before they had reached the Castle Craven high-road.

"Was that the brother—upstairs?"

The Venerable, walking with a kind of solid straightness down the middle of the lane, and looking neither to the right hand nor the left, nodded his big head.

"It was."

"Laid up?"

"In a manner of speaking."

Lance had no more questions to ask for the moment. His impressions were eating into a black surface like sparks into tinder. That fellow upstairs knocking on the floor, and Mary's flinching, and her remaining below with them in spite of the summons? The various impressions merged, and he was ready with another question.

"What's the matter with him?"

The Venerable answered with one word, and Lance's head seemed to swing up and round.

"That! Good God!—I felt——"

They were on the high road now, old Pybus on the path, and Lance on the crown of the road, head up, eyes at gaze.

"I'm glad you have told me, grandpater."

His voice had a quick resonance.

"Anything more?"

"Oh, much more, my dear."

"Is there! I should have thought that that was enough. How did it start with him?"

"Boredom, poor lad. But someone else set it alight. It's an extraordinary piece of—sex psychology."

"How?"

"Another man."

"I see. Some stupid sot."

"Not at all. Wilfully."

"Wilfully? But—why?"

Old Pybus stopped dead for a moment, stared at the path, and then walked on.

"So damnable—that you would say—Incredible. Yes, almost incredible. Sheer, filthy sexual spite. And pressure, a kind of brutal, chuckling persuasion."

He was aware of Lance swinging nearer to him across the road.

"What the devil do you mean, grandpater? Not?"

"Just a kind of lust, my dear, which being repulsed—turned to this filthy retort."

"What, with Mary?"

"Yes, with Mary."

Lance stopped as his grandfather had stopped a moment ago.

"Do you mean to tell me, grandpater, that some—some—deliberately set out to turn that poor blind devil into a drunkard—because—Mary——"

"I do."

"But it's unthinkable; it's too damnable to credit."

"My dear," said the Venerable, "did nothing ever happen to you? A month ago, didn't sex scorch you? Doesn't the beast sometimes breathe in the faces of all of us?"

But for a while Lance was unable to believe it. The thing seemed too monstrous and too ugly to be real. It sounded like the worst sort of melodrama; it was a horrible smudge across the surface of the night. Yet he had only to look at his grandfather's face and the set of those blue eyes to know that the thing was a reality. And when he did realize it, it was with a silence, a feeling of mute, tense fierceness that was like the setting of ice.

"Who is the fellow?"

He was told, and his disgust deepened. He had nothing to say.

5

The Venerable lit the lamp. Lance had left him at the door of the cottage, and he had turned back into the darkness, and old Pybus, after rubbing his chin with the back of his hand, observed that the fire was *in extremis*. He went for some wood and, kneeling down, busied himself in resuscitating the blaze, poking in pieces of firewood and piling small coal about the young, crackling flames. His face had a silent and deliberate gravity, for the rekindling of the fire was to him mystical and significant, an act which had been sacred and symbolical ever since man had ceased to be a raw-fleshed beast. For a fire suggested the immortality of effort, an eternal cleansing, a warmth in the bosom of life, youth, age renewing itself. He could understand the guarding and renewing of fire upon the altars of old time, and see in it an upward act, the burning flower of mystery. Yes, even this cottage fire had its mystery, and when it was well ablaze, he drew his chair close, and warmed his hands at it. The clock ticked on. And he sat and wondered whether he had lit a blaze in the heart of youth, and if so—whether it would burn with that fine, mystical meaning. He believed that it would; he hoped that it would.

And presently he heard the door open and close. He did not look round or change his attitude, but remained very still in front of the fire. Lance drew up a chair and sat down beside him. They shared the fire and the silence.

CHAPTER XXXI

I

IN some of the little London coteries Lance had heard books
and the makers of books discussed. "So and so was so
subtle," or perhaps the word was "intimate," or some other
precious adjective which suited the high-brow pose of the
moment. Women seemed to love the word "subtlety," and
Lance had known a phase when consciously and cleverly he
had tried to be very subtle until the Venerable had let off one
of his squibs. "What is this subtlety they talk about?" Nor
had Lance been able to convince his grandfather that some
forms of subtlety were anything but the self-conscious culti-
vation of the obscure. "You want people to say, my dear—
'Oh, that Pybus fellow—is a deep young devil—damned
clever'." They had argued, and the Venerable had produced
W. H. Hudson's "Far Away and Long ago" and had made
Lance read pages 34 to 38, and then had asked him to say
whether the picture of death and the child was not completely
convincing and wonderful. "Where's your so-called subtlety
there? I see nothing but a beautiful naturalness, interpretation
—or recording—without affectation." Lance had replied that
the child's mind was not the man's, and that the weavings of
consciousness became much more intricate; and the Venerable
had agreed. "But still there is a naturalness, my dear, a
simplicity, more notes—no doubt—in the sound pattern. If
you—get—all the notes and in the right order. Things
may only seem obscure when we fail to see them clearly.
Obviously. Don't be a fogmaster."

Old Pybus may have been verging on the prosy, and his
preaching of naturalness not wholly in accord with his mysticism, but when the strange, romantic occasion came to Lance
he found it compounded of naturalism and mysticism. It
had the eternal duality, body of matter and body of soul,
physiology or any sort of ology you please and that mystical

essential which still eludes all the ologies. Also, it was all so absurdly simple. You felt the urge and you behaved with a kind of inevitableness, but not quite as the behaviourists allow. From the moment of his sitting before the Venerable's fire he seemed to become a most unsubtle and yet sensitive creature, and all that happened to him and in him, appeared as natural as the reaction of Hudson the child to the presence and the prospect of death.

When Mary drove her decrepit old two-seater into the Saracen yard the car's decrepitude touched him. That Lance was not there by accident but by design was obvious to both of them, yet without any suggestion of flagrancy. He just happened to be there. He made it appear natural that he should be there. He did not offer to help her in any way, but his challenge was direct.

"May I wander over—some afternoon?"

And she, with a box of eggs in her hands, was supremely wise as to his appeal, though she did not visualize all that lay behind it. She looked at him for a moment with one of those upward and discerning glances, and if she divined a kind of young ruthlessness in him she may have felt that towards some people and things it would be tempered always with the artist's tenderness. He would not be ruthless to a dog or a tree or to one particular woman. His ruthlessness had discernment.

She accepted his naturalness and returned it.

"If you happen to find me rather busy——"

"That's understood. I want to meet your brother."

Again she gave him that upward look. Was he quite sure? Or did he assume that she would understand?

"Yes, come and see him."

She went away upon her affairs, conscious of having divined behind his quiet and unsmiling seriousness a romantic fierceness; nor did she quarrel with the impression. It might be a kind of fierceness that appeals to a woman. It would have the quality of a flash of light. It would cleave the obscure and the ugly. And somehow there came to her in Castle Craven High Street, a memory of the young man on the white horse with his thundering troopers behind him. And she consented. She accepted that vision of youth in its panoply and in all its martial passion. It had a primitive rightness.

But when, with an air of serene casualness, youth told age that it was going to "Marions," age foresaw things, or felt very sure that it foresaw them. For it seemed to old Pybus that certain happenings would become inevitable, and he, too, consented. Youth must cut with the sword. In its shining harness there must be at such a season no crack or crevice of humour. It must have the stark, white face that would be laughed at in the pages of *Punch*; a smile for the gently effete, people who have finished, and have little left in them but a clown's half-amiable and half-acid chuckle.

"Can I borrow a stick, grandpater?"

The Venerable, who was smoking an after-dinner pipe, looked up from the book he happened to be reading.

"I should think so. You'll find 'em behind the kitchen door, such as they are."

Certainly, old Pybus's sticks were without pretensions. There was the old malacca cane without a ferrule, and the cherrywood that had a kink in it, and the plain ash that was still very much ash, and unusually heavy. Lance chose the ash stick, and the Venerable made a note of it.

"You like 'em heavy, my dear."

Lance had nothing to add to the simple act of choosing.

"May have tea over there."

"All right."

He went out and across the Castle Field, and old Pybus got up to watch him. Lance prodded the grass with the ash stick, and to old Pybus it was not a stick, but a cavalryman's thrusting sword, and for a moment his grandfather felt both anxious and exultant. Age is apt to shrink from violence and to avoid it, for with the falling of the leaf and the passing of the year—the old wise consciousness asks for gentler happenings. But the Venerable was still the old Roman who, in the force of his youth, had sometimes stabbed at life with the sword. He watched his grandson disappear round the angle of the Castle's wall, and then resumed his book and his chair by the fire. But he did not read his book. He fell into a stare of thought, and so long did it last with him that he was ten minutes late in posting himself in his usual place in front of the brass gong.

2

Lance opened and closed the gate of "Marions," and walking up to the porch, stood for half a minute before ringing the bell. The door was open and in the passage hall he saw an old blue cloak and a brown mackintosh of Mary's hanging on the pegs, and a couple of sticks, an umbrella and three old golf clubs thrust into a brown drain-pipe. He was very much aware of these things as her things, the properties of her stage. That strip of brown linoleum was trodden by her feet, and no doubt she sometimes polished the round brass card-tray on that little oak table.

He was conscious of a stillness that belonged not only to the heavy, grey November day, but to his own self-consciousness. He turned about to look at the garden, seeing the two little lawns grey with moisture and stippled with worm-casts and fallen leaves. The brick path needed weeding. A bed of snapdragons still bloomed spasmodically. Beyond the hedges the Brent Valley showed as a dim and bluish void, all vague as to detail.

His feeling was that the house must be empty. Looking along the passage he could see the door of the sitting-room ajar, and when he put his hand to the brass bell-handle and pulled it, he expected to hear no more than a little clangour somewhere in the distance, a summons that would be unanswered. He heard the straining of the bell wire and the distant tinkling of the bell, and then a voice—sudden and a little querulous:

"Who's that?"

The voice came from the sitting-room, and before Lance had begun to explain himself, it was heard again.

"Is it you, Bob, old man? She's out—somewhere."

Lance stepped into the passage. He felt that he had to make an immediate reply to that unexpected challenge.

"Is Miss Merris in? I've walked over from Castle Craven."

Then followed a little silence as of surprise, but Lance fancied that he could hear a chair pushed back.

"My sister's out somewhere. Who is it?"

"Lance Pybus. Is that Mr. Merris?"

The initiative was his and he took it. He walked up the passage and pushed open the door, to see a man in bagged and creased grey flannel trousers and a blue coat with brass buttons looking towards him and the open door. Merris was sitting in front of the fire, his chair half-turned away from it, and in the attitude of a man surprised and about to rise to his feet. His blind face, with its drooping eyelids and little black beard, had a curious and slumbering uneasiness.

"Forgive me for coming in. You know my grandfather—I think."

The man in the chair remained silent and unsure. His thin face was half in the shadow, and it had the sinister elusiveness of a face that is unfriendly and not clearly seen. His attitude was a little furtive, and unwelcoming.

"Old Pybus, the porter at the Saracen?"

"Yes," said Lance quite gently, "Old Pybus, the porter. Do you think I shall find your sister—out there?"

Merris's blind eyelids seemed to stare like shuttered windows. He put a hand and fingered his beard, a strange and half-senile gesture, hesitant, almost surreptitious. And Lance was conscious both of repulsion and pity. He noticed that the thin hand had a slight tremor.

"Afraid I'm worrying you. I'll go out and try and find your sister."

The lips made a movement in the midst of the black hair, but no sound came, and feeling like a man oppressed by the faint and stuffy smell of a sick room, Lance turned about and escaped into the garden. But no sooner was he out in the open air, and in quest of Mary, than that feeling of disrelish vanished. He did not understand why or how. His impression of the brother as a poor frowsy thing from which his own clean aliveness shrank a little as from an unpleasant and decadent sottishness, did not pass over in any way to the sister. He might and did exclaim—"Poor devil!" but he did not think of the sister as "Poor Mary." And somehow his reaction to the brother's tragedy—for tragedy it was—quickened that other impulse until it ceased to be a mere impulse and became a seeing and a feeling and an understanding. He saw the woman in Mary as he had not seen her before. He saw her in a way that he would never forget, so that his seeing of her became one of those associated memories which would never fail to produce in after years a tremor of tenderness.

She was not in the garden, and he tried the orchard with its rank, green grass and alleyways of old trees. Nor was she in the orchard, but through the thinning lacework of one of the hedges he saw her in the little sloping field below the beech woods. And he stood still for a moment, watching her with a quick and sensitive curiosity, and a feeling of strange inevitableness.

But he did not see her merely as a bare-headed girl in a tawny yellow jumper moving about among the chicken houses, and shutting up the birds for the night. Already—and almost insensibly—he had come to visualize her with more fullness, much as an older man sees a woman when looking for that which is woman in her and not mere sex. She had courage; she was fastidious; she could loathe a job and yet stick to it, and yet at the same time she possessed that rare flexibility which makes for understanding. And Lance, standing there among the old trees, felt that he knew quite a lot about Mary, and yet that she retained her mystery, an exquisite unexpectedness which never becomes familiar. She was one of those immortals who would retain their wonder at life, just as the Venerable had retained it. You would go on loving that wonder in her, those eyes behind the eyes. You would not regard her as a mere body, and so—in time—cease to regard her—because mere bodies become nothing more than bodies.

Going to the gate in the hedge he passed through it. He wanted to call to her as he felt towards her.

"Mary."

The naturalness of it slipped out of him. She was about twenty yards away, fastening the gate of one of the wire runs. She turned and faced him, and his claiming of her as Mary. His impression was that she smiled.

He moved forward a few steps and paused.

"I have seen your brother. He told me I might find you out here."

She slipped the key of a padlock into a pocket of her jumper. And from her manner of looking at him he got the impression that she knew that he knew. He was conscious of a feeling of expectancy.

"I have just finished. We'll go in and have tea."

Her voice had a quietness, and as she came down the grass slope towards him, he felt that the Mary in her consented. It was not a self-conscious mechanism that joined him, but the intimate, live, mysterious creature who was flower and fruit and perfume. He stood still, waiting.

The strange thing was that he had nothing to say to her, nor did she look as though she expected him to say anything. They drifted down through the gate and into the orchard, each conscious of the other's consciousness, and mutely and gently accepting it.

But in the porch she paused, and her glance touched his face, and he divined in her a little tremor of something, distress or apprehension.

"Do you mind locking the door? I'll go and see to the kettle."

He was startled, but in a moment he understood, and he lingered behind her with a deep look in his eyes. He closed and locked the door, and hanging his hat on a peg, and slipping the ash stick into the brown drain-pipe, he entered the sitting-room.

"I found Mary. She was shutting up the chickens."

The brother's blind eyelids flickered. He moved uneasily in his chair.

"Better put something on the fire, hadn't we?"

"I'll do it. Mary has gone to get tea."

And Lance established himself on the hearthrug close to her blind brother.

3

Lance talked. He realized during the first half-minute that it was one of those occasions when you had to talk, for the blind face at the other end of the hearthrug had neither the will nor the wish to help him. It was both vacant and mistrustful. It suggested the face of an eavesdropper. It had a curious and embarrassing stillness.

When Mary came into the room with the tray she looked at both men a little anxiously. She was struck by the contrast of those two profiles as seen against the light of the fire; the one was alive; the other had a sulky deadness. She knew her brother so well by now, his dissemblings, his suspiciousness, his air of listening like a man outside a door. For months they had been playing this horrible and surreptitious game, and if she had not grown to hate him it was because he was so helpless even in his cravings.

Lance turned to her, smiling.

"You've a piano here."

She looked at her brother.

"Gil's."

And then her eyes met Lance's and he understood.

"I say, Merris, do play to us—afterwards."

The eyelids quivered.

"I'm not in the mood. Sorry."

Lance did not look at Mary, but he leant forward and took the kettle from the fire, and held out his other hand for the teapot.

"Let me do it."

She surrendered it silently, and went to the window that looked towards the orchard. The vista of grass and old trees had a dimness, though twilight was not yet. She pulled down the blind, and Lance noticed that act of hers, and seeing

her turn towards the other window he was struck by a something in her eyes, a look or apprehension.

"Tea by firelight—is that the idea?"

She answered that she disliked the November twilight, and
pulled down the other blind, and he wondered whether she
was shutting things out, other possibilities, incursions. He felt
sure that it was so and in him that inevitable tenderness towards her seemed to leap and glow. He put the kettle down
in the fender, and went to place the brown teapot on the tray.
She was standing there now, with the tips of her fingers resting
on the edge of the table, her face very grave and thoughtful.

"I'll do the waiting, Mary."

Her eyes looked quickly up at him, and then glanced aside
at her brother.

"Gil has that little table."

"Right. I'll get it."

During tea Lance tried to draw Merris out by talking to him
about music and the tendencies of modern music, for he had a
young man's prejudices and enthusiasms, and was ready to
confess that Beethoven was to him no more than Czerny's
Hundred and One Exercises pompously elaborated. He
abominated the eighteenth century school. It was like
Pope's poetry, sententious, artificial, insincere. But Merris
was still unaccountably suspicious, and seemed to hang those
swollen white eyelids of his superciliously in front of the
fire. And did Lance include Bach in his condemnations?—
and Lance had to allow Bach a rolling solemnity. He tried
the moderns, and asked Merris what he thought of Albeniz
and such pieces as Cordova, Seguidillas and Cadiz, and
Merris was rude.

"Never heard of the chap. Some new pose—I gather."

Lance said that Albeniz had extraordinary colour, a flamboyant and gaillard sumptuousness; but Merris was not
interested, and Lance gave it up. He stayed on for half an
hour, smoking a pipe with Mary's permission. He had offered
Merris his pouch, and the fellow had refused it. "Thanks,
I'll smoke some of my own stuff presently, if you don't mind."
He appeared to make a point of not smoking with Lance,

sitting there with an air of sulky patience, and waiting for this chatterer to go.

When his pipe was finished Lance pulled out his watch, and said that he had work to do. He stood over Merris for a moment as though waiting for a hand.

"Good night."

"Good night," and the blind man began to feel for his pipe.

Mary went with him to the porch door, and closing if after them, wandered down with him to the gate.

"I'm glad you came. You mustn't mind——"

"I'm afraid I bored him."

She was looking into the distance, her hands resting on the gate.

"Everything bores him—poor Gil, everything and nothing."

"Doesn't he touch that piano—now?"

"No."

"We must get him back to it."

She swung the gate gently to her as he passed out, and turned to linger.

"If one could——"

"May I try, Mary?"

"If you will. He used to extemporize. He had real genius—of a kind."

"I'll try."

And though she did not thank him, he knew somehow that he had more than her thanks.

For a few seconds she listened to his footsteps in the lane, and then went back and locked the door, and with a feeling of self-compulsion re-entered the room. Her brother was leaning forward, holding a piece of flaring paper to the bowl of his pipe, and the glare of it lit up the black and white sullenness of his face. He turned sharply, throwing the burning spill into the fender.

"What's that chap want?"

She stood by the fire, looking down at it and at him.

"To be friends."

"I don't like him. He puts on airs. Talking to me about music. An old hotel porter's grandson."

Her stillness was the stillness of self-control.

"You must have noticed his voice, Gil. Don't you know the voice—of a man—when you hear it?"

He flared up. Why hadn't she used the word gentleman? Yes, he could recognize the amateur gentleman all right, the half-educated fellow who could talk with vulgar niceness. And who was the chap, anyway? And what did he do? Sponge on his old grandfather?

She turned aside, and began to clear away the tea-things. She stifled a hot resentment. His poor, sottish selfishness hurt her, but she would not allow herself to be hurt. She answered him quietly, and with an air of finality.

"You are quite wrong, Gil. Why shouldn't we have a friend? I have asked Lance to come again."

He muttered something, something that was crassly offensive, but though she looked with sudden hurt contempt at him, she let it pass.

"Very well."

"If he comes here again—I shall go up to my room."

"As you please."

4

The Venerable happened to be in when Lance came back from "Marions" and he saw his grandson return the ash stick to its place behind the kitchen door. Nor was Lance particularly communicative. He sat down in front of the fire for five minutes, but his silence was neither self-conscious nor deliberate; it concealed nothing; it was just a part of his mood. And old Pybus went on reading his book until Lance had found something that had to be said.

"Pretty stiff problem—that brother of hers."

Old Pybus laid his book down on his knees, and for fully half a minute nothing more was said. They sat and watched the fire. Had cross-word puzzles been popular in the cottage you might have concluded that they were hunting some particularly elusive word. But Lance was thinking how words changed their temper, and that the crude application of a word to a situation or a person became inadequate when your vision ceased to be a cocksure stare. Not so very long ago he would have applied the word "swine" to Mary's brother; but when your crude impatience was checked you saw in all creatures of Gadara the presence of a devil, not the old-fashioned, anthropomorphic devil, but obsession, an hypertrophied appetite, some pitiful disharmony.

"I tried to talk music to him. Supposing, grandpater, one —got such a chap back to his piano?"

The Venerable reflected.

"Yes, and the keeping him there, my dear, with such a gap in the consciousness? I don't know. But it ought to be tried."

Lance's head went up.

"I am going to try—that and other things."

CHAPTER XXXII

I

FOR some days old Pybus was just a little sad. Possibly he felt himself to be a spectator, the old fellow in the chair at his cottage door watching the lusty young things at play. For the moment he had no tale to tell to his children, and one of them went in and out with a face of fierce dreaminess; and yet the Venerable's philosophy was capable of quietism; you sat and watched and waited for your bird to perch, and because of your stillness the thing would happen.

Perhaps, in the Venerable's case, it was bound to happen, for the Lance who went to "Marions" and the Lance who came back from it were not one and the same creature, and the Venerable would wonder how matters were between Mary and his grandson, and what they said to each other, and how they looked when they said it. Probably the brother was making things more than difficult, but then a love affair should not be too easy. For in the falling of the leaf and before the last leaf should have fallen, old Pybus felt moved to preach a sermon upon matrimony, though it would begin with "My children," and end with a blessing. Oh, old-fashioned fellow, damning marriage as an adventure, and hailing it as a sacrament, the growth of an exquisite comradeship; and seeing in "progress" nothing but a return to a point on the opposite curve of the circle!

Did the Venerable wish to see Lance and Mary consummate that comradeship? Undoubtedly he did; yes, and in spite of the world's tendencies towards adventurous singleness, and that top-heaviness that used to be called the artistic temperament. Artistic fudge! Old Pybus would argue that your creative artist is not a juggler behind the footlights, but a quietist, and the greater the craftsman—the greater the quietist; a man who looks through a window, a housed creature, a thing to be protected and planned for, and encompassed with serenity. Of all men the artist needs a mate, but a very particular mate, and the Venerable—having pondered upon life, wanted Lance to marry. He wanted him to marry Mary, for he divined in Mary that particular woman. So, during those November days, he went about with an air of sage attentiveness. He had left the core of the problem to youth, for the very passion of youth is a solvent of problems, and though it was November, old Pybus felt thunder in the air, emotional thunder, and some time the clap of it would be heard. It would break over the muddled head of that poor blind devil, and over the head of Mary, and over the head of someone else. Were ash sticks carried without a purpose? But if Lance got hurt——?

While Lance, prodding the turf of Mary's field with that self-same stick, and devotedly probing the problem, and finding himself prodding the air as well as the more solid turf, would fall back upon the seemingly obvious protest.

"You can't go on like this—Mary. You can't chuck your life away."

And looking over his head she would reply that—somehow or other—you couldn't drop certain burdens. They were fastened to your shoulders—and you would not be happy if you let the cords be cut, and then sneaked off into the future.

She perplexed him. So quickly had their intimacy ripened that he felt that he could say anything to her—and she to him, but the saying of things can be like throwing a stone into still water. She was still water. She gave him the impression of the inexpressible, of the subtlety of feeling that cannot be rendered into words. He felt resistances that were not calculable. And sometimes when she spoke—and gave him back words after he had pressed words upon her, he was made to think of little drops of blood escaping. She tantalized his increasing tenderness, all that strove for her—and with her.

He would try to fasten to a promise.

"Look here—if we can't get Gil back to the piano—away from that other thing—will you agree——?"

But she would not agree to anything. She would look both

frightened and obstinate. She was being assailed on three
sides, and she had her moods of bewilderment. The whole
emotional scheme was a little blurred. She had endured for
so long that any movement of revolt seemed difficult. She
was female, and he male.

Obviously the first and urgent move was his, but when he
hinted at it and its necessity, she seemed to flinch.

"No, not that way. I'd prefer——"

Always he felt himself growing reticent when she flinched,
not because he was surrendering his inspiration, but because
he hated to see her eyes grow big and troubled. With all her
endurance and her courage she was amazingly gentle; she
seemed to have a horror of the violently physical.

And he would prevaricate.

"Oh—all right. But that is what ought to be done. You
are too gentle—Mary."

"You'd like to call me cowardly."

"Heavens, no. I'm not such a crude beast. But I have my
view."

So for a week or more the affair fluctuated, though Lance's
efforts to break down the brother's blind hostility, and to
push, lead, or flatter him back to his piano had little result. It
was as though Merris resented Lance's aliveness, his power to
see, the very patronage of his coming and going. Caged up
in his perpetual darkness Merris's psychic perceptions were
unpleasantly acute. He felt in Lance a rival, a male personality
impinging upon his own orbit; he was jealous of him, furiously and sullenly jealous. Of course, the fellow came to see
Mary; he wanted Mary, and all this pretence about pianos and
persuasion was humbug, and offensive humbug.

"The chap thinks I'm a fool."

Such was the reaction of the romance upon Merris. He
glowered sightlessly upon fortunate, masterful youth; he
behaved as though Lance bored him; he would blunder out
and grope his way up to his room. And his mental and
emotional reactions were as awkward and recalcitrant as his
movements. He was conscious of being preached at—though
the harangues were disguised in the language of friendliness.

He would sit up there and brood. He would show these two! They were preaching a sort of decency to him, while amusing themselves, and giving expression to their romantic energy by combining against him and shutting him up. He was not to be allowed. Damn them—both! His crave, and the ironic malevolence of that crave, had an inevitableness. Idiots!

Mary might keep the doors locked and the windows fastened after dusk, but that good friend, that fellow with a sly yet robust sense of humour, was not to be discouraged.

"Gil—old lad."

"That you, Bob?"

"Have a drink?"

A piece of string was let down from an upper window, and incredible though it may seem, that was how it happened.

2

Snow had fallen. It lay on the hills and on the hedgerows, and crusted the branches of the trees; it had covered the fallen leaves; but the clouds that had spread this whiteness had passed, and the blue of the sky was cold and serene and still.

Lance, from the hollow of the "Marions" lane, saw the great red winter sun hanging in the black branches of the Woolshot beeches. It was like the blaze of a beacon, and the branches of the trees were trails of smoke, and behind him Castle Craven—faintly blue upon its white hill—glimmered its windows at the sunset. He was conscious of a great stillness, but it was a stillness as of suspense. In staring at that great red circle he, too, seemed to reflect its redness. The cold, still air felt strained.

There were tracks in the snow: footprints, the arrow-heads of birds' feet, the marks of a rabbit. He noticed them, and the red berries on the thorns and briers, and the way the snow hung pocketed in the hedges. Coming to the white gate he paused there with old Pybus's ash stick sloped like a sword over his shoulder. It was both less and more than a sword. The very face of him had a kind of fierce alertness, a young pallor.

He looked at the window, at her window. He went in and through the orchard, and in and out among the old, gnarled trees which seemed to make quaint gestures as he passed under them, his head cocked, his eyes frosty, as though looking to meet his enemy there. Youth under arms! In the upland field he saw the patterning of Mary's footprints linking the wire doors of the runs and the brown houses, and he noticed that there were no footmarks but hers.

He went back through the orchard towards the cottage, and at the window looking towards the orchard he saw her face, a white oval behind the glass. She was standing there watching him, with glints of firelight in the room behind her. He raised that stick of his.

"Mary."

Her lips moved. She disappeared. She had gone to meet him, to unlock the door and let him in. He stood in the porch kicking the snow from his boots.

"Anything happened?"

"No."

"I'll come in. May I?"

"Gil's upstairs."

"Still?"

"Yes."

They did not look directly at each other, and with apparent casualness he moved past her, and she closed the door. But he seemed to be aware of her eyes and their expression, and of the elusive shadowiness of her face. She was not flesh, but a complex of emotions, a mysterious creature reminding him of a woman in one of those old pre-Raphaelite pictures, large-eyed, full-throated, strange. She seemed to shrink and draw back into the dark passage as though eluding the instant issue. His masterful, young passion was so much less subtle than her reaction to it and its possibilities.

"I'm sorry about Gil. It's damnable."

She made a movement with her hands.

"Yes. Go in. I'll see to the fire."

He gave her a quick and searching look as he turned to the door.

"No need—Mary. I mean—the other thing. I know."

Almost she was the victim of a dramatic indecision. She was agonized with hesitations. She let him go into the sitting-room, and while pretending to be busy in the kitchen, she stood motionless by the fire, staring at it. She had a horror of violence. She had so schooled herself to surrender and to the patient suffering of things, that she trembled a little when this young, dramatic chivalry of his came striding and clanging. She shrank from the wrench, while divining its necessity and its romantic ruthlessness. So this was romance! Of course—— And to steady herself she began collecting the tea-things, cup by cup, and saucer by saucer, and with the sugar-bowl in her hand she seemed to be counting the number of white cubes in it. Was there no other way? And supposing——? But how absurd, these tremors and tendernesses and vacillations, these primitive qualms! She would go in and tell him, reason with him.

The kettle was steaming, and the tray ready, and she had no excuse for further loiterings. She picked up the tray and carried it out into the passage. The door of the sitting-room was half-closed, and she pushed it open with her foot, to see Lance at the orchard window. His figure had a dark and poised intentness; it looked very black against the afterglow and the snow.

He turned sharply, and with a jerk of the arm pulled down the blind, but not before she had seen something moving in the distance between the trunks of the fruit trees.

"All right—Mary. Don't worry."

The tea-cups jiggled on the tray as she placed it on the table. She was aware of Lance moving towards the door.

"It's all right. Tea in five minutes."

She made a swift glide as though to intercept him.

"Oh, please. Not that way——"

He stood holding the door. His face had a masterful but quiet fierceness, and on this most dramatic moment in their lives she realized him and his maleness, and all that they would mean now and in the future. She seemed to see as in a dream, with time effaced, and a life's happenings crowded into one swift picture. She stood mute, motionless, staring at him, and her face became like a child's plaintive and consenting. She felt a kind of inevitableness and accepted it. She found herself supposing that things of the heart happened in this way, like a tower falling, and that afterwards you had to sort out and replace the pieces. Yes, the afterwards—and so often the afterwards—was the woman's!

She had the feeling of clasping something to her, something that scorched and hurt, and yet had a quiver of exultation.

"Oh, my dear——"

She saw his eyes as he closed the door.

"Stay there—Mary. Don't look."

She heard him go quickly down the passage and out into the snow.

3

She heard voices, voices which had the sharp crack of branches snapping under the weight of snow. She could not hear what was said, which was well, for such words were like fierce blows, and not for her.

"Keep off—you young——"

"You—swine."

There were other sounds, like a stirring of nature, a vague movement as of wind and chafing branches, and she stood with her hands to her bosom, fearfully attentive, trembling. She knew—she could imagine. She was conscious of a kind of age-old primeval fear, the fear of the woman shut up, crouching, hidden, while men tore at each other. And she—she the civilized—soft-thinking woman—was involved in it, and so furiously involved that she felt her fingers curving to clutch. Her lover was fighting; he was being hurt. How would things go? That great tawny beast of a man——! Oh, horrible, the horror of humiliation, of his being thrashed, of his coming back to her beaten, ashamed, her young rider on the white horse. She could not bear to think of him being smashed and mauled. She must look.

Stooping she raised a corner of the blind. The sky was a suffused redness, and against it the fruit trees were sharp and black; the snow appeared tinged with the sky's redness. She saw the two figures half-way up one of the orchard aisles, knotted together, striking, twisting, jerking from side to side. She closed her eyes and dropped the blind.

But a moment later she had to look again, and it seemed to her that in the passing of those few seconds the sky had grown pale, and that the orchard was full of the dusk. The two figures had broken apart, one lying prone on the snow, the other standing, and with a little catching of the breath she realized that the standing figure was Lance's. Oh, thank God! The figure on the snow moved; it rose on its hands and knees; it made an effort to crawl. She saw Lance——

Again she dropped the blind. She became aware of her heart beating, and its contractions were so strong and rapid that she felt shaken by them; she seemed to quiver like a piano when powerful chords were struck. She sat down on a chair behind the door. She felt strangely stifled, but strangely exultant. Oh! romance, violence, the old rage of chivalry, the beast trampled upon, the white knight triumphant! So, things sometimes did happen that way. But how dark it was! The room was growing dim. She must have lights, lights for him, not the lamp, but candles, firelight. There were candles on the mantelpiece, and she hurried to light them, only to find her hand so shaky that the match flame and the wick seemed to be playing hide and seek. She had to steady that right hand, holding the wrist with her left hand. But how absurd, how dearly and splendidly absurd! She felt herself swept by a gust of tenderness. The candle flames seemed to waver. She knelt down and stirred the fire to a blaze.

A moment later she heard the porch door open. She rose with one swift movement. The light was dim in the passage, but she could see his face.

"Oh, my dear, you're bleeding."

He laughed, or she had the impression that he laughed.

"Oh, probably. It's nothing."

His voice had the hard breathlessness of a man who had run a race. He was all torn about, collarless, shirt ripped open. There were red blurs on chin and forehead.

"He'll never come here again. I could have killed him."

"Oh, my dear."

She caught his right arm, pressing it between her hands. Her face winced for him.

"You're bleeding. I'll get water. Come, come and sit down, by the fire here——"

His red mouth seemed to smile at her.

"Am I a very horrible object, Mary? Well—he was worse. I'll go into the kitchen—and clean up."

"Oh, my dear, no. You're—you're—— No one but me—will ever have seen you like this—It's my part."

She compelled him towards the chair by the fire, and he looked down at her with an amused, devoted fierceness. So, it was her part, and all this violence and blood——

"Mary."

He let himself relax into the chair. A cushion was under his head. He watched her go out of the room, and the very air seemed stirred by her solicitous, sweet haste. He lay back and smiled; his bloody face lost its grimness.

4

The Venerable had forewarnings. Was it because the white breasts of his pigeons appeared to have a redness when he fed them, or because that flaming winter sun went down in a whorl of fire behind the ash trees and the Castle? But he remained off duty—he was remaining off duty more and more these days, and his world humoured him; he sat by the fire; he let his thoughts go back to the days of his own romance. Oh, yes, there had been a romance: a girl in a white muslin frock sitting under the old thorns on Hampstead Heath, a pale, fragile, fey-eyed thing; but old Pybus's romance had never gone beyond the May flower. He had wondered often what he and Miss White Muslin would have made of marriage, and now he was wondering what these two children of a later generation would make of it, were they to marry.

He was knocking his pipe out on the bars of the grate when Lance came in. The lamp was lit, and when old Pybus saw his grandson's face, he turned again to the fire and waited.

"It's all right, grandpater."

"All right. Good lad. You——"

Lance came to lean on the back of the Venerable's chair.

"Oh—I got him. He had the best of it for the first half minute. He must weigh two stone more than I do. But it was just rough and tumble. By God! He hurt me, and though he hurt me I felt I had him. He couldn't last. Fat, and too sodden. Besides—I was raging."

Old Pybus, with his empty pipe stuck between his teeth, nodded a big white head.

"You got him."

"He could just about crawl when I'd done with him. I made him crawl into the lane. Oh, he's finished—all right. He got the knock from me. He'll never go near the place again."

His grandfather sat and smiled.

"How's Mary? Was she much——?"

"Oh—a little. But she was splendid. She washed my face for me. It needed it. But, grandpater, I have never felt so good before, knocking that beast into grovelling pulp."

"You beloved savage! But that's just what was wanted. You can kiss the top of my head, my dear."

It was kissed.

CHAPTER XXXIII

I

THIS thunderclap had other reverberations. It had both closed and opened doors, and to a blind man it uncovered a vision of a young Zeus holding the lightning.

To Mary it was an opening of windows, deep breaths of clean, free air, the death of an evil thing, the beginnings of that most difficult and delightful experiment in self-expression, a duet between two young moderns.

To Lance this romantic storm ushered in blue water and a curious awareness of a something in himself which was both sacred and immortal, though a man cannot judge of that which is immortal in himself until he has come to the season when he faces his own mortality. He loved, but he was at the very beginnings of the great sacrament. All that he knew was that the image of woman had two lamps burning before it, wonder and compassion. Nor could the Venerable help him here. There was no one to tell him that Mary would gather to herself memories of poignant and beautiful appeal—that she would be the one creature to whom he would turn always with an uprising of infinite tenderness. That she would be—just Mary. That she would be something more than mother, wife, or child. That—always—she would have a little veil of dear and exquisite mystery. Youth does not foresee or forefeel these things; it cannot do so. Life grows. Nor could Lance tell that before the face of Mary—seen or conjured up— the violences and ruthlessness and angers of a forceful maleness would pause and stand still. He would feel that tremor of tenderness and compassion, a going out to her of all that was strong and fine and gentle. Because she was gentle, because her eyes and hands drew him when, like a hurt or angry child, he was ready to stamp and to rage. Because she was just Mary, a creature immortally wise and gentle and courageous, exquisitely imperfect, and therefore sensitive to her beloved's imperfections.

For—in the beginning of things he saw her both vividly and vaguely. She was May to his April, a little older, a little more mature, in the fullness of the setting of the fruit of suffering. She could look at him attentively; she could show a brave frankness.

"Don't be so infallible, dear man. We are still—groping."

She could tease him gently, and when the Venerable listened to her teasing he would have the air of smothering a sly and exquisite chuckle.

"Good girl. Don't let him grow a solemn face. Make him forget that he is too damned clever."

But at the moment the White Knight appeared dominant, and rode his horse magnanimously, and saw the issue before him as clear as a white shield. Woolshot had been tumbled out of the saddle. It had been trodden on and mired. It had effaced itself, gone upon a holiday, caught the Orient Express, and rumour had it that the Tawny Beast was hunting other tawny beasts somewhere in Africa.

Meanwhile the other half of the problem remained, and to the young handler of lightning it could not appear insoluble. Merris had to be got back to his piano. Obviously. Also, a little ruthlessness might be necessary. Splashes of cold water interspersed with little bursts of applause.

Lance used a quite modern frankness.

"Look here, sit down and play that thing of Ravel's to me."

He had Merris out of his chair and by both elbows.

"Come along—there's a good chap. I want that piece of music."

That Mary's brother had surrounded himself with a fog of hostility was but the mere skin of the problem. Lance thought that he could unravel the business, or peel off that sullen husk. Merris needed stimulating. He needed lifting out of that sordid self-absorption in which he sat like a flabby and spoilt child stubbornly glowering in its pram. It was not that Lance was unimaginative towards the other's blindness and his cravings, but he looked at them, so to speak, over Mary's shoulder.

He had talked to the Venerable.

"It's a case for a cold tub at six in the morning."

"Frightfulness, my dear?"

"One quarter of frightfulness to three-quarters of persuasion. I want to get him to realize——"

"You do."

"Mary."

The Venerable was moved to suggest that if Merris had not realized Mary and her fundamentalism—it was rather late in the day to attempt it. Self-expression was the only thing. His music.

Lance said: "Exactly," but the word was inadequate. Merris had to be put back to his piano, and to be persuaded that there was nothing in heaven or earth more potent and precious than his piano. He would have to improvise himself back into a world of clean sounds and feelings.

"Don't you see it in that way, grandpater?"

"And the appreciation, my dear?"

"We can give him it—but not too much of it. Can't he be made to realize that the world is still full of ears?"

"Beginning with his own."

Lance walked over from Castle Craven each afternoon. He was working in the morning and at night, and in spite of these distractions his work had moved forward. Or perhaps it was because of them. All that he could say was that the working of his inner consciousness was changing; it seemed to be losing a dreadfully facile cleverness; it cost him more effort; it was as though the well of his inspiration had deepened and the bucket had to go deeper. But he was getting that deeper water. The thing on paper had a rightness, an inevitableness. It astonished him; it seemed to come up out of the dark, and from mere vapoury nothingness change to light.

Usually, during those December days, he would open the white gate of "Marions" about dusk. He would see the various December twilights: a sky that was grey or opalescent or steel blue, and the winter blackness of the beeches, and the wet bronze of the leaf carpet and the rusty bracken. On the hillside, Mary would be putting those unromantic fowls to bed, but the wire runs and the brown houses had an air of impermanence. If there still was work to do he would help her.

"How is the piano to-day?"

"Two hours this morning."

"Splendid."

Her face looked smoothed out. Going down through the orchard they would loiter and hold hands, and pretend to look at the sky or the stars or the old trees. Some things were so very near, other things still very remote and problematical. There was a tacit understanding between them, an open mindedness. He had said to her—"I'm just nothing yet; what the world calls: 'A fellow who writes,' but I am going to be something. So—you see." And she had answered: "Not quite clearly—yet." Which was understandable, and he understood it, and bore with it because of the gentleness that was his for her sake. You could not rush and overwhelm her loyalties. Possibly he had begun to suspect that some things are worth waiting for.

"Next year—you'll get out your colours and brushes."

"No time."

With his arm over her shoulders he looked down at her serious, sweet head.

"There must be—yes—later on. It isn't as though we both scribbled. I'm not going to be a little Jack Horner. I'm learning about the duality of things."

"What's that?"

He smiled, and digressed.

"Just the way the hair grows on your forehead."

"I can't help it."

"Thank God! There are such lots of things you can't help, Mary, and so I can't help them either. You make me just stand and stare."

Yes, Merris was the problem, his as well as Mary's; though Lance could never quite overcome his feeling of distaste, of physical shrinking, his dislike of that blind, flaccid and sallow face, with its beard and its air of nervous, sneering boredom. The fellow was both tragic and unwholesome, and Lance had a wish to put him out in the rain to be rained upon, or to let

the north wind blow through him. Heavens, how it blew
and rained that winter! Even when there was some blueness
in the sky the north wind seemed to be trying to push Castle
Craven over the edge of the hill into the Brent valley. Lance
had to sit with his oil-stove close to his chair, and to rub his
hands over it, and the Venerable was paying for the oil.

2

But between them, with some assistance from old Pybus,
they did contrive to persuade Merris back to his piano. On
Sundays the three of them plotted a little music causerie; nor
was it all artifice, for Merris had hands and a temperament, and
he could smother the sound of the wind in the trees. He had a
preference for northern music, that of the Scandinavians and the
Poles. He liked to play by firelight, for he had that peculiar
appreciation of atmosphere which survives the loss of vision,
and may be exaggerated by it. Also, he had a dislike of being
watched, and an uncanny instinct for knowing when backs were
not turned. Mary and the Venerable on the sofa, and Lance
on a couple of old cushions, watched the fire, and listened.

It was sufficient to say—"Play this" or "Play that," and to
remain silent. He knew better than any of them the how and
the why of it, and like all interpreters of sound and colour,
was apt to resent polite chatter. He was more approachable
when nothing was said about his music, and it was listened to
and appreciated in silence. He would just go on playing, and
if the darkness had the silence of sympathy, he was satisfied.

Lance came quickly to understand this passion for silence,
and its sensitive significance. It was as though Merris resented any sort of interference. He had snapped Lance up on
one occasion.

"That thing makes you hear the Vistula running, and the
wind in the poplars."

Merris had turned on his stool.

"The wind in the rain-pipes—if you like. Music isn't
pictorial. Damn all Village Blacksmiths."

So Lance learnt to be silent, and it was this delicate silence of his that began—as it were—to surround the darkness between them and to create a nascent intimacy.   Lance explained it to the Venerable by saying—"The chap likes to be listened to. Naturally.   It's his method of self-expression.   We'll get him by listening."   But, as a matter of fact, the reactions were much more subtle and obscure, and not so easily rationalized. For Lance had a peculiar effect upon Mary's brother; he was both a stimulus and a provocation.   He had appeared as an interloper, a vigorous young male thing setting the darkness vibrating.   He might sit there silently, but Merris seemed to see his silence as a self-assured, attentive, critical face.   There were many moments when he hated Lance.   He seemed to divine in Lance a compassionate arrogance, a tolerance that referred to him as a "Poor devil."   His very playing was an attack or a retort, a passionate and bitter challenge, to that silent, unseen youth.   The very intimacy that began to grow up between them had a curiously acid sparkle.

Also, he was jealous of Lance.   His very helplessness had made him very dependent upon his sister.   He was possessive. His blindness had cramped and narrowed his nature.   He would suddenly behave like a peevish and spiteful child.

"It isn't my music, Pybus—I'm not quite such a fool."

Mary had left them alone together by the fire.   She was busy in the kitchen and Gil—moodily aggressive—had refused to play.

"Not wholly your music.   I agree."

"Well—don't forget it."

Lance smiled, and was astonished to find that Merris seemed to divine the fact that he was smiling.

"Don't grin."

Lance looked hard at the blind face.   He had begun to discover that an impartial frankness was the best counter to Merris when he was in one of his irritable moods.

"Well—do you grudge Mary a friend?"

He thought that he detected a sneer quivering under the curves of those thin nostrils.

"You are an exacting beggar—you know.   Mary has a life of her own.   She's not your slave."

And then—of course—the brother looked plaintive.

"Yes, rub it in. I'm a parasite, a damned nuisance. You'd like me out of it."

Lance picked up the poker and prodded the fire.

"Shut up, Merris. Don't talk like that—about her."

Nevertheless, Merris did respond to the stimulus. Here was this fellow who was writing a book and bringing over chapters for Mary to read. In the evenings Merris could hear her turning over the pages.

"What's that you're reading?"

"Lance's novel."

He did not ask her to read it aloud. He was just a little afraid of Lance's novel, just as he was more than a little afraid of Lance. And like a child he was moved to insist upon his own particular trick. His pride sat itself down at the piano. Moreover, there were other indications of a quickened self-regard. He became less of a sloven. He was driven into Castle Craven to have his hair cut and his beard trimmed. He indulged in two new suits. He would sit in front of the fire, cleaning and polishing his nails as though those hands of his were master-hands and worthy of deference.

3

The Venerable, observing the three of them, and loving the two of them, while pitying the third, felt himself fumbling with a Chinese puzzle that fooled his old fingers.

He wanted Mary for Lance; but would Mary be obtainable without her brother? And did either Mary or Lance understand the ruthlessness of marriage: its sacred exclusiveness, its intolerance?

But he was soon made to realize that Lance understood it. They were walking back to Castle Craven in the wet darkness, with a north-west wind making a bluster in the hedges. Old Pybus, in black oilskins and sou'wester, looked like a large-sized boy of fourteen bobbing along beside his grandson. Lance was head-in-air, in spite of the wind and the rain.

"What do you think of Merris, grandpater?"

There had been times when the Venerable had thought of Merris as better dead, but he did not say so to Lance; some solutions are too obvious and too easy.

"More grip, my dear."

"Yes, he's cleaner. But you can't assimilate him. What I mean is——"

He took off his hat and shook the rain out of the brim, and the gesture was prophetic.

"I'm sorry for the poor beggar—but, you see—he's hostile. I suppose it's natural. He has had Mary all these years."

The Venerable trudged along the path with his hands stuffed into his pockets.

"Just so. If you want Mary——"

Lance's silence implied that he wanted Mary, and meant to have her, not only for his own sake, but for hers. Also she had to be persuaded that one husband was more precious than twenty blind brothers. It was nature. But, then, Mary's trouble was the very fact that she was Mary.

"I can't see her—leaving him in a corner of his own. But that is what must happen, grandpater. I won't have anything else. Of course, I accept responsibility. It's up to me to help to put him in a comfortable corner. That's the situation."

Old Pybus grunted.

"It is."

They arrived at the high bridge over the Brent, and the light from the bridge lamp glistened upon the Venerable's black and polished figure. The Brent was in flood, adding its moist roar to the sound of the wind in the beeches, and on the crown of the bridge it occurred to old Pybus that life and youth were like the river. Flood water, not to be denied, tearing to the sea. Life solves its own problems either with a gentle gliding or with violent haste. Some things—or perhaps all things—are inevitable.

"Have you said anything to Mary."

"Not yet."

Old Pybus appeared to shake the rain out of his eyes.

"Try to be gentle. But it's inevitable—of course. You two together."

The Venerable hated meddlesome people, but he did feel curious as to Mary's inward tendencies. She belonged to a world that was still dominated by the idea of sacrifice, by the vision of a figure hanging upon a cross, and old Pybus had come to doubt the soundness of the sacrament of sacrifice. It had begun with a bloody offering to a god, and had become the mystery of god sacrificed. But how often was the sacrifice nothing more than a pathetic surrender to some other creature's egotism. It was a sacrament which had appealed to women, or perhaps it had been forced upon them by the maleness of all orthodox creeds. Or perhaps it was a natural, emotional urge in woman, the bearer of children, the nurturer of children? That Mary had this sacrificial passion in her was fairly obvious, and old Pybus wanted it for Lance and not for the other fellow; and here was another problem. Mary might obstinately refuse to come down from her cross.

Going over to "Marions" one Sunday, with Lance left at home in the throes of a "situation," old Pybus stumbled innocently upon a scene. It was frosty and clear and very cold, and getting no response from the cottage, the Venerable was setting out upon an exploration, when he heard the two voices. And there, in the orchard, was Merris sitting on the green seat, and looking as though he was glued to it. He was without an overcoat. He had the air of a thoroughly sulky and rebellious child, clutching its perch, and refusing to be carried indoors.

But the very absurdity of the scene was suggestive, the defiance of that blind figure, its air of stubborn and rebellious malignity.

"I'm going to stay here—I shan't be wanted in there. I'm superfluous."

The Venerable's eyebrows bristled. His inclination was towards a good leather slipper well and truly applied to that incorrigible manchild's spiritual posterior. But he went softly back to the porch, and waited. Poor, jealous, cunning child! Were two or perhaps three lives to be denied completeness because of a blindness that lacked grace?

A robin, shrilling in the cold sunlight, fixed a black eye upon old Pybus, and the Venerable, whistling a response to the bird on the bough, found other eyes upon him.

"Oh—Venerable!"

He smiled upon her, perhaps, because she was not smiling. She had the air of a patient nurse pushed beyond her forbearance.

"Lance is in the throes. My opportunity——"

She looked through and beyond him.

"And my child's rebellious."

He stood aside to let her pass, while he absorbed the significance of that word "child." A child was so final. And was that her feeling?

"Tantrums? Supposing——"

She went past him, and turning in the passage, looked at the sky through the bare branches of the apple trees.

"You see—he's jealous—What would you say?"

"I'm prejudiced, my dear."

"How?"

"In your favour—and in Lance's."

It was as though he had stripped the problem of its veil of sacrificial sentiment, and had done it wilfully. He saw her face stiffen. She understood.

"You men are greedy. What could you say?"

"Not greedy—always. Not in that way. Besides—one has a right."

"Lance?"

Old Pybus nodded.

"Surely? But only—if—— Well, I'm meddling, my dear. But only you can tell."

She stood very still and her eyes had a like stillness.

"How could I do it? He has no one. He's so pathetic, even when he's—impossible. And yet—you must know. He's in the orchard."

Said old Pybus—"I'll go and fetch him in. You'll catch cold there. Go in."

But though he had spoken softly to her he felt less gentle towards the brother. Blind, petulant, grudging whimperer! Insane egotist! He walked on into the orchard in a Roman rage, and paused to observe that figure on the seat. He was shocked, for the fellow was weeping, exuding tears from under those drooping eyelids, sitting there gripping the edge of the seat, his blind face wet and plaintive and futile.

Old Pybus gave a toss of the head. Damn the fellow! Damn his weakness, his egotism! Prometheus set on a garden seat, and tearing his own vitals! But was not this sort of weakness the most exasperating and frustrating of vices?

He walked across the grass, feeling it brittle and frozen under his feet, and laid a square white hand on the brother's shoulder.

"We're waiting for you. Come in."

The blind face winced.

"But I don't want to come in."

The Venerable's hand transferred itself to the coat collar.

"Get up. You're no better than a baby. You want slapping and putting to bed."

4

That is where a man may differ from a child. A child may forgive and forget, and a man may not, especially if he is vain, and a weakling. Merris was led by the Venerable through the orchard and into the house, with a back and a neck that were as stiff as a steel rod, and a face that was frozen. He moved his feet with a kind of careful shuffle. He guided himself to his chair and sat down in it, his hands on his knees, the whole of him expressing a rigid sulkiness.

Mary was in the kitchen, and old Pybus, after a glance or two at that sullen face, and gauging the depth of the room's silence, felt moved to apply the slipper once again.

"Does it ever occur to you to think of your sister?"

Merris's hands gripped his knees. He seemed to stiffen himself.

"Is it any business of yours?"

Old Pybus's white eyebrows bristled.

"It's what I choose to make it. The trouble is—that you are too sorry for yourself. We're sorry, but you are sorrier."

It ought to be the other way about. Supposing you reflect on the fact that your sister has some right to a life of her own."

After that there was silence, a congealed stillness, until Mary came into the room with the tea-tray and was met by that chilly atmosphere. She looked at the fire and at the two figures. She put down the tray, and kneeling between old Pybus and her brother, reached for the coal tongs.

"You are letting the fire down."

The Venerable bent forward to take the tongs from her.

"Apologies, my dear. Let me."

Trudging homewards later under a frosty sky, with the stars ashiver, he still felt a little inward warmth over the using of the slipper. Life should be nine-tenths persuasion, and one-tenth frightfulness. Certainly. And Mary had not exercised frightfulness. Merris had the temperament of a child, of a little, strutting, sulky boy, and if the devotion of ministering hands could not move him, well—a cut with a cane might cause him to take notice and reflect. The Venerable held canings to be inevitable. You chose the rare and particular occasion. You switched a forgetful pride. You found the raw place, and when you had stimulated it you applied the unguent of a wise sympathy.

So old Pybus thought, and prophesied a possible reaction; but the effect of those few simple and curt words was to be other than he imagined. The quality of a reaction is a question of blood, breed, texture, temperament. He had switched Lance on occasions, and the quick blood had answered generously. But Gilbert Merris was not Lance.

"May do him good," thought the Venerable. "Whom the Lord loveth——"

The stars blinked above the Venerable's head. He had mixed mysticism and pedagogy. "May do him good." But our psychology is still apt to be unexpected. We are like boys playing with chemicals, mixing things in a test tube. There may be a boiling over, or a surprising colour change.

"May do the beggar good."

Later, the Venerable would be caught wondering whether he would have done the thing—had he known or foreseen.

CHAPTER XXXIV

I

AT Christmas Lance went to Windover. One of Probyn's cars came for him, and with it a letter to the father of all the Pybi, who read it with an air of benignity, and then put it away in his pocket.

"Good of Probyn. No, I'm not coming. You two ought to be together."

So Lance dispossessed the chauffeur and drove the big blue car over the winter roads, and knew that he had never felt so comradely towards his father as on this day of winter sunlight and blue black distances. They had exchanged simple and gracious gestures, and were to come together not as father and son, but as two men of the world, ready to respect each other's reticences. For Lance had been to the wars and could boast of trophies. Also, he went to Windover as a lover and a son, and as a young man who had set himself to do this difficult thing and was accomplishing it. Above all, he carried in his breast pocket that glorious letter from John Richmond, a letter such as a man either writes or receives perhaps twice in a lifetime. It was epic. It referred to the first half of the recreated "Rust"; also it pinned upon Lance's coat the red badge of courage.

"Your book and your pluck balance each other. I'll publish you in the autumn. Go ahead."

When they were within five miles of Windover, Lance pulled up and resigned the wheel to the chauffeur. "I want to look at the country. Don't make a smudge of it." And leaning back in a corner he recalled a phrase of his own in the second chapter of "Rust." "The speed-smudge of modern life," and as the big car glided graciously along the undulations of the road it gave him a sense of restrained power. He watched the country, the grey-green hills burnished by the sinking sun, and the black woods, and the ploughed fields which showed a tinge of purple. The landscape had a beautiful strangeness while remaining gently familiar. Or, was it that he saw things differently, because he himself was both the same and different? He watched for the old house. In the avenue of beeches a red sun flashed and vanished behind the rhythmical grey trunks of the trees, and when he saw the house it seemed to stand in a blur of gold dust. It satisfied him.

His father, hatless, and wearing a rough tweed overcoat, came along the terrace from the library window. They shook hands with an inarticulate but smiling shyness. The chauffeur dealt with Lance's suit-case, while father and son walked back towards the library window.

"I thought—the Venerable—might be with you."

His father's voice had a note of diffidence.

"Yes. He was pleased, pater—but he thought——"

"I see. You and I."

"Yes."

As they turned to enter the french window, Probyn's hand rested lightly on his son's shoulder. His face had a shy radiance.

"Well, here we are. Have tea in here. Go in."

But Lance stood back, and, with a little courteous hesitancy, waited for his father to enter.

"How's the mater?"

"Not so well—as I should like. Had to rest in the afternoon."

"Oh," said Lance, with a twinge of conscious self-reproach —"I hadn't heard. I'm sorry."

"She will be down in five minutes."

Probyn closed the window, and Lance stood on the hearthrug, staring at the fire. He had become suddenly aware of his father and of his father's room, and of his father as a man who felt and could be hurt, a very human creature. There had been a something in his father's voice when he had spoken of his wife. And Lance felt the warmth of the fire on his face.

"Pater——"

"Yes, old chap."

"I want to say something—I think I have learnt a good deal—lately."

Probyn stood stiffly by his desk.

"Never too old.   Same with me, Lance."

"I've been a bit of a prig to you—sometimes.   I'm sorry."

Probyn was having trouble with his eyeglass.   He cleared his throat, and then appeared to remember that he was still wearing his overcoat.

"That's all right.   Suppose I may have been something of a city father.   Think I'll take this thing off."

"I'll put it in the hall for you."

"No, don't you trouble.   That's all right, old chap.   Hallo, here's your mother."

They were both holding the coat and looking at each other with a kind of affectionate shyness when Lance's mother came into the room.

2

He went to her quickly and kissed her.   And in that moment, and with an inward catching of his consciousness, he had realized her difference.   It was his mother, and yet not his mother.   She was thinner, less vivid, more spiritualized.   There were little lines as of pain between her eyebrows and at the angles of the eyes, and the eyes themselves had a look as of apprehension.

"Oh—Lance——"

He kissed her again on the forehead.

"I'm glad to be here, mater.   I'm sorry—such a long time. Oughtn't you to sit down?"

She seemed to cling to his hand, and hers was moist and hot.

"I'm getting an old woman—my dear."

He pushed one of the big brown arm-chairs towards the fire, and Probyn placed a cushion in it.

"There you are, old girl."

Lance, with a queer, glowing, and infinitely grave face, stood looking down at his mother.

"Anything else I can get you?"

She looked up at him with those apprehensive, asking eyes.

"No—just sit down, Lance. Take a cushion on the floor—like you used to. Remember the old nursery? And making toffee?"

Lance sat down on a cushion, and then turned to glance up at his father.

"Where are you coming, pater?"

"Oh, here—just here," said Probyn clearing his throat.

3

The most remarkable thing about that Christmas reunion was the fact that money was not mentioned. The Golden Fleece appeared to have been put away in a cupboard, and its effulgence ceased to cast a glare. Though, on Christmas morning, while lighting their pipes and discussing a walk through the woods, Probyn produced an envelope, and with an air of casualness while squinting at the bowl of his pipe, placed the envelope on a corner of the desk.

"Might be useful. Token of goodwill."

He was a little flushed, and a little apologetic, and Lance taking the envelope and examining the contents, unfolded a cheque for five hundred pounds.

"Pater——!"

"Just a sign of goodwill, old chap. Hope you'll accept it—in the spirit in which it is given. Not a bribe, you know."

Lance put the cheque in his pocket and struck a match.

"It's very good of you, very generous. I didn't come here—pater, you know——"

"That's just it," said his father, "that's just it."

No more was said, but Lance produced John Richmond's letter and handed it to his father, and pretended to read *The Times*, while Probyn shared his son's panache. Because Lance supposed that his father would be pleased, perhaps he watched Probyn screwing the monocle into his eye, and taking the letter to one of the french windows where the light was

better.   Nor was there any strutting of Lance's self-love, no
petty notion of rubbing the thing in.   He wanted his father
to feel pleased.

"Rather a decent letter, pater?"

Probyn removed his eyeglass.

"Yes—by Jove—yes.   Congratulations.   Splendid."

He glowed.   He looked at the winter landscape and
thought; "Well, if this fellow Richmond wants to do the
big thing—I'm in with him.   Supposing I put down a thousand for advertising?   Have to do it—gracefully—of course.
Nothing blatant."

He stood fingering his tie, and then turned to scrutinize his
son with a mingling of curiosity and secret satisfaction.   So
this was the kid to whom he used to bowl a shilling composition cricket-ball, with a gravel path for a pitch, and the wicket
chalked on a very new brick wall.   Extraordinary!   Hadn't
everything been rather extraordinary, the Golden Fleece,
knighthood, Windover, the resurrection of the Venerable?
But Lance and Lance's book were more extraordinary than
anything else.   Life seemed to be both amazing and simple.
Amazing, because suddenly a fog seemed to lift, just as the
mist cleared on an autumn morning, and you saw the world
serene and sunlit and somehow—strangely clarified.

"One of the most—gratifying letters—I have read.   I'm
delighted."

Unconsciously he made one of his little, stiff, civic bows.

"May I keep it and show it to your mother?"

"Of course."

They went out and walked.   It was clear and frosty, and
the beech leaves were crisp under their feet, and beyond the
fretwork of black boughs were great gouts of blue.   The
very air had a quiet candour.   And treading among the dead
bracken, or following the grass tracks between the green furze
banks, with the sun aslant upon the heave of the hillside, they
seemed to walk into a new awareness of each other.   It was
not expressed.   Largely it was inexpressible.   Lance did not
arrive at the conclusion that his father had come by a philosophy
of life, but he was aware of his father looking at things, a tree,

or a piece of greensward, or at a cushion of bronze-brown
leaves caught between two old massive roots, as though he
took a pleasure in looking.   That is to say, he was beginning
to look at beauty with eyes that discerned and loved.

"I always like that bit of blue hill over there——"

Lance followed his father's pointing stick, thought of a
craftsman's phrase, but did not exploit it.

"Yes—very good."

"I'm rather worried about your mother, Lance."

There were questions and answers.   They talked almost
casually, as Englishmen will, but it was the casualness of concealed feeling.   Diabetes, insulin.   Oh—yes, the doctor men
were quite encouraging—but then—of course—one did worry.
And the man in Lance was old enough to understand that at his
father's age—there were worries—suspenses—deep-rooted
associations which felt the tremor.   And he conceived towards
his father a gentleness, a feeling that was almost protective.
He had not quite understood his father.   He began to see
something of the Venerable in Probyn.

Happening, after tea, to pick up a book from his father's
desk he found it to be an anthology of old flowers and gardens
—"The Old World Pleasance."   His father had inserted
several slips of paper to mark particular passages, and had
scribbled pencil notes upon the slips.   Lance read:

> "Bring hether the Pinke and Purple Cullambine
> With gelliflowers,
> Bring Corronations, and Sops in wine,
> Worne of Paramoures;
> Strow me the ground with Daffadowndillies
> And Cowslips and Kingcups and loved Lillies,
> The pretty Pawnce
> And the Chevisaunce
> Shall match with the fayre flowre Delice."

Lance read his father's notes.   "Thought the gelliflower
was a wallflower.   What are Sops in Wine?   Also, the
Pawnce and the Chevisaunce.   Memo, make inquiries for an
old herbal.   N.B. Thomas Hyll says that the marigold follows
the sun, turning its face.   Observe—some time—if this is so."

"'Ranunculus.   This flower is one of a very unsociable

o

nature, and will not thrive mixed with or standing near any other sort.' John Lawrence, 1726. Mem. Try them by themselves in a pot or stone vase."

Lance smiled. From this little book of his father's drifted a faint perfume; a smell as of old herbs and of happy associations. How very simple and pleasant and childlike to watch a marigold flower turning with the sun, or to attempt to persuade that very unsociable plant—the ranunculus—to be socialistic and tolerant of crowds. Better than sticking postage-stamps into an album, and squinting at them through a magnifying glass! Probyn in his "Old World Pleasance" had become a humanist.

4

Old Pybus, feeding his pigeons on Christmas Eve, saw Mary and her grey car arrive in the Saracen yard. He had a bird perched on the crown of his hard felt hat, and one on either shoulder, and Mary was reminded of a mystical figure of the Trinity.

"What, shopping?"

"Yes, Christmas."

"Have tea with me. I can give you a better tea than they do at the cake shop."

"I know. Well, may I? In half an hour?"

The pigeons were round his feet, and above the roofs the winter sky glowed red. Her face had a faint flush. She appeared happier, as though some of her confidence in life had been restored. The Venerable, looking at her as she looked at the sky, was made to think of the shepherd's jingle upon red sunsets and red dawns.

Yes, undoubtedly things were better at "Marions." There appeared to have been a definite reaction, and that application of the slipper had stimulated a blind pride.

"How's the brother?"

She smiled.

"I left him improvising a carol, a kind of 'Good King Wenceslas' as one of the moderns might have rendered it."

"Splendid," said old Pybus. "You might have brought him with you."

"He was quite happy. The girl is getting his tea. I have a few things to buy."

The Venerable nodded his head, and the white pigeon rose from his hat.

"Hallo, there goes my panache! I'll have the kettle boiling in half an hour."

The kettle was old Pybus's affair. He watched it taking its time to boil on the sitting-room fire, but he was in no hurry, and he was thinking of Merris and the seeming finality of Merris's blindness. To feel the fire and not to see it, to smell a rose and to know that the darkness conceals a flower! But was it not possible for a man to create or collect about himself a world of sound, and to make of himself so sensitive an instrument that the sense of sound might satisfy him? Could Merris do it, or was he better dead?—for there was no other alternative worth choosing. But take a man's natural vanity; you might feed it and clip it as you fed a young yew hedge and then use the shears. But who was going to handle the shears? And if your green stuff grew rank and pulpy, and no one troubled to clip it, the result might prove unlovely.

"That's it," thought Old Pybus; "one would like to be a sort of little peripatetic deity. But you might take yourself too damned seriously."

He glanced at the clock.

5

Merris also was sitting in front of the fire, and with an air of unusual sleekness, a well-brushed head and a trimmed beard. From somewhere he had routed out a black velvet coat, and his tie was a little profuse and the colour of amber. A lamp stood on the table, throwing the shadow of his head and shoulders upon the strip of wall beside the fireplace. He was leaning forward slightly, listening, and now and again he would rub the palms of his hands together like a man rolling tobacco. He was not conscious of the gesture. It was expressive, part of his anticipatory mood, or as though he were stroking a pleasant thought.

Sounds of activity came from the kitchen, a girl's going to and fro over the tiled floor, the clink of a cup, the clatter of a knife dropped upon a wooden table, and to Merris these sounds had the quality of music. They were part of his sensuous aliveness. When the girl broke into an indifferent whistling of the winter's most popular dance tune, his lips mimicked the notes.

She came down the passage.

"Shall I make you some buttered toast, Mr. Gilbert?"

He turned head and shoulders towards the door.

"Please, Nelly. What's that you're whistling?"

She looked at him round the edge of the door. She was a plain young woman with a broad face, and coarse black hair, but her voice was not unpleasant. She was smiling, and the smile was both sensual and sentimental. She had a very large mouth.

"'Pansy Eyes'—Everybody's playing it. It's rather nice."

"Fox-trot?"

"We Charleston to it, Mr. Gilbert, up at the Rec."

"The Rec! What's that?"

"The Recreation Room—up at Castle Craven."

"Oh—I see."

They laughed; but the girl's laughter was more like a titter.

"Wonder if I could play it on the piano?"

"You do play—so lovely, Mr. Gilbert——"

"Look here, Nelly, you shall whistle it after tea, and I'll try and vamp it on the piano—— I used to dance."

"Did you, Mr. Gilbert?"

"Believe I could dance now. There's the old gramophone and one or two jazz records."

"Oh, Mr. Gilbert——"

"We'll push back the furniture and try. Hurry up with the tea, Nell."

He might have added: "Before Miss Mary comes back," but the conspiracy was suggested and understood. The girl gave a little wriggle of the shoulders and hurried off to the kitchen. She had no lover; no lover had come her way, and she wanted a lover. Merris, blind though he was, and perhaps because of his blindness, had for her a strong enticement.

Merris stretched out his hands to the fire. He felt the warmth of it, and that other warmth—the nearness and the consent of a woman. He divined it, felt the little snuggling, secret thrill of it in the warm darkness. He moistened his lips. There is a sort of physical pride in man that exults and swells itself out in the presence of such an adventure, and Merris's pride had been wandering alone like a street-walker. Mary had cut him off from that other crave, and his very blindness was a crave, a dark void asking to be filled.

The girl brought in his tea and placed the tray on an oak stool beside his chair.

"I haven't made you any toast, Mr. Gilbert. I thought——"

"Take too much time. Had your tea, Nelly?"

"No, sir."

"Have some with me. Get another cup."

His voice caressed her. He could not see her face, but he imagined it as smiling and confused and flushing with consent. He heard her slip out of the room, and when she returned he was aware of her moving about in the darknesss. The curtain rings jingled. He understood. She was making sure that the curtains covered the windows.

"Got your cup?"

"Yes, Mr. Gilbert."

"You had better pour out for both of us. You can sit on the tuffet, can't you?"

He felt her close to him, her arm almost touching his knee.

"That's lovely. We shall have to keep our ears open."

Said the girl:

"Miss Merris has the car. It's a noisy old car—too—isn't it?"

6

Mary locked the blue doors of the little old coach-house, and crossed the brick-paved yard to the rustic gate, which opened into the garden. The sky was powdered with stars, and a little, brittle breeze moved the apple branches across those points of silver. A shutter creaked, but the unrest of the winter night was to her a quiet breathing, and in front of the porch she lowered her heavy basket to the ground, and stood at gaze. She could see Castle Craven as a crown of lights upon its hill, and each light was like a little friendly eye. She could say to herself that she was happy, if to feel smooth and cared for is to be happy. She could say: "I have endured. I have striven to help, and help has come to me. And here is music."

She could hear her brother playing. He had struck a few tentative notes, and then three full sonorous chords, just when she had paused to look at the lights of Castle Craven. In putting down her basket she had felt herself discarding a burden.

Poor old Gil! He had seemed so much more of a man during the last three weeks. And what a relief it was to be able to come home without having to hold your breath—and to wonder! Was anything more sordid and soul-rotting than suspicion, that almost surreptitious stealing in upon his blindness? And she had Lance.

She stooped for the basket. In it—among other things—she had Gil's Christmas present, a new pipe and half a pound of his favourite tobacco. Blessed stars—blessed simplicity.

She turned and tried the door, and found it locked. She had raised her hand to the brass knocker when she heard the girl's footsteps.

"That you, Miss?"

"Yes, Nelly."

"I thought I'd lock the door, Miss."

"Quite right."

"Shall I take the basket, Miss?"

"Thanks, Nelly. You can be getting home now—if you want to. I have a little present for you here. It's Christmas Eve."

CHAPTER XXXV

I

PROBYN'S car turned into the Saracen yard and came to rest with its long blue bonnet within six feet of the inn's side door. This door was painted white, and Lance and his father were in the act of putting the fur rug from their knees when the white door opened and showed them the Venerable, carrying a little black tray. On it were two plates surmounted by two tin covers, the Venerable's dinner, or his two silver caps of maintenance.

It was a singular occasion. The chauffeur got down to open the near door, and Probyn, being next to that door, was the first to leave the car. Both Lance and the chauffeur saw that particular act. Probyn's simple and quaint *beau geste*. It embodied a ritual. Probyn, in his long coffee-coloured over-coat, stood at the bottom of the two steps, and holding out his hands, claimed the privilege of carrying his father's dinner-tray.

And the Venerable consented. He recognized and sur-rendered to an act of grace. Probyn, carrying the tray with something of the air of a knight bearing his lord's sword and spurs on a black cushion, walked down and across the Saracen yard with his father. It was the most silent of ceremonies. Neither of them had uttered a word, and Lance, who had remained in the car, knew that he had witnessed a notable act.

He got out, folded up the rug, and placed it on the seat. The chauffeur, a pleasant person with very English eyes in a rosy face, stood solemnly staring.

"You had better get some dinner, Payne."

"Yes, sir. What about your suit-case, sir?"

"You might carry it down to my grandfather's, the cottage at the bottom of the passage."

"Yes, sir. The way the gentlemen have gone, sir?"

"That's it."

But Lance had seen more than an old fellow in a black coat and striped trousers standing in a doorway, holding a tray. He had been absent at Windover less than a week, and he had returned to see the Venerable as he had not seen him before, as a very old man. Just those few days, an insignificant lapse of time, and yet the thing had happened. Or had he returned with eyes that could be startled by the change, though the change must have been there. The little sturdy figure had appeared to him indefinably old and shrunken. The white head had seemed less massive and vigorous.

He walked slowly down to the cottage. His heart was open to both those other men. He was aware of a little spasm of sadness, a beautiful, wise sadness. He saw his father stretching out his hands for that tray.

"Salve—pater——"

Pausing outside the door to glance up at the Venerable's white pigeons on the red and grey roofs, he was moved to a gentle wondering. Mystery of wings, and mystery of blue sky, and mystery of spirit! O, most splendid of mysteries, redescending upon the earth with the sound of wings invisible! Was man mere clay, man—the mystic, man the magnanimous and compassionate? A little, old, black dinner-tray, and his father's hands!

He heard voices.

"Your dinner will be getting cold."

"You are going to join me, Probyn."

"Of course."

"Then—I'll go up and order——"

"No, no; on no account. I'll go myself. We'll have what you are having."

Probyn came out of the cottage and met his son. They looked at each other. They were son and father. They smiled.

2

It began to rain after Probyn's car had left. Old Pybus had gone on duty, and Lance, after unpacking his suit-case and looking at the landscape through a wet window felt most strangely like a small boy in need of comfort. The little room struck raw, and his mood was penetrated by a like feeling of rawness. He and his father had talked for a while before the fire, and Lance had raised the question of money.

"Do you mind how I use that cheque, pater?"

"Just as you please, old chap. It's just a bit of paper."

And Lance had said: "Did you notice how old he looks? I hadn't realized it before. It shocked me."

Probyn, leaning forward to warm his hands, had answered very slowly.

"He is a very old man. Of course—both of us—would rather—— But he's the sort that likes to die in harness."

Looking at the wet landscape Lance felt strangely sore. He was thinking of that little old man standing where the brass gong hung like a halo. And for three months this little old man had given him bed, bread, and meat and, how much more than these, the courage to endure, an inward vision. The old Roman at his post! But in Lance there had arisen a sudden passion to succour, to protect, to cherish. He felt it towards four people, Mary, his mother, Probyn, the Venerable; but at the moment its strongest urge was towards the Venerable.

"He's the sort that likes to die in harness!"

The ardour of youth in arms confronted the shadow of the inevitable. A very old man! And suddenly he realized death and its physical finality as a blotting out of beauty, even as that rain was blotting out sky and hill. He had never seen death. He was as a child, and he stood there remembering those poignant pages of Hudson's book which the Venerable had put into his hands. The thing touched him now as it touches all of us—though our lips may remain sealed, and we stand inarticulate, incredulous, questioning. Absurd emotion! How crassly obvious. Had he, then, been so full of his own affairs that he had not realized the obvious, or suffered himself to see that figure of Old Mortality? And what did it mean to him?

Lance put on a raincoat and an old cap and went out into the rain. He knew quite well where he was going. He was going to Mary. He was running to her in this moment of almost childish bewilderment and pain as he would run to her through life, to his beloved, his mother-woman, the one creature from whom he would unthinkingly exact tenderness, soft touches, understanding. There was that in him which seemed to know without knowing, as a child knows. He wanted this sense of elemental soreness touched and soothed. He wanted to express something. He wanted her and self-expression.

He noticed neither the mud nor the rain. He sought her cottage like a scared small boy making for home. His problem was hers; she had no riddles of her own, or he had forgotten them. He found himself at her door, knocking.

It opened. She was there in the dim, wet, winter light. He saw her eyes, and did not translate their expression into any selfless language.

"Mary——"

She looked at him, and somehow her hands went out. She had for him that strange, indefinable something. His tremblings were hers, his angers, his bewilderments. There were things that she set aside.

"Oh, my dear——"

He put his head down on her shoulder.

"Oh, what a kid I am! I want to tell you——"

3

She had taken him into the kitchen and there they had sat side by side on a couple of wooden chairs, with the kitchen range showing its black teeth at them like an idol with a head full of live coals. She had listened. She was sufficiently unpractical to understand him and his moods. She knew that she would never ask him to be Young Logic, and that she

would love him the better for his sensitive outbursts, for there
was a part of her that was made of moonlight. Common
sense, with her fat arms in the washtub, cheerfully bids the
man-child not to be a fool. Oh, those stupidly cheerful
people! With one hand pressing his head against her cheek,
she suffered him to express his self-realizations.

"But don't you think that his last few years will have been
rather happy years?"

"But one takes so much for granted. One gets so absorbed."

She smiled over him, one of those half-whimsical—half-
tender smiles, which are to a woman's face what the genius
of the artist is to the portrait. Of course he took things for
granted. He was taking her for granted. He was absorbed
at that very moment in intimate and personal emotion. She
was his one and complete Mary: a mirror, a voice, his own
individual conception of her as Mary. But she could say
of him: "You dear, funny, lovable old child." She could forgive him for failing to feel that she had a particular and poignant problem of her own.

"I expect we look at things rather differently."

"But do we?"

"When you are old. I think old people feel the chill of the
unknown. They want to feel warm and human and sociable,
and near to those they love. They ask for kindness.
Wouldn't one?"

"I suppose so. But then—the Venerable has done all the
giving."

"Oh, no, my dear. Besides—I'll tell you how I came to
understand. Gil had to go to one of the leading oculists, and
when the doctor found out that we were rather poor he would
not take any fees from me. He was an old man. And I
was rather young, and uncomfortable, and I tried to persuade
him to let me pay. I remember a look—almost of pain and
of appeal on his face. He said: 'Young lady, I am an old
man. May I not be allowed to do something for the love
of the thing? What is money to me?'"

"Yes, that's rather fine. It touches one."

"Besides, it's so natural."

But she had Gil in the other room, and her thoughts passed from lover to brother. She was troubled about Gil, without being able to decide what it was that troubled her. Her eyes were fixed upon the black bars of the range and the red glow behind them, and she was made to think of faces in the fire, monstrous faces, fantastic masks. Gil puzzled her. He had the air of being much better friends with himself, and she should have been glad; but her gladness was clouded. She had divined a something in the house, as though she was meeting drifts of elusive perfume, or as though a face smiled at her, and then smiled differently when her back was turned. She had caught glimpses of her brother in a mirror.

She made a movement.

"Are you coming to see Gil?"

"Of course! How's the music?"

She rose and stood looking at the black bars and the live fire behind them.

"He seems much more cheerful."

A sprawling figure in an arm-chair, that was Lance's first impression of Merris. He was struck by the length of the fellow's legs, and the feet in light blue socks cocked on a footstool. Mary was saying, "Here's Lance," and Lance saw a head turned on a cushion, and that blind face looked curiously sleek and complacent.

"Full of plum pudding?"

Yes, a kind of sleek smirk, a languor which somehow suggested arrogance, a stillness that condescended. It was a complex of impressions. And that facetiously—"Full of plum pudding?"

Lance moved to the fire. His responses were casual.

"I prefer mince pies."

"Find 'em inspiring? Mary tells me you always write on a full stomach."

"I suppose that's so."

"How do you manage the blood to the brain?"

Mary had left them alone together, and Lance sat down with an air of deliberation. He looked attentively for a moment at the velvet jacket and the amber tie, and the little clipped beard, and those blue socks complacently solacing themselves. And then he turned his eyes to the fire. He was embarrassed by a sudden quickening of the dislike he had always felt for Merris. He did not want to look at him. He did not want to be very near to him. Physically—the reaction might be described as a distaste for a man who did not wash. But why this facetiousness, this almost smug lounging in front of the fire, a suspicion of something swollen? Mary had used the word: "cheerful," but it struck Lance as being inadequate, perhaps consciously so. A one-word atmosphere is like a picture that is all blue or all red, and Merris might be the colour of raw flesh, but he was clothed. Lance wondered.

Was it Merris's music? Was this velvet coat pose? Had the fellow conceived a "soul child," and was he swaggering like a young mother? If so—he—Lance supposed that it was all to the good, and the beard could not be helped, and the amber tie was a coloured gesture. He said: "How's the piano, Merris?" and saw Merris's long fingers go up to caress his beard.

"The piano is very well, Pybus, thank you. And how is the pen? Does it fountain as it should?"

"I use a steel nib. Ladies—medium point."

From Merris came a kind of chuckle, a dry sound, like leaves blown about.

"Symbolical of sex—I suppose!"

There was silence. Lance had travelled beyond the "Damn the fellow" mood, the Englishman's natural reaction. Irony implies a subtle self-conceit. To condescend is to provoke an echo. And Lance, frowning at the fire, did suppose that he had condescended to Merris, and that the fellow was sufficiently sensitive to feel and to resent it. But that did not explain Merris's transfiguration, the suggestion of a sleek chuckle.

"You ought to do something with your music."

"Think so?"

"I do."

"Then—there cannot be any doubt about it."

When a man attempts irony he challenges you to rag him,

but Lance heard Mary enter the room, and with her she seemed to bring the muteness of a smothered question. Lance felt self-conscious. It would be little help to her to find them like a couple of pert and squabbling children. He stood up, and looking at his watch by the light of the fire, remembered his grandfather.

"Going?"

"Yes. I'm expected—there."

His eyes said more, and turning in the doorway, he looked back at her brother.

"Good night, Gil. I meant what I said about your music. I know you think me a confounded prig."

He saw Merris's profile against the fire.

"Same to you, Pybus. Good luck to the steel nib."

Mary followed Lance out into the passage, and taking from a peg the old raincoat she wore when at work in bad weather, she held it up to him. Saying nothing—he helped her on with the coat. It was she who opened the door, and let in the raw wet night.

"England——"

His hand touched hers. He felt the droop of her, a sudden tiredness, a questioning of life. She looked into the wet, dark drizzle with wide eyes.

"I'm coming a little way."

"No hat?"

"Does it matter?"

He slipped an arm round her. She had comforted him, and he in his turn felt that she asked for comfort; that she was discouraged, and troubled. They went through the gate into the lane, and his sense of her nearness was poignant and very precious. Never had she seemed so near, or so ready to lean.

"What did you think of Gil?"

He was aware of her looking up into his face.

"Seems more pleased with life, doesn't he? I suppose it is the piano, and self-expression."

"I wish I knew."

The note of distress and of doubt in her voice shocked him.

"Don't you know?"

"No."

"He isn't getting that stuff——?"

"I've wondered. But how——? Oh, my dear, it makes me feel so sordid. This eternal watching and suspecting."

He held her closer.

"Look here, Mary—this can't go on. I want you to let me do something about it. You have given too much of yourself. It is time someone else did the giving."

"But what can one do?"

"Be intelligently selfish. There are places where Gil could be cared for. I could arrange it. I know someone who would help."

He felt her stiffen.

"One of those anonymous places! I couldn't. You see— I promised myself——"

He paused, and standing still, he felt the rain on his face. He was conscious of a sense of a struggle, of the wilful lover in him urging a claim. He was conscious, also, of her leaning against him with a kind of pathetic rigidity, and it seemed to him that two men in him held her. His mouth touched her hair. It was all wet with the rain. And there ran through him an instant, infinite tenderness.

"Mary, I'll do just what you wish. But, my dear, I want you to be happy."

She pressed her wet head against his face.

"It's so hard. Be patient with me, oh—be patient. There's a something that pulls me. I can't help it, Lance. I'm made that way."

He said: "I know. It's just because you are Mary."

4

When man has become civilized he is a gentle opener and closer of doors, and Lance found the Venerable asleep in his arm-chair in front of the fire.

Lance did not wake his grandfather, and stepping softly to look at him he seemed to see a little old, tired child curled up in the chair. His sleep was very soundless and still, and his breathing so shallow that for a moment Lance wondered which sleep it was—the sleep of to-day or that of the great to-morrow.

Slipping out of his wet mackintosh, and kneeling first on one knee and then on the other to take off his shoes, he sat down on an old green plush footstool close to his grandfather's feet. The Venerable's head, reposing on a red cushion, had a mystical whiteness. His hands were crossed over the lower button of his black alpaca coat. And Lance looked at his grandfather's hands; always meticulously clean, and with a skin that had none of the branny harshness of old age; they had—or seemed to have—on this last night of the old year—a tenuous pallor. They were typical, the hands of a very clean and proud old man; but to Lance they were much more than that. They were the hands of a worker, hands which had bestowed upon him a worker's benediction, and the blessing of human understanding. "Great old man—even in his sleep," thought Lance, and felt in his pocket for that cheque of his father's. He unfolded it, and holding it with both hands, seemed to consider it, as though the words and figures were mystic symbols. His father's signature, too, "Probyn Pybus" with a flourish of the two Y's and a looped line drawn beneath it—was a sign in the heavens. Lance smiled; he was smiling at the Lance of yesterday, and looking with a ruthless self-knowledge at the Lance of to-morrow. "Till he took me in hand," he reflected, "I was just damned clever, a precious young highbrow. I suppose he taught me to feel."

And then the Venerable woke up without Lance being aware of the opening of those very blue eyes. Old Pybus looked at his grandson, and at the piece of paper held by his grandson's fingers. He too smiled.

"I think I have been asleep, my dear."

Lance did not move, nor did he attempt to conceal his father's cheque.

"So you have, grandpater. And now you have mentioned it—I want you to do more sleeping. Getting up at six on a winter morning isn't necessary."

Old Pybus drew up his feet and sat erect in his chair.

"Probyn gave you that, my dear?"

"Yes, he's a Pybus, grandpater. And I took it."

"Because?"

"Yes—in a way. And because—I think I had a glimpse of what was at the back of his mind. I suppose one learns to take things—though I seem to have been doing nothing but taking. Mary gave me a hint."

"On—taking?"

"Partly. But—grandpater—don't you think you could retire? What I mean is—I feel—that it's my turn—our turn. You see——"

Old Pybus laid a hand on his grandson's shoulder.

"My dear—I understand you. But I like doing things. Old people do, you know. They treat me very gently here. I'd like to go on doing things. I shall like it all the better for knowing——"

Lance—slowly and softly folded up his father's cheque.

"You're an old war-horse, grandpater. But—I wish——"

"Well, my dear, the wish is the thing that matters."

CHAPTER XXXVI

I

WHEN a north-east wind blew over Castle Craven it blew bitterly, and the old town would turn up a grey collar and huddle itself under the hurrying sky. The halliards of the flagstaff on the church tower kept up a monotonous clapping. The roar of the wind joined the roar of the river. The Venerable's pigeons sought out sheltered corners, the warm side of chimney stacks, the angles of dormer windows. In the Brent valley and on the hills, landscape and sky gave the impression of movement, the trees blown all one way, and looking as though they were trying to run from that bitter blast, but were rooted to the ground by terror. Lance, at work in his upper room, kept the oil stove very near; paper and pen were cold, and now and again he had to hold his hands over the stove.

As usual, old Pybus got out of bed at six. He had an alarum clock on the table beside him, and Lance would hear the clock's reverberations, and tumble out into the raw gloom to light a candle, and hurry downstairs in trousers and shirt to forestall his grandfather and put a match to the fire. The Venerable felt the cold. On these mornings his face had a grey, pinched look, and he would rub his hands to get the blood moving in his fingers.

"I wish you would stay in bed, grandpater, until the room is warm."

But the Venerable was obstinate. For ten years or so he had gone on duty at half-past seven, and the Saracen Inn was his ship. He had to see what that lubber of a lad was doing, whether the doorstep was as white as it should be, and the hall and the lounge clean and tidy. He examined every ash-tray, sorted out the letters and tucked them under the tapes on the green board, gave the brass gong a polish, and kept an eye on the fires. As he had confessed to Lance, he liked doing these simple things, and though he had no fear of death, he loved the day's rhythm, the realities of its routine. His mysticism did not lack hands.

At half-past seven he would walk off up the yard, wrapped up in a black overcoat. Lance insisted upon the overcoat, for the yard had a draughtiness on these winter mornings, and as likely as not the Venerable would loiter to whistle to the pigeons. He began the day by throwing out the crusts and two handfuls of seed to them. And at night Lance would carry the oil stove into his grandfather's bedroom half an hour before the Venerable went up to bed. Until this winter old Pybus had scorned a hot bottle, but he had been persuaded to allow that it warmed your feet and helped you to fall asleep.

2

That north-easter was not blowing on the night when Mary came up to Castle Craven to share a little *festa* with Lance and the Venerable. It was the Venerable's birthday. Probyn had been over in the morning with his conception of what a birthday present should be, Probyn the practical, the wool merchant, whose fleece was turning to goblin gold. He had brought a fur-lined overcoat, six flannel shirts, the same number of thick pants and vests, and a precious copy of Gerards Herbal. He had swallowed a glass of sherry and some emotion. Even in the late nineteen twenties England and a Pybus could be old England and old Pybus. Cars might blow their trumpets, but there were some walls that had not fallen.

Lance had ordered the dinner, and had tipped the Saracen cook. Also, he had managed to procure flowers, a posy for the Venerable, and violets for Mary. Also propped against old Pybus's glass was the dedication of "Rust," lettered in old-English type by Mary. "To the Venerable."

Old Pybus was wearing his famous made-to-measure suit, and the tortoiseshell glass with the black silk ribbon.

"In honour of you, my dear. This is how we did things at Trinity when Lance and I were up. Hallo—what's this?"

He had been manœuvred into his own chair and kept there with his back to the table until George, the head-waiter, appeared in person with the soup-tureen.

"It's a little previous, grandpater. Mary worked it in ivory black."

Lance was referring to the dedication and not to the soup, but his grandfather took the half-sheet of vellum-paper into his hand, and the paper trembled just a little.

"Thank you, my dear. The more one wants to say—the less there is to be said. But it's a great gesture."

He looked across at Mary.

"So your colour-box is out at last. Ivory black instead of rose-madder or vermilion. You must keep the rose-madder for Lance."

He laughed.

"Moods and a colour-box. But at my age! Now—just how old am I? Ought I to tell?"

"Does it matter, Venerable?"

"Unless I want to boast about it, my dear. But I think not. Supposing we wish "Rust" as many editions as I have had birthdays."

"How the highbrows would hate me. Seventy shameful editions!"

"Offer them the chance, my dear, and see them jump."

He was in great spirits, for here were these two young things sitting down with an old fellow on his seventy something-th birthday, and looking at him lovingly. They were gentle to him, not with the patronage of youth, but with a fine and delicate courtesy, because that old body of his was growing frail. And he had nothing but a few hundreds to leave to either of them. His amber had no such fly in it. He was the Venerable, the head of the house, their ancient of days.

And certainly he was not dull. He shared and enjoyed their glances. He sat there like a Benedictine, with a little twinkle of tender teasing in his blue eyes. Here was romance, the romance of reality, the quintessence of human mysticism, a marriage of mind and emotion.

They drank red wine. George had warmed it, and it was bland and mellow, and the Venerable felt that red wine was sacramental. When Lance poured him out a second glass, old Pybus appeared to reflect for a moment before raising the glass. He made a little bow to Mary, and a little bow to Lance.

"Your health, my dears."

They touched glasses.

'*Sanctus simplicitas!* I wish you both something better than happiness."

He did not wish them the absence of any shadow, for shadows have their uses, nor was he thinking of their particular shadow. The man with the blind eyes had been left at home with his piano, though Lance had suggested his joining the party. There need be no ungraciousness in a refusal, but Merris had been ungracious. "No, thanks. I'm not part of the celebration." He had refused with a little smirk of irony, but without spleen. But there may have been some significance in their forgetting of Merris on that particular evening. He was less than a shadow. If they thought of him at all, they thought of him at his piano, absorbed in the sounds of his own creating, a human disharmony which would have clashed with the *leit motif* of this particular occasion.

Lance had left his chair to pour out the Venerable a glass of port when there came a knocking at the door. He stood with the decanter poised, and with a downward smile at his grandfather.

"I can guess what that is."

"George in a hurry?"

"I divine a deputation. The staff of the Saracen presents its compliments and congratulations to Mr. Pybus."

The Venerable made a movement as of sitting erect and ready in his chair.

"Better see, my dear."

Lance passed the decanter to Mary, and went to the door. He had a smile ready, but the smile was not needed. He saw a girl standing there, and on her face was something indescribable, a kind of sullen, wet horror.

"I want to see Miss Mary."

Lance held the door open.

"You had better come in."

The girl's eyes were fixed in a stare upon his collar.

"No—I won't. I want to see her out here. Something's happened."

3

Lance had brought the little aluminium saucepan from the kitchen and placed it on the hob of the sitting-room fire. It contained their coffee, but they were not to drink that coffee. He turned to look at the Venerable, who was sitting very erect in his chair with an air of almost grim attentiveness. They could hear the two voices out there in the darkness. Mary had closed the door.

Old Pybus's eyes met his grandson's.

"Something?"

Lance nodded. He felt that there was nothing to be said while those moments of tension lasted. Something—yes—something! It was the girl who was doing most of the talking; her voice, hysterical and slightly shrill, seemed to hammer at the room's silence with a couple of emotional fists. Her words came in snatches between sharp spasms of breathing.

"He just wanted to enjoy himself—that's all. Don't look at me like that. Yes—I can feel you looking. How was I to think of such a thing happening? You shut him up—you did. He never had any fun. Oh—dear—oh—dear! I just wanted him to have a little fun. Oh, my God! He's lying down there. No—they didn't stop—blast them. When I saw—I just ran. Yes—up here—I'm about done."

Old Pybus, as though some blind instinct was groping in him, felt in his pocket for his pipe. He looked up as Lance made a sudden movement towards the door. He held up a hand.

"No—my dear."

"Grandpater, did you hear? She said——"

"Yes—I heard. We snap like dogs when we are in pain. Be still."

The wailing voice began again.

"He was just merry—he was. 'Nelly, I'll race you,' he said, just like that. How was I to know that he was going to do such a thing? I saw the lights of the car coming—and I shouted to him and ran after him down the road. He didn't seem to hear the car."

Said that other voice, Mary's voice—"You say he didn't seem to hear. Yet he could run. You must tell me—how bad he was. It's everything."

"Oh, Miss, it's cruel."

"No, no,—don't you see? Did he know that car was coming?"

"I don't think he knowed—Miss. He wouldn't have done it, would he—on purpose?"

The door opened and Mary came in. She did not look at either of them, but at the chair on which she had left her hat and coat. Her eyes were like two dark hollows in her white face. She stood there as though bewildered.

Lance went to her.

"We heard. We couldn't help it—I'll go, dear."

She pointed to her coat.

"No—I must go. Could you send people—a doctor?"

Old Pybus got out of his chair.

"Lance—you——"

"Of course——"

"I'll see to the other things."

Lance held Mary's coat.

"I'm coming—dear. I must. Where did the girl say?"

She seemed to set and stiffen her throat and shoulders.

"Between the bridge and our lane. On the main road."

They went out together past the dim, half-defiant, half-cringing figure of the girl.

"Nelly, you must come."

"Oh—I couldn't, Miss. It's too horrible—him lying there—on the grass."

"You must. You must show us. Hold my hand."

4

They took the path by the Castle Field and down through the hanging beech woods, Lance first going to the Saracen yard to borrow a hurricane lamp which was used in windy weather. Returning, he met his grandfather, buttoning up his coat, and ready with the matches that Lance had forgotten.

"What a night, grandpater."

Old Pybus's face was strangely impassive.

"Some things—are better—as they are. Have they gone on?"

"Yes."

"I'll send the other people to you."

Lance found the two women waiting for him where the path turned by the old sally-port of the Castle and a wind-blown ash spread its branches like a sheltering hand. The lamp threw a pool of light, and Lance held it so that their faces were in the shadow. The girl, huddled against the wall beside Mary's erect and waiting figure, was crying into a crumpled handkerchief.

"I'll go first—and light the path for you."

He was aware of the stillness of the trees. There was a smell of moist and rotting leaves, and here and there a root writhed like a snake across the path. The branches of the beeches lost themselves in the blackness above, and he had a curious feeling of being closed up in a little shell of darkness with those two following figures. He had things to say to Mary, tender, reassuring things, and he could not utter them because of that snivelling girl. She had not the virtue of silence. The river below them was full of the winter's hurry, and superimposed upon its chant were the blurtings of tragedy.

"He only had two glasses—I'll swear it, Miss. We just turned in—so to speak."

Lance winced. He heard Mary's sharply agonized: "Oh, be quiet." Yes, why couldn't the fool be quiet; or did tragedy demand a pitiful, blubbering clown? But what a culmination! The girl's blurtings had painted the crude picture, those two going off together in the darkness, the common pub below the bridge, Merris's red mouth and blind eyes, the fever in him, the hurried—greedy gulpings. He had come out from the place, playful, inflamed, like any hobblede-hoy, to stagger about the dark road, to dare the girl to an absurd race. What a picture! The very word "pub," public-house, smelling of that vulgarity that is so English or Nordic, beer, sweat, a steamy—stuffy room, mouths adhering to cheap glasses, gin, sawdust, silly laughter, silly voices!

He heard Mary say: "I don't blame you, Nelly. Try to be quiet." And suddenly the situation was saved, and snatched away from that smell of beer and of beastliness. He understood that in Mary there was pity, some strange and compassionate mercy shown to this other woman. Something quivered in his throat. Oh, thank God! And again he heard the river running, and smelt the fragrance of those autumn leaves, and somehow the night was clean. Ah, Mary! He wanted to face about and touch her, gather something that was hers and put his lips to it. She was greatness; she was woman.

They came down to the bridge over the river, and the bracket lamp on the parapet showed an empty curve. Lance paused. He had the calmness of pity. He was inspired.

"Nelly—how far down the road—was it?"

Her voice came back to him with a dull gentleness. She too was absorbing Mary.

"About a quarter of a mile, sir, I should say. Just where there's an oak tree in the hedge."

"I'll go on ahead."

He looked at Mary, and Mary was silent, but her silence thanked him. He went on.

Holding the lamp shoulder-high he came to the place where Merris lay where the car had flung him. The road was empty. There were the hedgerows and the dim shape of the oak tree, and a curve of green grass. Merris lay on his back with his arms spread. His face was untouched; it expressed sleep, a strange tranquillity.

Lance put the lamp on the grass and knelt down. It was the first time that he had seen death, but even in his innocence he seemed to know that death was here.

5

He put out the lamp, and Mary, marking from a little distance the sudden vanishing of the light, divined it to be a signal.   She stood still; she closed her eyes for a moment, so that the inward darkness of realization matched the outer darkness.   She spoke to the girl.

"Nelly, you can go home."

The girl stood and shivered.

"Did you see the light go out, Miss?"

"Yes.   You can go home.   You need not come with me any farther."

She went on alone, and Lance, hearing her footsteps, stood wondering whether she had seen and understood.   His impulse was to go and meet her, and yet he remained motionless, holding the lamp.   She was very near.

"Mary——"

She was just a dim shape in the darkness, and he was surprised at the stillness of everything, at the strange and almost secret way things happened.

"Mary."

"You put out the light?"

"Yes, you saw."

"Oh, my dear, how I have failed."

Her cry of distress went through him.   He put the lamp down on the grass.   She did not resist his arms; she let herself be taken and held; she gave herself up.

"Beloved, what are you saying?   You gave everything."

"He's dead.   Did you hear what she said to me?   That I shut him up, that he was dull, that he wanted to enjoy things."

"Oh, my dear, and you were gentle to her.   It wasn't so. You're not to think of it in that way."

"Oh, poor Gil!"

He took her face between his hands.

"Mary, my Mary, it's not true.   You were perfectly wonderful to him.   You're wonderful to me now.   You always will be.   What more could you have given?   Oh, don't tremble like this."

Her eyes were closed.

"Hold me, Lance, hold me; don't let me go. It's all dark."

"I'll hold you, Mary, always. Put your head down, dear."

She did not weep; she made a kind of broken murmuring, and all the while his lips were pressed against her hair. He just held her and loved her.

6

In a little while she grew calm. She looked up into his face, and stood off, but with her hands upon his shoulders.

"I'd like him taken home."

"I'll bring him home. They'll be here—very soon. But you?"

"I'm going home."

"But, Mary, can you—alone? I can't let you——"

"I can," she said. "I wish to."

"Dear, you're brave."

She made a little movement of the head.

"Oh, one has to be. It's all rather dim and strange at present. I feel as though something had hit me, and dulled me. I'd rather go."

He was loath to let her go.

"But—Mary——"

"I want to do things. It helps, to do things. Stay here—for me—Lance—my dearest, and bring him back."

"It's as you wish. I'll run on after you when they come."

Holding his hand, she turned and looked at something that was like a shadow on the dim grass.

"Poor Gil. I'm going now, dear. You'll wait."

7

Later, Lance was glad that Mary had gone, for hard upon the heels of Law and Medicine came a little rabble from the river alleys of Castle Craven, intrigued by the rumour that someone had been smashed up. A grey-headed sergeant of police, pushing two women aside whose heads strained forward into the little circle of light with looks of greedy curiosity, joined the doctor and a constable. "Stand back, will you." There were three or four children poking about among the legs of their elders. Headlights glared. The driver of the ambulance, who had left his engine running, remarked to someone, and that someone happened to be Lance: "They do like the smell of blood."

Lance looked fierce. He saw these pushing, peering figures as cattle round a feeding-pen. He went and stood beside old Pybus, who had come down with the doctor. The Venerable was as muffled up in silence as he was in his big, black coat.

"I'm glad she didn't stay. I'm going on, Venerable."

His grandfather nodded.

"What does she wish?"

"She asked to have him there."

"Better tell them."

The doctor was drawing aside, and Lance took his place, and spoke to the sergeant. He said what he had to say, and the sergeant, looking up over a big shoulder, observed that there would be an inquest, and that the Castle Craven mortuary was more useful than a private house. Lance did not argue. "It's Miss Merris's wish, sergeant. I promised," and the sergeant—with an air of philosophic and official tolerance—replied with an "All right, sir." Lance was feeling restive. He shouldered somebody aside, and stood by his grandfather.

"I'm going on. Will you see that they—do what she wishes, grandpater."

Old Pybus touched his grandson's shoulder.

"I will, my dear."

Lance ran. He was glad of the darkness and of the raw night air in his face, and glad to lose those glaring headlights and the little swarm of surreptitious, craning figures. The smell of blood! A thrill! Someone smashed up! Just like Brooklands, with a rushing and a jostling round the circus rails. Did a crowd ever think? And yet people could be so extraordinarily decent. But when he came to the "Marions" lane he dropped to a walk, feeling somehow that he must tread softly up this little path of many memories. His consciousness was Mary's. His restiveness, his resentments and his scorns died away in his consciousness of her tragedy. "Oh, my dear, how I have failed!" He would never forget that cry of hers and the way it had moved him. As if she could fail a man! Why, she was as unique as the Venerable.

He came to the gate and paused. He saw the winter hedges, hazel and thorn and holly, the bare fruit trees, the two old yews, and set behind and among them four lighted windows. She had lit her lamps and her candles, and he was made to think of torches, a pyre, the whimsies of her tragic tenderness. No house, dark and dubious and secretive. She asked for light. She had willed light, and the sensitive manchild in him applauded her. He went through the white gate with a swelling of the throat.

The door under the porch was open. He went in. He seemed to know instinctively where he would find her. She was sitting in front of the fire, elbows on knees, her face between her hands. She looked round and up at him with a dark silence of the eyes.

"They are coming?"

Her eyes went back to the fire, and kneeling beside her, he too, looked into the heart of the fire.

8

All was over. The lane was empty, and old Pybus stood in the porch, buttoning up his coat.

"I shall stay here to-night, grandpater."

"Quite right, my dear. She ought not to be left alone."

"She says that she is going to sit by him all night. She thinks she's failed. As if she could fail! If she can keep awake, so can I."

Old Pybus realized that he had forgotten his hat. His big head was so very full of other matters.

"My hat, my dear. Left it in the sitting-room. Yes, you keep your vigil. I think I'll be getting back now."

Lance went for his grandfather's hat. Their voices had been hushed, and so were his footsteps, for death was lying under a white sheet, but Mary had ears.

"Grandpater—I forgot; you'll have to walk. You ought to have gone back with the ambulance."

"Walking won't kill me, my dear."

"I wish I'd thought. I'll come with you as far as the end of the lane."

And at the end of the lane they parted, Lance turning back to his vigil. Old Pybus loitered for a moment, looking at the lights of Castle Craven and seeing the old hill town as a fantastic birthday cake upon which life had stuck some seventy candles. And life and death had conspired to give him a present.

"I'm not sorry. No—I'm damned if I'm sorry."

Suddenly he heard his grandson's voice coming to him from the darkness of the lane.

"Grandpater."

"Hallo."

"I'm sorry your day ended like this. But many happy returns of other days."

Old Pybus raised his hat.

"The same to you, my dear; the same to both of you."

He went upon his way with great content.

CHAPTER XXXVII

1

LIKE the disciples in the garden of Gethsemane, Lance Pybus slept, though he had watched with his invisible Mary through the first watches of the night. The fire was grey ash, and the lamp had burnt itself out when he woke in his chair to find Mary standing beside him. A little light was sifting through the curtains, and her figure was wraithlike.

"Mary!—I'm sorry—I've been asleep."

She touched his cheek with her hand, and her fingers were very cold.

"Why not? You were here, and I felt you here. And now we begin the day."

He took and held her hand as he rose.

"Dear—you're very cold, and I have let the fires out. I'm quite an expert at fires. Where shall I find things?"

"I'll show you."

She pulled back the curtains from the window looking on the orchard, and they saw the trees like ghost trees between a dim grey sky and the frosted grass. The day was coming up, a beginning of things and an ending of things, and they stood to watch the orchard coming to life and the trees ceasing to be ghosts. And in the chill of the winter dawn they drew together with a calm and quiet consciousness of new horizons.

She was the first to move.

"Come. We'll light the fires, and I'll get you some breakfast."

He kissed her softly on the forehead, a salute of honour.

"Always—and for ever, Mary."

2

When Lance went out into the lane a winter sun was shining upon glistening hedgerows and frosted grass. A thin blue sky covered the zenith.　The earth felt firm and clean and ringing under his feet.

He lit a pipe and looked across at Castle Craven.　What a day!　It was one of those live and vivid mornings in the midst of winter, and he walked fast, full of himself and of those other selves.　The day was both to-day and to-morrow; it envisaged many morrows; it had sunlight and blue sky.

He took the path up through the beeches to the Castle Field.　The clock in the church tower struck nine.　He saw the Venerable's pigeons flashing white wings, and lining the roof tops.　Dear old Venerable!　He entered the cottage and saw the fire alight and cheerful, and his grandfather's breakfast things still on the table.　Old Pybus had gone on duty; and Lance, with a glance at the fire, closed the door on that familiar and quiet room, and walked up through the Saracen yard to the white door in the red wall.

He opened it; he walked half-way along the passage, and stood still.　He saw a figure lying on the floor below the big brass gong.　A woman was kneeling; a waiter and a boy were bending forward.

The kneeling woman looked up into Lance's face.　He was gazing at his grandfather and not at her—though he was aware of a sound of weeping.

"He'd just been upstairs to carry down a bag.　He came and stood here—just as he always did.　I heard something fall."

Lance was staring.

"He must have struck the gong as he fell.　It was flashing and swinging when I rushed out.　But doesn't he look grand and peaceful?"

Lance knelt down.　He saw nothing but the Venerable's face, tranquil, vaguely smiling.

THE END